When Blood Reigns

I0673443

By
Barbara Custer

Night to Dawn Magazine & Books LLC
P. O. Box 643
Abington, PA 19001
www.bloodredshadow.com

Print ISBN: 978-1-937769-49-9
Digital ISBN: 978-1-937769-50-5

Front cover Illustrator: Dawné Dominique
Back Cover Illustrator: Teresa Tunaley
Editors: Gemini Wordsmiths

Printed in the United States of America
Worldwide Electronic & Digital Rights
1st North American, Australian and UK Print Rights

To Michael, who left this world much too soon. Love you forever.

I would like to thank Gemini Wordsmiths for all the work and patience they demonstrated during the developmental edit to prepare When Blood Reigns for submission. Hugs go out to my fellow scribes at the Hatboro Writers Group for their good humor and support with critiques, and to Jonathan Maberry and the Writer's Coffeehouse for teaching me an appreciation for zombies.

Finally, to Dawné Dominique, thank you for designing a lovely front cover, and Teresa Tunaley, thank you for your help with the back cover and other Night to Dawn projects.

Prologue

Alexis trembled, struggling to regain consciousness.

In her half-dream state, terror filled her mind – terror and fuzzy images. Her body lay stiff, her fright immobilizing. Images from weeks prior faded in and out of her memory: a Kryszka soldier smashing through a bedroom window of her mother's home, using a Kryszka plasma gun to kill the intruding soldier, and her asthmatic sister, Robin, holding her chest, as if struggling to breathe, face and hands blue and ice-cold, but dead from the stress of the attack.

Alexis woke and slowly opened her eyes to see nothing but pink and white floodlights hovering above her. As her vision cleared, she made out an off-white grid floor. Beige and white slate tiles on the walls. A sign to her left translated in bold red symbols to, "Warning: No Unauthorized Entry." The air thickened with the smell of antiseptic. She tugged at her arms, but fright had not made her immobile. Her hands were tied down by cables that secured her to a table, and she felt the poke of a needle in her arm.

Could the Kryszka be keeping me here? Do they use IVs? They must, she realized, as she turned her head to see one of the creatures transfusing blood from an IV bag hanging on a pole into a catheter in her left shoulder. Another bag containing yellow fluid dangled from a hook just below the blood; she guessed this one contained saline solution. When she tried to sit up, she felt the wires pasted to her chest; black wires led to a monitor that displayed her blood electrolyte levels and her vital signs in color codes. Red for heartbeat and blood pressure, blue for oxygen saturation, and green for electrolyte levels.

As her vision cleared, she peered around the stark room. Another screen caught her attention. This one posted her urine output, blood cell count, and cranial pressure in white lettering. Machinery whirred behind her in a slow, steady hum, and ... *why do I need a cranial monitor?* Whatever had gone wrong with her must have affected her brain.

More recent images came rushing back to her. The tanned guard who first questioned her had said she could be useful. Perhaps he was plying her with hypnotic drugs so he could get information out of her. Or maybe – and she liked this idea much better – her Kryszka lover, Yeron, had found her and brokered a treatment plan with the guard.

She recognized the Kryszka adjusting her IV as Zoltar, who had carried her to the questioning room. Perhaps he was a doctor, too; according to Yeron, many Kryszka had double careers. Unlike the white lab coats worn by doctors she'd once worked with, he wore standard Kryszka attire – a navy blue tunic. His stoic expression betrayed no emotion. His olive skin made him appear Mediterranean, but his ruby red eyes, coarse red hair, and pointed teeth defined him as Kryszka – and alien.

She tried to sit up again, but the pressure of the bubble-wrap bands chafed her arms and hurt her. More memories came back: the execution of her renegade fighting partner, Shively, being interrogated by guards, and the pain of shocks to her hands. *Why was I saved?*

"I would cease struggling; your vital signs are unstable." No emotion. *Just the facts, Ma'am.*

Zoltar held an empty syringe in one hand while answering Alexis's confused look.

He had given her a series of injections to stimulate her brain, which would help her learn his language quickly; but even after this procedure, translating from English to Kryszka would take brainpower. She'd never learned linguistic nuances, such as contractions or idioms.

"Tell me everything that happened, starting with your first encounter with my people."

Her mouth felt bone dry, but she decided she could talk. Alexis drew in a deep breath.

"All right. I will begin with the day Yeron came to my hospital ... clinic, to work ... about three years ago, my time." At Zoltar's frown, she added, "I am sorry ... I never learned how to convert our time to Kryszka-years. Yeron lived at the hospital because a bomb set off by Eigil, the Kryszka renegade, destroyed his own people's underground compound. Yeron thought he was the lone Kryszka survivor, but then humans continued to disappear or mysteriously turn up dead, the same as when Eigil was alive."

"Renegade meaning ..."

"Yeron called Eigil and his followers 'renegades' because they caused so much trouble."

"I see. Do you think the deaths happened because of the renegade Kryszka soldiers?"

"Yes, but my coworker Laurel was involved, too. Before all this, Yeron and his partner, Doctor Joe Hoffman, were running clinical trials to try to eradicate incurable human diseases. Because I have severe rheumatoid arthritis as you can see from my misshapen limbs, I applied for their program. There was a long waiting list.

"Laurel was a respiratory care nurse working on my team, but she made serious, sometimes fatal errors, so our supervisor assigned me to watch her. One afternoon, I came back from lunch and caught Laurel tampering with a woman's tracheostomy tube, causing her to asphyxiate. Laurel's eyes widened as if she had suddenly realized what she was doing, and she panicked. I tried to revive the patient, while Laurel paced the room, crying 'What did I do?' This was the final blow, and management let her go."

Zoltar was disgusted by what he had heard about Laurel's actions. His upper lip curled and he wrinkled his nose. Not that this surprised Alexis. According to Yeron, Kryszka body language was similar to that of humans.

"Around other people Laurel appeared catatonic, almost possessed," she went on. "Other times, she would burst into a fit of rage at the slightest provocation. I was afraid she would come after me, so I decided to spend a couple of days with my mother and younger sister, Robin. They lived in Royerstown, about 24 kilometers from my home."

Zoltar shook his head, frowning. "That was a mistake. If someone wants to kill you, they will study your routine, and they will find the names and addresses of your relatives."

Alexis averted her eyes.

"Any information is accessible if you search hard enough." Then his voice softened. "Go on."

"As you figured out, Laurel did her homework. She found the addresses of ten people she thought had wronged her ... and this became her hit list." Alexis swallowed hard.

"My mother went to work that evening. Usually, a friend of the family cared for Robin, but she had died – she was on Laurel's hit list – so that night, I stayed with Robin. Robin had severe asthma and emotional challenges, so we tried not to leave her alone.

"Robin started panting and wheezing, and her emergency medicine did not help. I was about to call a paramedic service, but I heard the creak of careful footsteps from the roof, right above the bedrooms at the back of the house. Robin stared at me, eyes wide and fearful; she pointed toward the ceiling and babbled about monsters. I gave her the quiet sign with my hand to my lips and went to check.

"In my mother's bedroom, I saw a Kryszka soldier ... she had breasts, long hair, and feminine features ... outside the window. Suddenly the window shattered inward, showering the bed and me with slivers. She lunged at me, mouth open wide, sharp teeth bared, and threw me on the bed. The torture was brutal; she shoved my back against the glass fragments. She was hungry ... salivating so much that she never saw me reach for my pointed tool ..." *Damn, what was the Kryszka word for "screwdriver? "*...that turns screws. I stabbed her in one eye with it. She backed away, screaming, and dropped her gun. I was bleeding and her saliva got into my wounds, but I managed to grab her gun. So I killed the soldier and took Robin through my mother's garden, intending to get help from her next-door neighbor. It got much worse. Another Kryszka soldier outside spotted us and opened fire. I killed that one, too, but the plasma set fire to the garden. While my injuries were serious, the sound of the gunfire terrified Robin. She repeatedly gasped from the smoke and suffered a fatal asthma attack."

"Oh, my ... Alexis." Zoltar's voice was pained, his eyes misty with sadness. "Finding her dead must have been horrible for you."

Alexis gulped, her voice faltering and her eyes circled with the white of shock. "It was."

"How did you fight with your deformed limbs?"

Alexis shivered, her voice back in control. "You do what you have to. It helped that your plasma gun was a forgiving weapon. The human-made guns were not designed to be fired by the physically disabled. Too heavy and too much recoil.

"My mother's neighbor, Fenimore, heard the commotion and called for help. Medical personnel transported me to Yeron's floor at the hospital. By then, I was bleeding badly from the glass fragments lodged into my cuts. Her drool had infected my wounds, and the tests showed alien venom. So Yeron injected me with a drug called CX249, which he designed to counteract this poison. Yeron believed that this poison had spread to my brain because my left side became numb. The drug counteracted the effects of the venom, but it awakened previously dormant parts of my brain, and I found myself able to move objects just by using my mind."

Zoltar nodded. "Telekinesis."

"Yes. The police hailed me a hero, but I never understood why. I didn't feel like one because I had let my sister die. But the severity of my injuries necessitated my admission to a room in Yeron and Doctor Hoffman's research ward. They developed a compound called 248AR, which would put my arthritis into remission. It helped me for a short time but did not last, as you can see."

"That you prevented those rogues from harming other people made you a hero." Zoltar's voice tinged with admiration. "What happened to the other victims on Laurel's hit list?"

"Four of them died, plus Robin who was not on her list. The rest survived, some with injuries like mine. My coworker Johnny was one of them, so was my former mate, Mark. Both are dead now. Shively, my neighbor who worked for my father, was another survivor. He was gentler than a lamb with me ... helped carry my trash and groceries. That all changed when he helped form a team to search out the underground compound housing these renegades. We assumed that more were being trained to attack.

"During my recuperation, an army of creatures looking and smelling like dead humans attacked a ..." *How do they say "mall?" Never mind.* "... a group of stores. Yeron had infiltrated an Army website and got videos of these creatures attacking and biting humans. He later figured out that these were live humans poisoned by vischlausk. Realizing that humans did not have the technology to manufacture vischlausk, he suspected renegade Kryszka. Yeron, the other survivors and I feared that these monsters would invade our clinic next. We called the 'dead' people that attacked, 'walkers.' We chose Shively for our leader because he belonged to an underworld group called the mob, and his contacts provided us weapons and a safe house. He is not the first mobster to run afoul of the renegade Kryszka soldiers, so his friends decided to help ... at least while they had the funds."

Zoltar took it all in, eyes thoughtful.

"Yeron showed me the proper way to use a plasma gun. Falling in love ... well, it just happened."

"Interesting." Zoltar regarded her with the intensity of a scientist studying a unique specimen. "Tell me, Alexis, did other humans share your fondness for Yeron?"

"A few, like Doctor Steve Leicht, my internist, and Doctor Joe Hoffman." Alexis smiled. "Most people feared Yeron because he was Kryszka, and they remembered the awful things Eigil and his soldiers had done. When I met Yeron, I saw a kind man, the kind of person who would open bottles for me. We used bottled water at the clinic, and when you have severe arthritis, opening anything is difficult."

Zoltar lifted his brows. "What happened to Laurel?"

"The police considered Laurel a primary suspect because the people who had enraged her ended up in the clinic hurt or dead. When police officers searched her home, they found three women chained in a pit, a dog roaming the house, and human remains in the freezer. Laurel was not there.

"Shortly afterwards, the walkers broke into the clinic, and I stopped thinking about Laurel. They exuded an odor of dampness and newly turned earth, but they were live humans injected with toxic levels of a chemical called vischlausk, which destroyed their inhibitions. They could walk, breathe, and attack, but think only at the basest level. Whoever administered the vischlausk must have smeared them with secretions from corpses. The infection I have ..." she searched Zoltar's eyes,

5

trying to gauge his willingness to believe, "… must have come from those creatures."

Zoltar nodded in agreement.

"Your infection most likely came from bacteria found in cadavers. I am surprised anyone would use vischlausk on humans. Most renegades kill with disintegrators."

"Someone forgot to tell that to the rogue guards. The walkers overran our floor, coming at me, Yeron, my former mate Mark, Shively, and … my mother."

"Your mother?" Zoltar's eyebrows shot up. "Kryszka parents and children fight in the same battle, but I thought that humans and their relatives never did so on the same team."

"Our military does not allow relatives to fight on the same branch at the same time. My mother happened to be in the ward when the walkers attacked. She had never used weapons, but she learned fast. Mark had a vicious temper, which is why we separated. He had hurt other people and me badly, but Shively insisted on having him on our team, although I never understood why. As much as Mark terrified me, I had to find a way to put my feelings about him aside."

Alexis exhaled deeply. "It comes down to one thing, Zoltar: You do what you have to."

Chapter One: Laurel Feeds

Woehar's Underground Laboratory, May 28, 2010, 9:00 p.m.

The burning came and went, depending on the amount of painkillers flowing through Laurel's bloodstream. She lay on her air mattress, eyes fixed on the domed ceiling lights. She thought about her mother's civil moments, like the time she had taken Laurel and her sisters to the shore. While her sisters built sand castles, Laurel gazed at a piling in the ocean. During the day, while they feasted on hot dogs and soda, the breakers covered the top of the piling. After sunset, after her mother had bagged the leftovers and later when the moon cast its first slivers upon the gently lapping ocean, the tide went out, and the piling stood above the waves, its face like a gargoyle with jagged teeth.

In her pain-filled mind, the burning became the piling and the painkillers, the tide. Right now, the tide had gone out and agony as sharp as rusty nails twisted through her hands and feet. Long stretches without painkillers meant her Kryszka keeper, Woehar, was having a bad day. Worse, the huge pink ceiling light morphed into a skeletal face with a blood-red grin, ruby red eyes, and a crooked nose. It was Abaddon, the same specter who'd taught Laurel about death and punishment during his first appearance at her parents' home years ago. It had been weeks since she'd last seen him, but she'd recognize his face anywhere. Ghost-voices whispered from the light, but Abaddon's was the loudest. *Prepare for some bloodletting,* he ordered in his gravelly voice.

Footsteps. Woehar's cleats in the hall shattered her reverie. Light, clicking steps meant she was in a good mood. Loud, clonking steps warned that trouble was coming. Woehar was stomping to the door.

The panel slid open, revealing her gloomy face. Her red eyes smoked with fury.

"Whatever's wrong, I told you everything I know." Laurel's voice quivered.

"Yes ... well, none of it worked." Woehar's eyes blazed with wrath, but no hunger at least not yet. "I sent over two hundred humanoids to your clinic and the surrounding area. They destroyed the stores, part of your clinic–hospital, and killed over thirty people. I did not count the injured. No one who matters died."

"What about Alexis?" Laurel asked as she thought about the one person on Earth she hated most.

Woehar burst into raucous laughter. In the soft light, Laurel could see her glittering teeth drooling saliva. Drooling meant bloodlust, and the brunt of it would come down on Laurel. "My brother Yeron taught Alexis how to use Kryszka plasma and she destroyed my specimens. When her legs gave out, she killed from the floor. When she could not shoot, she fought by using her telekinesis." Woehar sighed. "The plasma gun and her mental powers turned our invalid into a warrior."

"I find that hard to believe. Last time I saw Alexis, her hands were deformed by arthritis." Laurel's lips quivered. The fact that Alexis could handle any gun, let alone Kryszka weapons, had repercussions Laurel couldn't face. It was the equivalent of Yeron giving her keys to the White House. "What do you mean by mental powers?"

"Whatever chemical Yeron administered to Alexis, it gave her the ability to move things and people with her mind the way we Kryszka do. I did not realize this until it was too late. Mark did not accompany Alexis to her training and the microchip only records activity near our human comrade."

Laurel gulped. Things had gone worse than she had expected. "What about the vischlausk ... the stuff that could make your brother violent?"

"I sent three soldiers to the hospital to inoculate Yeron with vischlausk. They tranquilized him, but Alexis and her friend, Shively, interfered before my soldiers could inject the vischlausk. Shively killed my officers and confiscated the vischlausk, while Alexis nursed her beloved Yeron to consciousness. Yeron, Alexis, and their friends are alive and healthy."

Black tumors of rage bloomed inside Laurel, making her forget her fear of Woehar and the pain. "That bitch gets away with everything."

Woehar smiled. "Not everything. She lost her position with the hospital."

"Yeah, right. I bet people are offering her handouts."

"They are, especially my brother. He is so much like our father. Both of them admired the human ... how you say ... spirit." Woehar's anger returned, but she directed it toward her family. "Yeron deserves to die because he betrayed our people when he taught Alexis and her friends how to use our weapons."

"Alexis would never let someone like Yeron near her."

"She has, Laurel, she has. The microchip recorded Mark chastising Yeron and Alexis. He caught them in bed, naked."

"Either Yeron brainwashed Alexis," Laurel said, "or that bitch fell down a well of shit and came up with diamonds. Both of them wrecked our operation."

"Maybe not." Woehar gave her a malignant grin. "They just think they did."

"They did. You said Alexis and her buddies destroyed your specimens and officers."

"They destroyed the ones I sent." Woehar's eyes measured Laurel. "I can make more, but right now, I must give your pain medicine. Be quiet a moment and let me think."

Laurel winced as Woehar injected a syringe into her left buttock. Moments later, the tide of relief came back in, and the burning stopped. Woehar then released the ties that restrained Laurel. She remained still and turned her eyes toward the domed light. Abaddon's face bobbed and smiled. *It's all right, Laurel. You may talk. Deflect her attention away from you.*

"Are you planning a punishment for Alexis?" Laurel gave Woehar a savage grin. "Like I used to with the girls I brought into my home ... before I came here. Let me know when you're ready to get her."

"I can best hurt Alexis through the people she loves. When I get done with her, she will wish she had never been born," sneered Woehar.

"Good. Then I'll roast her." Sheer ecstasy surged through Laurel at the thought of cooking Alexis over a slow fire. Alexis's wiry frame, though wasted around the arms, offered delectable muscle. She rolled her tongue across her lips. "When do we begin?"

Woehar drew in a sharp breath. "My assistant Draekh will give you your last gene fusion tonight. He suspects that a chemical imbalance causes your visions of Abaddon, and that this should resolve after your bodily changes are complete. If the treatment gives you the powers I expect, he and I will administer it to all our specimens. By the time Alexis and her buddies leave their clinic, you and my other augmented specimens will be ready."

"Fine, but Abaddon is ...?"

"Be quiet." Woehar moved a finger to her lips. "Someone is visiting."

A tall, older woman dressed in glittering navy entered, her robe whispering with each soft footstep. According to Woehar, most Kryszka tempered their metals to get the desired color, though most wore blue. Laurel had to admire their skills and Woehar's sensitive Kryszka ears.

The pink light illuminated the visitor's shiny metal-plated tunic. The older Kryszka's eyes seethed with hate, directed toward Woehar. She let loose a spate of what sounded like gibberish to Laurel. Woehar shot it back and the shouting hurt Laurel's head. Laurel cupped her hand over her mouth, fighting hard not to laugh. It sounded like Woehar had gotten into big trouble.

After the senior Kryszka had her say, she stormed out to the hall. The panel closed, but Woehar continued screaming in her native tongue.

"What's wrong?" Laurel asked.

"Quyeba, the governor of the compound, found my other specimens. She and my parents were close friends." Woehar stomped around Laurel's table. "Quyeba said I am a disgrace to my family and no longer welcome here. She wishes I was dead."

Laurel gasped. "Did she really say that?"

"Are you listening?" Woehar grabbed a bed rail and shook it. "She thinks Yeron is dead, and during her tirade, she said, 'Yeron should live here. Sometimes the wrong people die.'"

"Oh, shit!" Laurel sat up, wincing from the pain in her feet. A million thoughts swam through her head: If Woehar left, how would she get pain medicine? What about Woehar's partner, Drake, or whatever she called him? Underneath it all, the question that had haunted her since her arrival at the compound hammered through her brain; what if Woehar's anger incited her bloodlust, and Laurel wound up on the short end of her food chain?

"I'll take you to my house," Laurel offered.

"Your house?" Woehar's voice came out brusque, her narrowed eyes saying, *bad call, you idiot!* "Your officers use primitive techniques, but they are shrewd. By now, they have searched your car and your house and associated you with me. Surely Alexis suspects and shared her suspicions with these officers."

"Alexis again," Laurel said between her gritted teeth. "That girl should die."

"Destroying her will not be easy." She tilted her head, regarding Laurel. "I should have anticipated this. Maybe I can find more specimens and this time, clone them before sending them above ground."

Laurel gasped. "This time ... what?"

"I should clone them. My androids erected another building adjoining this one, one large enough to support my equipment and specimens."

"Another building?" Laurel looked at Woehar. "Quyeba will be furious."

"It does not matter. If Quyeba or anyone else tries to enter this laboratory without my knowledge, they will die." Woehar grinned, showing her bloodstained teeth. "That is why I performed your gene fusion, to make you invincible to any intruder."

The panel whispered open again, drawing Laurel's attention, and another Kryszka, a male doctor, entered. At seven feet tall, he wore a flowy silver metallic gown that reached to his ankles. His birdshot pupils sent chills through her body. He'd chuck his first-do-no-harm rule in the nearest receptacle when he got hungry. More than once, Laurel had contemplated running, but Draekh and Woehar had weapons and telekinesis; Laurel had no way to defend herself. She couldn't run because of foot wounds inflicted by Laurel during a previous temper flare. With baleful eyes, she watched Draekh swagger over to Woehar and give her a noisy smooch. He then set his eyes on Laurel.

His fingers cradled a hypodermic needle. The doctor turned toward Woehar and asked, "Are you sure about this? Too many drugs can damage the specimen."

He spoke in English, but his thick accent made it sound like, *too many drocks can demmege the specimen.*

He regarded Laurel with piercing scrutiny and smiled. *If you're smart,* his smile intimated, *you won't ask for details.* It said it loud and clear without any accent.

Laurel backed off asking further questions, but she bit back a scream when the doctor plunged the needle into her forearm. Seconds later, darkness washed over her.

****

"Wake up," Abaddon's voice crooned. "We shall go for a stroll."

Laurel's eyes fluttered. She swallowed hard and paid for it with a burning sensation in her throat. She rolled her tongue against her teeth. All of them were sharp and pointy. Her pain was gone, and a primal hunger took its place. Fantasies of drinking blood and tearing flesh danced through her mind. She examined her hands, staring at what remained of her dirt-crusted fingers. Her nails had sharpened into talons.

She hopped to her feet. The sudden movement jarred the stumps on her toes, causing them to burn, as if on fire. The name Alexis came to mind, someone who deserved punishment, but she couldn't remember why. Over the last three years, she had been edging out over a mental abyss, walking on a bridge that narrowed with each step. On the day she lost her job, the bridge thinned out into a tightrope. Sometime during her stay with Woehar, the tightrope had snapped, and now a red haze surrounded her.

"I'm so hungry I could eat a bear," she said through the red cloud.

Abaddon's distant cackle sounded muffled, as if it came through a gauzy blanket. "That does not surprise me. Follow me."

Her gait shambling, Laurel followed a blurry form in the red haze. Paneled doors slid open and she descended an escalator into a room the size of a football field. She stood before rows of metal tables where human specimens lay restrained. Their cries sounded distant to her new ears. She guessed they were crying from hunger, pain, or perhaps terror. In any case, she knew that this visit would end in fun. She salivated.

The blurry figure nudged her to the front-most table. Tatters of a woman's shirt floated through the reddish mist. Someone had hiked one sleeve up over the prisoner's elbow, revealing tracks along her forearm. The dirt crusting her hair and forehead left a map of creases on her face, but the smooth skin around her eyes revealed that she was in her early thirties.

Long, ropy strands of saliva dripped from Laurel's mouth at the sight.

Get her, Abaddon's voice whispered. *Now is your time to attack and feed. Think of this woman as dinner, and this laboratory as your restaurant.*

They took another three steps. The prisoner wheezed high-pitched notes with each intake of air. At an earlier time, before Laurel's mutation and descent into madness, she might have recognized the woman as an asthma patient. *I can't do this.* A clawed hand clenched at her snarly hair. *This girl needs treatment. I'll ask Drake, or whatever Woehar calls him, for asthma medicine.*

Asthma medicine? Abaddon's laughter rang in her ears. *You're hungry, Laurel. Feed your bloodlust.*

At her approach, the prisoner let out plaintive cries. "Please help me," she begged, sobbing. "I can't breathe."

She coughed. Fine trickles of blood oozed from the corners of her mouth. Her breath came with sibilant wheezes; accessory muscle use accompanied each intake of air. Her eyes bulged like soup plates, one hand extended toward Laurel as if reaching for alms. Laurel continued tugging at her hair, wondering how she could harm a patient. The filmy figure watched her from the shadows, lips curled into a smirk.

Stabbing sharp as an ice pick knifed through Laurel's head. That and the trickle of blood jarred her primal hunger, and the thirst came on her with a burning force. *That's right,* the ghost voice whispered. *Give in to it. There's no fighting it.*

"Of course," Laurel said, smiling. "I'll be glad to help you."

The woman heaved a sigh of relief. Like most people, the prisoner interpreted Laurel's gentle voice as a sign of good intentions. The girls who'd lived with Laurel and knew her best knew that a soft voice meant imminent death.

Laurel grabbed the woman's arm as if to lift her off the table. She wrapped her arms around the woman's shoulders and bit into her wrist. The relief on the woman's face turned to terror. She shrieked, and her cries excited Laurel more. After savoring the sweet gush of blood, Laurel moved on to the muscle. As she swallowed each morsel, Abaddon rubbed her back.

"Draekh implanted a mixture of vischlausk and chromosomes from Kryszka and our animals," he said. "Woehar and I shall make several clones of you. Then we will see how long Alexis and her people last."

Laurel continued feeding. Somewhere above ground, a dog howled.

Chapter Two: Saying Goodbye

Jackson Hospital, May 29, 8:00 a.m.

At Jackson Hospital, where zombies had trashed several floors two days ago, Alexis Carofalo stuffed her belongings into a rolling suitcase. Her navy blue tunic and matching trousers were made of interwoven metal plates. The tunic enabled her to work its slits with her thoughts. The tunic openings were much kinder to her hands than the snaps and buttons that came with traditional human gear. Soft and flexible, the pants allowed enough room to move her splint-clad leg, and the metallic cuffs on her tunic lent stability to her wrists. *Perfect attire for my upcoming battles with the dead,* she thought.

Yeron told her the outfit had once belonged to his now-dead sister. Alexis smiled at this. So long as the uniform gave her mobility, she didn't give a damn if the devil had worn it. She patted her pockets, assuring herself that she had her mother's rosary beads and two plasma guns. Lighter than traditional guns and about the size of Glocks, these cylinder-shaped weapons had ergonomically-friendly, grooved handles, and fit nicely into her pockets.

She packed her suitcase. A lockbox containing a spare weapon went into a side compartment. Tissues as well as supplies she'd need for her "monthly" went into another, along with soap, shampoo, toothbrush, dental floss, and toothpaste. A bag of Reese's Peanut Butter Cups followed, along with her Eric Clapton CDs, Kindle, chargers, Advil, and a month's supply of her 248AR injections. She paused a moment, flexing her fingers, gnarled from arthritis. Though the deformities remained, the 248AR had chased the pain away. Her travel hair dryer and a photo of her parents and deceased sister, Robin, went in next. After murmuring a prayer with her mother's rosary, she slipped it back into her tunic pocket.

Urgent knocking on the door startled Alexis. Her mother barged in, dressed in a patient gown and robe. She clutched one side of her chest. Her breathing came fast, and sweat glistened on her pale face. Although she wore Jean Nate, her signature fragrance, the acrid stench of fear lingered under the citrusy scent. The redness in her shadowed eyes told Alexis she'd been crying.

"Mom!" Alexis rushed to her mother, arms reaching to hug her. Then she stopped herself, remembering that her mother had a broken rib. "What happened?"

"My neighbor, Fenimore, had a close call last night. He was at the Food Fair when those *things* broke in, but ..." She made a sign of the cross. "He had his gun. He hightailed it to his car. When he got home, three more of those things were staggering across his yard." She wiped her forehead with a tissue. "He made it in the house, and can you believe it? He still had his groceries. I don't know whether to laugh or cry."

Alexis laid a hand on her shoulder. "Is he hurt?"

Her mother shook her head. "He got away without a scratch after he shot the intruders. But you ..." She pursed her lips. "I'm so worried about you. When you're not chasing after dead people, you'll be cooped up in a cabin alone with those boys."

"I won't be alone." Alexis smiled. "Yeron will be with me."

"That boyfriend of yours frightens me most of all." Her mother's lips quivered and then her eyes brightened. "You love this man; I see it in your eyes. But he's not our kind, and his version of loyalty may differ from ours. He had no right to make advances on you. How will the hospital administration handle this?"

Like I give a shit. Alexis rolled her eyes and tried to keep her voice gentle. "Mom, the bosses here have more serious problems. Besides, I told Yeron he couldn't be my doctor. His partner Doctor Hoffman knows my medical history well, so I asked him if he could treat me."

Her mother's frown deepened. "Let me guess. Yeron has to continue treating you because the 248AR is an experimental drug."

Alexis gazed at the floor in silence.

"That's what I thought. How can you get married? No church will marry you."

Who cares about weddings now? Another eyeroll. "As you pointed out, I'm heading into danger," Alexis said, slowly, patiently. "None of us know if we will survive. So I need to grab what happiness I can."

"And Yeron makes you happy?"

Alexis's eyes twinkled with delight. "His brand of loyalty isn't so bad. He stayed with me when those zombies broke in and covered me when I shot the ones near you."

"That's true," her mother conceded. She canted her head. "Maybe Yeron will protect you. I hope so."

"He will."

"Even with Yeron, you can't fight without help. How will you get your medicine? Food? Electricity?"

"I don't know about electricity, but I'm sure Doctor Hoffman can send the 248AR and stuff by UPS or FedEx."

"Don't count on them. At best, each driver will need armed guards with him for every run. At worst, they might suspend deliveries altogether." Her mother nodded as if confirming this to herself. "Fenimore and I discussed you and your friends last night. Tyrone and Johnny have young children, and Shively's wife expects her baby at the end of August. You can't do this without outside help. So I decided to run the supplies to you. When you get to your cabin, wherever you're going, give me your address."

Alexis gasped, her brown eyes staring. "Mom, I can't let you do that! You're hurt."

Her mother shrugged, her jaw set. "By the time you need more medicine, my rib should be better. Besides, my Jeep Cherokee has four-wheel drive and off-road capability, and I can handle guns."

"I've got enough medicine to last a month." Alexis attempted a smile, but it came up lopsided. She fought back the tears. "I'm hoping by then we'll catch the people responsible for this."

"Alexis, honey." Her mother caressed her cheek. Her voice softened. "If you're going to lie, at least wipe your eyes. We both know this won't go away in a month or even a year."

Alexis grimaced. "I guess we do." Then she squeezed her mother's shoulder. "I love you for doing this."

"I love you, too." Her mother managed a weak hug. "Promise me you'll be careful."

"Of course, I will." Alexis tried to be calm, but her voice sounded dim and ancient. "Try to find time for happiness. Cook your neighbor a good ravioli meal. I bet he'd appreciate it."

Her mother drew in a deep breath. "Food's the last thing on his mind. But we're talking about you. After you catch whoever's making those walkers, I want you home safe. I'll do what I can to make that happen. Do you have a rosary?"

Alexis nodded, lips tremulous. She swallowed hard. "Yes, Mom, I'm taking yours."

"Good." Another hug, and her mother kissed her on the cheek. "Please don't be a hero."

Chapter Three: An Understanding

Jackson Hospital, May 29, 10:00 a.m.

Two men wearing bloodstained jeans dragged Yeron's blood analyzer onto a wooden trolley, and his centrifuge and laptop onto another. Shively, the leader of the mission, had hired them. Every five minutes, he shouted out orders, and the men cursed under their breath. They smelled sweaty and the 85-degree temperature did not improve the situation. So far, Yeron's suite, where he'd lived and worked, and the equipment in it hadn't been damaged from the invasion by the vischlausk-poisoned beings.

While the men lifted and shoved, Yeron wrapped his test tubes and unused syringes with bubble wrap and placed them into wooden crates. The culture media, slides, and chemicals went next, the labels unread. His mind kept reliving his romantic night with Alexis, with memories of her soft, silky body and rose fragrance. Love with her that night was like sinking into a romantic dream, until the next morning when her mother and the other survivors had surprised them in bed.

"Yo! Where do you want this stuff?" One of the men jerked his head Shively's way, his words slurred.

"Drop it off in the U-Haul at the loading dock." Shively jerked his thumb toward the door. "C'mon, let's move it."

"I will handle the glass supplies." Yeron grimaced at the sight of the men's unsteady gaits and rough laughter.

Shively cast his glittering blue eyes at him and shrugged. "Whatever."

Yeron loaded his boxes onto a separate hand truck, not wanting to trust the delicate equipment to these clumsy men. When one of them passed by, his breath reeked of liquor. He waited while the men headed for the service elevator. In the corridor, he stopped at a linen cart and retrieved an armload of blankets and pillows. With a deep sigh, he tossed a couple of pillows on his hand truck.

At the loading dock, the men shoved the analyzer and other machinery into the van. More stuttering and high-pitched laughter followed. Unintelligible comments flew when they noticed Yeron. How much liquor did they drink? Frowning, Yeron piled pillows on the floor. The cartons went on top, with the blankets draped over the sides. He shut the doors and the men padlocked them. Shively remained by the dock door, scanning their surroundings, icy smile tucked into place. Because of his tousled blond hair, one wisp up in the air, Alexis said he reminded her of Dennis the Menace, but Yeron thought he had the cold eyes of a killer.

The two men lurched toward the truck, but Shively planted himself in front of the cab. "Not now. Get coffee before you drive."

What coffee? Yeron furrowed his brows. "The hospital cafeteria is in shambles, but they may have a refreshments cart in the lobby," he told Shively.

"I hope so," Shively replied. "These guys are wasted."

Yeron shifted his focus toward the men. Ruddy complexions, husky builds, muscular arms. The still air carried the faint scent of decaying flesh. "I do not understand what you—"

"Look, I'm in no mood to explain." Shively's face reddened. "Go kill time with the others. I want these guys on the road before we leave. I'll call when we're ready to split."

"Right." Yeron headed inside and rode the working service elevator to the fourth floor.

At the landing, he took two steps and cringed at the dread gnawing at his heart. Despite the warm air, chills notched up his spine. Hands thrust in the folds of his tunic, but he forced one foot before the other down the hall. When he arrived at the utility room, a familiar being blocked his access to Alexis's room—not a vischlausk-poisoned being, but Matilda Carofalo, Alexis's mother. Pain lined her pale face, no doubt because of the broken rib, but her gray eyes clouded with anger.

"Matilda." His hands kneaded against his clothes, "I am sorry about the condition in which you found us yesterday."

"Are you?" Matilda was aloof and distant.

"Yes. If my father was here, he would give me a ... a tongue lash ..."

"Tongue lashing?" Matilda canted her head to one side.

Yeron nodded. "He would scold me for my lack of discretion. He schooled me to keep strong emotions private. If the wrong people saw Alexis and me together, they might use that knowledge to harm her."

Matilda heaved a deep sigh, then winced. "I'm glad you realize that," she said. "Finding you two in bed was plenty upsetting, so last night, I called my pastor. He told me that God didn't create the universe just for humans. He said that people from other worlds and humans should strive for a peaceful coexistence. That doesn't include relations between species, dammit!" She shook her head as tears spilled down her cheeks. "Alexis said you make her happy. I should let you and her be."

"But you cannot." Yeron kept his voice soft the way he might with an elder. "You wanted a traditional marriage, good health, and a lucrative career for her, and none of those things happened."

"You bet they didn't." Her face flushed. "Her background and yours are so different – how could you two wind up together? You're her doctor, for God's sake. Under ordinary circumstances, you'd lose your license to practice. I don't know how Administration will handle this."

"There is nothing to handle." Yeron paused, allowing his words to penetrate. The dark look in Matilda's eyes warned him to select his words wisely. "Alexis is doing well on the new medicine, well enough that another doctor can handle her care. She and I share more in common than you realize – our telekinesis and interest in medicine, among other things."

"Spare me." Matilda gave him a dismissive wave of her hand. Another deep breath, and her voice softened. "I must admit, though, you seem to care about my daughter. You stayed by her side when she shot at those beasts; and before that happened, you intervened when a woman from Personnel gave her a hard time." She managed a weak smile. "I appreciate that, Yeron."

Yeron bowed his head. "I did the best I could."

"Sometimes your best isn't enough." Matilda dabbed her eyes with a tissue. "Those monsters were awful, but last March – when I lost my other daughter, Robin – was worse. Know what made this morning so hard? Alexis is my only child now. It killed me to say goodbye. I'm so afraid I'm going to lose her, too."

"Alexis will survive. She is a tough little lady."

"That's the trouble." Matilda glared at him, arms folded across her chest. "Everyone emphasizes the word 'tough.' I focus on 'little lady.'"

So much for delicacy and tact. Yeron bowed his head. If he were human, he would have blushed.

"The post office and FedEx suspended service," Matilda said in a let's-move-on voice. "I don't think Alexis wants to accept that. The pharmacies here might have trouble getting her medicine, too. So Doctor Hoffman gave her enough to last a month. I told her what I'm telling you: One of my friends and I will deliver her medicines and anything else you might need."

"I beg your pardon," Yeron said, raising his hand, "but that will not be necessary. Alexis and I will find someone else to deliver the supplies."

"I doubt you'll find anyone else, and I'm not trusting her medicine to maybes and what-ifs." Her set jaw and determined eyes discouraged argument. "So we'll do this. I wish I could go with her now, but injury aside, I'm too old to chase dead people. Alexis can handle guns, but she shouldn't travel alone with those boys. Tyrone's respectable, but I doubt the others are. Especially Mark. Did you know he tried to kill her?"

The bastard raped her, too. He terrorized her so badly that it took hypnosis for her to remember what happened. Yeron tightened his fists inside his deep pockets. "I do. The others are safe, but Mark is a vicious man. I tried to convince Alexis not to go, but she has her own mind."

"Tell me about it." Matilda stared at him. Her hands dragged through her silver hair. "There's no talking to Alexis when she gets her mind set."

"I found that out." Yeron smiled. "Because of Mark, I am going with her."

"Then you and I are on the same wavelength." Matilda smiled back, but she continued tugging at her hair, twirling strands around her fingers. "So I need a favor. Promise me that you'll bring Alexis home safe. Promise me, Yeron."

So many things can go wrong, Yeron thought. *I should not make promises I might not be able to deliver, but Matilda looks ready to break. She does not need another reason to worry.* His inner conflict resolved, he met Matilda's gaze with his red eyes resolute as steel. "I promise I will bring Alexis home safe."

Chapter Four: Preparing for War

The Streets near Jackson Hospital, May 29, 10:00 p.m.

Suitcase packed, Alexis sat on her bed and clicked on her TV. The TV buzzed and snowy images filled the screen. She tried her phone and got a dial tone. Google and other websites popped on the screen after she booted up her laptop. She leaned back with a sigh of relief. So far, Yahoo, CNN, and other sites confirmed the zombies' destruction in Philadelphia, but not its surrounding towns. The walkers had managed to cut electricity in some areas and wreck a transmission tower or two, but the phones and Internet worked at the hospital. So far.

The photos the reports included depicted the ruins of the seventh floor, the cafeteria, and the emergency room, as well as the stores facing the hospital on the surrounding streets. *Bah fungule. I'm not surfing through some news website. I lived through this mess.*

Instead, she moved onto Facebook, where everyone "shared" reports from the news websites. Several people had posted graphic photos. Her favorite online stores posted alerts about delayed shipments to Philadelphia. No mail today, tomorrow, or next week. Thoughts of her mother circled through her mind, circling the way the zombies had before they moved in for the kill. How would she manage a drive to the cabin? Every so often, Alexis glanced at the photo of her parents and Robin. "Fuck it," she said, turning away from the computer.

She retrieved her rosary and recited the Glorious Mysteries. These prayers seemed appropriate because Yeron, her mother, and everyone else who'd accompanied her to this latest battle had survived. Another knock came from the door after she had finished praying.

Yeron came in, and she rushed into his arms. "Do not listen to any report," he told her. "The news will upset you."

"Not only that. Mom's planning to schlep medicine and other supplies to our cabin. What if her car breaks down and those *things* gang up on her? She's sixty years old, Yeron. She can't handle it."

"Those creatures are dangerous, but Matilda needs something to do. As unpleasant as what she proposes might be, the stress of waiting and not knowing if a loved one is alive is worse. That kind of worry kills."

Alexis wrung her hands, contemplating her mother's health when Robin took sick versus how she was now.

"I see your point," she conceded. "When Robin had her last asthma attack in March, Mom's blood pressure went so high she almost wound up in the hospital. She came through the invasion in good condition, in spite of her broken rib."

"Exactly. Matilda told me her plan, and I tried telling her that either Shively's friends or someone from the hospital can bring any supplies we might need."

"Can someone at the hospital do that?" Alexis searched his soulful red eyes.

Yeron shook his head. "We are doing this ourselves and no one at Jackson has the time to deliver supplies. Besides, whatever alternative anyone suggests, your mother has her own mind. As humans say, the apple never falls far from the tree. You are her only child now, and she fears losing you. Matilda made me promise to bring you home safely."

"My mother told you that?" Alexis's lips broke into a gamine grin that lit up her face. "She must like you. Next, she'll ask you to call her 'Mom.'"

"That is not going to happen." Yeron grinned. "Matilda spoke with me because she is desperate to keep you alive, and she knows I care about you."

"Can't Shively's guys transport my medicine?"

"They could." Yeron rubbed his forehead. "Shively's men showed up drunk this afternoon, and he thinks coffee will make them sober. They were rough with the analyzer. I did not trust them to handle the glass supplies. Would you want these men to transport your medicine?"

"No way. My mother's careful with anything she handles, so we work with either them or her. Shit," Alexis said through clenched teeth. "Before she left, she begged me not to be a hero. I don't want her to be one either." She shuddered and Yeron tightened his arms around her.

"Matilda can do this if she keeps her wits about her," Yeron assured her. "Last night, the walkers came at us on the seventh floor, a confined spot. This time, she will be driving a car. Cars go fast, my Steel Rose, and the beings with vischlausk poisoning shuffle."

"What about the renegade soldiers?"

"I hope that if she sees any, she smashes into them." Yeron's voice oozed bitterness. "I hate them for destroying my mother and father, and now they are after you. The promise I made to Matilda matters to me as well. I care about you a lot, especially after last night."

"Last night?" Alexis smiled up at him, batting her eyelashes. "Many things happened, Doctor Phil. Be specific."

Yeron laughed. "Before you fell asleep, we did this ..." he bent down and kissed her cheek, "... and that ..." he went for her lips. He wore the aroma of Irish Spring soap and his sinewy arms felt oh, so reassuring. She could spend the rest of the day in a lip lock with him.

"Oh, I'm sure we did other things, too." She giggled. "You should refresh my memory. Preferably away from the camera."

Yeron lifted his chin upward, his eyes focused on a white disk. To Alexis, it resembled a smoke alarm. He stood regarding the alarm a moment and then turned his eyes toward another disk above the window. "There." He gave Alexis a pleased-with-himself grin. "I dismantled both cameras."

"You did what?" Alexis's jaw dropped; her eyes bulged. "How?"

"I dismantled the wires with my mind. You could, too, if you did not daydream so much."

Alexis's cheeks reddened. "I do *not* daydream. I'm thinking."

"What about, dear?"

"I wonder how many zombies are out there and whether we'll catch the people who made them. More than that, I wish we could go to a peaceful island with a temperate climate, where these things don't happen."

"So do I, my Steel Rose. So do I." With that, Yeron released one hand, scooped her into both arms, and laid her on the bed. "We have time before Shively's guys sober up, so let us make the most of it."

****

Under a sky dark as tar, Shively and his gang left through the rear exit of Jackson Hospital. The power blackout cloaked the surrounding streets in shadow. Shively and Tyrone led them through an alley parallel to Jonasville Street, where the hospital was. Alexis stayed close to Yeron, teeth gritted, with Johnny to her left, and behind Shively. Mark followed close behind her. Despite Johnny's and the others' assurances that they could control Mark, she found herself shivering. She felt his intent stare on her, the way she had ten years ago right before he threw her on the couch.

"Brrrrrrr." She rubbed her arms, moving closer to Yeron.

The warm May air carried a stench like that of rotting tomatoes. At the end of the block, the full moon splashed silver over the buildings and bushes. Yesterday they had slaughtered an army of emaciated, wasted people who smelled like they were many days dead, monsters that had trashed Jackson Hospital's research floor. They knew more lay in wait; the offensive odor betrayed their secrecy.

Unease festered in Alexis's stomach. A creepy feeling nagged at her, like someone had eyes on her, biding his time, planning a surprise attack.

She glanced toward Yeron. The soldier in him had replaced the lover: squared shoulders, head erect, jaw muscles tight, and mouth closed. His ruby eyes shifted right and left. With the invisible eyes on her came an overwhelming sadness. *Don't be ridiculous,* she scolded herself. *It's not like he's snubbing you at some party. He's watching out for trouble and you should, too, so pay attention.*

Still, the feeling of being watched lingered.

Aw *ooooooooo! A*WOOOOOOOOOOOOOO!

Alexis let out a yelp, and this time, she *did* latch onto Yeron's elbow as if they were dancing at a party. The howling continued, loud and plaintive.

"Listen to that." She nudged his shoulder. "Those woods are crawling with dead and their stink's drawing the dogs."

"The dogs smell Kryszka renegades." Johnny's voice faltered. His wide blue eyes remained fixed on their surroundings. "I don't like this."

"Whether you like it or not, deal," Shively told them.

"That's right." Mark's voice raked her with freezing contempt. "We've had enough of your whining."

Alexis stiffened, then set her lips in a grim line. *Damn, I'm not spending the next several weeks listening to Mark's shit.*

With her telekinesis at the ready, she whirled upon Mark and unleashed a surge of psychic energy. Mark stumbled, fell against a brick wall, and then landed in a heap. He doubled over, one hand rubbing his right arm.

"Cut the shit, asshole," she warned him.

"Whoa!" Johnny brayed nervous laughter. "She socked it to you."

"Bitch nearly broke my arm." Mark scowled, struggling to his feet.

"Next time, she might hurt you bad." Tyrone's solemn face shone with sweat. "If I were you, I'd shut it."

Mark's mouth worked like a guppy's, and in the moonlight, his face reddened. Tyrone held his finger to his lips. Mark kept quiet.

The howling continued, sending liquid fear racing through Alexis's veins.

"Of course, the dogs will howl," Yeron said. "This street smells gamey."

"The animals sense danger, too." Alexis hugged her tunic around her shoulders. She had Yeron to thank for looting the plasma guns and uniform after his compound exploded. "*Weekly World Reporter* had a big article on dogs and how they smell scent."

Yeron did not comment. He continued staring ahead, his face impassive.

"I'd like to give those creatures a nice, long, dirt nap." Johnny scowled. "Too bad *Weekly World* didn't give us an easy way to make it happen."

"Do not worry, honey." Yeron smiled and stroked her hair. "I will not let you face those creatures alone."

"Be quiet, all of you!" Shively darted a withering glance over his shoulder. "There's something weird ahead."

Shively reached into his backpack for his binoculars and flashlight. Alexis and the others stopped and kept quiet. All eyes were on Shively. There was no sound coming from the houses; most of them were cloaked in shadow. No streetlights, thanks to the power outage. The dogs continued howling, long, melancholy wails. No other sounds could be heard except for the crickets. The air thickened with its rancid odor. Alexis slid her fingers around her plasma gun. Knees bent, she braced herself for an exchange of gunfire.

"Where at?" she asked.

"The back alley." Shively pointed and moved to his left.

Alexis and the others hustled after him. An acrid smell wafted from a garage near a doctor's office. The buzzing came next. The garage appeared intact, but the low beam from Shively's flashlight washed over a corpse. Swarms of flies buzzed around its skeletal legs and the two blood-spattered bushes that concealed the rest of the body.

Shively and Yeron slipped on rubber gloves. They yanked aside the brambles, revealing a gutted woman. Dirt crusted her hair and face. Her whole body had deteriorated into one gaping sore, with long, serrated gashes stretching from elbow to wrist. Her intestines hung from her torn abdomen. Someone – or something – had ripped her open and torn the flesh from her legs. The flies were forming black clouds over her remains.

"Ew!" Alexis recoiled, grimacing.

Johnny gagged and vomited behind her.

"If I were human, I would vomit, too," Yeron said as he gave Johnny a sympathetic nod. He then bent down, shining a light on the victim. "This reminds me of the atrocities Eigil and his soldiers inflicted on their prisoners. Someone sent us a warning."

"You calling on your buddies, Shively?" asked Tyrone.

"Nope, I've got them moving stuff to the cabin. Let the cops deal with this mess. I'm checking on my guys." Shively two-fingered his cell phone from the top pocket in his overalls.

"Enemy soldiers." Alexis shook her head, watching Shively make his call. "They're the brains behind this operation."

"You got that right," Tyrone said. "Whoever left this here wants us dead, too."

"That's why we shouldn't involve Alexis," Mark said. "We need people who can handle weapons without hurting others."

At the sound of his harsh voice, Alexis cringed. She backed away from him and leveled him with a glowering stare.

"Mark." Alexis forced calmness into her voice. "I know you're a meathead but try to fathom this. I sedated the things that grabbed you so they wouldn't eat your meathead brain for supper. That meant sedating you, too. Now if those burns hurt you so much, I'll kiss them and make them all better." Alexis's syrupy voice lowered as she glanced at him

Yeron scowled. "Alexis, do not touch him, even as a joke. You do not know what your meathead does in private."

"So what does he do in private, Doc?" asked Johnny. "Jack off in his didies?"

It wouldn't be the first time someone caught him doing that, Alexis thought, and she wrapped her arms around herself, skin chilled from the memory. "Johnny, who told you?"

Johnny cocked his head to one side. "A little birdie."

"Stop!" Tyrone slapped Johnny on the shoulder, laughing. "I can't bring you anywhere."

"That's enough." Shively glared at everyone, tucking his phone back into his pocket. "Let's get out of here."

And then gunfire erupted.

****

More shooting, and yellow rays shot inches away from them, blackening the brick siding of the office building.

"Get down!" Shively hollered.

Yeron whisked Alexis behind two Dumpsters, where they knelt. The others ducked behind parked cars. From overhead, plasma weapons cut yellow swaths across the street, scorching the pavement and cars. With each blast came the stink of sulfur. Alexis huddled against Yeron, peeking between the waste receptacles and scanning the buildings for signs of the shooter. The street appeared deserted. Then Yeron cupped his hand around the back of her head and turned her face skyward. The moonlight revealed two Kryszka renegade soldiers crouched on the roof of a federal bank across the street, guns trained toward them. Their dark helmets and body positions cast their faces in shadow. Johnny and Tyrone attempted to return fire, but their shots missed their target. Alexis raised her gun, not expecting better results. She hadn't counted on an assault by snipers.

"Don't." Yeron stayed her hand, his voice a faint whisper. "Let us use our minds."

Alexis thrust her psychic energy at the soldiers' hands. One gun dropped, and then the other.

It amazed her how easy mind maneuvers were becoming, but like many soldiers, these renegades carried extra guns. Alexis and Yeron never gave them a chance to reach for their backup weapons. In the next instant, the renegades bobbed and weaved toward the edge of the roof, then toppled over the side. No screams or shouts, just a whooshing sound, two thumps, and the clatter of metal.

"Come on." Yeron nudged her shoulder. "If we are lucky, they broke their necks. If not, maybe the fall stunned them."

Alexis bolted for the alley where their pursuers had landed. The shooters should have sustained serious injuries after a fall from a two-story building, but no one cried for help. Alexis surmised that maybe the fall knocked them unconscious.

She was learning to hate the word "maybe."

In the alley, one assailant lay prone, writhing in pain. The other got up shakily and raised his gun. Shively charged toward them like a panther, fired his sidearm, and the renegade's head exploded in a wash of blood. Tyrone shot the other in his neck. His movement stopped.

"Fuck!" Johnny waved his fist. "How come they survived the fall?"

"Good question." Alexis looked at Yeron. "You shoved them with your thoughts, too, right? One of them should have busted his skull."

"Their armor protected them." Yeron laid his hand on Alexis's shoulder. "Their training includes techniques to minimize injury during a fall."

"Techniques for falling?" Alexis's brown eyes widened. "What do they do, levitate?"

"No. Most people are too frightened to manage levitations. Our soldiers focus on landing feet first. At all times." Yeron smiled. "I know because I had to learn."

"Don't worry." Johnny laughed. "Your lover will catch you if you fall."

Mark, who had lapsed into stony silence, favored Johnny with a harsh glare. "This isn't funny, Johnny."

"Who asked you, candy boy?" Johnny asked, and shot him a

hard look.

"Guys ... stop." Shively jerked his thumb toward a black SUV parked in a small driveway, two blocks away from Jonasville Street. "There's Tyrone's Pathfinder. You driving, Tye?"

"Yep. We're leaving while we can."

"Good. My contact left a Hummer for us on the outskirts of Royerstown. I'll drive from there. Then we're heading out to the cabin in Merriman Trails."

Chapter Five: Laurel's Body Changes

Kryszka Underground Laboratory, May 29, 12:00 p.m.

After what seemed like forever, the reddish cloud faded. Laurel's eyes lingered over the bloodied remains of an older woman, the second person she'd fed on in twelve hours. The sweetness lingered in her mouth, but with it came an infinite sadness. Her eyes brimmed with tears. An unemployed respiratory therapist, she had healed people for a living. Why feeding should upset her now she couldn't say, but she belonged at Jackson Hospital, giving breathing treatments to people with asthma. Then she remembered; management had fired her in March. That, and a government agency suspended her license because of an inquiry into a patient's death. What had she done?

You can't unring a bell, a male voice whispered, and in the round overhead light, Abaddon's demonic face grinned at her. *Love what you are and feed.*

Feed? Laurel had consumed her second meal while Woehar disposed of the first. The green and white jumpsuit she'd snatched from a prisoner at Woehar's lab had turned maroon with blood. Her feet tingled. Looking down, she saw the reason. Dark green claws were poking from her stumps. A scream lodged in her throat. Instead, she licked her bloodstained hands.

A TV screen clicked on overhead. It portrayed a cage with thick, metal bars, large enough to hold a bear. Inside, a *settva*, a two-legged creature with green scales, sharp teeth, and yellow eyes, chewed on a Kryszka native's leg. Someone had tied the prisoner's hands and feet. He screamed until his vocal cords ruptured, and his voice became stridulous. Moments later, the man lost consciousness. Why didn't the prisoner use his telekinesis to protect himself? Maybe he couldn't. Laurel shivered.

Woehar stood beside her, rubbing her shoulders. She must have returned during Abaddon's visit.

"Did I do that?" Laurel turned her eyes away from the screen and traced her talons along the bones. Most of them were picked clean, except for under the ribcage and other hard to reach places. Her voice sounded hoarse. She tried reconciling her body changes with her former life as a respiratory therapist, but the cloying essence of meat called to her. "How can I eat raw meat?"

"The alterations in your chromosomes and metabolism reinforced your craving and gave you the ability to digest raw meat. As your body continues to change, your appetite will increase. Your teeth have gotten sharp." Woehar crooked her finger. "I will show you."

With the blood warming her stomach, and foot claws scraping the floor, Laurel followed Woehar to a mirror over a wall sink. The teeth didn't matter; she remembered treating asthma patients and adopting homeless girls. Where did that Laurel go?

"Look in the mirror." Woehar's smug voice invaded her thoughts. "What do you think?"

Laurel looked. The pink light bulbs threw light on her yellow eyes and stringy blonde hair matted with blood. The skin around her face had peeled, leaving behind greenish scales on her cheeks. Her parted lips revealed bloodstained, serrated teeth. She was turning into a *settva*.

Laurel opened her mouth to scream, but instead let out a dusty croak. "My skin ... my hands!" Her voice sounded as if pebbles had lodged in her windpipe. She flickered a glance toward Woehar's narrowed, forbidding eyes and forced a smile. "I look like Abaddon's bride."

"You think so?" Woehar frowned. "Why do you keep mentioning Abaddon? I told you, he is only a figment of your chemical imbalance."

"Chemical imbalance?" Laurel managed another faux grin worthy of an Oscar. "Whether he's real or not, I still look like his bride. If I had these teeth before, I could've made the girls living with me terrified." *Let me out,* a shrill voice cried inside her. It belonged to the human therapist. *Let me treat my patients.* She hesitated a moment, regarded Woehar's evil eyes, and then continued. "Did you go anywhere interesting?"

"Maybe. Draekh and I left a surprise, including the remains of your last meal, for Alexis and her buddies."

"You found them?" Laurel couldn't help smiling at Woehar's cleverness. "Where?"

"Your friends were skulking through a dirty alley." Woehar's smile broadened. "My surveillance camera sees all, thanks to Mark Adams, a hostile participant. He does not know it, but the computer chip I placed under his skin enables me to track his movements and those of the ones around him."

"Whoa!" Laurel admired Woehar's dexterity with technology. "While you watch Mark, I'll go after Alexis and her little clique."

"Not while Quyeba hovers over her precious compound." Woehar's voice dripped with sarcasm. "I shall distract our dear governor first and then you do what you please with Alexis."

"Don't worry. I'll get Alexis." Laurel salivated at the thought.

"Whatever you do, Alexis is not suitable for consumption," Woehar advised. "Yeron contaminated her with his medicines and her meat will make you ill. Draekh thought his chemicals might contaminate you, too, until he understood my plans. I want you well fed."

What happened to my job? What about my home? the caregiver inside screamed, but Laurel's mouth drooled. "So what are your plans, Woehar? I'm sure you had particular reasons for turning me."

"I did." Woehar's lips curled into a malignant grin. "My assistant Draekh and I will continue to pick up street people and other undesirables. We shall clone them and make new specimens for my vischlausk treatments. These people shall be your assignment."

"My assignment?" Laurel echoed, puzzled, eyes on the tables. Dozens surrounded her, each holding a person. "Do you want me to inject them with vitriol or whatever you call it?"

"Draekh and I shall administer what vischlausk we need." Woehar's red eyes glittered with madness. "We plan to process many specimens before we turn them loose. Your job is torturing them."

"Oh, dear, I must—" *help them,* Laurel started to say. "—think of some creative punishments," she said instead, clasping her hands. "I once tied a girl to the ceiling by the wrists. She hung for days without food or water before she died."

"No, Laurel, I want them alive. Feed them and give them water. Do everything you can to inflict pain without breaking any bones or causing internal injuries." Woehar smiled like a teacher encouraging a pupil. "Use your imagination."

Laurel glided past each table, sizing up the prisoners, and listening to their pained cries. If she could just treat their injuries as best as she could ... but the image of torn flesh danced through her mind. A bite in strategic places wouldn't crush any bones or injure vital organs, but might cause excruciating agony. If only she had her cigarettes, she lamented, since burns inflicted the worst pain. "Do you have an instrument that burns?"

"Will this do?" Woehar handed Laurel a scalpel with sharp edges. "If you squeeze the side buttons, the blade will get scalding hot and leave burns."

Laurel grinned. "Perfect."

Woehar grinned. "I will expect progress reports."

"No problem. I'll pretend I'm punishing Alexis." Straightening up, she took in her surroundings; she estimated at least forty prisoners. Laurel knew how to exact discipline. With scalpel in hand, she got to work.

Chapter Six: On the Road

Shively's Cabin at Merriman Trails, May 30, 4:45 a.m.

Tyrone sat at the wheel, eyes on the road, knuckles shiny with sweat. Beside him, Shively thumbed through a map while chain-smoking Marlboros. The air thickened with smoke, and Alexis had to keep clearing her throat. She could tell by the street signs and wooded areas that they'd gone somewhere northwest of Royerstown. It was 5:00 a.m., and the sun had come up, an orange ball of fire in the sky.

Alexis cuddled with Yeron in the Pathfinder's middle seat, hand clasped in his. Mark frowned in the cargo seat behind her, his eyes smoking with hate. Johnny, his seatmate, gave no sign of noticing. He had his nose in a *Weekly World Reporter* magazine. Alexis would have given her last Reese's Peanut Butter Cup for one of his wisecracks. Mark's face reddened with every glance towards Johnny. Any second, he'd lose it and get out his nail-studded baseball bat, and come after her with it the way he had ten years ago. The memory sent chills up her spine.

She touched the left border around her lips, where Yeron had last kissed her. Was he also thinking about their earlier tryst? His blank expression gave no clues. His culture and life in a Kryszka colony had schooled him well in hiding his emotions. *Never mind your trysts,* she scolded herself. *Quit woolgathering; find the renegades' compound, and shoot any walkers in your way. In that order.*

The silence in the vehicle was deafening, the stink of cigarettes worse. Shively exhaled plumes of smoke out the window while giving directions to Tyrone in a clipped, tense voice. Perspiration drenched his blond hair despite the breeze blowing through the open windows. Tyrone darted glances behind him at every traffic light. The dark brown circles of weariness around both men's eyes made Alexis wonder when they'd last slept.

The banter they had enjoyed leaving the hospital had stopped. The skirmish with the sniper had left everyone speechless. At a nondescript garage, Shively exchanged Tyrone's car for an olive green Hummer. The silence continued while everyone moved their bags to the

Hummer, and later at the IHOP where they had breakfast. The dread hovering over everyone did not allow them the luxury of idle chitchat.

Tyrone broke the silence by asking, "So where is this cabin, Shively?"

"Merriman Trails development in Grays Landing, off Route 85. It's not too far from the Trident Mall."

"The first zombie outbreak happened there this past March." Alexis offered a strained smile. "Maybe the scientists behind this are still close by."

"That's my thinking, too," Shively agreed.

****

Shively slowed the vehicle as they approached a smoke-filled wooded area. Between swirls of gray, officers and soldiers dressed in navy blue were dragging bodies toward the road. The musty smell in the car had been bad, but the stink of cooked flesh blending with the fumes from outside overrode the cigarette odor. The flames cleared further on, leaving behind battered limbs and bodies, scrawny figures in filthy tatters. They were squirming and moaning. Five walkers crawled into the street, forcing Shively to assume a serpentine course. One man with half of his face sloughed away loped toward the shoulder, and then turned toward another figure at his feet. He reached down and grabbed the man's left arm as if to help. Instead, he braced one foot against the man's back and yanked his arm. The limb tore off the way a chicken wing might, but blood spurted, and he devoured the flesh. The hapless man screamed through it all, his cries drowning out the chomping sounds.

Alexis shuddered. Yeron pulled her close and rubbed her shoulder.

"Oh, my God!" Her lips quivered. "What the hell's this?"

"That's a damned good question." Tyrone maintained his stoic demeanor, but jewels of perspiration nested in his eyebrows. Droplets ran down his mocha-colored face and neck. He was breathing hard. "Lord, help us."

"Fuck!" Johnny slammed the magazine on his seat. "What are the cops doing, playing pocket pool?"

"They are searching for people who can be saved," Yeron said, casting a glance his way. "They might cremate the dead to avoid a pandemic ... if they can find the time."

Alexis straightened up, her eyes on Shively and the others while twirling her finger through her tangled curls. "If not, will we have to do that?"

"If necessary," Shively said. "First, though, we'll kick butt. Then we'll nuke the renegades and find the place where they are manufacturing these monsters."

Tyrone arched his eyebrows. "How does our cabin play into that?"

"Aside from being close to Trident Mall, its bulletproof windows and electric fence will protect us." Shively nodded with a single, decisive dip of the chin.

"But we don't have electricity ... do we?" Alexis continued twirling her hair.

"We own a generator." At the next traffic light, Shively turned his head, smiling like a teacher encouraging reticent pupils. "We've got walkie-talkies, too, in case the phones don't work. Simple to use. Right, Mark? You're quiet. Are you all right?"

"Yes, sir," Mark replied in a distant voice.

About a half hour later, they doglegged up Mill Road, a narrow street. The willow trees leaned toward the road, their thick trunks splashed with maroon, marking battles between humans and creatures. At the dead end, Shively swung up a dirt driveway and parked the Hummer in front of a barbed wire fence. The young men slung their backpacks across their shoulders. Alexis and Yeron carried three bulky trunks between them, using telekinesis. They followed the others up the dirt road to a brick cabin; the trunks floated in the air ahead of them. Everyone shuffled into a living room, an eight-by-six-foot cubicle with vomit-green walls.

Alexis let her trunks drop and dove for the loveseat, Yeron beside her. Fiber filling poked out of the ripped, threadbare yellow cushions. Mark took the lone chair, a hardback affair with faded paint. Johnny and Tyrone sat cross-legged on the wooden floor. No comforts of home here.

"Guys, listen up," Shively said in his drillmaster's voice. He stood, hands on his hips, eyes sweeping over everyone. "First order of business; find that other compound. Get ready to march and ride. If the walkers come at us, we shoot. Alexis and Yeron will use the plasma guns."

Mark's eyes brightened with tears, and his lips moved up and down like a fish. Not that this surprised Alexis. Though he harassed people smaller than he, he crumbled around people his own size. She'd seen it at the hospital. Tyrone shot him a fierce glance.

"Johnny, you handle the radio and Geiger counter. The former Kryszka compound had higher levels of radiation, so this one might, too. If you pick up any strange signals, sing out. If you run into any dead walkers or Kryszka renegades, kill them. Let the authorities find the mess; don't make any calls unless I say so.

"Tyrone, Yeron, Alexis, and I will alternate on point. Tyrone and I will use the M16s. Alexis will use the plasma guns because the recoil of our guns would be too much for her. She and Yeron will fight with their mental powers and plasma guns. As for other chores ..."

Shively's eyes flickered back and forth, and then settled on Mark. "Mark, you get clean up and laundry. If one of us gets sick, shot, or otherwise, you fill their spot." His penetrating gaze probed the room again. "I will maintain the generator. Yeron, you run the lab and treat any injuries. Alexis, you're his assistant. Tyrone, you handle repairs for the Hummer and any broken plumbing. Johnny, you're in charge of the phones and computer. Everyone helps with the cooking. Questions?"

Johnny raised his hand. "What happens if more than one person gets sick or hurt?"

"Then we fight short. I assigned people based on their skills. Yeron and Alexis will work the lab because of their medical skills. If things get ugly, then we learn each other's jobs.

"Stay calm, and you'll get through this alive. Panic, and you may not." He paused, sweeping his intense stare across the room. "Room assignments."

He's acting as if we're in the army ... Another glance at the dilapidated furniture and weather-beaten floorboards, and Alexis rolled her eyes. *He's right.*

At Shively's command, she shuffled past a closet-sized office and through a hallway.

"Tyrone and I get the master bedroom." Shively waved toward the rear of the house. His hand shifted toward a door adjoining the office. "Yeron, you get the basement. There's a shower, lab supplies, and a sofa bed."

Yeron glanced toward the door, smiled, and nudged Alexis's shoulder. Alexis smiled back and watched him glide down the steps.

"Alexis, you sleep here." Shively knocked on the door facing her and then pointed to another across the hall. "Mark and Johnny, you share."

Mark banged open the door, stole a peek, and then slammed down his carryall. "Now wait a minute. I'm not sharing that closet with anyone."

"Be quiet!" Tyrone's eyes flashed at Mark. "This isn't a fucking party."

Here we go with the Mark Adams show.

Another roll of Alexis's eyes. Before she could slide her suitcase into the room, Mark shoved her, causing her to lurch against the doorway. "Alexis has way more room in here," he went on in a hateful, childish voice. "She gets special weapons, time with her ET boyfriend, and a cake assignment in the field. Are we catering to her whims out here or what?"

"What whims, bastard?" Alexis shoved him back with her thoughts. He stumbled. His hand grabbed the doorknob, seeking purchase, and found none. He landed on his butt amidst peals of mirth from the others. "Nobody got a cakewalk."

"Is that right?" Mark struggled to his feet.

"Nobody wants to bunk with you, asshole!" Johnny punched him, knocking him down again.

"Guys, stop," Tyrone warned, but his face lit up with a wan smile. "Alexis, does it matter which room you get?"

"Yep," Johnny jumped in with a devilish grin. "She wants to sleep with Yeron."

"Johnny!" Alexis let out a bray of laughter. At least the comedian was back in business.

"What's the big deal?" Johnny winked. "We don't mind you and Yeron indulging in kinkiness."

"This isn't a fucking honeymoon suite." Shively pursed his lips. His frosty eyes measured Johnny. "Alexis doesn't get to spend time with Yeron unless they're doing a job."

Thank you very much, Johnny. Alexis gritted her teeth. "Yeron needs the basement for lab work anyway. I don't care where I sleep, but one of us has to share."

"I'll sleep in the office," Johnny offered. "At least it means peace and quiet."

"Suit yourself." Shively shrugged. "Mark, I gave Alexis a larger room because she takes medicine and wears a leg brace. These items take up space. What's your problem?"

Mark sucked in a deep breath. "Nothing, sir."

"Good." Shively's eyes roved over everyone. "The bickering stops. *Now.*"

Thumping steps punctuated his statement. The basement door banged open. "Shively," Yeron called out. "I just spotted an army of walkers on my closed circuit monitor. They broke through the fence."

"Shit!" With a deep frown, Tyrone scooped up Shively's binoculars and peered out the window. "They're coming, ugly things looking deader than dead. How did they find our cabin?"

"Someone knows we're here." Shively gave a nervous wave of his hand. "Guys, the situation is bad. Get ready."

Baggage dropped, weapons appeared, helmets slid on, and balaclavas lowered. Alexis barreled toward the open gate with the others, down a narrow path, led by Shively and Yeron shouting directions.

Chapter Seven: Alexis's Specimen

Grounds surrounding Shively's Cabin, May 30, 2:45 p.m.

Several figures lay sprawled in the grass, their hands charred black. Alexis swept ahead of Shively, thrusting her mental shield and firepower at the ones still coming at them. Yeron glided past Shively on his left. Tyrone and Shively moved like panthers, battering the figures with lead, angling for headshots. Always a headshot; the creatures' infected brains governed their desire to attack and feed. Johnny nabbed the figures that lunged past the lead and fire, and Mark felled the ones approaching his periphery. They kept on coming, faster than Alexis could fry them. Bony talons angled for her face. She ducked, and Johnny's bullet sheared the head off her would-be killer. Yeron disintegrated another two walkers who were converging on her. Unbidden, images of her late sister's face flashed before Alexis; she poured her anger into a mind-shove that battered a walker reaching for Tyrone's shoulders. For what seemed like hours, the air rang with the rasp of breathing, and gunfire stitching across the field, and then ... silence.

The group stared at the smoke drifting from the tangled heap of bloodied bodies. Alexis estimated at least thirty dead, gross things in tattered clothes, crawling with bugs on rat-bitten faces. Worse, the bodies stank like charred carrion. Her companions looked as dirty and tired as she felt. "Hoffman said that a chemical—vischlausk—fried their brains and made them like this," she said. "Horseshit! These are walking dead. It said so in *Weekly World Reporter*."

"These walkers are live people, honey," Yeron said in a pained voice. "Joe Hoffman was right about the poison. I tried to tell you that."

"Bullshit." Johnny folded his arms across his chest.

"Then the bull's having a good shit," Shively said. "I found that syringe, the one with the vischlausk, the night the walkers attacked the hospital. The renegades used that chemical to make them wild."

Alexis shook her head. "They look mighty dead to me."

"They *smell* dead." Tyrone shrugged. "Maybe someone implanted a device in their head, something that makes them lunge and attack."

Alexis shifted her eyes toward Mark, who kicked at the forms, assuring himself they were harmless. No movement. He remained silent.

"While you debate this," Yeron said, giving Alexis an easy and open grin, "I found an intact specimen. A certain someone here sedated the creature instead of disintegrating him." He laid his muscular arm across her shoulders. "I will load it onto the Hummer for tissue analysis. You do not mind helping me, do you?"

"Of course not." Alexis glanced sideways, hoping no one would notice her reddening face.

"Look at that." Tyrone exchanged an amused glance with Johnny. "Her heart's going pitter-pat, pitter-pat."

"That's enough," Shively said in a gruff voice. "Move it."

****

Alexis exited the bathroom in a sweatshirt and pants, towel-drying her hair. She stumbled over something hard ... Johnny's booted foot. He knelt by the door to Mark's room, right ear against the wood, giggling. "Hey, Alexis!" he whispered, waving his hand. "Check this out."

Alexis groaned. "Check what out? Yeron needs my help."

"Your sweetie can wait. This is precious."

With a shrug, Alexis squatted beside him as far down as her brace would allow. Then she heard a man weeping. Mark let out a long, anguished sob, followed by *riiip!*

"Johnny, that's not funny." Her lips quivered. She glared at him, scared and angry. "This bastard raped and tried to kill me years ago. Now we're supposed to trust him with our lives."

"Exactly my point. Mark's up to something, so we ought to watch him. He shredded paper when you and he were patients on the same floor." Johnny cracked the door and peeked. Another giggle. "Former Mr. Tough Guy pisses in a diaper now. How do you like that?"

"Alexis," Yeron called from the basement doorway. "What are you doing? Please come down here."

"In a minute." Alexis turned toward Johnny, grimacing. "Mark can be devious; I found that out the hard way. But he never ripped paper or diapered when we lived together. Maybe when the renegade Kryszka nailed him, his kidneys took the brunt of the attack."

"Damn, you're clueless!" Johnny cackled. "The man's getting his jollies."

"What jollies?" Yeron stepped into the hall, eyes intent on Alexis and Johnny.

"Shhh!" Alexis pressed her ear closer. She tried to peek through the crack but Johnny blocked her view. Mark let out another wail, followed by the tearing of paper. She cringed, still drying her hair with the towel.

"Eavesdropping and spying at his door?" Yeron watched her, a puzzled frown on his face. "What is going on?"

"Mark's bawling and tearing up paper, that's what." Alexis kept her voice low. "He's great at attacking people he thinks can't defend themselves, but he chokes at the thought of real fighting."

"He cries because he is angry," Yeron said. "He was plotting terrible things against us just now. Vague threats, such as 'I will get them where it hurts the most.' I heard every word he said from the stairs."

"No shit." Johnny riveted his gaze on Yeron. "You must have the ears of a cat. Do other people like you have sharp ears?"

Yeron nodded. "All Kryszka have sensitive hearing, more so than humans. I was Mark's healer at the hospital. From what I observed, he is dangerous. He beat his second wife and molested her two girls. I warned Shively, but he said he had special plans for Mark."

"A child molester?" Alexis gasped. "Good Lord!"

"The man disgusts me." Yeron grimaced. "Shively wants him for insurance."

"What's this about Shively?" Tyrone emerged from his bedroom with a worried frown.

"Mark's ranting and ripping paper." Johnny grinned. "He pees and jacks off in his diaper, too. Goes after kids, and writes about it all in his diary."

"Are you serious?" Tyrone tiptoed behind Johnny and cracked Mark's door.

Alexis leaned closer, nudging Johnny's shoulder aside.

The overhead light gave her a clear view of Mark on his bed, back toward the door, a pile of magazines beside him. Already, he'd turned his floor into an exploding tickertape factory. His jeans bulged at the butt. The back waistband dipped, revealing blue and white plastic. Alexis caught a faint odor of urine.

"I shouldn't be here," Mark said.

Voice choking with sobs, he tore off the cover page of a current *US News & World Report*. The front cover picture depicted a cheerful politician, someone who never encountered zombies or renegade Kryszka, or understood that they lurked behind every alley and bush. Mark tore a strip of paper from the glossy cover page. His sobbing eased with the long, slow ripping sound.

"I'm an administrator and I have a job to do." Mark dropped the strip on the floor, unaware of the listeners in the hall. He ripped slowly and made each strip as narrow as possible. Alexis guessed that if he made them too narrow, they'd peter out before he reached the bottom of the page. Getting them right required a focused mind and precise hands, the same precision he'd used with his baseball bat on wives he viewed as miscreant. She knew, having been on the receiving end of his punishment. He'd left her a leg scar for a souvenir.

"I'll get them." His voice softened. "When they least expect it. You'd better believe it."

Riiip!

His hand stopped halfway down the page, and he burst into a fresh spate of weeping. Tyrone pulled the door shut.

His voice dropped to a whisper. "Did anyone *think* to tell Shively?"

Johnny shrugged. "Yeron said he warned Shively. Maybe that's why Mark's got a shit assignment."

Clomping steps came from the kitchen. Shively materialized in the hallway, face crimson. "Warned me about what?"

Alexis opened her mouth to answer and saw a glint in Shively's eyes. Despite his mob ties, he'd acted the gentleman with her, the kind neighbor who carried her trash. Shively's mob persona had replaced that gentleman, making him a boss with no tolerance for complaints or excuses. She lowered her eyes and rubbed her damp hair again.

"Mark's room is bugged," she said at last. It sounded like a good answer.

"Uh huh." Shively's glare measured each person. "Meantime, you're fooling around when you and Yeron have things to do. The rest of us ought to look for these bugs. Standing near Mark's door and giggling is a fucking waste of time."

Even as Shively spoke, Tyrone hurried to the living room to search.

"Mark's planning to hurt somebody," Johnny said. "Watch him."

"Let me worry about Mark." Shively surveyed the group. "Alexis, quit fooling with your hair and help Yeron. Johnny, give Tyrone a hand. I'll talk with Mark, and when I'm through, I better find everyone at work."

"Thanks for getting me in trouble." Alexis shot Johnny a harsh glance on her way to the basement.

"Anytime." Johnny grinned.

****

Yeron settled at the desk in the basement, sandwiched between his blood analyzer, centrifuge, and computers. Already, he had loaded most of his software. The machines covered half of the room, all of them running off Shively's generator, along with the lights, phone, and appliances. A cabinet by his computers contained walkie-talkie radios, hazmat suits, and gas for the generator. Alexis had to wonder how Shively's "friends" had managed to move so much equipment here so quickly. A sofa bed, bureau, and a desktop computer occupied the rest of the space. Two doors facing the stairs led to a bathroom and closet.

She then wheeled toward Yeron. "Don't you dare get sick, shot, or ... otherwise. I'll be damned if I'm fighting with Mark as a partner!"

"I want you healthy, too. I enjoy staying alive, and we should not trust a man who tears magazines, among ... other things." He gave her a tense grin. "Enough about Mark. I want the others down here. Joe Hoffman autopsied a specimen and sent me an email with the results."

"Email?" Alexis stared at Yeron with cow eyes. "So the Internet works?"

"So far, dear. At least the secure sites." Yeron smiled. "This safe house may not be pretty, but it comes with Wi-Fi. Shively's people loaned us a powerful generator and enough radios so your mother could use one."

"The uniforms, equipment, weapons, and the Hummer ... and now this cabin must cost a bundle." Alexis whistled. "Where are they getting this money?"

"A better question would be 'why?'" He shifted his scrutiny toward his machines, then back to Alexis. "One of the renegades attacked and consumed Shively's mob boss."

Alexis gasped. "Charlie? I remember reading about Charlie's death. I find it hard to believe that with his guards, he couldn't overpower the attackers."

Yeron shrugged. "People get overconfident. How did you know Charlie?"

"My dad worked for him. Despite what the newspapers said, Charlie had a good side. He gave generous gifts to my family ... paid my tuition for college." Alexis shook her head, her face flushing. "No one deserves to be mauled and eaten."

"You do not need to defend your sentiments toward Charlie." Yeron took her hands in his, caressing them. "Most humans judge too rashly, but you appreciate a person's good traits. I like that. Just know that Charlie's death gave Shively and his fellow mobsters sufficient motivation to finance striking down the renegades."

"I suppose they supplied the laptop, too."

"No, Johnny brought his laptop. He left it in the kitchen. I am sure if you ask him, he will let you use it to email your mother, or you could call her. I would advise brevity, though, since anyone can hack the Internet and phones."

"Shit, I'd forgotten about that." Alexis sighed. "I promised my mom I'd give her our address."

"Go ahead. Just be careful." Yeron smiled, with encouragement. "Matilda will be glad to hear your voice."

"Thanks." After snatching her phone from her pants pocket, she dialed her mother's number. She gave a thumbs-up signal when the call went through.

"Alexis?" Her mother's worried voice. "Are you okay?"

"We're fine." Alexis mustered cheer into her voice. *Mark's tearing up paper and we managed one go-round with the zombies. We're fine, all right. Fucked up, insecure, neurotic, and emotional.* "We've settled in. Yeron's answering his email."

Yeron looked up and grinned.

"Mumph." A long pause followed. "Did you see more of those things? Doctor Hoffman said the police are finding them everywhere."

"We saw a few." *Liar, liar, pants on fire.* "How's your rib?"

"It's better. A few, huh? You ran into a gang of them, didn't you?"

"Well ..." Alexis looked up at Yeron for answers, but he focused on a viewscreen filled with data.

"For God's sake, be careful." Her mother's voice grew shrill. "I worry about you."

"You should be careful, too." Alexis's voice bled with concern. She couldn't help it. "Call me before you come to the cabin. Get Fenimore to drive you."

"All right. Where are you?"

"We're at 125 Merriman Trails, off Route 85, in Grays Landing." A pause, and she heard her mother's scribbling. "I wish I could make this go away."

"But you can't. No one can. I love you, honey."

"I love you, too, Mom."

As Alexis hung up, Yeron smiled. "You do not lie well."

"It's hard to fool my mom. She can tell by the timbre of my voice how my day went. At least she knows I'm alive."

"Yes." Yeron focused his attention back to his screen. "Here is an email from Joe. He sent a report on a walker."

"Okay." Alexis then raced up the basement steps and yanked open the door. "Hey guys, get down here. Yeron's got information on the zombies."

The men rushed down the steps. They congregated around Alexis while Yeron turned his screen toward them. "This email came from Joe Hoffman," he said. "His analysis revealed putrefied blood spatters; also cadaverine and putrescine, chemicals released during decomposition."

"Zombies!" Alexis shuddered. "I knew it."

"Shut up!" Mark's harsh eyes spewed anger.

"Why don't you shut your face, candy boy?" Tyrone punched him in the arm.

"Thank you, Tyrone." Alexis caressed her prayer beads. "I hope everyone brought crucifixes."

Johnny snickered. "That works on vampires."

"I said a rosary before our big brawl on Jackson's seventh floor," Alexis overrode him. "It worked. We're alive."

"Zombies? Vampires?" Shively threw his hands up in the air and dropped them. "Why don't we go for the garlic and holy water?"

"Those things will not help." Yeron regarded Shively, scratching the back of his head. "Chanting ... praying, if you will, might. At Eigil's compound, my half-sister Becky prayed to a deity ... Jesus, and most of us escaped."

"Jesus is your best friend in the trenches ... your only friend." Tyrone bowed and folded his hands. "But guys, you didn't let Yeron finish his report."

"Sorry," Alexis said. "Go on, Yeron."

"The man exhibited severe malnutrition and high levels of an unknown poison in the blood. I believe this chemical is vischlausk, which causes neurological deterioration. The specimen can walk and breathe, but is capable of only the basest functions. His animal behavior and the layers of putrescine and cadaverine give the appearance of a dead man walking."

"Like the one your sweetie sedated." Johnny grinned.

"Alexis made my job easy." Yeron smiled. "Honey, are you ready to get my tissue samples?"

"No problem." Alexis slipped her rosary around her neck. "Give me a scalpel with a Good Grip handle and I'm ready to work. Yuck, yuck, yuck."

"That settles it." Shively smiled, sounding pleased. "You two work on the specimen." His eyes settled on Mark. "I didn't see any bugs. That tells me that a certain somebody leaked information to the wrong people, and those people sent these last visitors. I'm trying to figure out who talked. We'll break off for supper around seven."

He headed up the steps, followed by Johnny, Tyrone, and Mark.

"Baked beans and hot dogs. Shively and Johnny love the stuff." Alexis grimaced after the door closed behind them. She donned an isolation suit and gloves. "Where's the specimen?"

"I packed him in a body cylinder," Yeron said. "He is awake."

Alexis gaped at Yeron, stunned to silence.

"Close your mouth." Yeron laughed. "This thing attracted a lot of flies."

Alexis snapped her mouth shut and donned a mask. "I didn't mean to put him to sleep," she said. "I thought I destroyed him."

"Hitting the tranquilizing—the blue ray—is a common mistake for the novice soldier." Yeron unlocked the middle door. It opened outside to steps that led to the back porch. Behind the gate, the Hummer sat, shielded by the lengthening shadows of the afternoon sun.

After opening the trunk, he slid out a six-foot, coffin-shaped glass drum. Inside it, a hooded person—at least its face was human—thrashed against the glass. Its head whipped back and forth, teeth gnashing. Its fish-belly white fingers clawed at the air holes on the top.

Chapter Eight: Yeron's Analysis

Basement of Shively's Cabin, May 30, 4:45 p.m.

Yeron levitated the cylinder to the basement. After setting the container on a worktable, he opened the latch, releasing a horrible, rancid stench. Alexis stepped sideways while reaching for her gun. The being leaped at Yeron and then stopped when Yeron fired his blue laser. It slumped inside the container.

"Are you kidding me?" Alexis recoiled, one hand still on her gun. "That greenish yellow crap on his legs ... I've seen that on dead people. He might be smarter than the ones on TV, but he's still a zombie."

"We shall see." Yeron watched the person for signs of movement. So far, none. He handed Alexis a rag. "I sedated him so he cannot move. We will wash him first and then choose our samples."

Alexis averted her eyes, not caring to bathe a creature that had tried to bite her lover.

"Wear your rosary if it helps you feel better." Yeron smiled.

"Damn straight I am. How am I going to wash this thing?"

"With antibacterial soap, as you would any patient." Yeron handed her a bottle of liquid soap and a stack of moist rags. "Start with the legs. I will work from the head down."

Rag draped over her hand, Alexis glided down the left calf, wiping away the leaking pus. The seepage exuded a potent stench that reminded her of battery acid. The putrescence fell away, leaving behind emaciated legs cratered with congealed gashes, rat-bitten on the edges. Up around the groin, her rag bumped against an open gash where the genitals used to be.

"Ugh!" She dropped the rag. Churning socked her gut. She scanned the room for a sink, saw none, and instead puked into a trash can.

"Alexis, sit!" Alexis complied with Yeron's stern order. He knelt beside her, arm on her shoulders. "Sorry I gave you this chore, but I never bathed patients. Androids did that at the compound and nursing assistants do it at Jackson Hospital."

Alexis sank into a chair, doubled over, keeping the trash can within sight. "That thing isn't a patient, dammit!"

"I found a carotid pulse, so this thing is a live male."

"No, it isn't alive. Where did you get this 'he' crap?"

Alexis leaned over the trash can and upchucked again. The stink like rotting tomatoes kept her gut heaving. At least outside, the air and gun smoke had dissipated much of the odor. "Damn Shively. Why didn't he leave the lab work for Doctor Hoffman? I'm not doing this crap. We should be looking for the hidden compound and shooting the bad guys."

"Oh, Alexis!" Yeron stroked her hair and kissed her on the head. "You are so innocent about war. Most armies assign tasks according to one's skills, and Shively has us. Only I can perform surgery. You have fifteen years of experience working in a hospital. Johnny knows how to fix radios. Shively and Tyrone worked with surveillance."

He stood, watching Alexis, hand stretched out. "I have anti-nausea pills."

"Thank you." Alexis swallowed the proffered pills, watching Yeron's concerned face. "I suppose analyzing tissue samples might give us clues as to who's making these creatures and where. I'll get over it. I am over it. Just give my stomach time to settle."

Yeron continued assessing her with the curious eyes of a cat.

"Well ... I'm not going to rip books or piss in diapers anytime soon."

At that, Yeron chuckled. "You are prettier than Mark." His eyes twinkled. "Are you better now?"

Alexis nodded. She joined him at the worktable.

"I will finish bathing him," Yeron told her. "Prepare the slides and cultures. Get your supplies from the left cabinet on the floor. I will talk you through the procedure."

"Wait a minute. Shouldn't you monitor his vital signs? If this person is alive ..."

"I do not have the proper equipment. My Doppler enabled me to find his pulse."

"Are you sure it's a man?" Alexis bent closer to the cylinder. The thing looked so wasted she couldn't tell its gender.

"The person is a male. I can tell by the square jaw."

"Shit." Alexis retrieved the slides and other equipment. She set them up on a tray near the body. "Yeron, we should move it ... him ... to a hospital. He needs medical treatment, the kind he'd get in intensive care."

"Except for the vischlausk poisoning, this man is healthy. Enough to rip people apart."

"Oh." Nothing about the specimen looked healthy. It had to be a zombie. Alexis fingered her rosary, murmuring a silent prayer.

"Be ready with the slides when I request them. After we finish, I shall destroy him and dissect the brain."

With slides in hand, Alexis watched him make an incision down the right forearm. Blood and watery fluid oozed from the fascia. Yeron scooped out chunks of fibrous tissue. Blood samples went into test tubes. Footsteps plodded overhead as the men traced and re-traced their steps searching for bugs. Alexis kept her eyes on the man-thing, watching for fluttering eyes or fingers, signs of impending awakening.

It never happened. The specimen's respirations and heartbeat stopped after Yeron opened the stomach cavity. In its emaciated state, the blood loss and incisions hastened its death. Using a surgical saw he had brought from the hospital, Yeron made a cut across the crown of the head, from the bony bump behind one ear to the one behind the other. He then opened the cranium and extracted the brain for dissection. More samples for the slides ...

"Okay." Alexis placed the last sample with the others beside the microscope. "What now?"

"Give me time to analyze these specimens. I should have the results after dinner."

Alexis took a seat on the sofa bed, stifling a yawn. "Do you think that intruder at Jackson Hospital ... the one who masqueraded as a housekeeper and tried to get me ... planted a bug somewhere?"

"She may have. Eigil taught his soldiers how to install an im-plant under the skin or within clothing. I had inspected our uniforms before I cleaned them." Yeron gestured toward a tunic hung up on the rack. "Your suit is ready."

Alexis smiled appreciatively. "I think the renegades planted a bug in Mark when we were patients. Something that affects his behav-ior."

"Mark mistreated you, his second wife, and her children with-out help from anyone. He left Meadowood Hospital in a sordid condi-tion and tried to blackmail Joe into withholding your treatment. His paper shredding and other behaviors are worth investigating, but I do not have the equipment to evaluate him. Your X-ray equipment and MRI scanners cannot detect the kind of bugs my people make."

"Shit." Alexis glanced toward the specimen. Yeron laid the man's remains back in the cylinder and latched the hinges shut. "Shive-ly will never listen to my theory about Mark without an X-ray or some-thing."

"Shively is not stupid. He knows about Mark's past, and like

Johnny pointed out, that was why he gave Mark menial work." He draped his arm over her shoulder and drew her close. "You could make this easier on yourself if you slept down here with me. Then Mark could sleep in your room." He planted a kiss on her forehead.

Alexis leaned into him for the embrace. "Not with Shively riding his high horse. Besides, I don't want to sleep in the same room where we work on those specimens. But ..." She wagged her finger and gave him a wicked grin. "You could pay me a visit tonight."

"A visit, yes?" He smiled. "And suppose I wake Shively?"

"You won't. You're quieter on foot than I am."

"That is true." Yeron took her hand in his. "If Shively became preoccupied and I dissected our finds outside, would you consider sleeping down here?"

"That's two major 'if's.'" Alexis surveyed the room – the machinery, the sofa bed, the TV, and the refrigerator. The sofa bed could hold two adults. "We'll see."

"I grew up in an underground apartment not much larger than this room," Yeron said in a nostalgic voice. "We had limited space and we did not waste paper the way people do here. We never read paperback books. All reading material came from our version of the Internet. No bathroom tissue either; our toilets aspirated the waste with a vacuum and wiped the bodily orifices with disinfectant."

"Your life sounds idyllic until you factor Eigil into the equation."

Yeron's eyes took on a haunted look. "Eigil made our lives unbearable. He looked for guilty verdicts, and if you were innocent, he trumped up charges. The lucky ones got fried with his disintegrator and died. If you were luckier, you fled from the compound because in most cases he punished wrongdoers by feeding them to the *settva*. The *settva* animals resemble your prehistoric dinosaurs."

"Dinosaurs?" Alexis gasped. "Which ones?"

"A *settva* resembles a cross between a Tyrannosaurus Rex and an iguana."

"Holy shit! My internist Steve Leicht and his wife Becky have been underground ... he told me some horrific tales, but he never mentioned *settva.*"

"Steve and Becky do not know about them. The *settva* never posed any danger because Eigil consumed the human prisoners." Yeron's eyes became large pools of sadness.

Alexis caressed his cheek, wishing she could smooth away the pain. "I'm sorry you went through it. You must have lost some good friends."

Yeron averted his eyes. "I had two—Quyeba and Zoltar. They

had left our compound years before it exploded."

"It's too bad you lost contact with them." Alexis regarded him fixedly. "Quyeba or Zoltar might know something about these renegades. Did they tell you where they went?"

"They migrated to another compound," Yeron said, turning toward the readout on his viewscreen.

"Where? Steve told me that your citizens used pods for flight. That doesn't make sense. Your people couldn't build a working ship, right?"

"I think they could, but our home planet ... Kryszk ... could no longer support life."

"Right, then. I assume the departing citizens include your two friends. Did they describe this compound or given you an idea where this compound might be?"

"No." Yeron gazed at her with his sad red eyes. "It was too dangerous for them to give such details."

"Things can slip when you're talking. If you could recall the conversations you had with Quyeba, what you remember might help Shively and the boys find the lab making these walkers."

"I doubt it," Yeron replied in a mournful voice. "Where I lived, you had to be discreet. Besides, anything I say will remind our team of Eigil."

Alexis tried to picture Yeron as a criminal and couldn't. She loved this man, alien features and all. Lustful notions came to mind, but she would reserve those for Yeron's nocturnal visits. Instead, she shifted her focus toward her late sister.

"Those renegades destroyed Robin and my best friend, Delores. Nothing can bring them back; but if figuring out your friends' whereabouts leads us to this mystery compound, it would help me find closure."

"I never wanted anyone hurt. I hate the renegades for what they did to you, your family, and other humans. Before the first attack, the one that took Robin, I thought that Eigil and his renegades had died in the explosion."

"So did our officers." She kept her voice low. "Steve said your people stayed because they found Earth habitable. Let's say your contacts built another compound, thinking they could start fresh, and the renegades found this place. Might that be possible?"

Yeron's head bobbed up and down. "Quyeba was my father's assistant. Zoltar was her half-breed son. They moved to another compound long before my mother died."

"Quyeba." Alexis scratched her head. "That sounds Asian."

"She shortened her name after Eigil ordered her mate shot.

Her mate Lyrus was Zoltar's father and a human woman his mother. She adopted Zoltar after Lyrus died, and my parents took both of them into their home." Yeron's smile saddened. "I made Zoltar my brother. They lived with us until they left for the other compound."

"But they never told you where?"

"My father never asked and Quyeba never volunteered information. Not even clues. Eigil tortured people if he suspected they were hiding something."

"Eigil sounds like our Adolph Hitler. I assume other people wanted to escape from his dictatorship, so they joined Quyeba." Yeron's nod emboldened her to continue. "I suspect that's where we'll find the renegades and their zombies."

"Infected people," Yeron corrected her.

"Zombies."

"Infected." Yeron held firm. "That man had a pulse and respiration."

"It amounts to the same monster." Alexis's forehead puckered. "What if your two friends went bad?"

"Quyeba grieved over the loss of her mate and her son wanted to understand his human traits. They despised Eigil and would never befriend his renegades, but they watched what they said. Where we grew up, you dared not say too much if you wanted to survive."

"So I see." Alexis exhaled. "Steve never mentioned your connections."

"I never told my brother-in-law Steve because I feared he would tell his wife, Becky, and she might tell the wrong person." Alarm crept into Yeron's voice. His hands clasped her shoulders and his voice took on a pleading tone. "You must not tell Shively or anyone else. Quyeba and Zoltar are harmless."

Harmless? She doubted it. Sitting on the mother lode of sensitive information was tantamount to treason. Then she imagined officers poking and prodding Yeron, hypnotizing him in an attempt to decipher the information, or worse, shooting him. She shivered.

"Relax." She rubbed his shoulder. "I won't tell anyone. I think though we should look in places where your friends might go. For example, where did they go to hunt wildlife? Suggest that site to Shively but don't mention anyone's name."

Yeron appeared to consider this. "We did most of our hunting in wooded areas."

"Such as where? Philadelphia? Royerstown? Think hard about this. Once we find this place, we stand a chance at survival and getting on with our lives."

****

Alexis ate her meal in silence – platters of franks, canned carrots, and baked beans for everyone except Yeron, who dined on raw steak and fruit. Like most canned goods, Alexis's meal carried a tinny taste. She thought about her mother and her servings of homemade pasta. Beside her, Johnny let out an explosive fart.

"Johnny, get downwind." She waved her hand.

"Ahh! I'm getting off some good ones." He chuckled.

Laughing, Tyrone sprang up and clicked on the oven fan. "He blew a hole in his chair."

Alexis gave a rueful smile. Unpleasant as he smelled, the essence of "rotten-egg" Johnny made sense, unlike the foul odors from the walkers.

"You getting any weird signals?" asked Shively.

"Nope." Johnny lifted his leg and farted again. "Ahh!"

Alexis giggled. Mark scowled and continued eating in silence.

Yeron jumped. "I just heard my analyzer. The tests should be complete."

"Downstairs." Shively stood, holding his nose. "Don't go blowing up anything, Johnny."

That drew titters from everyone, except Mark. He shot Johnny a disgusted glance but remained silent. They stood by the desk while Yeron pointed to his readouts.

"Joe Hoffman has it right," Yeron said. "The brain damage is irreversible and severe, leaving the part that controls the basest functions, breathing, and respirations working. I know what the toxin is."

He paused, as if allowing his words to sink in.

"This," he went on, holding up a filled syringe, "is the solution the renegade used to try to poison me. For people like me, it induces aggression and a thirst for human flesh. I found large amounts of this toxin – we call it vischlausk – in the specimen's blood.

"My father tested vischlausk on an animal, a rat, and that animal clawed and bit anyone who stood too close. He tried to reverse the effect, but none of his formulas worked. No antidote for this poison exists, even in the Kryszka laboratory. Manufacturing vischlausk was a criminal offense until Eigil became Governor."

Tyrone raised his hand. "Suppose the renegades poisoned one of your good guys. Would he turn bad, too?"

"He might try to resist, but those primal urges will compel a Kryszka to attack. Most of Eigil's soldiers ingested the toxin, and it took minimal influence to persuade them to give into these urges."

"So this is a manufactured poison." Alexis mopped the sweat from her forehead. "What happens now? Do we sedate these people and ship them to the hospital?"

"You can't be serious." Mark spoke up from his corner, giving her a contemptuous scowl. "No hospital's got the resources to handle these people."

"Nursing homes?" Alexis turned toward the others for support. "A special unit can keep them sedated until someone finds an antidote for the poison."

"What's with the incisions?" Tyrone inspected at the glass cylinder with wide eyes. A Y-shaped incision stretched from the occupant's shoulders through the mid-chest to the pubic area. "Did you cut out his eyeballs, too?"

"One eye, plus his internal organs and fascia," Yeron told him. "His other eye was missing when we found him."

"Did you knock him out before you cut him?" Johnny asked.

"No, I gave him intramuscular Droperidol." Yeron indicated a bandage on the man's right upper arm. "It did not quiet him, so I had to use my plasma gun."

Alexis rubbed her arms, trying hard not to look at the cylinder. "Traditional sedatives won't quiet these people. The chemical in these guns will. Yeron sent Joe a report."

Murmuring erupted between Shively, Tyrone, and Johnny. Mark stood quiet, head down, hands shoved in his pockets.

"None of this was Yeron's fault." Alexis swept her scrutiny among the men. "The analyzer doesn't lie."

The murmuring stopped. They exchanged glances. Their faces went bug-eyed and pale. Johnny dragged his fingers through his moist hair. Tyrone folded his beefy hands; his lips moved in silent prayer. Shively drew in a deep breath, his face reddening. A tear worked out of the corner of Mark's eye and rolled down his cheek. Rubbing her arms and shivering, Alexis moved closer to Yeron. His arm draped around her shoulders.

"They're zombies," she said, looking up at him.

Yeron lowered his eyes, head bowed. "They are not zombies as most movies describe them, but the toxin induces a zombielike state. They do not respond to FDA-approved sedatives. Restraining them will not make them less dangerous. Alexis is right; the plasma chemical sedated them. We have a limited supply of that chemical."

Shively folded his arms across his chest, his head tilted. "I don't suppose you can duplicate this chemical."

Yeron cast a baleful glance at his analyzers. "Not without better equipment."

"Well, Alexis." Tyrone gave her a weak grin. "They might not be zombies, but they're damn close."

Alexis shuddered. "I didn't want to be close."

"It is what it fucking is." Shively's blue eyes became hard and resolute. "This week, we'll check out Trident Mall. We'll look for any clues about the underground lab that's making these things. Alexis, since you called it so close, you pick the menu for tomorrow night's dinner."

"Pasta. Something with decent gravy ... er, tomato sauce." Her mouth watered at the idea of homemade ravioli, but the ingredients involved required an extra trip that meant a potential clash with more walkers. She grimaced. "Canned pasta will do."

Chapter Nine: Ghost Ride

Trident Mall, Grays Landing, June 2, 10:00 p.m.

At 10:00 p.m., Shively drove Yeron and the others to Trident Mall. Nocturnal exploration meant less likelihood of detection by officers and surveillance cameras. Each of them nursed a thermos of coffee. Coffee, one of the beverages that humans drank that Yeron could tolerate, enhanced his alertness, as it did for humans.

The team had packed slides and other supplies to collect samples. They also brought their weapons, a Gamma Scout Geiger Counter, face masks with LED lights, and Maglites so they could work in darkness. Yeron couldn't help grimacing from the odor of urine permeating the vehicle. He tried to focus on the destruction outside.

A full moon splashed silvery puddles on the streets and the miles of treetops seemed endless. Every so often, a gas station or farm rose like a shadowy stalagmite in the gloom. Alexis nudged closer to Yeron, her brown eyes filled with dread. Everyone remained quiet, except Shively and Tyrone who were arguing over directions in whispers.

After an hour, they veered towards Route 83, a four-lane highway that led to the mall. All of the street lamps and traffic lights were out. A glance out the window revealed battered picnic tables, followed by large brick buildings. Yeron's previous videos of the Trident massacre had portrayed those buildings. Moments later, Shively parked under a thick cage of trees outside the mall perimeter.

"Stay behind the car until I tell you otherwise," he barked.

A rotten stench overwhelmed Yeron when he stepped out of the Hummer. His boots landed in mud the consistency of jelly. He pointed his flashlight downward and saw large yellow circles on maroon-colored paste. Blood.

Beside him, Alexis covered her mouth. "Ugh!"

Mark whirled around and shot her a withering glare. "Shut up!"

Johnny darted a fierce look at Mark. "Right back at you, asshole."

"Drop it a few levels." Shively reached for his binoculars, his voice low but his face granite. "Chill. About a half-dozen guards patrolling the place."

Alexis glanced toward the parking lot. "I don't see any officers."

"They are there, honey, about 300 yards away." Yeron pointed toward people clad in dark uniforms, by the front entrance. His years at the colony had schooled him in detecting distant movement, but Alexis and Johnny had no experience with reconnaissance. Both of them needed to learn if they wanted to survive. "These are not the officers we met; they look like rented cops."

"Rent-a-cops," Alexis supplied. "They do, but I bet they carry guns."

"Great," Johnny murmured beside him. "So what do we do?"

"We wait until they finish their shift," Yeron told him. "They will have to turn in paperwork, among other chores. That will give us enough time to get in without being caught."

"Most shifts change around midnight." Tyrone glanced at his watch. "Figure an hour and a half. They'll want to report to the next shift. That might give you a half-hour to get into the mall before the new guys show."

"Can we wait in the car?" Alexis asked.

"Nope," Shively told her. "We can't see from there."

****

The officers vacated the premises two and a half hours later. Shively gave the signal and at first, everyone followed him. Yeron took Alexis's hand and guided her toward the right path that led to the front entrance. Johnny went behind them.

"No." Shively shook his head as if he were speaking to people with limited intelligence. "We're going in through the side entrance."

Alexis grimaced, her voice tremulous. "Yeron wants to go through the front."

"Does it matter?" Johnny asked. "By now, the officers cleaned up this place. This should be a cakewalk."

"You think so?" Tyrone glared at him.

"What I think," Mark said, "is that we should dump these crybabies."

Yeron recoiled at Mark's approach. The urine stink came from him, overriding the essence of decay. "Speak for yourself," he said in a dry voice.

Johnny burst into noiseless laughter. Yeron smiled, but his lips froze when he made out the two large vehicles parked by the side entrance, visible in the moonlight. They looked like designer buses, the kind that Greyhound or other transportation companies might use.

Close enough to see but too far to make out any activity.

"Shively, any movement on the buses?" he asked.

Shively peered through his binoculars. "Nope."

They crept closer to the side entrance, staying within the shadows. Yeron scanned the lot and entrance for cameras, disabling them with his mind as they went. Without his ability, the officers would catch them on closed-circuit television. Still, they had to move fast. Ten minutes had passed since the first shift of officers left. The officers getting their report would arrive any moment and catch them. Everyone else shone their flashlights, illuminating the doors and the two vehicles.

The buses weren't going anywhere. They leaned near the mall entrance, the front ends smashed like accordions against the brick building. Some of the windows had been punched out and the tires were flattened. Dried blood spattered the sides of each bus. At the rear of one bus, a clump of fascia crusted with bone and blood hung off a window, looking like a zombie's face. Yeron's heart lurched in his chest. He gulped.

Something had punched out the glass doors of the mall entrance, too.

Behind Yeron, Johnny's Gamma Scout clicked away like a time bomb.

"Oh, my God!" Alexis grabbed Yeron's arm. "What's with the renegades and our buses? Don't they use pods?"

"Our pods can only transport six people at a time. Besides, your vehicles are simple to operate. I learned to drive a car within a week after I settled at your hospital."

"I gotta hand it to you for neutralizing the surveillance," Shively said to Yeron. He shifted his attention toward Johnny. "What's with the Scout?"

Johnny stared at his handheld device, eyes wide as saucers. "The radiation's bad. We'd better wear our respirators."

"How bad?" Shively asked, approaching him.

"About 200."

"I'm not taking any chances." Tyrone snapped on his facemask, as did the others. "Guys, lower your voices."

After donning his mask, Yeron scanned the lot again. No officers or guards. To an outsider, the asphalt might resemble an ordinary lot. No debris. The bricks along the side of the building had cracked where the buses had rammed into them. Despite the shattered glass, a padlock secured the door casements. Yeron crushed its tumblers with his thoughts. The shackle loosened and the padlock dropped on the pavement with a loud clang.

So much for quiet. Yeron shrugged.

Mark straightened up, giving Yeron another dark look. "Why don't you make a little more noise?"

Ignoring Mark, Yeron guided the doors open with his thoughts. Shively walked toward the doors and hesitated. "I doubt we've got much time to poke around, so I suggest we split up. Mark and I will check out the buses. Tyrone, bring the others with you."

"Now wait a minute." Mark's jaw tightened and his face reddened in the moonlight. Yeron pitied anyone who had to work with him. "I'm not getting on some broken bus."

"Oh, yes, you are," Shively said in a menacing voice. His cold blue eyes met Mark's. "We might find the drivers' logbooks on those buses. If we do, we can figure out where these buses were when the renegades stole them. I bet it's not too far from their compound. Besides ..." He gave Mark a shit-eating grin. "I want to know why you stank up the Hummer."

Johnny poked Alexis, and they giggled. Yeron's eyes drifted over toward the buses again, and he wondered if they would still be smiling after tonight's mission. He doubted it.

"Guys, let's go." Tyrone waved his hand, then crept inside, followed by Alexis, Johnny, and Yeron. The paucity of electricity cloaked them in darkness. Yeron grabbed Alexis by the arm and held her close. He set his Maglite to high beam.

Their flashlights threw shadows across the cracked brown floor tiles. Empty perfume bottles, scattered on the floor amidst dried blood spatters, glittered in the dim light. He imagined women and children fleeing for their lives, knocking over display stands as they went. For a moment, muffled screams assaulted his ears. Glass tinkling as the bottles clattered to the floor. A rose scent followed, and then skeletal shadows flittered along the burned out walls.

Alexis gasped. "I think we're being watched and not by the cameras."

"We probably are," he agreed.

The sounds and movements stopped, but the broken glass forced Yeron to choose his steps carefully. He trained his light toward the empty ceiling. The tiles were gone. The exposed wiring and cables dangled from the casements like snakes, reminding him of Eigil's ghastly compound.

"Damn!" Johnny shifted his gaze from floor to ceiling. "What is this place?"

"It used to be J.C. Penney," Alexis said. "Mom took Robin and me here."

Tyrone's eyes widened. "Well, someone trashed it good."

Yeron nodded with agreement. The Maglites illuminated empty racks littering the floors, holes burned into the plaster, bare bricks exposed. "The renegades attacked here," he said.

After he made a detour around the cashier's desk, Yeron headed to the open mall area. Blood splattered an overhead sign that read "Restrooms." Alexis stopped and glanced to their right. The sign pointed to a narrow hallway where the bathrooms would be. What was she thinking? Why would anyone want to use the facilities here?

"Hey, guys." Johnny pointed toward a Dunkin' Donuts sign. "This looks fresh."

Moist blood trickled down the glass doors underneath the sign. Tyrone held up his light while holding his nose with his free hand. "You got that right ... but ugh! The trash stinks."

Yeron started at the rustling sound. *Rats.*

The noise came from a metal wastebasket in front of the Dunkin' Donuts. Johnny headed a few paces closer and grimaced. "It smells like a dead rat."

"Probably is," Tyrone said to Johnny. "We'd better bag and tag it, in case Yeron wants to analyze it."

"No problem." Johnny raised his voice over the clicking from his Gamma Scout.

Yeron retrieved his slides from his pack. He slid to his knees and peeled samples from the doors for analysis. Judging by the thin texture of the blood, he suspected that more walkers had broken into the mall during the last 24 hours. The rustling grew louder.

"Alexis," he said, without looking up, "see what is making that noise."

No answer. Yeron darted a glance over his shoulder. Alexis was gone. Her pattering footsteps echoed in the silence.

"Alexis!" he shouted, setting aside his slides. "Where are you?"

"She probably went to take a piss." Tyrone glanced over from the trashcan. "She shouldn't have left without saying something."

"I should have gone with her. It is not safe to go anywhere alone." After Yeron stowed away his fifth slide, he straightened. More footsteps echoed from the gloom.

"Johnny, I will be right—"

"Ah, shit!" Tyrone's shout sliced through Yeron's voice. "Johnny, get back here!"

No answer. Tyrone stood by the wastebasket alone, holding a maroon-stained blanket with tongs in one hand and his Maglite in the other. Yeron's light washed over Tyrone's face which was dripping with sweat; his breathing was ragged. "Where did Johnny go?"

"I don't know. He hightailed out of here when he caught a whiff of what's in this trash." Tyrone's eyes dilated from fright. "Yeron, c'mere. This doesn't look like rats."

Yeron came closer, brandishing his light, his free hand on his gun. Tyrone lifted the blanket away from the trash. It reeked like meat that had spoiled in the hot sun. The rustling stopped, replaced by wobbling from the trashcan. The can flopped over with a loud bang and the bloated figure crawling out was most definitely not a rat. The figure struggled to its feet, looking many weeks dead. Its toothless mouth opened and shut, as if seeking food. Its skeletal limbs wobbled and flailed. Cracked leathery skin rode over bones and grayish tissue. Fetid pus oozed from the open sores. Tyrone recoiled.

"Jesus, help me!" he cried. "A real zombie."

"I can subdue it." Yeron squirted the figure with the tranquilizer button on his gun. He waited five seconds. Ten. A minute. A wee bit longer. The figure continued shambling toward Tyrone, while he backed away several paces. Somewhere behind him, more footsteps lurched.

Chapter Ten: Dead People Walking

Trident Mall, Grays Landing, June 3, 1:00 a.m.

In the ladies' room, Alexis's light roved over bashed sinks, dented stalls, and overflowing cracked toilets. Maroon stains splotched the doors and pilasters. At a sink, she tried turning a spigot that looked intact. No water. Sanitation be damned, she had to pee, and she needed her privacy. Why did she drink so much coffee? She'd forgotten about its diuretic effects when she had drained her thermos. After another glance around, she headed into a stall.

Plodding footsteps. Thumping at the bathroom door. Moaning.

Shit! Alexis finished her business and yanked up her pants. Out came her gun. She gagged on the sickening stench. In the gloom, her light cut jagged circles around three skeletal figures weaving through the door. Their bloated, pus-stained faces drooled blood and saliva, two of them bald, and the third with a hollowed-out skull. Two more figures lurched through, followed by others. All of them worked swollen, blistered jaws, their groans sounding like pebbles rattling in their windpipes.

Alexis screamed.

She couldn't kill them all, not with one hand carrying a flashlight. This was worse than the invasion at Jackson Hospital. Back there, she had daylight and the men with her. Now she only had her Maglite. She could pick them off with her thoughts, one by one, and maybe take out three, but the rest would be on her. Maybe she could sedate them with the blue ray. Then she'd step over them and run.

More walkers crowded the doorway. Alexis backed away from the door, step-by-step, stall after stall, firing the blue ray. The figures kept coming, their cadaverous faces relentless and hungry. *Oh, God, the sedative's not working!* She ducked inside a stall and climbed onto the toilet seat, bracing herself against the partition panels. On the panel, her light revealed a double toilet paper holder with a shelf; above, the head rail, and then a thick pipe running along the ceiling. Her right foot went onto the toilet paper shelf. She grabbed the edge of the panel, screaming from the pain flashing through her hands, and then hooked her left elbow around the head rail. The right elbow followed, both feet on the shelf, the figures closing in on her.

"Yeron!" she screamed. His sensitive ears would hear her cries ... unless the figures had gone after him and the others ...

Heart hammering inside her chest, she curled her arms around the pipe. Her elbows did the work. Though the plasma gun accommodated her crooked fingers, the thick metal pipe would not. Her movements were clumsy, but she managed to stand with one foot on the head rail and the other on a partition panel.

Left arm coiled around the pipe, she played her Maglite. The bathroom had tiled walls, but no windows. Debris crusted each brick. Bugs crawled on the grout between the tiles. Straining her eyes, she made out a vent on the opposite wall above the sinks, broad enough to accommodate an adult. The sink underneath it canted to the left. Trapped, she'd become a meal waiting for these zombies.

Slow groaning issued from the stalls. Shearing and tearing followed when the creatures ripped a door off its hinges. Alexis sprayed the fire ray on the figures, hoping she aimed true. The creatures let out mewling howls, but they didn't stop. Despite the smoke cooking off their charred skin, they ripped out the doors and panels, one by one. The rail and partition swayed under her feet.

Alexis hung onto the overhead pipe for dear life. She brought her knees around the pipe, seconds before the final panels fell with a loud clatter. Arms and legs wrapped around the pipe, she wriggled across the room. The rough hot metal stung her wrists and aggravated the numbness in her left leg. She'd injured it months ago when Kryszka soldiers broke into her mother's home. She shifted positions to get a better grip. Capital mistake. Her flashlight dropped, shrouding her in darkness. A muscle gave way in her left ankle, resulting in a pounding ache. She knew that before long, the ache would progress to agony, forcing her to let go.

"Dammit!" Tears flooded her eyes. "Mom ...Yeron, I'm so sorry." Sorry wouldn't cut it. Her mother and Yeron would take her death hard.

"Use your telekinesis," a man's voice called to her.

"It won't work. There's too many." The voice had a musical lilt like Yeron's, with a Kryszka accent. In the faint light, she made out the light wispy shape of an older man. *Oh, great, now I'm imagining things.*

"I am real," the specter replied as if reading her mind. "I understand your panic, but you will die unless you fight those creatures."

"How? I tried shooting them, but they're zombies."

"What you call them does not matter. One is right behind you and about to grab you. Think about how much you love Yeron and use your mental powers."

Dead fingernails grated on the pipe behind her. She imagined nights with Yeron and the feel of his tender arms, and dammit, she loved him. She refused to quit and die.

Ripples of emotion ebbed through her. With deep concentration, she mustered a force field around her and thrust a psychic twister shove. The scratching stopped. Something heavy landed on the floor below her with a loud thump. More howling. Alexis let her psychokinetic force loose with as much energy as she could manage. The wind brushed beneath her. A lavatory door became a flying torpedo. The louder moans told her that it had socked two of the creatures.

Shouts from outside the bathroom almost made her lose her concentration. Tyrone's booming voice, Yeron's worried one, and the sound of Johnny's ticking Gamma Scout. Light beams from the men's flashlights flooded the room, revealing a dozen or more walkers, their eyes on Alexis. No sign of her mysterious visitor. Bullets sprayed, dropping three of them. Sparks flew from their necks and spines. Yeron shouted something at Johnny and Tyrone and then mind-slammed the remaining walkers up against the walls. Lights tucked in their pockets, Johnny and Tyrone stood underneath Alexis, stretching out their hands.

"Let go," Tyrone called to her. "Johnny and I will catch you."

Alexis groaned. The numbness and aching in her leg and stinging in her hands were ungodly. Tyrone and Johnny tucked their Maglites in their pockets, placing their faces and outstretched arms in shadows. Her left leg wobbled ever since the Kryszka poison had affected her muscles. Now she imagined the men groping in the dark, trying to catch her and missing, resulting in her good leg being broken. Her weapons weighed ten pounds, making a total of 130 pounds, enough to carry a heavy wallop when she dropped. "Get Yeron. He'll levitate me."

"Yeron needs his levitation to control the zombies." Johnny's smart-aleck tone had fled his voice, and a pained plea had replaced it. "I know this is scary, but it's your only choice."

"You think so?" Alexis shook her head. "I've never read about anyone doing this, not even in *Weekly World Reporter*."

"I've done this many times in the Army," Tyrone said. "Let go. We'll catch you."

Alexis uncoiled her numb leg, then her right one. The pressure on her arms became unbearable. The floor rushed up at her, but she landed in the arms of the two men. They eased her to the floor. Her lame leg buckled, but Johnny caught her as fast as a cat.

"You okay?" Alarm edged in his voice.

"Not quite. I think I sprained my ankle." She looked up at Tyrone and Johnny. "I'm sorry I caused so much trouble."

"No need to be sorry," Tyrone's gentle voice soothed her. "Come on. Let's go—"

Sharp rapping on the door.

"Fuck!" Johnny shook his head.

Before anyone could answer, Shively barged in, waving his light. "We'd better haul ass. There're guards poking around, and ..." He trained his light toward the zombies. The creatures thrashed against the tiled wall, mouths opening and closing. "Son of a bitch!"

"You're telling me." Hand braced against Johnny's shoulder, Alexis gagged. The stink of charred flesh coming from them nauseated her. She took a step with her bum leg, which wobbled again, but Johnny held her fast.

"If we go," Yeron spoke up from the stalls, "I will lose control of these monsters, and they will attack."

"They won't catch us if we run," Tyrone said.

"Alexis can't walk," Johnny pointed out, eyes on Shively. "She hurt her ankle."

"So?" Shively's square jaw and narrowed eyes discouraged argument. "We have to split. I didn't say run. These monsters move slowly. Let the officers deal with them."

"Excuse me." Alexis cast a forlorn gaze at Shively. "Those creatures can move fast. They tore the stalls apart in here. They kept going strong after I tried frying them."

"These aren't the same monsters we fought before; that's for sure." Tyrone fixed his eyes on the row of groaning zombies, held against the wall by Yeron's mind. "If we shoot them, we'll attract the guards' attention."

"Tye, you and I can help Alexis to the Humvee if Yeron holds the walkers," Johnny offered.

"That would be best," Yeron agreed, his relief evident. "What about Mark?"

"What about him?" Shively gave a dismissive wave of his hand. "He's hauling our find to the Humvee. Now move it."

Tyrone grasped Alexis by her right shoulder, while Johnny held her left. "Okay, we'll help you to the car. Yeron will control the zombies."

The strong grip on her shoulders took the edge off Alexis's pain. She made her way out of the ladies' room, half-hopping, half-loping, by leaning on the two men. "Thank you."

"Hell, it's no trouble." Johnny chuckled. "Now if you weighed 300 pounds, we'd let you fall on your ass."

Alexis managed a weak grin. Shively sprinted to the exit, passing her as he went. By the time they made it outside, Yeron's light footsteps pattered behind them. He caught up beside them, darting glances over his shoulder.

Seconds later, gunfire exploded from inside the mall. Tyrone and Johnny picked up their pace, half-carrying Alexis. Her leg crumpled and stung each time she tried bearing weight on it. As they grew closer to the grove of trees, booming followed. Johnny stopped.

"What the fuck ...?" he cried.

"Keep moving," Tyrone ordered him. "We'll talk later."

Chapter Eleven: Yeron Sees a Ghost

Shively's Cabin at Merriman Trails, June 3, 3:00 a.m.

At the car, Alexis fainted. Tyrone and Johnny held her while Yeron climbed into the Humvee. After he levitated her inside, he eased her head and shoulders onto his lap. Johnny scrambled in and plopped beside them. The specimen, bound and tied with duct tape, rode in the cargo hold. Tyrone took the wheel with Mark and Shively up front.

It did not surprise Yeron that Alexis fainted. The circles under her eyes spoke of pure exhaustion. After Tyrone pulled out onto the road, Shively whirled around, his piercing eyes shifting between Johnny and Alexis.

"I'm not at all happy with the way things went down tonight," he said, unaware that Alexis was unconscious. "No one wanders by themselves, understand? That goes for you, Johnny and Alexis."

"I'm sorry, Shively," Johnny said, lowering his head.

Shively then dictated driving directions to Tyrone. As he did so, Johnny pointed toward Shively, then Alexis, and put his head inside his shirt and giggled.

"Alexis," Shively went on, turning around toward them again, "lose your hang-up about using the woods for a toilet."

Alexis did not answer. Her eyes remained closed, her head cradled in Yeron's lap. This time, Yeron burst into quiet laughter—inside his tunic the way Johnny did.

"How badly is Alexis hurt, Yeron?" Shively asked.

At that notion, the laughter died in Yeron's throat. "I did not do a thorough exam, but her ankle is swollen. I will wrap it in ice when we get back."

"Hope her leg's not broken," Shively said. "I wanted to find clues about this underground lab, but we can't go there again. Those officers made us."

Tyrone averted his eyes. His puckered lips made him look as if he had choked on a chicken bone. "Yeron took some slides and a spec-

66

imen. I gotta admit, Johnny got me pissed when he ran off, but he came through when Alexis screamed for help."

"That's true," Shively conceded. "And our visit to the bus wasn't a total loss. While Mark sniveled about getting on the buses, I found the drivers' logbooks. The books should note something about where the last drivers parked the buses before the renegades stole them."

****

At the cabin, Yeron left the specimen in the Hummer. He would get to him later. Alexis was his main concern. She did not stir when he mind-carried her down to the basement. When he laid her on his bed, she moaned but did not open her eyes. Her brace had come undone and hung by its Velcro straps around her swollen ankle. Dirt smudges covered her face and arms. Her chest rose and fell with deep respirations. She needed a shower badly, but her loss of consciousness drew a hard line of ice up Yeron's back and shoulders.

"Alexis," he shouted. "Wake up."

He leaned over, about to shake her awake, when a voice speared him to attention: "Son, leave her be."

Yeron gasped. The speaker, his late father, was a mere smoky wisp standing by the desk, but no one would mistake the authority in his voice. His dead father had visited before when Yeron worked at the hospital, but Yeron shuddered at his presence.

"Father," he said after he found his voice. "Alexis needs a shower and a thorough examination."

"She will get those things, but not tonight." The specter regarded Yeron with watchful eyes. "Alexis is a determined woman, but like many humans, she is superstitious. She froze when she first saw those creatures."

Yeron bowed his head and heaved a deep sigh. "I never should have left her alone."

"Perhaps not." His father's voice softened, offering a reprieve. "I reminded her that she had her telekinesis."

Yeron shivered. "Father, you saved her!"

"No, she saved herself. I encouraged her. Nevertheless, sleep is her way of coping with what happened. So let her rest when she can because the dangers are going to get worse."

"I expect they will, Father, because Mark is with us."

"So I see." The apparition shook his head. "If I were you, I would not discuss your plans with Mark."

Tell me something I do not know. His father's warning bumped Yeron back to a conversation he had overheard months ago, when he was treating Shively at Jackson Hospital. Shively had gotten into a heated discussion on the phone, his contact's angry voice loud enough for Yeron's sensitive ears to hear.

"*That sicko messed with my kid. Wax him, Shiv. That's an order.*"

"*Don't worry, boss. I'm on it.*"

"*How are you gonna do it from a hospital bed?*"

"*Don't worry. I got it under control. When we leave the hospital, I'm taking him for a nice, long ride.*"

Shaking his head and clearing his thoughts, Yeron reached for Alexis's wrist. He checked her pulse. Strong and regular. "Father, I am suspicious of Mark, too."

When Yeron looked up, the specter was gone. Alexis did not stir. The shower could wait. With a deep sigh, he wrapped her left foot in an Ace bandage and slipped a pillow underneath it. After he finished, he showered and climbed into bed with her. If his Steel Rose was that frightened, he did not want her sleeping alone.

Chapter Twelve: Autopsy

Cabin Basement, Merriman Trails, June 3, 10:00 a.m.

When Alexis opened her eyes, she found herself in Yeron's bed with his arm draped around her. Her left foot lay propped on a pillow. Someone had wrapped a bandage around her ankle and a bag of ice sat on top. She eased herself off the bed.

"Steel Rose." Yeron jerked awake, regarding her with worried eyes. "Where are you going?"

"I need a shower." Alexis removed the ice and tried to stand. She managed a smile. "I'm okay. No pins or needles."

The numbness was gone, but her left ankle ached. She limped to Yeron's bathroom. A glance in the mirror revealed dark shadows under her eyes. Her hands had swelled; bruises speckled her elbows. The damage could have been worse, considering that a dozen dead walkers had chased her up a pipe.

The voice. Alexis was hearing voices like her former coworker at the hospital—like Laurel, aka the Angel of Death—had. "Stop this," she scolded herself. "Keep it together."

She trembled. She couldn't remember how she had reached the cabin. Johnny and Tyrone were helping her to the car, and then— nothing. Was she blacking out, too? Laurel used to pass out whenever one of her mistakes resulted in a patient's death. The mumbling came next. Alexis used to catch Laurel talking to the air when she thought no one was watching.

God, she looked filthy. In Yeron's shower, she scrubbed away the grime, but nothing would erase the memory of those dead walkers.

"Alexis, are you okay?" Yeron called.

"I'm working on it." She hobbled out of the shower, wrapping a towel around her.

Yeron perched at the edge of his bed, dressed in pajama bottoms. "At least you can walk," he said, relief bleeding through his voice. "Any pain?"

"The ankle hurts," Alexis confessed. "I used your shower because it hurts to walk."

"You are better off down here," Yeron agreed. "Aside from the fact that I enjoy your company, Shively is in a foul mood. He is upset with you and Johnny."

"He's mad at me because I had to go to the bathroom and I went alone." Alexis furrowed her brows. "What did Johnny do?"

"Tyrone found one of those monsters in the trash can. Instead of helping Tyrone restrain the walker, Johnny panicked and ran. To his credit, he came back when you screamed for help."

Alexis rubbed her eyes and yawned. "Let me guess. Shively's pissed because Johnny ran in the first place."

"Shively had one thing right. That mall is too dangerous for you or Johnny to go anywhere alone." Yeron's voice softened. "I understand why you need privacy; but next time, I will go with you."

Alexis coughed. The memory of the walkers' odor made her gag.

"Please do. The idea of dropping my pants in front of the boys ... especially Mark ... spooks me. I'll never forget the ugly look on his face the night he raped me. So I'll tell you what. Next time I have to go, I'll say 'I have to change a tire.'" She hesitated, noting Yeron's puzzled eyes. "'Change a tire' will be my code phrase for using the bathroom."

"Change a tire." Yeron chuckled. "I will give you a dollar if you go upstairs and say that to Shively."

"It's not funny. Those creatures terrified me. That bathroom reminded me of a Halloween haunted house, but worse because the dangers were real. I'm hallucinating, too, like crazy Laurel used to, and I blacked out."

"Do not compare yourself to Laurel. You collapsed from exhaustion and then you fell asleep."

"That doesn't explain the voices. The one last night told me to use my mind over matter and remember how I love you."

"I love you, too." Yeron gave her a hug. "Did this voice sound like me but older? Did the shape cast a shadow?"

"No shadow. The voice sounded a little like you."

"My father Teodon has unsettled business, and that includes helping you. He frightened me the first time I saw him as a shape. He talked to me last night, too. So ... I heard the same voice."

"Oh, my God! Your father must expect something bad ..."

Loud shouts interrupted Alexis. The hallway door banged open. Tyrone flashed through the hall, clad in striped pajamas. The smell of something rotten drifted toward the basement. Buzzing followed. Shit of some sort had hit the fan. Again. Alexis looked down at herself, gulping when she realized she still had on the towel.

"Put this on." Yeron tossed her a blue nightshirt, yanking it from his closet with his thoughts. She slipped into the shirt while loping up the stairs, grimacing at the shooting pain from her ankle with each step. Yeron came up behind her.

A dead man had gotten into the kitchen. He threw a chair at Tyrone, who ducked. His grinning predatory face had turned the deep purple shade of a spoiled peach. The buzzing came from the flies covering his body. Alexis focused on the walker, mind-slamming him against the hallway wall. Shively sidled to her left, aiming his M16.

"Do not shoot it," Yeron cried. "You might cause an explosion."

"Who let that thing ... never mind, I'll hold him." Alexis remembered an article from *Weekly World Reporter* about someone wrapping a zombie in blankets to drag to the lab. With her strongest mental power, she nudged the creature, flailing and biting at the air, to Mark's bedroom. Greenish mold outlined the area where he crashed into the wall. More seepage dribbled from its legs and sores. Standing by the doorway, she levitated it into Mark's bed.

"What are you doing, bitch?" Mark shouted behind her.

Before she could react, Tyrone and Yeron barreled into Mark's room and wrapped the dead walker in Mark's blanket. The two of them lugged the monster to the basement. Mark stared at the secretions left on his bed, his face reddening, fists clenched.

"You stupid idiot!" he shouted at Alexis. "You ruined my mattress."

Alexis blenched. Part of her wanted to laugh; another part wanted to scream. "I learned the technique from my newspaper. It worked."

"Cheer up, Bucko." Grinning, Johnny clapped his arm over Mark's shoulders and punctuated his words with a rotten-egg fart. "No one will notice the smell from your diapers."

Mark smacked Johnny's hand away, shoved him toward the hall, and turned to close his door.

"Not so fast," Shively said. "Tyrone found that body in a trash can. We left it tied in the car. How did it get here?"

"Good question." Johnny smirked. "Markipoo did a shitty job with the duct tape. I bet he left a mess in the Humvee."

Here we go again with the Mark Adams show. Alexis gazed toward the basement door, then back at Shively. *I should have stayed in bed.*

"Nice save, Alexis." Shively flashed her a grin. "Go get some breakfast. Do something about that leg, too. It looks like your ankle's about to blow."

"Thank you ..." *I think. How the hell am I supposed to eat in this zombie stink? Dammit, my injection's due. Too bad I need food with my medicine.* Alexis glanced at the coffeepot, shook her head, then helped herself to milk and a couple of granola bars.

"Johnny, go down and relieve Tyrone so he can repair whatever's broken in here. Mark and I will clean the Humvee." Shively gave Mark a malignant grin. "Isn't that right?"

"Guess so." Mark's face bleached several shades redder. His hands balled into fists.

Alexis injected her thigh while keeping a wary eye on Mark. Every time things went wrong, he was behind it. "Fuck him," she said to herself.

****

After she donned a T-shirt and pants, Alexis limped down to Yeron's workstation. Clad in a hazmat gown, Johnny held the body by the feet. Yeron, also gowned, stood at its head, next to a stool. Yeron had duct-taped the body by the legs and calves to the table, but the tape didn't hold. The squirming persisted and the left leg ripped the tape off the table. The head thrashed upward, mouth biting at the air.

The walker's withered penis confirmed him as a male. Alexis had to wonder how Yeron would get tissue samples from a thrashing body. The torn, leathery skin stretched over the walker's rib cage and bald head. Cold cobwebs of bone peeped between the craters in his skin. Greenish black secretions seeped through the gashes in his legs and arms, leaking on the floor. Clusters of flies congregated around his gut.

"Ugh. This thing looks deader than dead."

"No shit." Johnny scowled. "Fucker's tiring me out."

"Alexis, gown up. Get the slides in my drawer. Then sit." Yeron indicated the stool beside him. "I will cut, but I need you to hold its head."

Alexis examined her hands. Yeron's prescription relieved the pain, but her hands remained gnarled and puffy. *How am I supposed to restrain a monster?*

"Use your telekinesis." Yeron nodded with encouragement.

"Okay." After retrieving the slides, Alexis took a seat next to Yeron. She rested her bad leg on the support bar below the table and focused on the body. Concentration didn't come easy, not with the odor coming from the creature. His head stopped moving, but his mouth opened and closed like a guppy.

"Johnny, stand back," Yeron ordered.

Johnny did not step back. He recoiled. Yeron made a Y-shaped incision from shoulder to shoulder, joining over the sternum, and down to the pubic bone. Instead of using his hands to cut through tissue, he guided the scalpel with his mind. Alexis swallowed hard; any second, she might upchuck those granola bars. A drop of sweat ran into her eyes. She blotted it with the side of her hood.

Johnny's eyes bulged. "What the hell ...?"

Yeron did not answer him. He continued steering his knife. The skin and tissue peeled back, exposing the ribs and abdominal organs. Alexis snuck a peek at the walker's bones and grayish muscles – a big mistake. It caused a break in her attention. The walker's head wriggled toward Yeron. Alexis summoned her concentration to hold it still.

"How ... why is he moving?" Johnny asked with a puzzled frown.

Because we're dealing with the supernatural, Alexis longed to shout.

"I will show you." Yeron reached for his forceps. "Alexis, are you all right?"

"I will be after we get a priest. He could undo the magic that's making these things move."

"Is that right?" Yeron smiled. Eyes focused on the body, he buried his surgical forceps into the grayish tissue at the neck. He wedged the pincers underneath the trachea. Seconds later, he withdrew his instrument, its teeth clamping a black capsule the size of a pill.

Johnny's mouth became an open O of surprise. "Damn!"

Yeron dove down two more times with his instrument and each time retrieved a capsule. The movement from the body stopped, but Alexis kept a mental grip on his head, lest he leap and bite someone.

"Relax." Yeron rubbed Alexis's shoulders. "Our monster cannot hurt anyone now."

Alexis stepped back, shifting her eyes between the body and Johnny. Johnny released his grip while staring at the three capsules. "What are those things?" he asked. "How did you find them?"

"They are microchips. Scientists at the compound where I lived implanted them into animals, androids, and sometimes people." Yeron lowered his eyes. "Usually in the nape of the neck."

"So that whoever gets the implants can attack?" questioned Johnny.

"Sometimes. My father used androids for surveillance. The microchips enabled us to program an android from a distance. Certain chips carry programming that enables the robot or body to operate plasma weapons. The ones for monitoring are flesh-colored to blend with the skin."

"Yeah." Alexis scratched her head thoughtfully. "I bet someone implanted a microchip into Meathead. Every time he's around, the zombies manage to find us."

"I noticed that, too." A puzzled frown crossed Johnny's face. "So why is he still with us? Shively must know he isn't right."

Alexis shrugged. "Shively blames it on coincidence. He'd never believe our implant theory without an X-ray."

"Shively has his reasons." Frustration crinkled Yeron's eyes. With forceps in hand, he laid the microchips in a metal box. "We should send this to Homeland."

Johnny gave a bitter laugh. "Yeah, right. Drop it off at the post office. It might reach Homeland by Christmas."

"Shively will get it there." Alexis headed to the base of the stairs. "Shively? Shively!"

Seconds later, Shively's booted feet pounded the stairs, followed by Tyrone's.

"Dammit, Alexis, you holler loud enough to wake the dead," Shively railed. "How many times ... what the hell's this?" His blue eyes became widened orbs.

"Microchips," Yeron told him. "Where I grew up, we used them for surveillance and construction. In the wrong hands, they can be dangerous."

"That's the truth." Tyrone's voice softened. "The walkers that exploded at the mall did so because we shot out their microchips."

"I'm not surprised," Alexis said. "Yeron found these in our walker's neck."

"To think we were shooting at them at the restroom." Tyrone mopped the sweat off his face. "If we'd hit the neck, those monsters could've exploded in that room with you in it, Alexis. God must love you."

Think about how much you love Yeron and use your mind over matter, Teodon's words echoed in her mind, and Alexis smiled. "I think so. He sent an angel to watch over me."

"He sure did." Yeron patted her shoulder. "Shively, this one should go to Homeland."

"I know someone who can handle this," Shively said. "Tyrone, we're driving out to Cherryboro tomorrow."

Tyrone nodded with his usual stoicism. "Why Cherryboro?"

"Those logbooks gave useful information, including the last stop the drivers made before the renegades stole the buses." Shively paused, sweeping his gaze across the group. "The original drivers stopped at Cherryboro bus terminal about thirty miles east of Trident Mall. That was their last stop, according to the log books."

"I can respect that," Tyrone said. "By the way, where's Mark?"

Shively shrugged. "Mark forgot to lock the case. The ties came loose and our walker trashed the Humvee. I tore Mark a new asshole for it. He's in his room sulking."

"Watch what you say around Mark," Yeron cautioned him.

"Damn straight." Tyrone nodded with agreement. "Something's off with that man."

"Markipoo and Shit Drawers are lovers, that's why," Johnny said, cackling.

"What?" Yeron scratched the back of his neck, eyes on Johnny. "Who is Shit Drawers?"

"Johnny calls Laurel that because she's lax about bathing." Alexis's hands shook, but she kept her voice steady and her gaze toward Shively. "Besides that, her errors caused patient deaths. Notice that zombies materialize when Mark's with us."

"Yeah. So what?" Shively gave her a sharp glare, his face reddening.

"We suspect that a renegade found Mark and implanted a microchip to spy on us." Alexis drew in a deep breath. There, she'd said it.

"You read this in ... let me think ... *Weekly World*." Shively folded his arms across his chest.

Alexis's cheeks flamed. "That's beside the point."

"Microchip implants for live people were routine at my compound," Yeron told Shively. "She could be right."

"Maybe that's why he acts so batty," Johnny offered. "He might not even know he's got one."

"Folks, you may have a point, but if you're right, any attempt at questioning him will be transmitted to the renegades. The less we say around him, the better. Personally, I think that he got pissed and talked to the wrong people."

"Wouldn't surprise me," Tyrone said, regarding Shively. "He hates being here, not that anyone loves chasing dead people. But Mark ... he was a child molester, for crying out loud. Let him go, Shively. Send him back to his mommy."

"Can't." Shively scowled. "We need insurance, and besides I'd want a snake like him close so I can watch him. So we'll watch what we say around him, but he stays."

"Okay." Alexis shrugged. *Whatever you say.*

"Listen up," Shively went on in his mob boss voice. "Day after tomorrow, we're touring Cherryboro. Alexis, you take point. Use your mind trick on the dead walkers, and we'll wax them. Everyone, be ready to haul ass." Without waiting for an answer, he headed up the stairs, followed by Johnny and Tyrone.

"Point position?" Alexis leaned against Yeron, her lips quivering. "I've never done point."

"I will be first behind you." Yeron held her close. "I will tell you what to do."

Chapter Thirteen: Laurel and Woehar Make Plans

Kryszka Underground Colony, June 4, 10:00 a.m.

While Woehar implanted microchips into bloated bodies with twisted limbs, Laurel squatted by the viewscreen, making chittering sounds. A man lay on the floor beside her, appearing to be asleep. His sweet scent called to her, and the changes in her body fueled her hunger. The DNA cocktail Woehar's doctor fused into her genes left her with scales, pointed teeth, and hulking muscles that ripped through the seams of her clothes, despite frequent upsizing. She now wore a tunic like Woehar. Her voice sounded low and guttural. Talons replaced her hands and feet. *What have you become?* The former respiratory therapist inside her screamed, but then the question left her like bats flying out the window.

She leaped at the man, sank her teeth into his cheek, and tore off the side of his face. The man thrashed and screamed. Laurel sank her talons through his skin and scarfed down the morsel, sweet as cake. He flailed, but his kicks batted like love taps. Wanting more, she angled for his throat. Blood jetted into her mouth. She licked and swallowed, despite Woehar's presence. The man's feet jittered, heels hitting the floor in a tap dance. Another scream followed when she tore into his chest, and then his movements and cries stopped.

Appetite sated, Laurel turned her gaze toward the viewscreen, which portrayed Alexis limping up a trail with five men following several yards behind her. The men were talking in hushed voices, with the exception of the one off to the side. Laurel couldn't make out his face, but she burst out laughing at the sight of Alexis's frightened brown eyes. She figured this was how a rabbit must look staring into the eyes of a cobra.

Woehar, who was implanting a microchip into a specimen, frowned.

"What is so amusing?"

"The guys made the bitch go ahead of them. When your creatures show up, she'll be the first to die." Another stream of giggles. "I wanted her dead, but it never occurred to me to throw her into a bunch of vischlausk-poisoned walkers. Her so-called friends are doing the job for me."

"No." Woehar's eyes narrowed, looking at the screen. "Yeron is guarding her like a prize. He is staying close so he can tell her everything she must do."

"Oh." The laughter died in Laurel's throat. Another glance at the screen, and she made out Yeron's profile off to the side.

"Watch what happens." Woehar's voice softened. "Her friends know what they are doing."

Minutes passed. Ten dead walkers materialized, shambling toward Alexis. *Alexis's toast,* Laurel thought, smiling. *Those ugly specimens could overpower someone her size.*

The first one stumbled. Then the second. Her smile faded as others followed, tumbling to the ground in a pile of arms and legs. Yeron and the others caught up with Alexis and opened fire. An explosion followed, and black smoke enveloped the bodies.

"Holy shit!" Laurel's lips quivered. "What happened there?"

"Alexis can levitate and that is why she went ahead of her friends." The words rolled from Woehar's mouth like a dirge. "Yeron knows about our microchips, and no doubt, he enlightened Alexis and her friends."

A question gnawed at Laurel, but she hesitated. The emotional climate on Woehar's face had darkened like a cloud about to burst. *Not the best time to ask questions.* Despite Woehar's harsh voice, transparent fear oozed through the contempt in her eyes. Her jaw quivered.

Laurel smiled, showing her jagged teeth.

"Alexis might be part Kryszka or some other species. Is that possible?"

Woehar appeared to consider this.

"No, she is human. But the chemicals that Yeron gave her to treat the poison can cause neurological side effects, and one of them could be psychokinesis."

"Dammit! That woman gets away lucky every time."

"Not this time." Woehar gave her a tightlipped smile. "I planned a surprise for our friends."

"More walkers?"

"Not only that. Your suggestion about bombing the cabin gave me an idea." She gave Laurel a cunning smirk. "Oh, this is good."

"How? When?" Laurel's eyes widened. "I bet that Alexis's friends know how to make the cabin secure. Come on, give it up."

"All in a timely manner." Woehar patted Laurel on the head.

"I can get into any building I choose, including the cabin. With microchips, these specimens can dig underground and into the basement where Yeron sleeps."

"You mean ..."

"Yes, they are digging underground as we speak. I am done with – how you say – 'cat and mouse.' I happen to know that someone Alexis holds dear is bringing supplies to the cabin in two weeks. That is when my specimens will deliver their surprise."

Chapter Fourteen: Alexis's Mother Gets Lost

Mill Road Gas Station, June 17, 3:00 p.m.

The first few reconnaissance searches at Cherryboro didn't expose any underground compound. Instead, more dead walkers with microchips came at them, shuffling from behind trees, shrubs, and limestone homes. Some of the infected buildings were sprawling estates, but apparently, the wealth hadn't immunized them against the walkers. Alexis and her friends continued to fight the walkers; a psychic shove from her or Yeron, plus a blast of plasma fire. Bullets from Shively and Johnny felled the ones they missed while Mark lagged behind everyone. Alexis and Yeron took turns walking point. *It's not so bad,* she tried to tell herself, heart thrumming inside her chest.

At the cabin one afternoon, she headed to her bedroom where her 248AR stayed cold in a small refrigerator. Seven syringes remained, enough for that many doses. *Not bad at all.* Forehead dripping with sweat, she retrieved her cell phone from her pocket, about to call her mother. As she did so, the worried voices of Tyrone and Shively filtered in from the kitchen. Something about "fifty magazines left." *Fifty magazines? Shively, Mark, Johnny, and Tyrone go through six every time we ride. Not bad, huh? Who do I think I'm kidding? I should call Mom.*

She began dialing, but stopped when the concerned voices faded to hushed whispers. Seconds later, footsteps.

"Alexis," Tyrone said, "Shively's on the phone with your mom. She's bringing your medicine and more ammo tomorrow, 2:00 p.m."

****

At 1:30 the next afternoon, Alexis paced around the kitchen table while Yeron and Johnny sat and stared out the window. No sign of her mother as 2:00 and 2:30 came and went. No calls. She tried to call her mother, but her phone brayed out static when she tried. No surprise there. The phones had poor reception every day, necessitating Shively's purchase of the walkie-talkie radios.

"You're going to wear a hole in that floor," Johnny told her.

"Sit."

"I can't. It's not like my mother to be late." Alexis dragged her fingers through her hair.

"She is not traveling alone," Yeron pointed out. "She may have run into—"

Buzzing blasted from Alexis's walkie-talkie radio. "Alexis." Her mother's voice barely made it above the static. "My Jeep broke down."

"Your Jeep?" A lead weight settled in Alexis's stomach. She pictured hordes of walkers congregating around her mother's car. Fingers unsteady, she pressed the "hold and speak" button. "Where's Fenimore?"

"He's in the hospital with atrial fibrillation. He loaned me his GPS."

"Where are you?"

"Somewhere close enough to you that I can use the walkie-talkie, in case the phone lines went dead. I'm at a gas station, but it's closed. So is the deli next door. I can't read the signs because they've crumbled."

"Oh, my God!" Alexis burst into tears. "Mom could be anywhere."

"Alexis." Shively had poked his head from the living room, frowning. "What's the matter?"

"My mother's car broke down. She came out here alone and she's lost."

Shively tore the radio from Alexis's hand. After depressing the "hold and speak" button, he walked to the rear of the house. Alexis followed him, trying to listen in but static drowned out the words.

Yeron, who had followed behind her, draped his arm over her shoulders.

"Shively told your mother to sit tight. We will go get her."

Alexis nodded, her heart bursting with gratitude that Yeron's alien traits had gifted him with sensitive ears.

"Do you think Mom understood him?"

"I hope so," Shively answered before Yeron could. His eyes settled on Alexis. He handed her the walkie-talkie.

"Keep talking to your mom. Yeron, Johnny, Tyrone ... let's go. We have to find Matilda. I'll drive."

Yeron accompanied Alexis, his hand cradling her shoulder. Johnny and Tyrone trailed behind them. Mark came out of his room as they passed and followed.

"What's up?" he asked.

"Nothing," Shively said flatly.

"Where are you going?" A whine crept into Mark's voice.

"Out." Shively maintained a poker face. "Stay here and guard the house."

"Whatever." Mark shook his head, mumbling, then headed back to his room.

"What's Mark's problem?" Alexis's mother growled.

"Nothing," Alexis said through clenched teeth. "He's being Mark."

"I don't trust that guy. At least Yeron is upstanding."

"Hear that, honey?" Alexis leaned against Yeron, smiling through her tears. "Momsy paid you a compliment." She depressed the "speak" button again. "How's your rib?"

"Sore. Nothing that a little aspirin can't handle."

"Matilda," Shively shouted from the front. "Have you seen any walkers?"

"So far, no," her mother said. "The streets are nasty, though. Lots of potholes and broken-down cars after you leave Royerstown."

"But no walkers. That's good," Shively said. "What did you bring?"

"I've got letters and *Weekly World Reporter* issues. I brought ravioli, salad, cannolis, and peaches. I have Alexis's medicine and chemicals for Yeron's lab, and five crates of ammo. That's what the delivery guy called it."

"Ammunition, a home-cooked meal, and medicine." Alexis breathed a sigh of relief.

They piled into the Humvee and Shively drove slowly toward the end of the driveway.

"I need more details about your surroundings." Tension edged into Shively's voice. "There are a million gas stations and delis in this area."

"I came up Route 85 as the GPS told me," her mother replied. "Then I lost reception. I turned right by a pylon at an intersection, hoping it would be Mill Road. I passed an old barn, came to a dead end, and took the next right ... and my car stalled. I managed to get it going and made it to this gas station."

"I know where you are," Shively said.

"How many miles?" Alexis asked in a wary voice.

"Only five ... fuck!" The Humvee screeched to a stop.

A jackknifed truck blocked the road past the stop sign. The trailer sat across the road, rear tire flat, and the cab pointed toward Shively's Humvee. A husky, tan-complexioned man in the cab was talking on a radio. They were losing precious time.

Alexis's jaw tightened. "Yeron ... can we levitate that truck?"

"I doubt it," Yeron said in a pained voice. "Vehicles like that weigh over fifteen tons. It would require six people like me to levitate it."

"I'm not sitting here all day." Shively twisted the wheel left and made a sharp U-turn. He headed back, driving on the grass. At the next street he cut right.

"I can handle the detours, but this street has a lot of potholes."

"Shively, I pray you make it." Tyrone's voice remained calm, but his mouth twitched. "If those walkers get to her mom, they'll wreck the car and take the ammunition in it."

"We're good as dead if that happens." Johnny licked his lips. "Why'd she come out here alone?"

"Because she decided she could," Alexis said in a weepy voice. "Look at this street."

"Shively, can't you go any faster?" Tyrone asked.

Shively shook his head. "If I try, I'm liable to wreck the Humvee."

"The walkers won't care." Alexis's voice cracked. "Mom doesn't have any time to spare."

Yeron sidled next to Alexis and pulled her close.

"You do not know that."

"We should have let Shively's men deliver the supplies. My dad must be rolling over in his grave."

"We will make sure she is okay when we find her," Yeron assured her. Despite his confident tone, Yeron's red eyes betrayed shock, as if to say, *I never meant for this to happen.*

Her mother's hushed voice crackled from the walkie-talkie. "Something's moving in the trees."

"What?" Alexis shouted.

"I mean the bushes." A long pause followed, and then her voice again, pleading. "It's one of those creatures. I've got my Glock."

"Matilda!" Yeron jammed his finger on the "hold and speak" button. The confidence fled from his voice, replaced by panic. "Stay in your car and lock your doors until we get there."

"Why? I can handle one walker."

"Most walkers bring their friends."

Matilda's voice came through again, but unintelligibly blurred by static.

"Dammit, she can't understand you." Alexis wiped away the tears running down her face.

More static, and overriding it, a scream. Try as she might, Alexis couldn't make out any words. Yeron's tight-lipped frown warned that he had trouble understanding her, too.

"My God!" She folded her hands. "Those monsters must be

breaking into her car."

"Hey, keep it together," Shively shouted from the front. "We'll find her."

They trundled up a road until it became blocked by battered cars. "Fuck!" He slammed on the brakes. "What the hell ..."

He swung the vehicle, driving around the cars on the shoulder and the grass, in a serpentine course. Another block, and there they were, four walkers bashing the windows of a Jeep. Not just any Jeep. Her mother's silver Cherokee. The fenders and doors were no longer silver but a grisly shade of maroon mixed with green. The driver's side windows had shattered, and two of the creatures were wriggling into the car headfirst.

"Mom!" Alexis screamed, bursting out of the Humvee. She ran toward the Jeep, ignoring the nagging soreness in her ankle. She used her psychic ability to pry the walkers from the car windows. Gray matter the texture of oatmeal spilled through wounds in their foreheads, but still, they moved.

"Guide them away from the car," Yeron hollered behind her. "Shooting them near the car may cause an explosion and harm Matilda."

With Yeron's help, Alexis led the gamey walkers toward an open field. Tyrone and Johnny fired, aiming for their heads. Shadowy stalagmites of smoke rose from the bodies. Alexis glanced toward the Jeep and its shattered windows.

"The hell with the smoke!" She rushed back toward the Jeep, Yeron right behind her. She grasped the door handle and yanked. Locked. She paid for her effort with stinging pain in her wrists. Her mother crouched, hidden somewhere in the Jeep. Alexis pictured her cut to ribbons, her face a rictus of pain, and unable to open the door.

"Shit! Dammit!" Alexis screamed.

"I have it," Yeron said behind her.

Two clicks followed. The door swiveled open, exposing ripped front seats. Shattered glass embedded in the vinyl glimmered, contrasted by greenish stains and beige secretions. Alexis's stomach churned. She turned her head and vomited onto the dirt. She took another look at the car. The rear seats were folded down, covered with shattered glass fragments. The coolers and crates holding the cargo that Matilda had brought remained untouched in the rear hold. *Dammit, those monsters trashed a car with my mother in it.*

"Mom!"

Moaning. Blood-streaked fingers poked out from under the rear seat cushion.

Alexis grasped the cushion, wincing at the pain in her hands, and decided to levitate it. As it rose, glass shards slid down the vinyl, landing on a wriggling blanket. Under the blanket, Matilda lay on the floor. The blanket moved away, exposing blood on her arms. Lots of it.

"Oh, shit! Yeron!"

"Wait!" Stepping up beside Alexis, Yeron peeled back the blanket. "Matilda, can you sit up?"

Alexis's mother shook her head. "I'm stuck."

"Hey, guys, come over here!" Alexis called toward Tyrone and Johnny, waving her hands.

Tyrone and Johnny sprinted to the car while Shively monitored the smoke for flames.

"Don't worry, we'll get her out," Johnny said.

Alexis stepped back, making room for the men.

"Momsy, try to move your leg," Johnny said.

Matilda tried to slide her right leg and grimaced.

"It won't budge. I squeezed under the seats to hide from the walkers."

"Your leg's caught under the front seat," Tyrone told her. "Stay still. Johnny, help me move it forward." Matilda let out a whimper as they did so. He then grasped her by the shoulders. "I'll lift you out, nice and easy."

"I will levitate," Yeron said. "You guide."

"Works for me," Tyrone said. The two men eased Matilda from under the seat and placed her on the grass. She had on a sleeveless top.

Bad choice of clothing. Alexis massaged her arms, trying to quiet the goose bumps. Blood trailed in ribbons down Matilda's arms, especially the right. *Why didn't she wear something with long sleeves?*

Yeron retrieved his enhanced surgical kit from the Humvee. Dropping to his knees beside Matilda, he retrieved the surgical thread from the kit. Johnny slid beside him, reassuring her in a soft voice. Alexis watched, hands pressed against her lips. *I should be helping.* Tears blurred her surroundings. The stabbing pain in her hands had come so fast, but that didn't matter now. Her mother had gotten cut trying to hide from the walkers. Another few moments, and they would've broken into her car.

Chapter Fifteen: Matilda Spends the Night

Shively's Cabin, Merriman Trails, June 17, 6:00 p.m.

"Matilda, a mechanic will tow your car to his shop for repairs," Shively said over a platter of ravioli and salad.

Matilda sipped coffee, keeping her bandaged arms away from the table. Alexis murmured a prayer, thanking God that her wounds had come from the glass.

"Thank you," Matilda said in a small voice. "How much will I owe him?"

"Nothing."

Matilda's chin jerked up. "Nothing?"

Shively set down his fork and met her gaze.

"You brought us supplies, meds, ammo, and this food. We'll get someone to drop off the car to your house. The repairs will take a few days, so stay with us for now. Tyrone or I will drive you home when the car's ready. You got cut pretty badly, so we don't want you driving by yourself now."

"I appreciate that." Her eyes blinked and her left cheek twitched. "Where shall I sleep?"

Yeron smiled. "You and Alexis can sleep on the sofa bed downstairs." At Alexis's sharp look, he patted her shoulder. "Do not worry, honey. I will not bring in any more specimens for a while."

"Thank you, Yeron." Matilda's voice cracked and a tear spilled down her face. "I shot those creatures through the head the way my neighbor Fenimore taught me. Why didn't they die this time?"

This time? Alexis flinched. *How many times has she run into these monsters?*

"The people creating them have enhanced their movements with microchips," Yeron told her.

"Microchips? Oh, *Dio Mio!*" Matilda's chest jerked with sobs. Alexis draped her arm across her mom's shoulders, wishing she could hug away the pain. "When those things came at me, my life flashed before me. I saw myself in grade school, jumping rope."

"I bet you did." Tyrone's head drooped. "No more driving out here alone. Next time, bring someone with you."

"Better yet, let someone else bring the supplies." Mark, who'd been silent, spoke with a somber voice, but his eyes held a devilish gleam. "That ammunition could've exploded. How much did you bring anyway?"

Matilda shrugged. "The delivery man stowed five crates in my cargo hold. I don't know what's in there; I didn't ask."

"Five crates sounds like a lot. I appreciate it." A crooked grin surfaced on Mark's ruddy face. He leaned back in his chair, hands folded behind his head.

"What's it to you, Diaper Boy?" Johnny's eyes narrowed to crinkled slits. "Why the sudden interest in our ammo?"

Alexis giggled. *You tell 'em, Johnny.*

Mark's face flushed a deep red.

"I was thankful for Matilda's safety. What's your problem?"

"You shit out of both ends." Tyrone glared at Mark. "Matilda brought that ammo for all of us." He turned toward Matilda, his voice kind. "The basement should be safe. No windows or vents. Make sure you keep the door to the outside locked."

****

"I shouldn't have come here alone," Matilda said as she climbed into bed. "Next time, I'll ask Doctor Hoffman or someone else to go with me."

If there is a next time. Alexis stretched, sliding her plasma gun under her pillow, where it remained snug.

"I should have helped more. Instead, I crumbled."

"You've got a tender heart, like me." Her mother smiled. "You always did. That's why I worry about you."

"I know." Alexis lay beside her mother, eyes on the ceiling of the steel gray laboratory. The lights from Yeron's machinery played soft red, blue, and green hues along the ceiling and walls. The colors soothed her, but a rancid smell, more pungent than the autopsy, left a sick feeling in her gut. It smelled like dead rats had decayed in the walls. She rolled toward her mother, who still lay awake.

Matilda regarded Alexis in the swirling, colored light.

"I understand why you love Yeron. He was so gentle with me today."

"Somehow I sense a 'but' coming." Alexis grinned.

"No buts." Matilda's gray eyes twinkled. "Whether I approve or not, I want you to be happy. If you can find happiness while the dead are terrorizing us, grab it."

"Thank you." Alexis heaved a sigh of relief. "Yeron's a jewel in a pile of dirt. Like this basement. It smells like an animal crawled in here and died three days ago."

Matilda shrugged. "Where else can we sleep?"

"There's the sofa—" Alexis jumped, startled by an underground rumbling. Crunching and rattling came next, loudest about three feet from the end of the sofa. She hopped out of bed and retrieved her gun.

"Mom, get up and get dressed."

Even as Alexis spoke, Matilda climbed out of bed, threw on a robe and her sandals, and backed toward the staircase. She stared at the floor, her mouth an open O of terror. "*Dio Mio!* What's going on?"

"I don't know, but I don't like it." Alexis donned her tunic and reached for her Maglites. "Go upstairs and wake Yeron. *Now!*"

Her mother sprinted up the steps, adrenaline overriding her injuries. Alexis backed toward the stairwell. The rumbling intensified, accompanied by the sounds of drilling and scraping. Heart leaping in her throat, breath panting, Alexis stepped up two steps backward. *Better turn and run,* a voice inside her screamed. *Something's trying to break in.*

It's too late to run, she thought better. *Whatever's trying to get in will demolish everything.*

"Oh, dear God, Yeron, where are you?" She absentmindedly massaged her arms. Her teeth chattered.

The linoleum beneath her feet buckled and then shattered. Spider cracks splayed along the cement with a popping, crunching sound, creating a chasm. Drifts of dirt sprayed over the remaining tiles. Something inside the chasm flashed white and exuded a foul odor. Alexis immediately realized it was the source of the rancid smell. "Jesus, help me!" she cried, summoning her psychic forces.

The chasm enlarged, forcing crumbling cement down into it. Bony hands dug up through the crevice. Her psychic energy enabled Alexis to keep those hands at the edge of the hole, but just barely. She counted twenty hands reaching toward her. Ten walkers.

"Yeron!" she screeched, but her voice came out a dry whistle. A bloodied hand broke through her force field and slapped the floor, inches from the bottom step. Alexis screamed, this time audibly.

"Dammit, Mom, get Yeron!" She fought to keep her force field in place. "Before they grind me into hamburger."

Chapter Sixteen: Basement Visitors

Basement at Shively's Cabin, June 18, 1:00 a.m.

Yeron lay halfway between deep slumber and twilight sleep, relaxing in a hot tub with Alexis somewhere. Surrounded by warm water, his lips against her silky skin, he brushed her breasts and shoulders with kisses. She straddled him, his thick rod nestled inside her. He hugged her, savoring the heat from her loins, the naked desire in her brown eyes, and her rose scent. The warm water sloshed around them. Zombies and renegades had no place here. Thunder rumbled outside, announcing the arrival of rain.

Sharp rapping at the door.

"Yeron!" a woman's voice shouted. "Get up!"

More rapping.

The pleasant images faded. Yeron's eyes snapped open. He was not in a hot tub after all. He had never left the cabin. Arms hugging Alexis's pillow, he gazed around her bedroom. The thunder came from underground. *Underground? From what?*

"Yeron!" Matilda's voice, panic-stricken. "The walkers got into the basement!"

Yeron bolted to his feet. The last vestiges of sleep vanished, replaced by gut-wrenching terror.

"Coming," he shouted, donning his boots and tunic. He grabbed his guns and Maglites on the way to the hall. He covered his ears but failed to mute the clattering, ripping sounds, followed by gravelly moans. Something scraped, the sound of dragging chains on dirt ... and ... what was this? He heard humming, the same noise he heard years ago when his home compound exploded.

"*Bah fungule,* my daughter's down there with them," Matilda cried. "Save her!"

Liquid fear sloshed through Yeron's veins. Swear words from the proper Matilda Carofalo who'd confined her frustration to "*Dio Mio*" terrified him more than anything.

"Matilda, I am going downstairs. The rumbling should have

woken everyone. Send Shively and Tyrone to the basement, and Mark and Johnny to meet us out back."

"We're right behind you," Shively's tense voice said behind him.

Something or someone had blown a hole in the floor near the basement steps. Skeletal, wasted creatures were trying to claw through the chasm, but Alexis's force field contained most of them. Not all. Because of the overwhelming number, two of the walkers had climbed out onto the cement. Yeron gagged on the smell of rot, but the humming frightened him more. It came from a walker who had broken through the chasm, one with a bashed-in face and worm-crusted eyes.

"Alexis, watch out!" Yeron shouted. "That walker has a creeper bomb."

Alexis did not answer. Instead, she faced him with panic stricken eyes.

"What?"

Comprehension dawned. Yeron had reverted to his native language. Seconds later, he realized that Alexis had not yet completely learned the Kryszka language.

"Alexis," he said, "one of them has a bomb."

"*A bomb?*" Alexis's mouth opened and she screamed. "Run!"

"No, Alexis. It will kill everyone here if it blows. I have to defuse it and I need your help."

"I can't do this." Alexis burst into a deluge of tears. She bolted up the steps. Her concentration broke, and more walkers clambered through the chasm. Yeron threw his own psychic force field over the creatures while blocking Alexis's path.

Yeron shook his head with frustration. He had not counted on Alexis crumbling.

"Pull yourself together!" His eyes became like fiery red lasers. His voice smoked with fury, but he could not help it. "Consider your mother and your friends. Do it quickly. Time is short."

Alexis faced him, arms folded across her chest, lips scowling, tears running down her cheeks. "You think I don't care about my mother. What do you expect me to do?"

"Shively and Tyrone will help me defuse the bomb." Yeron's voice lowered. "Levitate the other walkers and usher them through the basement door outside to an open area. Then Johnny and Mark can dispose of them. All of them must go except the one with the face gash."

"All right." Alexis gulped as if she swallowed a fishbone. She rubbed her arms and drew in a deep breath. After she levitated the basement door open, the walkers climbed through the chasm, clawing at the air, as if desperate to grab the nearest person. To Yeron's relief, they staggered for the door. One by one, she guided them outside.

****

Shively and Tyrone bounded down the stairs, wearing hazmat suits. Yeron guided the walker with the face gash to his table, ready to dissect. The humming continued, faint but distinct. The humans gave no sign of noticing the noise. Of course, they wouldn't, but his more evolved ears could detect it. The humans riveted their eyes on the door and the blasting sounds that came from outside.

"Restrain him." Yeron handed the men thick leather belts. "I need to confirm the type of weapon he is carrying."

"Confirm ... shit. I know how to defuse a bomb," Shively told him.

"The creep who made this one isn't human." Tyrone darted a glance toward Yeron. "Do what you gotta do. We've got him covered."

Despite the men's ministrations, the walker continued grabbing at the air. Shriveled gray flesh covered half of its face. On the other half, an open gash stretched from eyeball to chin, with bugs crawling through the fascia.

Yeron batted the bugs away and made an incision in the throat. The leathery skin tore when he tugged at it with forceps. Going deeper, he exposed the trachea, and underneath, the microchip and a black box with flashing green lights and yellow wires. The black box contained a creeper bomb, smaller than the one that had destroyed his compound, but capable of killing people. The flickering symbols displayed five minutes to explosion. Five minutes to defuse. Or die.

Frowning, Yeron moved over to his computer. He had saved his father's instructional software on dismantling a creeper bomb and access to the Net to use it, but it required a password to download. His red eyes narrowed and then widened. He chewed his lower lip between his pointed teeth, drawing blood. At the smell of Yeron's blood, the walker thrashed against its ties. Yeron turned back to the table and removed the microchip, quieting the walker.

After blotting the blood from his lips with his sleeve, he typed in his father's name. Access denied. He mistyped it. A second try also denied him access. The clock ticked away while he tried to recall a simple password. He tapped the membrane board and typed in his mother's name. He made it in. Yeron thrust his memories away and scrolled down the menu.

After he downloaded the software, the words, "HOLOGRAPHIC ASSISTANT" appeared on the screen, along with instructions to put on a set of headphones. He tapped the keyboard of the main terminal and reached for his bulky earphones. He moved to the bomb. He'd have to listen carefully to get it right.

The holographic assistant spoke into his ear. He listened and did as she said. He opened the box's housing. As he got to the primary explosive and detonator, the voice faded and static filled his ears.

"Son of a bitch!" he shouted.

"What you got? Static?" Shively shot him a look. His blue eyes bulged and rolled like those of a fear-maddened lunatic; his face drained white.

Yeron nodded, trying hard to listen to the assistant.

"Fuck this," said Shively, and before Yeron had a chance to react, Shively snatched the explosive.

"Hey!" Tyrone shouted. "What are you doing?"

"Cutting through this bullshit." Shively held the explosive up to the light. "Pulling the detcaps from the payload should neutralize any bomb."

"Not this one." He ripped the earphones off and, using his mental powers, Yeron pried Shively's fingers from the explosive.

"Drop it into the sink," Tyrone shouted. "Run water over it."

"Fuck that," said Shively. Snatching the bomb again, he tossed it quickly through the open door. Yeron shrunk in terror at the *woof* followed by a booming sounding like the explosion of an underground compound. Fire extinguisher in hand, Shively barreled outside, Tyrone behind him. Yeron grabbed another extinguisher off the wall. Flames erupted, licking the sides of the trees near the Humvee. Gunfire exploded; Johnny, Alexis, and Matilda formed a C-shaped circle around the walkers. At the sight of Alexis's mother, Yeron let out a low cry. *Matilda? What is she doing out here?*

It did not matter; he had to contain the fire. That meant putting out the flames and keeping the smoke away from the Humvee and the people destroying the walkers. Minimizing the damage necessitated intense concentration. They had a long night ahead.

****

As he entered the cabin, Yeron gasped at the sight of Matilda standing in the open door, hands cradling roses.

"What are you doing?" he asked. "You should be resting."

"I tried to rest until those walkers broke into the basement." Matilda sniffed her flowers and grimaced. "It stinks everywhere. I found about a dozen roses on one of the bushes. I hoped they'd help cover up the smell." She shook her head, giving a rueful smile. "Guess not."

Yeron sniffed the flowers and inhaled the scent of sulfur despite the floral aroma. Blood was oozing from two of her dressings.

"I saw you and Johnny quieting the walkers," he said, frowning. "Was anyone else with you?"

"Well ..." Matilda lowered her eyes.

"Tell me while I change your dressings." Yeron gestured toward the basement door.

"No basement." Matilda shook her head solemnly. "Kitchen."

"Very well. I will go get my supplies." Yeron sighed. "Wait for me in the kitchen."

In the basement, a high-pitched weeping noise and the sound of shredding paper assaulted Yeron's ears, presumably coming from Mark's room. Yeron proceeded back up to the kitchen where the faint odor of urine drifted from Mark's open doorway. He grimaced, holding his nose.

"Johnny went to meet Alexis, but Mark never left his room," Matilda told him. "She used her mind to control them and I got the ones Johnny didn't."

Yeron tightened his fists. "Dammit!"

"One of you guys shouted from the basement," Matilda continued as if Mark's behavior didn't faze her. "It sounded like a walker threw something that exploded outside. Then I saw you, Tyrone, and Shively run outside with fire extinguishers. You looked terrified, Yeron. You still do."

She clasped her hand over her forehead.

"Are we still in danger? Of course, we are. Why is Mark a part of this team? He's worthless."

"He is." Yeron lowered his eyes. "We have a good reason to keep him, but I am not at liberty to discuss it."

"In other words, I'm not supposed to ask questions." Matilda's gray eyes flashed with indignation. "Meantime, you gamble with my daughter's life."

"I cannot speak for the others, but I never let her go anywhere alone." Yeron spoke in a somber voice. "Tyrone, Johnny, and I watch out for Alexis in ways you cannot imagine. I found a bomb in one of the walkers, so I gave her a job that took her away from it." He cocked his head sideways. "Where is she?"

Matilda shrugged. "Sleeping, I think. Why?"

Yeron dragged his fingers through his thick hair.

"I owe her an apology."

"Because?" Matilda canted her head sideways.

"I came down hard on her because she panicked when the bomb hummed. One like it destroyed the compound where I used to live." Chills stirred in his shoulders, cresting at his neck. For an instant, he imagined himself back in Philadelphia, putting distance between himself and the compound when Eigil's bomb exploded. Images of his father's bloodied body flashed through his mind.

"*Dio Mio.*" Matilda crossed herself. "Alexis is fragile but she's not stupid. Your reaction was understandable and she realizes that. But Yeron, Mark's behavior – or lack thereof – will get someone killed."

Yeron focused on wrapping the bandage without answering. *She is right.*

"So I'm staying. I'll fill in when Mark does his no-shows. What do you say?"

Yeron straightened up and dropped his tape. He gazed at Matilda without answering.

"Don't stare at me." Exasperation edged into her voice. "I haven't grown a second head."

Yeron groaned inwardly. Matilda was asking his permission and this brought him to dangerous territory. As it was, any goodwill he garnered from her was conditional. The other men called her "Mom" while he dared not. Her demeanor toward him depended on how he answered.

Agreement would put her life at risk. Saying "no" would put her on the defensive, and she would come up with twenty valid reasons why she should stay. Though a competent warrior, dangerous variables existed, such as Shively's actions with the bomb and Mark's aberrant behaviors. Every time Shively planned a search mission with Mark in earshot, walkers invaded the chosen site. Perhaps he wore a microchip that transmitted the activity around him to the renegades; more likely, he leaked information to an enemy soldier. Could Matilda understand this and go home without protest? He doubted it. She worried too much about her daughter.

He heaved a sigh. "You should have this conversation with Alexis."

"Alexis is too close to the situation. I'm asking you."

The front door opened. Tyrone shuffled inside, hauling two fire extinguishers. Yeron exhaled with relief.

"We should discuss this with Tyrone, too."

"Hey, I had enough for tonight!" Tyrone slammed his equipment on the floor. "Now what?"

"Mark stayed in his room, so Matilda went out to help Johnny," Yeron told him. "She is offering to fight with us because Mark is a wimp."

"She's got it right about Mark." Tyrone whirled toward Matilda, his voice softening. "Mom, you can't stay here. You must know that."

"Don't tell me what I know." Matilda's voice raised a notch. "I can handle a gun."

"Mom." Tyrone lowered his voice and rested his hand on her shoulder. "You came through tonight, but what we're doing – any of us could get killed. Suppose it was you? Do you want Alexis to see that?"

Matilda lowered her eyes. A tear rolled down her cheek. After a moment, she shook her head.

"Maybe you have a good reason to keep Mark, maybe you don't. I'm afraid he'll get one of you killed. Think about that and ask yourself if your reason is worth someone's life.

"I'll sleep on the sofa." She handed Yeron the roses. "Give these to Alexis."

Yeron backed toward the hall, eyes on Matilda, and hesitated.

"Go." Tyrone waved his hand. "I'll watch her."

Chapter Seventeen: Reliving a Battle

Outside Shively's Cabin, June 18, 4:00 a.m.

Alexis curled up in bed, eyes shut, but sleep wouldn't come. Scenes replayed through her mind: a bomb exploding from the basement; Shively, Tyrone, and Yeron running to put out the flames; the walkers trying to break through her force field; Johnny and her mother destroying them. *Her mother?* What was she doing outside?

"Where's Mark?" she asked Johnny.

"He's busy pissing in his didies." Johnny turned to shoot at a walker with a shrug, as if Mark's bathroom habits were the most ordinary behavior in the world.

"Bah fungule, Mark," her mother shouted, and then fired at another.

The blasting sounds echoed in her head, punctuated by Yeron's shouting. She'd let him down, and an arrow of sorrow pierced her heart.

She tried visiting a safe place in her mind—her psychiatrist, Doctor Klein, had advised using this technique when circumstances overwhelmed her. Her mom's kitchen offered a safe place, where she'd eat a platter of homemade manicotti; a place where her wrists didn't hurt, and zombies were mere nightmares. The safe place offered a great refuge, but it didn't distract her for more than a minute. Shadows of misshapen dead bodies danced along the bedroom walls. Despite the air conditioning, the stink of charred flesh made her gag. Her arms rippled with gooseflesh at the imagined sound of gunfire and then ... footsteps. Real footsteps. A tentative knock.

"Alexis," Yeron whispered.

Alexis grabbed her Maglite and hopped to her feet. Clad in her nightshirt, she tiptoed toward the door. Alexis peered cautiously around the door as she opened it. Yeron held out his arms, one hand grasping a bouquet. He folded her against his chest. The anger had left his red eyes, but an infinite sadness had replaced it. She longed to hug him and make the night's horrors go away.

"I am sorry I yelled at you," he said, setting the flowers on her bureau. "This has not been easy for me."

"Of course, it hasn't." Her voice wavered. "I'm sorry, too, for not keeping myself together. This nightmare never stops."

"It certainly does not." Yeron's thick fingers stroked her hair. "Matilda told me Mark did not come outside. She wants to be his replacement in the team."

Alexis shook her head, heart thudding dulling in her chest.

"That's not going to happen. My mom's a capable shooter, but she can't run." Then her gaze dropped toward the floor. "Neither can I, but at least I can use my telekinesis."

"Tyrone convinced her to go home. She can run, but her ability is not the problem."

Alexis frowned. "Meathead's the problem. He always is."

"Not only Meathead. Shively, too. He lost control tonight. I had trouble dismantling the bomb, so he grabbed it and threw it outside. Tyrone said he would watch Matilda, but he may have volunteered so he could avoid Shively."

"My God!" Alexis crossed herself. "Does Mom know?"

"Matilda knows. She gave us good advice about Mark. You are fortunate to have her as a mother."

Alexis bobbed, smiling. "I'll keep her. What's with Shively? He's used to handling violence."

"Not the kind we face. We had better stay close to each other."

"No argument there."

"Alexis ... I need to be with you." He embraced her again and planted kisses on her cheek. "Your mother and Tyrone are in the living room. Your bed squeaks. So if we use your chair, can we make love quietly?"

"I think if we're careful ..." Alexis wrapped her arms around him and closed the door with her mind, "... we can shoot for the moon."

Chapter Eighteen: Video

Laurel lingered in a twilight sleep, drifting through a blood-red haze. She dreamed that she was back at Jackson Hospital working as a respiratory therapist, where an old man had suffocated after she attempted to wean him off the ventilator. Poor, poor thing. She'd wanted him to live, but she'd had a blackout. Things went wrong after her blackouts if Abaddon was involved. In the dream, the head nurse shouted at her, threatening to report her. Her head ached, and she ran out to the courtyard to escape the chaos.

She caught the hospital vice president snorting nose candy.

A smile crept across her face. The administrator's mistake offered a chance to barter for job security.

"You bad boy." She made a shame-shame motion with her fingers. *"Go straight to jail. Do not pass GO, do not collect two hundred dollars."*

The vice president twisted sideways with clumsy movements; he was not the authority figure she had seen before, but a walking withered corpse. Instead of pleading with Laurel not to report him, he grinned, revealing a blackened tongue and teeth. One bloodied eyeball fell out and dropped onto the grass. Laurel screamed.

"Stop your nonsense!" a woman bellowed behind her. "Now!"

Laurel's eyes flew open like window shades, as she snapped out of her dream. She realized she wasn't in Jackson Hospital; she was still lying on a table at Woehar's underground laboratory. The thing she'd become could not provide patient care. She only knew a craving for flesh and blood.

The lab held about 50 live occupants, each tied down to a metal table, but Laurel's eyes settled on a naked woman facing her. Someone had jammed a skewer down her throat. Its pointed end stuck out through her rectum. She lay in a puddle of blood, whimpering. Her sweet, cupric scent called to Laurel, who hopped off the table, her stomach rumbling.

Woehar blocked Laurel's access to the woman, her red eyes flashing with anger. Mealtime had to wait. Woehar's tantrum demanded her attention.

"I'm sorry," Laurel said in her harsh, grating voice. Her speech was getting progressively worse because of the chromosome fusion. "I had a nightmare."

"I will give you a nightmare." Woehar shook her fist, the one brandishing her plasma gun. Her chiseled face became a scrawl of fury. "Get one thing straight. When I first rescued you from that car accident, I did not do it out of friendship or pity. I needed a source of meat and a viable specimen for my *settva* experiment. So do not whine to me about your dreams or anything else. Do you understand?"

Laurel sensed that something had gone wrong. Again. Perhaps another botched attempt at getting Alexis; maybe Quyeba had caught on to Woehar's plans, and undermined those plans. Whatever happened, Laurel had grown tired of playing the whipping girl. Besides, her mouth salivated at the aroma of the skewered woman. She'd feed now if Woehar didn't stand in her way. A bittersweet scent issued forth from Woehar. Laurel found that peachy keen, for the thing she was becoming ate anything that walked. She tensed on her haunches, and a small, noisy growl rose from her throat. The scales around her mouth wrinkled back to show her long, white teeth.

Woehar's eyebrows drew together; her lips tightened. She cocked her gun. An invisible force slammed into Laurel's windpipe, knocking her to the floor. She landed on her shoulders and back, and oh, how that hurt! She howled.

"Do not think you can harm me," Woehar said in a cruel voice. "Not with my telekinesis and disintegrator. I will fry you first."

Laurel struggled to get upright, shuddering at the dark tumors of rage that blossomed inside her. Woehar had turned her into a monster, a horror worse than anything Alexis had ever done. One day, she planned to teach this bitch a lesson; but now, she had to play the role of a dutiful pet. "What happened?" she asked in a small voice.

"Matilda." Woehar spat out the name.

"Matilda who?" Laurel still tried for a little girl's voice, but the sounds came out hoarse and guttural.

"Do not play dumb with me, animal! I am talking about Alexis's mother."

Laurel stared at Woehar, eyes bulging, as she stood up.

"Oh, she's an old floor nurse ready to retire. She can't hurt you."

"Is that right?" Woehar yanked Laurel by the shoulders, birdshot pupils glittering. "Think again, stupid. Matilda may be old, but she is a warrior."

Warrior? She's got Matilda mixed up with someone else. Whatever. The sooner she unloads, the sooner I eat. Laurel rubbed her gut to soothe the gurgling.

"What did Matilda do?" she asked, humoring Woehar.

"Her vehicle broke down and my creations stumbled across her. She shot them, but they had the implant. So she used a radio to call for help. Alexis and her companions came to her rescue."

"You caught this all on Mark's microchip?" Laurel asked as she eyeballed the bleeding woman.

"Not the actual event but the conversation they had about it while they were eating. Watch and listen." Woehar backed away and clicked on a readout screen.

Laurel turned her eyes to the screen. It portrayed Alexis, Yeron, Tyrone, and Matilda at the table eating ravioli. Between mouthfuls, Matilda wept. Bandages covered her arms.

"Something cut her bad," Laurel said. "I bet that upset Alexis plenty."

"Minor injuries." Exasperation crept into Woehar's voice. "Yeron watches out for both of them. I find that interesting. I never imagined he would get along with a human like Matilda."

"What about the surprise you had for them?"

"Alexis and Matilda were in the basement when I sent my creations through the tunnel. The women were awake and able to get away in time. Yeron heard humming from a specimen, dissected it, and found my bomb. One of the humans threw it out the door. That bomb should have destroyed the cabin and surrounding trees." Woehar's voice rose as she spoke. "The fluid from the decaying tissues must have ruined the bomb."

"You could be right." Laurel's halfhearted nod indicated that she didn't give a damn about bombs, Matilda, or any of Woehar's problems. Despite her appetite, she had to humor Woehar to get dinner.

"Matilda's an old lady. She doesn't have the speed or the reflexes to chase your walkers."

"The woman in our video has a lot of muscle. Someone trained her well. She may move slowly, but she knows how to handle a gun."

"What are you gonna do now?"

Woehar sighed.

"Matilda and Alexis are at the cabin, but the kind of specimens there will pose no challenge. I will need sophisticated microchips that will enable my specimens to use guns. Then we will learn how fast Matilda is. I am determined to capture and kill her. Her death will distract Alexis. Capturing Matilda will not be easy. She does not discuss her plans around Mark. The others avoid him, too."

"Probably because he stinks and he's mean to them."

Woehar shrugged.

"So what? We know where Matilda lives. I can send my soldiers to her home."

Laurel snickered.

"Draekh and I must talk." Woehar hefted the prisoner by the skewer and thrust her Laurel's way. "Do what you please with her."

Laurel drooled. The scolding could be forgotten. For now. She fell upon the prisoner.

****

"I'm still hungry."

Laurel eyeballed the other prisoners. Her gaze settled on a teenage girl in soiled dungarees and a tattered T-shirt. Blood streaked her forehead and the crotch of her jeans. An IV fed her vischlausk. Like the others, she reeked of urine and feces. Eyes on her china-doll face, Laurel saw herself at age fourteen. Back then, her parents had disciplined her by duct-taping her to her bed, locking her in the closet, and forcing her to wear diapers. The fear lurking in the girl's eyes intimated that she'd endured similar horrors at home long before her arrival to the laboratory. Something inside Laurel shuddered at the sight.

At Laurel's approach, the girl let out plaintive cries. *A runaway, hoping to escape beatings by Daddy Dearest.* Laurel didn't need anyone to tell her why the girl ran away. The torn underwear and the bloodstains on her crotch told Laurel that someone had raped the girl. Her stomach gave the familiar rumble that urged her to feed; but a small portion of humanity that remained begged Laurel to help the girl escape. The closer she came, the louder the cries. It would be so easy to cut the ties and yank the IV to set the girl free.

The trouble was, Laurel couldn't see any way out of the laboratory. The vischlausk had already done its damage just as the *settva* fusion had done with her. That and she was damned hungry. The sweet scent of blood called to Laura, and she couldn't resist it.

"Damn you, Woehar," she whispered as she fed. "I'll get you for you've done to this girl and me."

Chapter Nineteen: The Grim Reaper Visits

Outside Shively's Cabin, July 6, 2:00 a.m.

Matilda's stay stretched on for two weeks while Yeron, Shively, Tyrone, Johnny, and Mark repaired the basement floor. She assumed kitchen and laundry duty while Alexis played "gofer." Every so often Shively and Mark hollered at each other. Alexis would settle for any job that took her away from the shouting. Sometimes she and Matilda stopped work to shoot at stray walkers approaching the cabin.

"Alexis, I'm so proud of you for fighting off those monsters," Matilda said the day she left. "You are your father's daughter."

"You're not so bad yourself, Mom." Alexis smiled and managed a big hug.

Matilda stood back, regarded Alexis, and a tear slid down her cheek.

"I can't leave you. I'll stay and help when Mark does his no-shows."

"Matilda." Tyrone's voice was firm. "We've been through this before. It's too dangerous out here. We agreed that Alexis doesn't need you hurt ... or worse. Remember?"

"I know ... but Alexis is all the family I've got left," she said. Something inside Alexis twisted at the pain in her mother's voice.

"Mom, I'll be all right." Alexis swallowed hard, fighting back her own tears. "Yeron's got my back."

"I know." Matilda blotted her face and met Yeron's gaze. "Promise me you'll take care of my girl."

"I promise." Yeron shook hands with her.

"Okay, let's get rolling," Tyrone said, heading for the Humvee.

A pall settled over the cabin after Matilda and Tyrone left. Shively headed to the office to pore over the logbooks from the buses. Johnny clicked on the TV but got snow, so he retrieved a DVD to watch a movie.

"Hey, what are you watching?" Alexis asked.

"*Star Trek*," Johnny inched up the volume and sat cross-legged on the floor.

Alexis drew the shades and plopped on the sofa; Yeron took a seat beside her. In the background, Mark continued shredding paper in his room. Shively's hushed voice filtered from his office. She guessed that the cell towers had reception. With a shrug, she tuned out the sounds and focused on the television.

About ten minutes into the movie, Shively burst from his office, hollering, "Fuck! Shut off the blasted TV!"

Shively's face flushed crimson. His blue eyes flashed with fury. Alexis clicked off the TV with her mind and settled her eyes on Shively.

"Did you get a call from home?"

"Worse than that," he snapped, and the anger in his voice told her that something had gone deadly wrong. "My supplier ran into big trouble. Next time we need ammo, everyone will have to pony up cash."

For a moment, Shively stared at her, Johnny, and Yeron, and then he stomped outside. Alexis peeked out the window and saw him retrieve a Marlboro from his shirt pocket.

Johnny shook his head.

"What the fuck was that about?" he asked.

"Maybe his supplier got killed ... by walkers or enemy mob," Alexis said, rubbing her chin. "If that's the case, we're on our own."

"I overheard enough to hear that was what happened," Yeron told her. "He is furious with Mark, too. While the rest of us repaired the floor, Mark whined and bawled and didn't help much. Shively slapped him in the head several times."

"Why'd he bring Mark here?" Johnny asked. "He's useless."

"I tried to tell that to Shively," Yeron said. "He did not listen."

Alexis gave an exasperated sigh. "He wants Mark close so he can watch him."

"Bullshit." Johnny folded his arms.

"He needs Mark for insurance," Yeron said. "If the fighting gets overwhelming, Mark will become a, ah, a sacrificial lamb."

Insurance ... sacrificial lamb. Understanding dawned, and Alexis hugged herself, shivering.

"Whoa!" Johnny gave Yeron a sharp glance. "Is that what he told you?"

Yeron nodded while dragging his fingers through his thick hair. His lips jittered.

"He called it insurance, but I overheard Shively on the phone, months ago when all of you were in the hospital. Mark molested the child of a Mob boss, and this boss ordered Shively to eliminate him."

Alexis gasped. "Dispose of him? How? He keeps saying we need Mark for insurance."

Yeron sighed, his face drawn with shadows in the dim light. "He said he was taking Mark for a ride after his discharge. That along with insurance, dear, means that when things get ugly, he sacrifices Mark so we get away alive. Please do not say anything about this."

"But you told us, honey." Alexis returned to her seat next to him, arm around his back. "Shively can be brilliant – he helped rescue my mom – but his plan's liable to backfire."

"She's right." Johnny's spectacled eyes flitted between Alexis and Yeron. "Mark may act like a crybaby, but he's not stupid. By now, he's figured out what Shively planned for him."

Alexis shuddered. "If he has, God help us."

"Does Tyrone know?" Johnny asked.

"I think he does," Yeron said. "I suggest we watch out for each other when Mark's around. And stay out of Shively's way."

****

At midnight two nights later, Alexis jerked awake after a nightmare. She couldn't recall the details, but she heard thumping and moaning. For a moment, her heart hammered until she recognized the voice. Mark. Shaking her head, she grabbed her flashlight and tiptoed to use the bathroom. On the way back, she stopped outside of Mark's room. The moaning and crying grew louder behind the closed door. She turned the knob silently and cracked the door, just enough to get a view of Mark sitting on his bed, stroking himself, eyes shut tight. Her hand jittered from fear, and she snapped off her light. Before she did so, she noticed three clothespins on Mark's mattress by his side. Alexis shivered when she considered what the purpose of those clothespins might be.

She bypassed her bedroom, not wanting to sleep so close to Mark. She proceeded toward the basement door ... and then headed back toward her room. *The hell with it. He's not worth it. I'd better sleep and get ready for our next search for the underground lab. Let him whine all he wants. Let Shively deal with him.*

Voices. Tyrone and Johnny. They were playing cards since they couldn't sleep, and there was no TV. Part of her longed to join them. Another part wanted to crawl in bed with Yeron for some serious lovemaking. Sometimes, she longed to lash out at Mark. Other times, she cringed whenever she passed his bedroom, gagging on the foul odor seeping into the hallway.

Mostly, though, she felt too tired and scared to care. Her hands stung every time she typed or opened test tubes, activities that required more concentration than she could muster with telekinesis.

And each day threatened the possibility of someone coming home in a body bag.

****

On the third night, Alexis awoke to rain pounding against the windows, occasionally backed by an explosion of thunder. The generators had shut down, draping the cabin in darkness. Lightning splashed across a purplish sky. In her mind, God was weeping over the deaths left by the renegades and walkers.

Pounding on her door speared her to attention.

"Wake up!" Shively bellowed. "The generators are out of gas, and the fence's got no juice to fry the walkers. They're heading toward the cabin."

Alexis glanced at the clock on her phone. Its lit face said it was two in the morning. After slipping into her tunic, she snatched up her guns, grabbed the Maglites, and scurried to the kitchen. As she stretched her arms, the first tentacles of pain crept into her hands. She grimaced. Yeron, who was drinking a cup of milk at the table, looked up and saw her face. He gave her a worried glance. She attempted a smile, but he shook his head. The 248AR had lost effect and her arthritis symptoms had returned.

The men congregated by the table, slugging down coffee. Alexis took her pain pills with orange juice and scarfed down a cereal bar.

"Look at that." Tyrone nudged her shoulder and pointed toward the window. "Blood moon rising."

Alexis squinted. Despite the heavy rain, a patch of red peeped from behind the clouds. She shivered. "You've got that right."

"Let's go, Sleepyhead," Johnny sang out. "Didn't you hear Shively?"

Mark yawned.

"Take your time, Alexis," he said in a pleasant voice. "The rain ought to slow them."

Why did Mark act so considerate? She'd better get on her knees and prepare for the second coming of Jesus. Mark's uncharacteristic kind behavior meant that the world had come to an end.

"It should," she agreed. "Creatures like those avoid water."

"They are not zombies, Alexis," Shively said. "Everyone, stick your weapons inside your coats."

Alexis complied.

"Why did he tell us to do that?" she asked Yeron.

"Moisture can ruin weapons, including our plasma guns."

They piled through the door and sprinted toward the gate. Thunder continued, and the rain worsened. The putrid air made Alexis gag. The walkers, greedy for blood, sighted them ten yards up the path. No time to assume position; Alexis reached into her jacket for her gun. Tyrone grabbed his M16. The creatures carried sticks. No, not sticks.

Bolt action rifles. Something hot flew by Alexis's head. The creatures were shooting at them!

Their bullets went to the side. Yeron mustered a mind-punch to knock their rifles aside. He couldn't deflect all the guns so easily; there had to be at least thirty. No doubt, they all had implanted microchips which enabled them to use firearms. The rain came down in torrents, causing Alexis's Maglite to provide only a modicum of visibility. Any second, the slushy ground would yield, causing a backbreaking slide.

Tyrone and Shively moved ahead, pointing their M16s. Five creatures closed in on Alexis, giving her an uncomfortably close view of their black-pitted eyes and gaping maws ringed with fleshy chunks. Her heart leaped, and then she went on automatic. An unlikely warrior with stiff joints and a pharmacy's worth of medication, she squeezed off plasma fire with deadly efficiency. Yeron moved ahead of her, gunning down ten more charging their way. Johnny fought alongside Alexis, angling for three more.

In the next instant, everything went wrong.

For Alexis, it happened in slow motion and yet so fast.

Johnny stumbled over a rock. One creature's bony talons dug deep into his flesh, with a grip stronger than any human's. The talons ripped through Johnny's skin with the same ease as Mark had torn his magazines. Blood sprayed from Johnny's mouth, revealing his doom. The creature's eyes held a silvery gleam, and the breeze carried its stench of flyblown meat. Its bony fingers closed around his wrists and ankles and pulled off his boots. Johnny's attacker and its two friends disappeared in a spray of fire from Alexis's gun, but by then the walkers had done their damage.

Johnny needed medical attention and fast, but more walkers were closing in. *We want fresh meat,* their gutted eyes expressed, *even if it's tainted with medicine.*

Chapter Twenty: First Aid on a Battlefield

Outside Shively's Cabin, July 6, 6:00 a.m.

Johnny lay on the rock, blood gushing over his face and neck, chest heaving. Yeron knelt by his side trying to staunch the bleeding. Yeron had come prepared with an IV, she noted with relief. It went into Johnny's forearm. Alexis would have given her last cent to rush Johnny to Jackson Hospital's ICU with its sterile equipment, but the walkers didn't allow time for such arrangements.

The walkers grunted for communication, their pale faces surrounded by blood-streaked hair plastered to their foreheads. Beetles crawled over their leathery skin, and hoards of flies formed dark clouds over any open wounds. Hand gripping his weapon, Shively pumped bullets into their throats. The ones chasing Alexis and Tyrone disintegrated under a cloud of fire and bullets. Smoke billowed from the downed walkers.

Skeletal talons reached through the smoke for Tyrone's back.

"Tyrone, watch out!" Alexis screamed, re-aiming her gun toward the walker about to claw Tyrone.

Tyrone whirled around as his attacker exploded in the flames issuing from Alexis's gun. Yeron shouted her name. She reeled back from the recoil, turned, and faced five walking corpses covered with flies, worse than anything she'd seen at the hospital. Engrossed as Yeron was with Johnny, he still tried to protect her. The creatures disbursed, limping and dragging their feet, before bursting into flames. The rain doused the fire before it did real damage.

After that, the woods went quiet. Alexis collapsed to her knees, panting.

"Alexis, are you okay?" Tyrone shook her shoulders, but her huffing persisted. "Yeron, get over here! She's hurt."

"I'm all right," said Alexis as she gazed over toward Johnny.

"Good," said Tyrone, "because he's busy."

Johnny moaned. Alexis struggled to her feet, leaning on Tyrone's elbow.

"I have to ... got to ... help them."

"Alexis, sit." Tyrone's eyes bulged like soup plates. Alexis's brace had come loose, and she hobbled more than the walkers did. Her face had blanched white, and the pain in her wrists had gone to white hot agony. Why wasn't her medicine working?

Alexis shook her head. "I said I'm all right ... just having breakthrough pain." She cast her gaze sideways toward the piles of still bodies. Shively stared at them, his face parchment pale, smoking a cigarette.

"Shively," Tyrone called.

Shively did not answer. He kept staring at the corpses.

"Shit," Alexis said. "Tyrone, Shively looks bad."

"He's okay. Shively!"

"What!" Shively snarled, eyes smoking.

Another groan escaped Johnny's lips. Shively forgotten, Alexis limped toward Yeron and Johnny, Tyrone behind her.

Gone was the Johnny with the raunchy humor. Alexis faced a battered man lying in a pool of blood, his face a rictus of pain, his eyes bright with tears.

"Alexis ..." he began. "I'm not gonna make it."

"Yeron will be able to help you." Alexis faked confidence she didn't feel.

"You think?" He tried to smile, but blood spilled from his lips with the effort.

"Alexis." Yeron nudged her shoulder. "Where is Mark?"

"Mark ... shit." Where happened to him? He'd followed her outside and then disappeared.

"Those things must've gotten him, too. He's not here."

"Dammit! Johnny needs a blood transfusion. He and Mark have the same blood type."

"Blood type?" Alexis shot a glance toward Tyrone, her voice stuttering. "Johnny needs blood. Hoffman said I'm A+, and ... you are?"

"I'm B." Tyrone shifted his eyes toward Yeron. "I think Johnny's A, so Alexis can donate. If you need more, Shively's O, the universal donor. Right?"

"Wrong. Alexis and Shively have positive blood," Yeron told him. "Johnny has A- blood. So does Mark. I will call rescue services for a Medevac and tell them we need A- blood." He snatched his cell phone from his tunic pocket. "... Assuming my phone works."

"What's the big deal about negative blood?" Tyrone asked.

"The wrong blood type could kill him." Alexis's demeanor crumbled into miserable sobs. *"That's* the big deal. I hope Yeron can get through to the Medevac."

"Alexis." Johnny's hand flapped against her knee. "Tell Carol I ...." another groan.

"... love her?" Tyrone asked.

"That's probably it," Alexis said. "They've got two kids – five and three. Johnny, keep it together. Your kids need you."

Johnny's chin dipped slightly. "Guys, tell Carol I'm sorry, and that I ..." As his voice faded, his eyes rolled back. Alexis palpated his throat, but he had no pulse.

"He wants us to tell Carol he loves her," she said to no one in particular.

"That may be a problem," Yeron said. "The phone is still non-functional. I could not get through to Emergency Services, not that it matters. He is gone."

"I can pray for him." Alexis got to her knees.

"Forget calling God," Shively shouted behind her. "God left the phone off the hook."

"God doesn't work that way," Tyrone said. "It might be a test of faith."

"The hell you say!"

"The hell I don't say," Tyrone barked.

"Shively, these 'things' knew what they were doing." Alexis walked up to a corpse that appeared intact. She kicked it with her boot. "I think the renegades implanted microchips and sent them here somehow."

"Ask your loverboy there." Shively glared at Yeron with disgust. "What am I supposed to tell Carol? 'Sorry' doesn't cut it."

Alexis noticed Mark's absence. Again. *Why isn't anyone mentioning Mark? Did I stumble through hell's gate? Had Mark gotten killed? Tyrone and I had come close to becoming dead meat ourselves.*

"There's nothing you can say," Tyrone said, his face long and his eyes filled with sadness. He touched her shoulder. "Alexis, I owe you my life. You stood tall."

"Not tall enough." Alexis pressed her fist against her lips to keep them from quivering. "I screwed up with Johnny."

"Johnny wasn't your fault."

"Okay, let's cut the sentimental crap," Shively snapped. "Shit happens."

"Only if we let it," Tyrone told him.

"Back off, Tyrone. I'm not in the mood." Shively's voice reeked with anger. "Candy Boy pissed all over us and left us out to dry."

"Mark?" Alexis questioned, as she shifted her gaze toward

Shively. "He was with me when we took on those things."

"That's right, he was." Shively moved his gloved hand over his sunburned face to mop the sweat. His blue eyes blazed with indignation. His fists clenched.

"When they brought out their guns, he took off and let us fight shorthanded. His stunt got Johnny killed and almost got you and Tyrone. I see everyone's got that 'I told you so' look. Save it."

So Mark was the reason Johnny died. No, that can't be right. I want Shively to be wrong, so he is. Something in Alexis's mind shifted, jarring an overwhelming urge to scream. Instead, she moved toward Yeron. He caressed her and kissed her forehead, but his comfort did nothing to ease her chills.

"It was an ugly fight. Are you sure Mark didn't get killed?"

"Did you see him fighting?" Shively favored Alexis, Tyrone, and Yeron with penetrating stares, but they had no answer for him. "Of course not. That chickenshit hightailed it out of here."

"I knew he was unstable," Yeron said.

"That sounds like an 'I told you so,'" Shively said in a menacing voice.

"And what if it is?" Yeron gazed at Shively, defiance creeping into his eyes.

Shively darted him a withering glance.

"Fuck you. I've got to talk to Johnny's wife, assuming the cell towers are working."

"They are not," Yeron said. "She has a walkie-talkie, but it may not be set to the same channel as ours."

"I'll give it a try." Shively sighed. "Alexis, you look beat. Get some rest. Tyrone, take her back to the cabin. Yeron and I will handle Johnny."

****

"Those two were ready to kill each other," Tyrone said to Alexis, once they were out of earshot of the rest.

"Yeron's upset, like the rest of us. He'd never hurt anyone."

Tyrone shook his head.

"You love this guy and he cares about you, too. That won't make him human. Something bad is going down between Shively and Mark, too. Be careful."

Caution belongs in another universe, Alexis opened her mouth to say so, but then a roaring sound speared her to attention. "Hey! What's that?"

"What's what?" Tyrone stopped in mid-step, causing Alexis to bump into him. "Shit, it's the Humvee!"

He ran in the direction of the sound, with Alexis behind him.

The Humvee came roaring in their direction. *The Humvee?* She didn't realize that the fighting had taken them so far from the cabin. Tyrone pumped out one carefully aimed shot. Poor technique could cause such shots to ricochet, but he hit his mark, flatting one tire. The vehicle weaved sideways and skidded into a tree. When they got to the wreck, they saw Mark Adams behind the wheel, wearing a shit-eating grin.

"You bastard!" Alexis shouted. Her exhaustion took a backseat to her anger. She forgot about her grief over Johnny. She forgot about everything except Mark, proud thief and deserter. Still behind Tyrone, she sprinted to the vehicle. Tyrone laid his beefy hand on the door handle.

"Shit," he muttered. "The door's locked."

"Does anyone have an extra set of keys?"

"Yes ... usually Shively, but he's busy with Johnny. Can you work the lock with your telekinesis?"

Alexis peered into the cab.

"Maybe, but my power doesn't work consistently for fine movements."

"No problem. I'll smash the window." With that, Tyrone raised the butt of his gun and aimed at the passenger window. The smile disappeared from Mark's face like fingerprints wiped away with bleach. He opened the driver's door, hopped down onto the grass, and ran.

"Oh, no, you're not going anywhere," Alexis cried. Fatigue had set in, but she managed enough psychic energy to cause Mark to stumble and fall.

Tyrone, moving with panther speed, caught him, yanked him by the arms, and shoved his face into the dirt.

"What's the big idea?"

"I never wanted this mission. Shively bullied me into coming along."

"You listen to me, and listen good." Tyrone now held Mark by the collar, knee wedged against his tailbone. "Johnny's dead because of you. Thanks a lot, pal."

"Stop! You're hurting me." Mark broke into a spate of sobs, tears running down his dirt-streaked face. "I never wanted anything to happen to Johnny, but face it. We're fighting a losing battle. Besides, I've got a hospital to run and two children who depend on me."

"Two girls your ex-wife doesn't let you visit. Just cut the crocodile tears." Tyrone nodded toward Alexis. "See if Mark stowed anything."

Alexis heaved open a back door with her mind and poke under the seats.

"Hmmmm, we've got a cache of bullets here, and here ..." Alexis recognized Yeron's safe, filled with firearms and ammo. "We've got the plasma guns. Meathead was too dumb to learn the combination." Ignoring the sharp pain, she used her hands to pry up the backseat cushions. "Grenades, by golly. Shively will want to hear this one."

"He sure will," Tyrone agreed. "Isn't that right, Mark?"

"Maybe he will and maybe he won't," Mark said in a juvenile tone. He shot hostile glances toward Alexis and Tyrone. "You think you're brilliant, don't you?"

"We know that you're lower than whale shit," Tyrone replied.

"Don't waste your breath on him," Alexis said. "Mark can't help that he's got shit for brains."

"Right you are. Get up, Shit-for-brains." Tyrone yanked him by the collar. "I need you to change the tire. Then we'll go back and wait for Shively."

"It's still raining," Mark whined. "Besides, I don't know how to change a tire."

"Too bad." Tyrone fished a key from his pocket. "Alexis, if I were you, I'd get chow and lie low. Things are going to get ugly."

"Things have already gotten ugly, but ... I get it." Alexis accepted the key. Her feet sloshed in the puddles as she half-ran, half-loped to the cabin. She figured that Yeron would be gone for several hours. She decided to eat a late breakfast and lie down for a nap.

Chapter Twenty-One: Mark's Disciplinary Session

Shively's Cabin Kitchen, July 6, Noon

A booming voice surprised Alexis out of a sound sleep.

"Alexis!" Shively bellowed. "Get out here. We're having a meeting."

Another meeting? Alexis yawned and rubbed her eyes. *Can't it wait? I'm not in any mood for any damn meeting now.*

Even Tyrone, seasoned fighter that he was, feared Shively. What happened to the kind Shively who helped rescue her mother and made sure she had a functional car? The compassionate neighbor who used to carry out her trash or help her with groceries when her hands hurt? That man had fled, chased by armies of bloodthirsty renegades and walking dead. You would have to be crazy to make a career out of destroying such creatures.

Brows knitted together in a frown, Alexis toddled to the kitchen where Shively held most of his talks. Shively lounged beside the table, Mark shaking before him. Tyrone stood gazing out the window, frowning. Shively wore dungarees and a raggedy, black sweatshirt; his chair faced Mark. His Glock hung by his belt, dangling in its holster from one post of the chair. Alexis presumed the Internet was working because Johnny's laptop sang "You've got mail!" every few seconds. Satisfied that everyone appeared okay, Alexis joined Tyrone by the window.

"Don't bother with the email," Shively told her. "We've got some dirty work ahead of us."

He leaned back, tilting his chair. The gun swung in its holster like a pendulum.

"The only thing I demand is teamwork. Working together is the only way we can survive. Does everyone understand?"

"Yes, Shively," Alexis and Tyrone answered in unison.

Shively rocked again; his gun continued swinging. He regarded Mark intently.

"What do you say, Candy Boy?"

"My name isn't ..."

"I'll call you what I damn well please." Shively rocked harder, and his gun swung faster. "Tell me, Candy Boy, why did you try to steal our ammunition?"

Mark's face turned dead white. His mouth dropped open.

"Answer me, you piece of shit." Shively jutted his finger at Mark. "I've never seen you cover anyone when the walkers attack. One time, you never showed, and Matilda covered for you. Now this. Lucky for the rest of us, Tyrone and Alexis caught you and found our stuff."

"Shively, I ..."

"Johnny died because he needed a transfusion. He never got any blood because you bailed and left us fighting short. The phones aren't working, and Johnny's wife lives too far away to use a walkie-talkie. Informing her about Johnny by email is dammed insensitive. Is any of this getting through?"

"Look, I panicked, okay? I promise ..."

Moving faster than Alexis could believe, Shively snatched up his gun, pointed it, and fired. The boot on Mark's right foot exploded. Fragments of leather, blood, flesh, and bone splattered Alexis's pants.

This can't be happening. I'm imagining the whole thing.

Mark screamed. He looked down at his shattered right foot with horror-stricken incredulity and bellowed at the top of his lungs. The bullet had partially severed the foot from the leg. Alexis could see bone splinters peeping from the gash near the ankle; she felt her stomach churn at the sight.

Shively grabbed Mark by the shoulder and pointed his gun at his face. "Quit bawling and act like a man."

Mark loosed loud, hoarse sobs and pushed away from Shively. The blood gushed from his wound and spilled on the floor.

Alexis opened her mouth to shout, *"Shively, don't do this!"* but her lips tightened shut. She contemplated batting the gun with her mind. Intervening would be so easy, but the darker side of Alexis concentrated on Mark and held him still. *Mark wrote the ticket that punched Johnny out of here. He tried to steal our ammunition, which would have gotten me killed. I won't let him get away.*

Quick as a cheetah, Shively's head whirled, madness stamped in his eyes.

"Are you folks having any problem with me finishing the job?" he asked.

"No problem." Tyrone's frown deepened. "The lowlife has it coming."

"The bastard deserves to die," Alexis said in a thin voice. "Finish him in the woods."

"Can't. The woods are too risky because of the walkers."

With that, Shively got off another blast. He scored a clean shot, and the bullet sliced through Mark's neck. His head lolled to one side. *His head?* The bullet must have severed an artery because a lava pool of blood spurted from the wound. Her concentration broken, Alexis grabbed the doorjamb to keep from sliding on the blood spilling on the floor. Seconds later, Mark dropped to the floor with a sickening thump.

He could have AIDS or something, Alexis's mind screamed. Black dots appeared before her eyes; the room spun in a sidestroke fashion. She clung to the doorjamb, willing away the dizziness, and managed to regain her control. She didn't want Shively to interpret fainting as a sign of weakness. Her father had told her stories about the cruelty of the mob, but Alexis thought his pain meds had caused him to hallucinate. Now she knew better. With her telekinetically holding Mark ...

What have I done? She shifted her gaze toward Tyrone, his face stoic and unmoving. He returned her gaze and shook his head. Alexis remained silent.

Shively placed his gun back in its holster.

"Tyrone, dump this trash. Alexis and I need to talk."

"Okay." After donning rubber gloves, Tyrone shoved Mark's corpse into a body bag and dragged the bag toward the door. As he moved past Shively, he gave Alexis a sigh of fervent relief.

Alexis scanned the counter for extra gloves and rags. She found them wedged between the radio and refrigerator. "I'd better clean ..."

"Yeron can do that. We need to talk."

Alexis regarded Shively, trying hard not to gag on the acrid smell of blood cooking on the stove burners and ceiling light bulbs.

"I lost control now, and you hate that, right?"

"I didn't say ..."

"I don't give a rat's ass what you say; I can tell by the fear in your voice. Killing's against your religion. I understand that. But Mark posed a dangerous liability. He got your work buddy slaughtered. You might want to factor those things into your prayer hour. However you feel, we gotta get past it. I'm the one in charge, and you're a damn good fighter. We haven't found that underground lab or the people making these walking dead. Can we work together?"

"Yes," Alexis murmured between numb lips.

"I lost control. Would you agree?"

Alexis hesitated. *At least give him points for honesty.* Responding "Yes" might make her seem weak, and ergo, a liability. Saying "No" would brand her a liar.

"I could have stopped you with my psychokinetic power, but I didn't. When we were married, Mark chased me with a studded baseball bat. He tried to blackmail the doctors into withholding my medicine. He's done so many other terrible things to me ... and now this, with Johnny. So I understand why you whacked him, but I wish you'd finished him off in the woods like I asked." The words tumbled out, and oh, how cruel they sounded.

"The woods would have been less messy." Shively gave her a wintry smile. "But you can't be choosy during times like these. The fighting's going to get worse when we find those responsible for these attacks. I don't expect your approval, Alexis, but given your history with Mark, I need your support. Are you with me?"

Alexis fell silent. She got to wondering where Yeron would dispose of the body, and if the police would find it. She hoped not. Any competent medical examiner could determine not only the cause of death, but the type of bullet and firearm used. Police interrogations would follow, a trial, maybe even jail time, and jail time would break her mother's heart. And, speaking of her mother, she'd be dead if Shively and the other guys hadn't intervened. Somewhere in this hellish pool of horror into which she'd stumbled, she'd found real love with Yeron. He'd do everything he could to keep her safe, but it behooved her to be careful. Careful, yet ready to run.

"Yes," she said at last. "You helped save my mom's life, so I'll stand by you. But ..." she wagged her finger. "I believe my former coworker, Laurel, is involved in this, too."

"You could be right." Shively nodded with agreement. "You're damned efficient on the battlefield. And smart. I just wish you'd quit treating this predicament like a tale from that sleazy magazine, *Weekly World Reporter.* "

"I'm making progress in that direction."

"Perhaps you are at that. Take a shower and rest. Yeron will be finishing up his written report on Johnny. He'll help me clear this mess when he gets back."

"All right. Thanks." Alexis stepped carefully through congealing puddles of blood to get to the hallway. No amount of scrubbing would erase this testimony to violence. Could she ever sleep in her bedroom again? Not for a long time.

With a change of clothes in her arms, she headed to the shower. She lingered under the hot water for an hour. She'd stay there all day if it would wash away the stink of death, but the memories branded themselves on her brain. Calling her mother might help. She rinsed and dressed.

She walked the hall and then the steps to the basement, feet wrapped in plastic. She retrieved her cell phone from her pants pocket. *Yes, chatting with Mom will make everything okay.* She dialed. No ring. She'd forgotten about the phones being down; and besides, what would she say?

"Hi, Mom, I'm calling to say hello."

Or: *"Mom, I miss you."*

Neither would fly. It was midmorning, her usual time to call, but her mother would hear in her voice that something had gone wrong. The timbre in Alexis's voice always portrayed the truth.

One place in the cabin offered the semblance of a safe harbor: Yeron's quarters. A true refuge eluded her, but the basement offered a convincing facsimile because Yeron was there. He listened without judging. He'd help her find a way to work past this nightmare.

Alexis swallowed hard, aware of an intense thirst. Yeron's basement quarters looked anything but romantic, with tables of analyzers and other machinery, and an unmade sofa bed in the corner. No comfort food in the basement fridge, except for a stash of Reese's Peanut Butter Cups and bottled water. Upstairs, Tyrone had stocked the house refrigerator with plenty of food, but the grisly sight and stink of the bloodbath nauseated her. Only a sweet taste might do.

She remembered she needed to take her medicine with food. In the basement, she kept snacks and bottled water in a box marked "Alexis's goodies." After helping herself to a Reese's Chocolate and water, she slumped on the sofa bed. She downed her pills with the water, cushioning them with the chocolate. She reached for more Reese's pieces, chasing them with water until she drained the bottle.

"What am I doing?" she asked aloud. "How can I eat after what I've done?"

Don't be ridiculous, a voice inside scolded. *Without food, your medicine will tear up your gut; Hoffman and Yeron said so. Yeron will help you cope with what happened.*

"That's what I'll do," Alexis said aloud. "When he comes back, we'll talk about Mark."

But her eyes grew heavy from the repetitive sounds of timers and buzzers. She curled up on the bed, and moments later, drifted to sleep.

Chapter Twenty-Two: Yeron and Alexis Strategize

Yeron's Cabin Basement, July 6, 2:00 p.m.

Sometime later, Alexis woke up to use the bathroom. When she came out, Yeron stood by the sofa bed, looking at her. "Alexis, what happened with Mark?"

Alexis shuddered and swallowed hard, and regarded Yeron. His surprised look sent chills down her back. This harbor offered only the illusion of safety. She'd better scram. Forget this whole operation and seek asylum with her mother.

"I'm sorry ... this was a bad idea." With that, Alexis tore off toward the back door, the one that led outside.

"Alexis!"

Alexis kept going. She wasn't in any mood for judgments or lectures. Not after what happened today. Not now, not ever. With intense concentration, she forced open the basement door. Sunlight blinded her.

"Alexis!" A distant shout.

Moving toward the thicker brush, Alexis sized up the woods, determining the best path. The straight stretch ahead would lead her right into the area where the walkers had attacked them. The narrower path to her left led to the main highway, she recalled.

She felt her pockets. No guns. She'd left then on Yeron's desk before wrapping her soiled tunic in a plastic bag so he could clean it. This realization came before the sensation of invisible hands tugged at her. *Oh shit. Yeron's using his mind control.*

She fought his pull with her own mind, but Yeron had one foot and eighty pounds on her. Of course, his extra size gave him the advantage over her. That and the fact that he'd grown up with the ability, while she'd only developed hers recently. As if drawn by a magnet, she drifted back toward the basement, tracking dirt in with her booted feet. The door closed behind her. Yeron caught her by her tremulous shoulders and guided her to the sofa bed.

"I am not accusing you. Shively wanted me to clean up and

warned me not to ask questions. I found something among the debris from Mark, and thought you should see it."

"Oh?" So a scolding wasn't forthcoming after all. She allowed a ghost of a smile. "You may cut off your mind force. I'm not running anymore."

The force field evaporated. Yeron kept his arm around her shoulders. The feel of his sinewy arm took the edge off her shivering. He then withdrew a folded glove from his pocket. Opening it, he produced a capsule-shaped device.

Alexis studied it, furrowing her eyebrows, then looked up at Yeron. "This looks like the implants you found in the walkers."

"This one has a camera." Yeron held the microchip up to the light. "The two long wires inside transmit activity and sounds back to the source, that is, the people scanning the microchip."

Another wrinkle of her brows. To Alexis, it looked a grain of rice.

"I wanted to tell you that our suspicions about Mark were correct," Yeron continued, his voice softening. "When I found your room empty, I became worried. I just want to know what happened."

"Shively told me to catch a nap. I couldn't. Lying in bed next to a floor soaked with my ex-husband's blood isn't conducive to restful sleep. It's sick! Do you understand that?" Her voice rose with each word. "It's sick!"

"Easy." Yeron held a finger to his lips. "Shively is upstairs, asleep."

Alexis grimaced, but nodded.

"I cleaned the mess," he told her. "I assume you saw Shively shoot Mark, and I am sorry you went through that."

Yeron's arm snaked around her tighter, hugging her against his chest. The feel of his smooth chin against her head soothed her tremors.

"There's more. I've got to talk with a priest. I want to go home to my mother. I can't sleep upstairs anymore."

"My Steel Rose, I would love you to sleep here with me, but why do you need a priest? Why leave at all? Assuming that the renegades have marked you, they will look for you, no matter where you go."

Alexis turned toward Yeron and noticed his sunken eyes – only now they were haunted, too. She wanted to love him and forget that this morning had ever happened, but not yet. Confession was in session. "I'd love to sleep here. I love you very much."

"I love you, too. Having you is like finding a steel rose in this nightmare. All that blood reminded me of life at Eigil's compound. Both men, Eigil and Mark, behaved like rabid wolves."

"I was no better. Tyrone and I were present during the shooting. Tyrone didn't bring his gun, so he had to go along with Shively. On the contrary, I could have stopped Shively with my telekinesis. Instead, I encouraged him to kill Mark. I said Mark deserved to die because he tried to steal our weapons. I wanted him dead because of what happened to Johnny."

Yeron kissed her forehead and stroked her hair. "Johnny was a good friend to both of us."

Alexis's voice quivered.

"Johnny died because of Mark. That doesn't make Shively's behavior okay. I'm trained to save lives and yet I held down Mark so he wouldn't get away. What does that make me?"

"You acted out of grief." Yeron caressed her shoulder. "If Mark had succeeded in stealing our weapons, all of us would be dead. You and Shively did what you deemed necessary."

"I doubt if Mark's mother or the police would understand that," she said, rubbing her arms. "Where's Tyrone?"

"Tyrone went to his room. He said he had to pray."

"I should do that, too," Alexis said. "Mark picked on people he thought couldn't fight back. Like the time he attacked me with his baseball bat, raped me, and tried to force Hoffman to withhold my medicine. Now his actions caused Johnny's death. Shively had a point."

"Shively used a sloppy technique." Yeron frowned. "I would have drugged or brainwashed Mark."

"I wish you were here. I pleaded with Shively to whack Mark in the woods. He didn't listen. Why not?"

"I am not sure, but we must consider the repercussions. Mark's family will figure out what happened. So will the healers familiar with Mark's temperament. If the renegades implanted a microchip to track Mark, they will know, too."

"Oh, shit!" Alexis massaged her head and leaned back. "If the police get wind of this, they'll say I was aiding and abetting. Do you think Shively and I will go to jail?"

"I doubt it, Alexis. The police have too many other problems to investigate the death of a man whom everyone despised. You should not run." His voice was pleading now. "Because of Mark's implant, his death will draw the renegades, including the people who want you dead. Do you understand that?"

"Yes, I do, and I love you for not judging me." Alexis regarded his rugged features, the way his fiery curls surrounded his ivory complexion. His pointed teeth flashed as he spoke. She saw them as mere imperfections, like scars or blemishes. His right leg pressed against her left. *If I'd married Yeron instead of Mark, I would've been much happier. I love this man.*

"If we survive and you still want to see clergy, Becky and my brother-in-law Steve introduced me to a great minister," Yeron told her. "I found him approachable and he works with people devoured by violence. First, we have to get through the next few weeks or longer to find the people creating these walkers."

"It doesn't matter. I can't undo what happened."

"Why would you try? Mark tried to steal our weapons. I would declare the shooting as self-defense. Johnny would agree."

"He might if he were alive," Alexis conceded, ignoring the inner voice classifying Shively's action as murder, with her and Tyrone aiding and abetting. "Johnny hated Mark. He used to work for Mark at Meadowood Hospital until Mark forced him to quit."

"I heard about that." Yeron cupped her face in his hands and turned it up toward his. "I had another reason for suggesting Steve's minister other than easing your conscience."

Alexis contemplated her gnarled hands, stark reminders of the damage stress could do when love went sour. Granted, her aunt had the same condition, but her symptoms flared up after a fight with Mark.

"Go on," she pressed.

"You must know how much I love you." With that, Yeron brushed her face with kisses. Her arms pulled him close. They piled onto the sofa bed, Yeron on top. The voice of doom quieted, silenced by the anticipation of lovemaking. Somewhere in her nether region, she felt something hard bulge from his groin.

He backed away, breathing hard.

"My Steel Rose, I enjoy our trysts, but I want something permanent with you. My DNA and your former union with Mark will prohibit a traditional church union, though. These could pose problems for you."

There is that, Alexis wanted to tell him, *and my track record with marriage.* But with the bulge pressing against her and his lips roaming down her face, the rising heat in her loins made it hard to think clearly. At the moment, her past belonged in another century.

"Mark and I got an annulment, so no issue there, but our state won't go for it. They'll want blood tests and other bullshit. But problems have solutions."

"What would you suggest?" Yeron smiled, bracing his elbows on either side of her.

"Shively could help us find a rogue priest," she said, smiling. "As for the state, I could fudge my blood tests."

"You talk too much." Yeron kissed her deeply, his tongue gliding across her lips. Their boots sailed across the room. He slipped off her top, then her pants, and then her lace bra. She fingered the bottom of his sweatshirt, trying to nudge it up.

He shed his sweatshirt, his pants, and his underwear, and tossed his clothes onto the pile. "I know you love me. You love with all of your heart."

The horrors which haunted her were shelved under a wave of desire so strong it amazed her. Her hands caressed the cords of muscle rippling between his upper arms and chest. Her legs curled gently around his hips. They were lying on the bed where she would sleep tonight. Every time she slept in that bed, she would think about his cool, muscular skin.

His fingers stroked her G-spot. Something vibrated from his touch, sending shudders to her very core.

"Yeron, I love ..." and then she exploded in orgasm, the shock-waves rippling to her limbs. Liquid coated her sex, and in the next moment, he penetrated her. He carried her over to the computer chair and sat. She settled on his lap, straddling him. By the light of the nearby window, she got a close-up view of his figure, his arms and shoulders, his white, corded skin.

Alexis cuddled against him, enveloped in his vanilla scent, his rod wedged inside her. She needed this closeness and looked forward to sharing the sofa bed with him for the whole night in a wraparound caress.

After they were both sated, she sank against him, her body melting into his, still in the chair. She planted a kiss on each side of his face, then looked into his eyes.

"Loving you came naturally," she said, smiling. "You don't even have to hypnotize me."

"You hypnotized me." He pulled her back against his shoulders, with her legs still wrapped around him, and carried her back to the sofa bed. He made love to her again, this time with him on top.

"I love you," he said afterwards. "You are my Steel Rose."

"I love you, too," Alexis said, and God help her, she did love him. No human Justice of the Peace, let alone a priest, would sanction such a union unless Yeron could pass himself off as human ... which he couldn't. *Figure it out as you go along,* her voice of reason piped up.

"I recommended Becky's pastor because he accepts her and Steve's union as valid, despite her being a half-breed," Yeron told her. "He might certify ours. If you want, you can talk to him about Mark. But none of this can happen until we find the renegades who are poisoning people with vischlausk. Becky's pastor does not have warrior skills. Asking him to drive out here to perform any ceremony may risk his life. Can you wait until we go home?"

"I could, but we may not survive out here either. Time is growing short, and what little we have left, I want to spend with you."

"I hope we have more than a little time." Yeron leaned on his side, facing her. "You suffered a lot with your health, your sister's death, and the loss of your job. The deaths today added to your grief, but I need you to stay strong. I lost my parents and a sister to Eigil's renegades. So I want you to promise me something."

Promises, promises.

"Go on."

"Things are going to get ugly if we find the renegade colony," Yeron said, looking at her. "Promise me that no matter how bad it gets, you will not give up the fight to survive."

That's a tall order, honey. When my time's up, God expects me to clock out. But there was no denying his pleading look and earnest voice. Alexis met his gaze with steel, resolute eyes.

"All right. I promise. If we're lucky, the renegades will run out of ammo."

"They are too resourceful for that." Yeron took her into his arms again. "Shively is getting careless; that much is clear. My brother-in-law Steve and I spoke. He said he is coming down to help tomorrow, but Shively will remain our leader."

"Dammit." But Alexis knew that Yeron was right. She had expected Shively to eliminate Mark, but not in the kitchen. Between that and the incident with the bomb, she had to wonder if Shively was losing it.

"Do you think Shively will mind my sleeping down here? He specifically said the cabin wasn't meant to be our honeymoon suite."

"Shively has enough on his mind with the deaths today."

"I understand his actions. Part of me applauds him, but his technique stinks."

"It does." Yeron's eyes grew somber. "Despite his recent actions, we must treat Shively as our leader. Can you do that?" Worry crept into his voice, concern that Alexis's emotions might interfere with her ability to fight.

"Shively came through when the walkers ganged up on my mother." Alexis averted her face. "I'll remind myself of that fact whenever I'm around him."

"You cannot do that because your eyes betray your guilt over Mark. I shall not leave you alone with Shively anymore because he might see it and question you on it."

"Thank you," Alexis said, and breathed a sigh of relief. "I'm glad we found each other."

A dull ache had settled in Alexis's wrists and thumbs; her arthritic symptoms had returned despite the treatments. So far, no one knew, even Yeron. She had her own secrets and she guarded them well.

Go away. Alexis put her head against Yeron's chest. His heart beat in her ears, and the pain *did* subside. They were on the sofa bed for an hour before sleep came.

She wondered how people at home would handle her and Yeron as a couple. Steve wouldn't mind; his wife was half Kryszka. Her mother was trying to accept him, but her version of God and religion precluded interplanetary unions, as Yeron called them. Then again, whom she married wasn't her mother's business. She promised herself to work on the details if she survived her confrontations with the renegades and made it home to her mother.

What am I thinking? Her internal voice of reason returned, but its authority had gone, and a plaintive, lost cry replaced it. *Am I setting myself up for more heartbreak? I don't understand anymore.*

Be quiet and enjoy the ride, she answered. She was drifting, now, floating toward a sweet darkness free of bloodshed or pain. She let herself go with a smile on her face.

Hours later, her phone woke her out of a sound sleep. Yeron had left – probably to use the bathroom or go to the kitchen. She snatched up her phone, relieved that the lines were working.

"Alexis, this is Hazlett," the voice on the other end said. "It's about your mother. There's been a fire."

Chapter Twenty-Three: Alexis Comes out of Remission

Yeron's Basement Laboratory, July 20, 6:00 p.m.

Alexis was asleep again when Yeron headed back into the basement. He smiled when he saw her beauty. Her smile and lilting voice had drawn him out of a twilight world of loneliness. She had much love to give, enough to fill the gaping hole left by his mother's death. But the wild way she thrashed in her sleep left him with an uneasy feeling in his stomach. The disquiet lingered.

Smile, Becky used to tell him. *God sent a woman who loves you for yourself.*

Although most Christians frowned on interplanetary unions, Becky embraced her half-breed status and incorporated it into her faith. Yeron's upbringing did not acknowledge the existence of any god, but now he felt differently.

He learned about spirit worlds and deities and the reality behind them each time his deceased father exited his spirit world to help him and Alexis. *God sent his father to help,* Becky would say. God believed Yeron deserved love.

I told you so, Becky would add, smiling. *I'm always right.*

Yeron smiled at the notion, grateful Alexis did not share Becky's fondness for helium balloons. He had given up on preaching to Becky about the dangers of helium long ago.

He jumped at the sound of a low-pitched hum, which caused Alexis to shift on the sofa bed. Her hand dropped on the bed and she groaned. Although she did not wake, the pain in that moan was unmistakable.

The hum, coming from his computer, was an alert to indicate movement outside. Yeron turned his attention to the viewscreen, which showed an unkempt stranger behind a rose bush, just beyond the electronic gate, relieving himself. *I do not need to watch that,* Yeron thought, but he preferred seeing that instead of another swarm of walkers.

He returned his attentions to Alexis. That groan. That was the reason for his disquiet. Two weeks ago, when Alexis scrubbed the kitchen table, a tight grimace formed on her face. The "boys," as she called them, had left tomato stains that stuck to the wood. The other day as Alexis passed Yeron in the hallway lugging an armful of laundry, he saw the same grimace. She spent a lot of time in the bathroom, too. Was the medicine making her sick? He hoped not.

Chapter Twenty-Four: More Skirmishes with the Walkers

Shively's Cabin, August 10, 10:00 p.m.

The dragging weeks ushered in more conflicts with smart walkers, creatures that were capable of using rifles. Yeron's brother-in-law, Steve, who was Johnny's replacement, came down to join their fight. The walkers' foothold held strongest at Route 363, a winding road five miles south of Allentown. Just yesterday Steve skittered sideways and plunged face down when his boot snagged on a broken tree limb. The walkers seized the opportunity and clawed at his shoulders with their blood-streaked, bony fingers. Yeron was too busy disarming a clutch of walkers to their rear to help. Alexis squeezed off shots slowly, but with deadly accuracy. Her firepower drove away the walkers before they did real harm to Steve. Shots hitting them in the back of their necks caused the microchips to explode. Steve kept thanking her while she helped Yeron stitch his cuts.

"Just be glad these plasma guns are ergonomically friendly," Alexis said to Steve once they were back at the cabin with the others.

"Aw, shit." Tyrone laughed. "Yeron set your ass on fire, that's what."

Steve and Alexis burst into laughter.

"This is no fucking joke," Shively shouted. "We're using up our ammunition for nothing."

"Nothing?" Steve echoed. "Isn't the Gamma Scout showing any radiation?"

"I'm getting zip. No radiation. I can't believe one stupid microchip enables these walkers to use firearms. Yeron, did you think to get another tissue sample?"

"I thought plenty," Yeron told them. "Maybe my test on our latest samples will give more information."

****

Yeron gazed at his current specimens. An image from his microscope told him "how" the walkers managed to shoot with rifles. He cursed in his native tongue.

"What's the matter?" Alexis asked as she stepped up behind him and wrapped her arms around his shoulders.

Yeron cut his eyes toward the sofa bed, indicating a perfect way for Alexis to help him escape the present horror. But he shook his head, trying to refocus. The misshapen cells he had seen demanded his attention. Now.

"These cells came from an android," he said at last.

Alexis gasped. "Are you serious?"

"I am as serious as the fight that almost killed Steve. Look at the cell structure." Yeron stepped sideways and nudged Alexis toward his chair. He double-clicked the cursor to enlarge the images.

Alexis studied the screen, frowning. "They look like ordinary blood cells."

Yeron cranked up the zoom feature. "Do these two samples look the same?"

Alexis peered closer and shook her head.

"Something dented the ones on the right ... like sickle cells. Is this fake blood?"

"Not fake. Manufactured. The Kryszka laboratories use a chemical similar to the control samples we use to calibrate our machines. They can alter its appearance to resemble human blood."

"Shively won't like this." Leaning forward again, Alexis braced her hand on the lip of the table. She stood and winced.

That was the last straw for Yeron. "Alexis, what is wrong?"

Alexis looked up at Yeron with an engaging smile.

"Nothing. Except for an occasional breakthrough pain, I'm as right as rain."

How is rain supposed to feel? Steel Rose is having more than breakthrough pain.

Alexis's lie did not surprise him. Most people lied to their doctors, let alone to their lovers. Steve once said that for every pack of cigarettes a patient admitted to smoking, he multiplied the number by three. People lied about compliance with medicine, too. Perhaps they wanted to be seen as "good." More likely, they were lying to themselves and avoiding the truth about their disease. As a healer, Yeron recognized most lies.

Except when your mother told one, a voice whispered inside him. *Consider how badly her joints used to hurt, but she convinced you she was okay.*

That is right, he thought back at it. *Except when Mother lied. Your exception has been duly noted.*

"What are you taking for the pain?" he asked Alexis.

"Tyrone sprung for a bottle of Advil before we left the hospital." Alexis wagged her finger toward the screen. "We'd better tell the boys about this cell finding."

"In a minute." Yeron held firm, determined not to be distracted. "You have had a lot of breakthrough pain lately. I suspect that you are coming out of remission. A simple blood test would answer my question."

"I said I'm okay," Alexis responded, firmly.

"If you are okay, why do you grimace every time you exert yourself?"

"Yeron, I know my body." The warmth in her voice faded. "Leave it alone."

"I cannot." Yeron's voice amplified a notch with each word. He hated scolding like a shrewish old woman, but he could not help it. "My mother tried to hide her symptoms, too. If I had called her on it, she might still be alive."

"I'm not your mother." Alexis's brown eyes blazed. "Besides, Woehar shot your mother."

"That is true, but she suffered from an infection that generally afflicts only humans. If she had owned up to her symptoms, my father could have helped her. Prompt treatment would have made her alert and better able to protect herself from Woehar."

Alexis pursed her lips.

"Yeron, now is not the time –"

"Hey, folks, cut the bullshit!" Shively hollered from the top of the steps. He stomped down the steps, two at a time, with Steve and Tyrone behind him. "Take it outside."

"We are not quarreling." Yeron met Shively's gaze. "We are having a discussion."

Alexis's face blushed beet red. She backed into a corner, eyes on the floor.

"The hell you say," Shively countered. "I bet Alexis calls it a fight."

"He wants me to get a blood test because my hands hurt," Alexis said, her face still downcast. "It's not necessary. I don't have any fever."

"You are afraid of what I will find."

"I take Advil before missions," Alexis said, as if that justified her refusing the blood test.

"How much? Enough to tear up your stomach?"

"Time out!" Steve stepped forward, clapping his hands. "We've got a nasty situation, folks. Let's not make things worse by arguing." He glanced sideways toward Tyrone. "How much?"

"What the bottle prescribes. With her Reese's candies." Tyrone shrugged and winked at Alexis. It occurred to Yeron that Tyrone was widowed for some time and might long for female company. That wink and the possibility behind it gave Yeron chills.

"Yeron." Steve waved his hand. "Let it go."

Shively shrugged. "Alexis is a big girl. If she says she's okay, then she is. She's lived with her condition a long time."

"All right." Scratching the back of his head, Yeron pointed to his screen. "The left blood sample has healthy, human cells. The right has darker colored cells, each with a sickle shape. This latter sample came from the last walker I dissected. This analysis tells me our specimen was an android. Androids have enough intelligence to handle most weapons."

"Holy shit." Shively whistled. "Our renegades must be stepping up their invasion."

"It would appear so."

"The Gamma Scout didn't show activity." Tyrone rubbed his chin and regarded Shively. "What's next, Boss?"

"Keep looking for evidence that a city is close by, but fan out," Shively said.

"There has to be radiation – people found plenty of it in the first compound where Yeron grew up. It would sure help if we knew where to look."

"That will not be easy," Yeron told him. "Expect to run into landmines and traps. The renegades will do what they can to conceal their underground city."

"That's true. We had hell to pay to break into the first compound." Steve mopped the sweat from his forehead. "That entrance could be anywhere."

"Forget looking in the cornfields," Tyrone cackled. "Especially if you're talking about a trap door. The monsters won't appreciate it if a cow shits on their trapdoor."

Titters rose.

"How about if we ask the folks living in Cherryboro," Steve said. "I bet they would notice something weird."

"Yeah, right." Shively shrugged. "With our luck, the people of Cherryboro saw a lot of weird stuff and will still slam the door in our faces."

"If someone reported hearing strange noises in their basement ..." Alexis said, "Yeron and I will look for a panel there ... if we can."

"We will." Yeron then lowered his head, when he became aware she was addressing the others and not him.

"I'm getting some shuteye," Shively said. "Everyone, be up

early tomorrow."

"Good idea. I'm beat," Tyrone said. "You coming, Steve?"

"Not yet," Steve said. "It's my turn to pick up supplies. I'll make it quick."

"I'm watching a movie," Alexis said. The TV snapped on and she flicked through its channels, working them with her mind. Yeron stopped and looked again, his eyes opening wide. Telekinesis to work a television? What happened to the remote? Then he remembered that it had gone missing when they moved her belongings to the cabin.

"Steve, I will go with you," Yeron said.

"Good idea." Steve followed Yeron to the Humvee, darting glances over his shoulder. "I did Alexis's blood test last night while you were in the shower. She knows the results."

"You did?" Yeron gaped at Steve, stunned. "She never told me."

Steve shrugged. "Alexis will tell you about it when she's ready."

"Ready for what? What do you mean, *ready?* Ready to eat, ready to go out ..." Yeron's eyes went wide with dismay. Humanity's unwritten laws about behavior were endless, and he had broken one with Alexis. What made him think he could forge a lasting relationship with her?

"Yeron." Steve plopped behind the wheel with a sigh. "Alexis watched arthritis cripple her Aunt Susan. The kind she and her aunt have is hereditary. It's frightening. She's not mentally ready to face the possibility of being sick again."

"The arthritis has gotten worse. I saw this coming for weeks, even before you arrived."

Steve nodded in agreement. "That doesn't surprise me."

"The stress from the deaths of Johnny and Mark may have triggered the relapse. You and Tyrone should get confident using plasma in case Alexis gets seriously ill."

Steve sucked in his breath. "That should not be a problem. Teodon taught me about plasma when we were at Eigil's compound. Tyrone's a quick study."

"Good." Yeron sighed. "Sometimes I think we are on a suicide mission."

"That idea crossed my mind, too." Steve kept his eyes on the road. "I'd hate for Becky to have to raise our kid alone. At least she's got her job, her brother, and close friends to help."

"Alexis does not have siblings, friends, or employment. I cannot imagine her eking out an existence just on disability." Yeron shuddered at the notion. At first, Matilda would sell her soul to make sure that Alexis had medicine, but if she died, that would leave Alexis on her own. In his mind, he visualized Alexis going without medicine to pay for groceries and vice versa. "That was one reason I came with you. I want to revise my will."

"You're going to need to revoke your old will and draft a new one. I can set you up with my lawyer through email, if I can get online. I assume you want to add Alexis in your will."

"Yes. I want to split my assets between Alexis and Becky."

Steve's freckled face paled. He stared at Yeron with eyes bulging like soup plates. "Are you sure about this?"

Yeron nodded. "If I die before Alexis, the amount I leave her will be enough to support her. I do not plan on dying any time soon, but if I do, I want her secure."

"All right. I'll call my lawyer, but please, don't tell Alexis. She hates the idea of going on disability, said as much, and discussing her financial problems will upset her more. If you want to patch up your disagreement, you'll need a peace offering."

"Peace offering? Such as what?"

"Something to show her you care. It doesn't have to be expensive. Think it over."

Peace offering. What qualifies as a peace offering? As Steve drove on, Yeron mulled over the suggestion.

They stopped at the supermarket, and Yeron continued thinking about an appropriate gift for Alexis. They took turns handling the grocery cart and watching for walkers.

Yeron's gaze shifted toward the plant aisle. Last time Alexis came with him, she lingered by the rose bouquets without buying. A furtive glance at her meager bank balance told him why. Alexis's medical problems made her eligible for government disability, but the humans' primitive computers, exacerbated by damage to the electronic towers caused by the walkers, precluded swift payment. The poverty of Alexis's finances swarmed with emotional landmines, so he paid for her share of the food without saying anything. The idea of looting jewelry from the Trident Mall crossed his mind, but he dared not risk attracting unwanted attention. Instead, he elected a crystal vase with a dozen red, long-stemmed roses for his love.

****

Alexis lay curled up on the sofa bed, asleep, a movie in progress. At Yeron's approach, her eyes snapped open. She watched him with wary eyes.

"Alexis, I am sorry I scolded you. I love you and want to make it up to you." He set the vase with its bouquet at her feet. The air thickened with their floral scent.

"Red roses?" Warmth edged into her voice. "Oh, my ... these are beautiful! How did you know I wanted roses?"

"I notice ... things." He caressed her shoulder. "Is there something you want me to know?"

"No! I mean ..." Alexis's brown eyes betrayed unspoken fear. "Did Steve talk to you?"

"Steve has nothing to do with this, but we need to discuss the circumstances that may have contributed to our disagreement. If you have unresolved concerns about my background, now is the time to say so. Perhaps your church ..." The words spilled out before he could stop them, inviting another possible confrontation.

"Yeron!" Alexis leaped to her feet. She embraced him, leaning her face against his chest. "I never meant to keep anything from you." She pulled her head back and focused her eyes on his. "I wanted to concentrate on the walking dead and find easier ways to destroy them."

"I can understand that." *I do not believe you, though*, he added silently.

"Thank you for the roses." Alexis smiled and hugged him again. "I guess I'd better level with you." After snapping off the TV, she retrieved an unmarked manila envelope from a bag underneath the sofa bed. "Look at these pictures."

Yeron snatched up the envelope, spilled its contents, and thumbed through the photos. They were of Matilda's home – or what remained of it. In one picture, smoke billowed from a limestone shell, its charred window casements testifying to violence. Another showed a burned-out bookcase and the tattered remains of a floral sofa. The walls wore gruesome shades of black, gray, and smoke. Ditto for the huge mounds of ashes that covered the floors.

He got to thinking about his own mother and the way she had died. Her killer had set fire to her bedroom, the room where he and his father had found her, charred. He shivered at the memory of choking on the acrid smoke.

"I got a call from Officer Hazlett the day Mark and Johnny died," Alexis told him. "Three renegades with guns broke into my mom's house. The guard watching her house took one down, but the other two killed him. She awoke and caught one sneaking through the kitchen ..." her breath caught in her throat "... and she knocked him out with a frying pan."

"She ... what?" Yeron arched his thick brows. "Most renegades wear protection on their heads."

"Mom used a cast-iron frying pan," Alexis told him. "Those pans pack a hefty wallop, and she thumped him hard several times on the back of the neck. Then she ran over to Fenimore's house. The third renegade must have set the fire."

Yeron sat beside her, photos in hand, stunned into silence.

"I kept it quiet," Alexis went on, "so we could focus on our own renegade problems."

"I understand, but I wish you had told me. Those renegades were using Matilda to get to you." He frowned. "Where is your mother now?"

"According to Hazlett, she's in a safehouse. Mom's okay, but Hazlett advised against phone calls or emails because the renegades might tap our lines or trace the calls. He did agree to relay messages."

Yeron's chin jolted.

"That she killed a renegade with a frying pan is impressive."

Alexis shrugged. "Her adrenaline must have kicked in. In spite of all that, she worries about me. She knows I'm hurting. This thing with my hands and my lack of finances is a big hassle. I can't expect any disability payment because the government hasn't approved my application. I'm still waiting for their decision."

"If we get a good day on the Net, maybe I can access your file and find an explanation for the delay. I was hoping that the 248AR would enable you to return to patient care." Yeron's hand caressed her cheek. "Your mother cannot help you financially because she will need her own money now to buy a new house and furniture for it."

"Not only that. My aunt bled out a chunk of Mom's savings before she died, mostly for medical expenses. Sometimes the money disappeared without any explanation. I know because I used your backdoor technique to break into my mother's bank records." She rubbed the back of her neck. "My counselor Doctor Klein emailed me and begged me to arrange a session by phone. I don't have the time when I'm chasing monsters."

"You should make time. Why are you worried about your mother's bank account now?"

Alexis heaved a deep, haggard sigh.

"I haven't had my period since we got here, so I was going to ask her for a loan to get um, prenatal care. I should have told you about that, too, but ..." she clasped her head. "I hate sounding like a stupid high school kid."

Yeron drew in a sharp breath. Exciting as the possibility was, her scarred Fallopian tubes made any chance at pregnancy unlikely.

"The last months have been brutal," he said. "The stress can affect your cycle. Did you do a pregnancy test?"

"Not yet. Steve said he'd get me a home testing kit."

"The results should give you peace. Whatever you find, you have to be honest with me."

"I can do honesty. I'm sorry I didn't mention Mom sooner."

"No need to be sorry. Let us get through tomorrow and stay

alive."

Alexis nodded. "I'm working on it."

"I would enjoy becoming a father, but not at the risk of your health. Your arthritis has gone out of remission and pregnancy may cause complications."

"Tell me about it." Alexis shuddered. "No tests tonight, okay? I'm not ready for more surprises."

"This will not go away. You know that, right?"

With a brief bob of her head, Alexis rooted through her bag again. She retrieved her rosary beads, the ones her mother had given her.

"I want to fall asleep with you holding me, but first, I need to pray. Whatever we find tomorrow will be unpleasant. I've wanted to meet my would-be killer, but now that we're heading toward a show-down, I'm scared."

"Sure." Yeron stepped away and took a seat before his computer. He never understood how those beads helped Alexis, but he now appreciated the Higher Power and the spirit world. He hoped the Higher Power would send protection Alexis's way.

While Alexis prayed, Yeron downloaded a file that contained his will, reviewing areas that needed changes.

Chapter Twenty-Five: Discovery of an Underground Laboratory

Farm at Cherryboro, PA, August 21, 9:00 a.m.

The next morning, they drove down Route 363, the highway leading to Cherryboro, the walker stronghold where the renegades had allegedly stolen the buses. They wore lead vests, and helmets with Plexiglas masks, and underneath, balaclava caps. The helmets protected against noxious gases.

This time, Shively bypassed the cluster of sprawling homes, past a school and a church, and parked the Humvee close to a wooded area. He flipped on his Gamma Scout. Silence. He slid out of the vehicle and crept into the woods, Yeron behind him with Alexis at Yeron's side. Steve and Tyrone took the rear, the group forming a star pattern. Despite the bright sun, a strong breeze took the edge off the intense heat. Alexis's lips moved in silent prayer. Yeron longed for the day that they could stop fighting walkers and make a home together.

Rustling branches. Plodding footsteps.

"Get down!" Shively hissed under his breath. "Shut up!"

We are being quiet. Yeron glanced at Alexis. A smile crept across her face. Grim as their circumstances were, she held onto her sense of humor.

The footsteps grew louder. A black bear rumbled past them without looking their way. Yeron guessed that their suits concealed their scent. Most Kryszka considered bear meat a delicacy, and Yeron planned to capture a bear later – alone. Alexis understood his needs, but the others did not.

Beeping sounds cascaded from the Gamma Scout.

"We're close," Shively said in a low voice. "Alexis and Yeron, use your mind trick. If you stumble on anything that resembles an entrance, sing out."

"I guess we sniff out this door like dogs," Alexis whispered.

"No, we *look* for a flat panel," Yeron told her. "The seams are so thin you need the eyes of a cat to find it."

"Shit!" Alexis rolled her eyes. "Why don't these people use entrance and exit signs?"

Yeron laughed. "The renegades will not make it easy, Steel Rose. Even the good citizens want security. The explosion taught them a lesson, one they kept in mind when they built their new compound."

"Less talk and more searching," Shively whispered over his shoulder.

Where was this entrance? The row of trees seemed endless.

Farther past the woods, the trees gave way to a cornfield. Clicking sputtered from Shively's Gamma Scout. Yeron curled his fingers around his gun.

The cornfield appeared deserted. It didn't matter. The territory might teem with renegades or walkers in a heartbeat. Yeron stayed close to Alexis.

"You two spread out," Shively whispered back to them. "Probe for an entrance."

"I prefer to work in pairs." Yeron pulled Alexis closer.

"It's okay. I'll stay within your sight," Alexis told him. "My gut tells me that we'll find something in this cornfield." She looked over at Shively. "Where are you getting the most static?"

"Nowhere more than any other spot. I can't pinpoint any compound with this thing. Yeron, you grew up with these people. Where would you build a hiding place?"

"I would hide where I would least likely be detected," Yeron replied, sarcasm edging into his voice. "Say ... underneath a church. Like the one we just passed, but out here in the woods, away from people."

"Don't know, but he has a point, Shively," Tyrone said. "What say you?"

"Ah, fuck!" Shively muttered. "Do you guys see any other churches? Give me a ... Alexis! What are you doing?"

In the second it took for Shively to speak, Alexis disappeared between the cornstalks. Yeron did not notice anything except the rustling leaves.

"Alexis!"

"I'm searching for an entrance," Alexis shouted. "Will you guys shut up and let me ... ah, shit!" More fumbling and rustling, and then something, or someone, dropped with a soft, *thwump*. "No kidding."

"Alexis!" Yeron tore off into the direction of her voice, the others behind him.

Yeron arrived, with Tyrone and the others behind him. He helped Alexis struggle to her feet; her gloves and pant legs were coated brown.

"I'm okay. I stumbled over something and fell into a pile of cowshit."

"Cowshit?" Tyrone chortled. "Did you have fun playing with the turdies?"

"Har-har-har-de-har-har." Alexis's face reddened.

If looks could kill, Tyrone would die, Yeron thought. Titters rose from Shively and Steve. At this point, her face had blushed the color of roses. Despite his best efforts, Yeron found himself smiling. Then a question surfaced in his thoughts, wiping away his smile: *why did she fall?*

"Define the 'something,' you fell over," he said.

"I tripped over a rock. It's round and pink."

Propping herself between two cornstalks, she tapped something round with her left foot. Yeron made out faint humming. Squatting, he wiped away inches-thick layers of dirt and manure to get to the source of the humming. Moments later, he exposed a dirt-streaked rock. He wiped it down with disinfectant, revealing not a rock, but a pulsing pink light.

"This might lead to our underground city," he said.

Shively edged closer, crowbar in hand. "We could play it one of two ways. Tyrone and I dig our way in ..."

"The hell we are." Tyrone pointed a shaky finger toward the light. "Look at that thing. There's no way to dig around it."

"I'm thinking that light's sitting on a trapdoor. If I'm right, Yeron and Alexis can open it with their mind over matter. Whatever we do, you've got radioactive fallout, booby traps, and renegade Kryszka laying in wait."

"I doubt it," Steve said. "Alexis would've been dead already."

"I will go alone," Yeron said. "People admired my father, Teodon, and these soldiers might recognize me. I can fend them off until you open fire. If we are lucky, I will be able to negotiate."

"Once they realize you're Teodon's son, you're dead," Shively said.

"It depends on who I meet. Most people, including some of Eigil's soldiers, admired my father because of his medical skills," Yeron said. *Especially Quyeba and Zoltar,* he added silently.

Shively shook his head, frowning. "I doubt anyone you meet will give a shit now."

"You may be right, but at least you will get a chance to prepare your weapons."

"Great." Alexis rolled her eyes. "Here I stand, covered with shit while you guys argue."

"Safety is our first concern, honey," Yeron told her. "Shit is a minor inconvenience."

"Yeron gets off a good one." Tyrone laughed.

"Be quiet!" Shively hissed.

"Shively, allow me to captain this part of the operation," Yeron told him. "I will try to open the panel. Gather Alexis and the men and take them with you a safe distance away – just in case there is a danger under the panel."

Shively shrugged. "Go for it. Come on, Alexis."

Yeron watched the team follow Shively to the edge of the clearing. He then stepped toward the pulsing knob and underneath, the faint outline of a trapdoor. He tugged hard at the door with his mind. It lifted with absurd ease, exposing a metal staircase. Kneeling, he shone his flashlight inside the opening. He sniffed the interior and listened carefully. No smells, sounds, or signs of movement. No flashing lights or vibrations, such as what he might hear with a Kryszka landmine. He then created a force field, something to shield himself and the others from potential danger when they descended the stairs. The radiation ... he had forgotten about that. Even from where he knelt, he heard the Gamma Scout spewing out ticking sounds. No worse than before, but still there.

"No obvious threats," he called to the others. "We can proceed."

The others dashed across the field as he crept down the steps. Shively joined him at a landing, followed by Tyrone, Alexis, and Steve. Their flashlights splashed bright yellow shadows on slate-colored walls. They opened a trapdoor on the landing and revealed a second stairway. They kept moving, with no light to guide them other than their Maglites. A wall panel faced the stairs. Yeron opened it with his thoughts, revealing a room about 3500 square meters. They stepped in and shone their lights on curlicues, faces, and other shapes etched in the slate tiles on the entranceway, unmistakably Kryszka.

Alexis paced the room, her brow creased in deliberation. The chamber looked like a deserted warehouse, but the engravings and glazed slate, the metal that gave Kryszka walls their sheen, indicated it was a Kryszka laboratory. Yeron proceeded to the opposite wall to begin searching for signs of recent activity until Alexis had opened a crevice in the left wall. She moved cautiously through the opening, and the others rushed in behind her. It led to yet another, larger room, this one filled with analyzers, data processors, and readout screens with Kryszka symbols. An overhead vent blew cool air, causing three chairs by a terminal to sway. There was no apparent sign of life.

But invisible eyes drilled into the back of Yeron's neck, sending shivers up his spine.

"Okay." Alexis scratched the back of her head. "We found our underground colony. Where are the renegades?"

"They were here." Shively shook his head. "They must have

seen us coming and hightailed out of here. Fuck!"

"They couldn't have gotten far," Tyrone said.

"They did if they used escape pods," Yeron told him. "Finding them now will be difficult."

"They decided to retreat." Alexis heaved a wistful sigh. "Maybe they will leave us alone for good. Ya think?"

"If you think that, you've been reading that fantasy, *Weekly World,* again." Shively frowned.

"She could be right," Steve said. "Yeron, *are* Kryszka known to retreat when things get ugly?"

"It's an individual decision and depends on the person's temperament. The average citizen might, but Eigil's minions will not." At that, the shivers crested at Yeron's neck. No one had retreated. He knew this as well as his own name.

"So where do we go now?" asked Tyrone.

"We look for another compound," Shively said. "Tomorrow, we'll pay the folks who own the cornfield a visit."

They retraced their steps until they stepped above ground, no one saying a word. Shively stayed at the lead, Tyrone and Steve behind him, Alexis and Yeron to the rear. At the Humvee, Yeron wrapped a blanket around Alexis and helped her into the seat. He then shut her door, walked around to the opposite side of the vehicle, and hopped in beside her.

"I'm glad we made it back here alive," Alexis said, smiling.

"So am I," he agreed. "I sensed that unfriendly people were watching us. I will not say anything to the others until I have evidence; but we have to follow up with this."

"I suppose you're right. In the meantime ..." Alexis smiled. "I need help cleaning my beshitted clothes."

"Beshitted." Yeron enunciated each syllable for fun but became distracted. The otherworldly feeling kept nagging at him, a sense of eyes bearing into his back.

Chapter Twenty-Six: Alexis's Illness

Underground Basement at Shively's Cabin, August 25, 7:00 a.m.

When Alexis woke, her stomach juices were churning. Her mouth filled with saliva ... not her usual gagging around dead bodies, but the gut-wrenching rumbling she felt when she had the flu. Yeron lay fast asleep, exhausted by the all-nighters spent writing lab reports. She bolted upright, grabbed her pocketbook, and ran to the bathroom. At the toilet, she vomited.

Better now. The rumbling subsided. Nerves, no doubt the same reason she hadn't gotten her period since the beginning of the mission. The daily marches, irregular meals, the fruitless search for the laboratory, and the skirmishes with walkers had wrought havoc with her gut and menstrual cycle.

Nausea relieved, she rooted through her pocketbook. It contained a home pregnancy test kit. Steve had sprung for the kit after she confided her suspicions back when she had applied Steri-Strips to his wounds.

"It's the least I could do after you watched my back," he told her. *"Whatever you find out, be honest with Yeron."*

"I will," she'd promised him.

The instructions with the kit were simple, the test painless. The absorbent dipstick went into a cup of her urine. Alexis remained on the toilet, staring at the stick as the moments ticked by.

The digital readout had a "plus" sign. Pregnant.

Alexis drew in a deep breath and exhaled hard.

"Shit!"

This wasn't supposed to happen. Doctor Fitzpatrick, the man who first diagnosed her arthritis, told her that scarring in her Fallopian tubes had made conception impossible. A second opinion during Doctor Hoffman's evaluation gave the same results.

The site of the blood test Steve insisted on doing hurt plenty. Pain, like a poison arrow, shot through her wrists every time she wriggled her wrists. She knew from experience that it only took minutes to review a lab test result. By now, Hoffman was preparing to deliver grim news. Although he'd lost his *I-Am-God* demeanor months ago, his newfound empathy didn't include tolerance toward half-breed births, especially with those from mothers with medical problems. Steve had once said that Hoffman tormented his wife, Becky, about her half-Kryszka genes. *Why, oh, why hadn't she used birth control?*

She tiptoed back to bed, praying her movements wouldn't disturb Yeron. *Touchdown,* she thought, sliding under the sheets. *He's sound asleep.*

Movement to her left. Yeron was awake, propped on his elbow, looking down at her with concerned eyes.

"Was the test positive?" he asked.

"Positive." Alexis's voice was monotone. "I'm sick to my stomach, and I don't think it's just the pregnancy."

Yeron jumped up, reaching for a thermometer. "I am taking you to the hospital."

"Uh-uh!" Alexis shook her head. "We're already fighting short. I'd feel awful if I left and something happened to you or the others."

"If you are as sick as you appear, you are in no condition to fight. You may pass out or lose the baby."

"A hospital won't guarantee my safety, as we learned at Jackson. They might not know how to handle a half-breed baby." Besides, she was okay according to Tyrone's "10-minute rule." He once told her any symptom lasting less than 10 minutes didn't count. Her training in patient care would call this flawed thinking, but that training happened in another lifetime. She allowed Yeron to place the thermometer in her mouth, hoping that there would be no fever. Yeron then palpated her abdomen.

"Don't poke my stomach." She talked around the thermometer. "It makes the queasiness worse." The thermometer beeped. Alexis removed it and stole a peek. "Temperature normal. Please, no hospital. Not yet, okay?"

"All right, no hospital." Yeron lowered his eyes. "I have always wanted a child, but not at the expense of your health. I love you and do not want to lose you. So please ... at least drink lots of water. Your lips look parched."

****

Her queasiness had settled by the time Alexis got up to wash her face, but the deep circles under her eyes and drawn cheeks whispered the threat of incipient illness. Her normally tanned complexion was bleached pale, as white as Yeron's. She'd never looked this bad from arthritis; something else was brewing. The emphysema patients she'd treated at the hospital looked better. In the kitchen, Tyrone was scrambling eggs and bacon. The spicy bacon aroma stirred up the rumbling in her gut. She helped herself to a box of Wheat Thins.

"What's with the crackers?" Shively stood beside her, pouring what passed for coffee into a Styrofoam cup.

"I'm not in the mood for eggs."

"You look like hell."

"Thank you for sharing." Alexis offered a cheerful smile. "May I eat in peace?"

"Aw, he's pissed because we found an empty lab." Laughing, Tyrone scooped some eggs onto a nondescript plate.

"Crackers are the best thing for a queasy stomach," Steve said. "Ignore him."

"Think I will." Alexis reached for the milk, a gallon-sized jug. Why did Shively buy such large containers? She pried the lid and tried to lift the jug. Brutal agony stabbed through her wrists.

Okay, let's do the mind trick. She lifted the bottle and poured a glass without spilling a drop. *I'm getting better at this.*

Tyrone glanced up at her with a broad, toothy grin. Yeron gaped at her, concern in his red eyes. Steve, who had his head in a book, twitched.

"What are you doing now?" Shively gave her a bug-eyed look.

"Pouring myself milk. The arthritis meds stopped working, so I improvised with another way to lift the container."

"Shit." Shively drew his hand through his moist hair. "Steve, what's up with her blood test?"

Steve tossed his book aside and sighed. "I sent her specimen to the lab and I'm expecting a report from Joe soon."

"I might as well wait for the fucking check in the mail. Alexis, you belong in a hospital."

"I tried to tell her that," Yeron said, "but my Steel Rose has her own mind."

Damn straight, Alexis thought, but she bit back her sarcasm.

"Don't worry, Doctor Phil," she smiled at Yeron. "We may have run the renegade soldiers out on a rail. If the others agree, I'll go to the hospital."

"Good point," Tyrone said. "Yeron, do you think the renegades are gone?"

"Another compound exists," Yeron told him. "We may have killed some of the renegades, but I make no guarantees."

"No guarantees, huh?" Shively's blue eyes flickered back and forth. "Alexis should be on bed rest. We're running out of ammo and money to buy more. The supply from my organization has dried up; everyone's desperate for weapons. So we gotta pony up. Anyone got spare cash?"

Alexis furrowed her brows, frowning. She'd gone several months without an income. Her mother paid her mortgage from the $7,000 Doctor Hoffman had given her, his way of compensating the fighters during the walker invasion at the hospital.

"No cash," she said, "except $200 in my bank account. I owe you for food and utilities, so I'll write your supplier a check. Okay?"

"Nope." Shively's jaw was set, lips tightened. "My man expects cash on the barrel head. Besides, I already got you for the food and stuff."

Alexis's mouth dropped open, surprised. Who was her benefactor? Why, Yeron, of course, because he loved her. As for the others, Tyrone didn't carry extra money, though he sprung for her Advil. Steve Leicht's medical malpractice premiums put a lock on his wallet. Her eyes settled on Yeron.

Her face flushed deep red as she struggled to get the words out. "I owe a certain someone here lots of cash."

"You do not owe me anything." Yeron laid his hand on her shoulder.

"I'm out, Shively." Tyrone's voice saddened. "Sorry."

"So am I." Steve shifted his gaze toward Shively. "Without cash, we can't buy more weapons. It's time we moved on. It's not like we can rob a bank."

"That's exactly what we're going to do." Shively's blue eyes narrowed into squinty triangles. His voice chilled like ice. His frost radiated in every direction. "I don't know about banks, but you, Tye, and I can filch guns from the folks living in those fancy houses near the deserted compound."

Alexis opened her mouth to protest and gripped her stomach as another ripple of nausea passed. What if they got caught and landed in jail?

"Fuck, Shively, we don't know that they're rich," Tyrone spoke up in a firm voice. "Besides ... it's just wrong."

Damn you, Shively! Alexis clenched her fists inside her pockets and winced at the stabbing pain. She relaxed her fingers.

"It's not right to rob someone and leave their family defenseless," Steve pointed out.

"Too bad." Shively's eyes narrowed. "It's them or us."

"Maybe we can, ah, borrow them from a store," Yeron said.

"Borrow?" Shively laughed acrimoniously. "Newsflash, Yeron. No store will loan you any guns. They're probably hoarding the weapons for themselves."

"I think he means looting." Alexis looked at Yeron. At his nod, she continued. "Trident Mall had a gun shop. Maybe we'll find something useful among the ruins."

"Nice try, but someone's probably already looted the firearms," Tyrone said. "The demand for weapons has gone way up because of the walkers."

"I'm sure it has." Steve grinned at Alexis. "We should still look."

"Steel Rose may be right." Yeron spoke up, his arm hugging Alexis's middle. "The ordinary citizen will try to avoid that mall. They might grab guns off the shelves and run, but they would be too scared to think about searching the stockroom."

"Yeah, well the officers might still be watching for vandals or looters," said Shively. "They made us when we were there. Next time, they might try to arrest us."

"That was over two months ago." Alexis waved her hand. "By now they forgot about us."

"Good point," Tyrone agreed. "With what's been walking the streets, most people have a short attention span."

"I doubt those officers do." Shively's voice softened. "Okay, we'll comb this area one more time for walkers or renegades. If we find any, we'll loot the mall. If not, we'll go home to our families. Fair enough?"

The others nodded their assent. Was the nightmare over? Alexis prayed it was so.

"Thank you, Shively." She swallowed hard, fighting another surge of nausea. "Guys, I feel like shit."

"I can tell," Yeron agreed. "How much are your wrists hurting?"

"A lot." Alexis looked down at her hands, not caring to admit that the vomiting and weakness scared her more than anything. "I'd rather sleep, but with one of us home, it will be that much harder to fight off walkers."

"Stay put." Shively patted her on the shoulder. "We'll get by."

"Of course, we will." Yeron planted a kiss on Alexis's cheek. Hand cradled on her shoulder, he ushered her down the basement stairs and lowered her onto his sofa bed. *Their* sofa bed.

"Did I ever tell you that you are beautiful?"

"Don't try to distract me. I can hear the fear in your voice." She drew in a deep breath. "We're both scared about this baby."

"I worry about your health. Do not feel guilty about accepting help. I earn more than enough money for both of us."

"I realize that." Alexis crawled under the covers and looked up at Yeron. "Doctor Hoffman is eating the cost of my medicine. Mom's paying my bills from her savings because the check she expected to get never arrived. I'm hoping to get reinstated at Jackson Hospital."

"That should not be a problem. According to Joe, a lot of nurses and other employees quit since the invasion. When he posts a position, he gets few takers. The walkers gave Jackson a bad reputation." Yeron caressed her stomach. "First, we get through today. Shively wants you to stay here and I agree with him."

Alexis's eyes glittered with unshed tears.

"I'm going to worry about you every second until you're back."

"Then do your prayer ritual. It helps you relax."

"All right." Alexis tensed at the foreboding in her chest. Somewhere, they had missed a vital link to the renegades. "I'll say my prayers and rest, but I want to keep my plasma gun with me. And frankly ..."

She heaved a sigh. "When you get back, I want to make the most passionate love we've ever made. Once Hoffman examines me, he'll put me in the hospital for a long time. Any plans will have to wait."

"All right." Yeron kissed her forehead. "Try to rest."

After Yeron and the men left, Alexis said her rosary. She opened the computer to download a movie, thought better of it, and crawled back into bed. God, it hurt to move. The room spun before her. The darkness crept in only seconds after she slipped under the covers.

Chapter Twenty-Seven: The Renegades Invade

The Woods near Shively's Cabin, August 30, 2:00 a.m.

Alexis did not stir until suppertime, when Yeron's kiss woke her. Her eyes snapped open. She peered at his worried frown.

"What happened?"

"We found dead bodies, but no walkers or renegades," he told her.

"No walkers?" At that, Alexis jumped up and hollered, "Yaaaaay!"

In the next instant, her head spun. She pitched and yawed. Yeron grabbed her by the shoulders and eased her to the sofa bed.

"Have you eaten anything while we were gone?"

Alexis slumped forward, elbows on her knees, and shook her head.

"Steve picked up dinner – raw steak for me and cooked steak sandwiches for everyone else. Let us go upstairs. You must be hungry."

"Not really." The queasiness in her belly increased at the thought of food.

Shively's voice and Tyrone's laughter, plus the clopping of boots overhead, gave her a headache. "I'll eat a little later. Okay?"

Yeron placed his hand against her head and frowned.

"No, not okay. Your eyes look sunken and your tongue has gone dry. Dehydration is serious, and worse in pregnant women. You have to eat and drink something."

Shit. Alexis wrinkled her nose.

"All right, I'll try."

The men piled into the kitchen, guzzling beer, overjoyed that their search had revealed nothing. The conversation centered around plans for getting back to everyday life. At Yeron's insistence, Alexis ate a cheesesteak and chased it with milk and two helpings of ice cream. Her nausea and headache subsided and she found herself laughing at Tyrone's jokes.

After dinner, the lovemaking came and went, and Alexis fantasized about everyday living with Yeron. Getting used to the idea of living with him was easy and she was anxious to begin. No doubt the pregnancy added to her health problems, but she promised herself to soldier through it, no matter what any doctor said. She had broken many of her self-imposed rules—taking part in Mark's shooting, lying to people she loved, but she would never consider having an abortion.

Having drawn those conclusions, she fell back to sleep. Her head rested on Yeron's chest. In her dreams, Yeron cradled a baby boy in his arms. The baby wore bandages on his chin, as he was recovering from a minor operation. Yeron's CD player belted out classical music with trombones in the background.

The trombones blasted in her ear, and when Alexis jerked awake, the blasts were coming from Yeron's computer.

No, not trombones. Alarms.

Alexis jumped up, fully awake now. Already, Yeron had donned his coveralls. He raced up the steps, hollering, "Shively! Tyrone! Steve, get up! The renegades are coming."

The surveillance camera glowed with an eerie brightness, making loud noises sounding like *doom, doom, doom.* Each blast telegraphed terror through her soul. She scrambled to the screen, which showed navy-clad figures trekking toward the cabin. *No more walkers,* she pleaded. *We've had enough, okay? These are live people ... and, oh, no, they're soldiers!*

She saw that they were Kryszka soldiers clad in navy tunics and matching helmets with see-through face shields. Renegades. Their hostile eyes and brandished guns warned that they hadn't come to pay a social call.

"Yeron!" she screamed, "We're in so much trouble. God help us!"

Voices upstairs. Clomping of booted feet. Moving in pantherlike fashion, Yeron glided back down the stairs and reached for his tunic. He tossed a tunic her way.

"Get dressed. Hurry!"

The pain in her hands flared with each movement. The tunic slid on; thank God for small favors. Yeron stood beside her, helping her fasten her boots and helmet. She didn't know someone could move that fast.

"I managed to wake the others. It was not easy because Tyrone and Shively, and even Steve, drank a lot of beer last night," Yeron said in a low voice. "They decided we were safe, so they celebrated."

"That's right, they were acting pretty goofy." Alexis heaved a deep sigh. "As the old saying goes, *like good old Art thinking the street was safe but gets hit by a car instead.*"

"Do me a favor," Yeron began. He slipped C4 explosives under her garment sleeve. One minute he was naked, and in the next, he was dressed and armed. "If you confront these soldiers, do not translate that to Kryszka. They will shoot you."

"Oh, my ..." Alexis shuddered. "Yeron, I don't intend to confront any renegades."

"Here, drink this with your medicine." Yeron handed her a cup of milk. Alexis swigged it with her pills and followed it with an injection. Cursing under his breath, he rooted through his equipment.

"What are you looking for?" she asked.

"Something you can wear over your stomach, in case there is radiation. I did not think to buy you a lead apron." Yeron retrieved half a lead apron from a cabinet. "Use this. It is heavy, but it will protect you."

Without waiting for Alexis to reply, he wrapped the apron around her waist and secured it with Velcro. The surveillance camera showed the Kryszka soldiers on their march, faces grim and determined. They knew how to inflict pain and kill.

"Let us go. We must hurry before those soldiers reach the cabin."

"Who's 'they?' What's this about renegades?" Tyrone sprinted down the steps.

His eyes settled on the monitor. "Holy shit!"

"No kidding." Shively came down behind him, hitching up his gun belt. He yanked open a closet door and dragged out five black gas tanks. They looked like the kind Alexis saw her patients use but twice as thick and taller. The regulators had two dials with Kryszka numbering. One dial affixed to a vinyl wand; the other attached to the tank.

"Don't worry, guys," Shively said. "Each of us gets a tank. We'll off these bastards with helium."

"You got that right." Steve came up behind Shively. "My family used these tanks to fight their way out of Eigil's compound. We can do it, too."

The markings on the regulators showed that the tanks were full. Helium would kill the renegade soldiers. Then a horrible thought surfaced from her subconscious, like a skeletal corpse rising from its crypt. Those tanks looked heavy. Could she carry one, let alone manipulate the tank and tubing? Maybe. Her telekinesis might help if she didn't need it for other chores. Then another thought, even more horrific, clawed its way to her consciousness. If helium was fatal to the Kryszka...

"We can't use these around Yeron," she cried.

"It'll work out." Tyrone's voice was firm. "He's our best fighter."

"He can't fight if he's dead." At that, a lump rose in Alexis's throat. She longed to explain how much she loved this man, that she could not raise his child alone.

"Don't use him as a sacrificial lamb."

"Steel Rose, I brought a helium-proof mask after Steve used helium tanks at Eigil's compound," Yeron said. "It enabled me to survive. The renegades may be wearing helium-proof masks, too, but ... maybe not. Whatever happens, I shall be here to drive you to the hospital."

"No one's sacrificing anyone." Shively shifted his gaze from Yeron to the others. "These bastards made the walkers and caused the slaughter. After we gas them, we keep moving. There's more waiting to ambush us, so we gotta stick together."

He passed out the tanks. Steve looped a mesh strap around one and slung it over Alexis's shoulder so that the wand rested in the crook of her elbow.

"There you go. You okay with all this?"

"No," Alexis whispered. "I'm worried about the baby. What if he, or she, is susceptible to helium?"

"Yeron and I will cover your back. Stay cool."

****

Shively sighted about a dozen renegades outside the electrified gate. He and Tyrone moved in, dodging plasma fire as they went, with Alexis behind them, and Steve and Yeron behind her, covering her back. The Kryszka continued squeezing off plasma, setting brush on fire, narrowly missing the two men. They then dropped when the team had gotten close enough to shoot with the helium spray. They weren't expecting it. The fight seemed easy until the blaze approaching the team spread, flames licking their way toward the fence surrounding the cabin.

"Call the police!" Shively shouted.

Tyrone snatched up his walkie-talkie. Alexis stayed close to Yeron. He moved at a steady pace, mask in place. Flames sprouted up behind them. What was this ... the cabin catching fire? Thank God she hadn't left any valuables there. Then she remembered ... her medicine! Steve carried an extra dose, but that was it. Worse, they left ammunition at the cabin – not much, since they were running low – but enough to cause a massive explosion. Already, the smoke was searing her throat. The churning in her gut came back with a vengeance.

"Yeron," she managed between heaves, "I ... I ...."

"Later, Alexis. I am trying to contain the fire with my mind." His tone edged with tension. "It is difficult, but it can be done. I need your help."

"I think I'm going to ..." *pass out,* she was about to say, but then white-hot agony flared up in her belly. She clutched her stomach, and the movement cost her. Pain knifed through her hands.

She tore off the path, passing Steve and Tyrone, who crawled as if in a daze, their eyes bulging. After lifting her mask, she coughed, vomiting what felt like a pint of hot red blood into the bushes.

"Dammit!" Another spurt of blood jetted from her mouth. She was going to die right here, not from Kryszka fire, but from an old-fashioned stomach bleed. At least her death came by a gentle approach. Bad as the pain was, she'd suffered worse from her arthritic flare-ups.

"Alexis!" Yeron shouted from somewhere behind her.

"Yeron, I had to vomit." Her voice came out a thin whisper. *How will Yeron and my mother get through my death? Is Mom safe? Will Yeron and the boys survive?* These questions and others surfaced, but she'd never find the answers.

Grimacing at the pain slicing through her fingers, she gripped the metal cross on her rosary, breaking the chain. Then she scrawled "Yeron" in the dirt, and paused. If she died, so would her child. One more hurt piled on the other. She finished with "I love you," sank to the ground, and rolled onto her side.

Blue lights surrounded her, and a force tugged her shoulders. *So this was what dying is like. How much will God punish me for what I did to Mark? Would the times I protected Tyrone and the others garner me any mercy?* She tried pleading for forgiveness in a prayer, but the words didn't come. Her focus encircled Yeron, her mother, and the boys. Her last thought, before the blue faded to black, was that she'd tried her best.

Chapter Twenty-Eight: Searching for Alexis

The Woods near Shively's Cabin, August 30, 4:00 a.m.

Fire trucks and police cars wailed up the path. Their lights cut red and blue swords against the trees. Yeron dropped to his knees, keeping his face close to the ground where the air was clearer. *Where is Alexis?* She had started to tell him something and then bolted. Somewhere behind the funnels of smoke, he'd heard her holler, "Dammit!"

Relieved, he sprinted in the direction of her voice. She hadn't gone too far; her voice was clear and audible. The path led to a narrow clearing where the fire had not yet spread. He passed Tyrone and Steve, who were talking with firefighters as they grabbed hoses and equipment from their trucks. Shively was ... where *was* he? The billowing smoke blurred Yeron's vision. His feet slid. He steadied himself and glanced down. That was when he noticed the pool of bloody vomit and the words in the dirt: "Yeron, I love you." And then something else caught his attention.

Green beads on a metal chain glimmered in the grass.

He walked around the vomit and the message, careful not to step in either. He bent to see the shiny object. They were Alexis's rosary beads. He reached for them and then stopped. If she had met with foul play, he did not want to contaminate potential evidence. She had worn them around her neck. *Maybe she dropped them when she fell, or when a disintegrator ...*

The blood. All that blood.

She was saying goodbye.

Steve's crackling voice drilled into Yeron's mind. He snatched his walkie-talkie, hoping someone had found Alexis.

"Yeron." Steve's voice crackled through the radio. "Where's Alexis?"

"I am looking for her," Yeron shouted. "Who called the police?"

"Tyrone did because of this fire. He said he couldn't get

through to the local police, so he called Officer Hazlett. He noticed Alexis's morning sickness, figured out that she is pregnant, and he told Hazlett. If something happened to Alexis, Hazlett will have to notify her mother, and she'll insist on riding here with him. Don't tell me she's missing."

"She is not here. I found her rosary in a pool of blood."

"Set up a triage – there may be others injured and find her." Steve's harsh, rasping voice tinged with anger and worry. His breath came fast. *"Now!"*

Yeron sagged, his head drooping. All at once, he felt old, tired, and used. "Steve, did you understand me? Alexis shouted something and then she was gone. She vomited blood and wrote out a cry for help."

"Is that so? Are you telling me that she's out there alone, sick as she is?"

"I do not know. I think she may have gotten sick, panicked, and bolted."

"Great. We promised to have her back home in one piece." The deep sigh spoke of Steve's frustration and worry. "We have to find her. Alexis has an infection - aspergillosis."

"What?" Yeron stared at his radio. That didn't sound right. Alexis hadn't shown any fever, cough, or other signs of infection. "What did you say?"

"You heard me." Steve's voice smoked with tension. "Joe sent me the results of Alexis's blood culture. She tested positive for aspergillosis, a deadly fungus found on human and animal corpses. Even with treatment, her chances of survival are fifty-fifty, and the pregnancy will worsen her odds. We should have shipped her to the hospital weeks ago."

"She refused to go ... until today." Yeron moved farther into the clearing, but he saw no sign of Alexis. "Her sickness came on so fast. She never complained of any fever, swelling, or shortness of breath. She was tired, but that's common in pregnant women."

"Her case is an exception. I'm glad you and Alexis found love ... but dammit, she had health issues. How could you let the pregnancy happen?"

It is easy, Steverino. My penis is superior to any penis on Earth. Yeron shook his head. *Stop this. Alexis might be dying.*

"Answer me!"

"Her doctors said that her scarred Fallopian tubes would make pregnancy impossible; so we did not take precautions." Yeron blotted the perspiration from his forehead. "Steve, it happened. I tried to keep her safe, to protect her and the baby. I covered her back through this entire mission. This time, she got sick and ran before I could intervene. She scribbled in the dirt, 'Yeron, I love you.'"

"Good Lord." Steve lowered his voice. "How can I tell her mother? Matilda hated that Alexis joined our posse. She'll go into hysterics, which will make it twice as hard to concentrate on any search."

"I realize that. Can the police help us?"

"I called Officer Hazlett, too. He's flying to the station in town by helicopter. When he gets here, I'll talk to him." His voice tightened. "Get ready to duck the shit when it hits the fan."

****

A few minutes later, Steve trudged through the path, face grim. With the help of the firefighters, the flames petered out, but a gauzy curtain of smoke blanketed the sky.

Tyrone followed Steve, cradling a stack of plasma guns in his arms.

"I counted fifteen Kryszka dead. I've got their weapons."

Moments later, a car came up the path and whined to a stop by the fire trucks. Yeron pivoted, gun at the ready. His jaw dropped. Hazlett got out, accompanied by a bloodhound. His partner, Julia McDevitt, followed Hazlett with Matilda in tow. Both officers lugged large black suitcases. Matilda had on a blue shirt and dungarees. Her husky olive-complexioned face had new worry lines, but the fire in her eyes rang true. Mother Tiger wanted to bring her injured cub home.

"What's Matilda doing here?" Tyrone whispered, nudging Steve.

Before Steve could answer, Matilda rushed forward, stubby legs pumping like pistons, lips huffing. To Yeron, she looked like a rocket engine ready to lift off.

"*Matilda* wants to know if her daughter's alive." She shifted her bloodshot, fury-filled eyes between Yeron, Steve, and Tyrone. The air thickened with tension.

"What have you done with her? You had a nice cozy setup here so she could fight your dirty war. You promised me you'd keep her safe, but you couldn't keep your pants zipped around her. Now she's seriously ill, hurt somewhere, and *pregnant*."

Yeron inspected his pants, but the Velcro fastening them had not come undone. His trousers were on, snaps snug. He met her gaze.

"I beg your pardon, but my clothes have nothing to do with this."

"*Bah fungule!*" Matilda's voice cracked. "Tyrone told the officers about your baby and they told me. How could you two allow this to happen? Especially Alexis, given her health problems?"

"Shit happens." Tyrone's eyes riveted on Matilda. "Speaking of missing, where's Shively?"

Yeron tried to peer through the smoke-filled area. The weight of despair on his shoulders caused them to droop. "I do not see him."

"I'm not asking about Shively." Matilda stared daggers at Tyrone. "I'm worried about my daughter."

"So are we," Steve shouted, "but your badgering isn't helping."

After that, Steve's mouth snapped shut. He shot Yeron a look that said *I don't believe I said that.*

Matilda snarled, pulled back her fist and walloped Steve across the face.

"Don't smart off to me, young man," she managed, but her breath came out in short, ragged puffs. She shook her hand from the pain and fell silent. Steve withered.

"Time out, folks." Hazlett raised his hands. "Yeron, what were Alexis and Shively wearing before they went missing? Speedy here can sniff out anything."

The bloodhound whiffed at the air, as if to reinforce the message.

They all gazed toward the cabin. Smoke billowed from the cabin and rose from the skeletal remains of the trees. Alexis's clothes were in the cabin. Maybe something had survived the fire. At least she had her beads ...

"Shively wore his uniform," Yeron told the officer. "Alexis had her prayer beads with her, but the chain broke and I saw them in the grass. I didn't want to touch them. Will they help?"

"They might. Where are they?"

"There." Yeron parted the bushes and pointed to the field where Alexis had gotten sick. They walked over in single file and then stood in a circle around the blood and vomit puddles. The blood had congealed to a paste. The rosary beads lay nearby the puddle. They looked at the message, which looked like someone had fingered it in the dirt.

"She was trying to say goodbye," Yeron said softly.

"Yeah, that's what I think, too." Steve fixed a steely glance on Matilda. "Let's hope the renegades aren't holding her in Cherryboro because that's an hour's drive from here. We'd better move it."

Matilda remained silent. Frightened as she was, she wanted to lash out at the first person she met. The officer squatted by his dog and spoke while the bloodhound bent its head, snout close to the rosary beads on the grass. Speedy sniffed the beads, wandered about, and sniffed the air. Yeron watched. The bloodhound sprinted into the clearing, Hazlett running beside him, his hold tight on the leash. Yeron and Julia followed behind closely, with Steve, Tyrone, and Matilda at the rear.

Could any canine have found my half-sister, Becky, during her imprisonment in Eigil's compound? Probably not. Eigil shot all invaders, human or animal. Yet humans relied on dogs for search and rescue. Speedy scurried ahead, determinedly. Very little escaped a bloodhound's nose and Hazlett had trained this one well.

After about an hour, they came upon a cornfield, where Speedy stopped, sniffed, and then proceeded through the cornstalks at a slow pace. Yeron and the two officers followed behind the dog at the same pace. Moments later, Speedy stopped again and pawed at the ground. Julia bent over and then straightened, eyes on the group.

"Well, this light's interesting. Where does it lead?" Julia shifted her gaze between Yeron, Tyrone, and Steve. "Don't all speak at once."

Yeron squatted beside Speedy and looked down. A pink light pulsed from the ground. He gasped. Heart thudding in his chest, he darted a glance toward Julia.

"Another underground compound."

"Or laboratory," Steve said. "We found an underground lab with machinery at Cherryboro, but no people."

"Did it cross anyone's mind to inform us?" Julia asked.

"We did not think it was necessary." Yeron lowered his eyes again. "We assumed the renegade Kryszka decided to retreat."

"We assumed wrong." Instant alarm filled Tyrone's face. "They set up shop somewhere else."

"I was afraid of that," Yeron told him, but somewhere in the deepest part of his brain, something niggled at him. *Did I let Alexis distract me?*

"Hey, guys, we're not pointing fingers." Hazlett held up his hand. "You should have notified us, regardless of what you found, but you didn't. So let's have a look, but with caution since we don't know the levels of radiation. Does anyone have a Geiger counter?"

"Shively had a Gamma Scout, but he's gone and so is the equipment." Fetching a sigh, Steve ambled over to Yeron. "You go first. I'm prepared to shoot, and I've got my helium tank, but I'm worried about hidden landmines. We have no way of knowing how much radiation there is."

"I'm after you guys." Tyrone stepped up behind Steve.

"Now wait," Matilda insisted. "I'll go first. If my daughter's down there, I want to know if she's hurt."

"I'll go first." Hazlett placed a restraining hand on her shoulder. "I bent the rules bringing you here, but I'm not taking you down into an underground tunnel." Matilda scrunched her nose up at him. "Don't make me sorry I let you come." He settled his eyes on Julia. "Watch her. If she makes a move, sing out into your walkie-talkie."

Yeron glanced at Matilda. He longed to say that he shared her fears about Alexis, that he could lose the one person who made his life worth living. But Matilda's gray eyes flashed with anger. Her good will had depended on Yeron keeping Alexis safe, and he had not. Who gave Tyrone, a security guard, not in the field of medicine, the right to ply Alexis with anti-inflammatory pills? The high doses, along with her other problems, must have caused a stomach bleed.

"Officer, I will help you with the suitcases," Yeron offered. "Assuming you need them."

"I appreciate it," Hazlett replied. "They've got pressurized suits."

Is the potential for noxious gases that bad that we need pressurized suits? This is a suicide mission! Did Alexis realize this? The lead weight of despair settled around his shoulders, a fear that he might never see Alexis and his unborn child again.

He had gotten halfway down the ladder when he looked up at Steve.

"This is a recovery operation, not rescue, right?" asked Yeron.

Steve gave him a measured look.

"Do me a favor. Don't let Matilda hear you say that."

"Do you think I enjoy saying it? If Alexis dies, then our son or daughter will, too. Pregnancy will not exempt Alexis from torture."

Steve stopped at the second rung above him. He gave Yeron an intent gaze, his face distorted with terror and his eyes red with grief. "I went through it when Becky was a hostage and eight months pregnant. I know this seems impossible, but think positively. Despite her condition, Becky fought as well as we all did, and so did Alexis. Your Steel Rose can protect herself."

"Not anymore." Yeron groaned. "You said that she has aspergillosis."

"That's true," Steve said, "but Alexis is well versed in the Kryszka language and plasma guns, skills that Becky didn't have. I'm hoping that the guards will want to interrogate her. If they do, then maybe ... just maybe, they'll provide what treatment she needs so she can answer their questions."

"That is a big *if*, Steve."

"By now, I bet, she's invented nicknames for her guards."

Yeron groaned. Alexis had been a quick study on the language, but not the taboos against using slang. Lovers might invent "play" names the way he and Alexis did with each other, but most Kryszka considered nicknames offensive. Such behavior might provoke a hostile guard into shooting her.

"That is what I fear."

Speedy brushed against his leg, drawing his attention. The dog scampered down the rungs, followed by Hazlett and Tyrone.

"This is a weird setup." Hazlett shone his flashlight. "I hope they've got another exit further out in the field. Otherwise, they'll be in big trouble if there's a fire and this way out is blocked."

"They do not use fire doors," Yeron told him. "Many walls have hidden panels. The residents know how to open these panels with their minds. If you do not know this information, the soldiers assume you are an interloper. They may shoot you."

"This room looks like the lab at Cherryboro. We checked it out," Tyrone said, "and found zilch."

"We're not at Cherryboro now." Hazlett stepped sideways while his dog trotted past some machinery, continually sniffing. "Yeron, if we are to succeed, you've got to forget your feelings for Alexis, forget about her mother. Our priority is to find your missing buddies and bring them home. Speedy can help, but you've got to look for those panels. Start looking."

Yeron scanned each wall, and the floor just in case he found any clues, such as footprints. Then he watched Speedy weave his way through a maze of machines, stepping over wires and cables, sniffing the floor and the air. Earth animals sensed danger long before humans or Kryszka did, but Yeron did not need an animal to tell him the enemy had set a trap. If he wanted to find a doorway, he would have to think like the renegades did.

The hostile soldiers would not treat sick humans. They sought humans for killing and consumption, and invented cruel methods of torture. No exceptions. Their warehouse for storing prisoners no doubt employed sophisticated security. The kinder ones presumed him dead from the explosion at Eigil's compound months ago. The cruel ones preoccupied themselves with torturing humans and would capitalize on deformities, like Alexis's misshapen fingers. That was what she faced. By now she was dead ... unless she happened upon a kindly guard. *Quit speculating!* He chided himself. *Concentrate on the search.*

She made friends easily; as a patient, she had endeared herself to her caregivers enough to get pro bono treatment. Perhaps her outgoing nature and knowledge of the language might garner leniency, but Yeron dared not indulge in delusions. So how would the renegades discourage intruders? At the destroyed compound, an officer suffered critical injuries from poisoning after stumbling into a trap. This time, he feared, the renegades might resort to death-dealing measures. He would do well to be extra cautious.

Perhaps they had planted landmines behind the wall. Maybe they built a force field superior to the ones within the old compound, something to neutralize traditional Kryszka weapons. If that were the case, any intruder would die. He had to stop thinking of the horrors they could conceive of and instead concentrate on the task at hand.

Speedy let out whimpers in front of the largest clutch of machines. His tail went halfway down and his ears perked up. He stood in front of the machinery, blocking Yeron's access, sniffing.

"Easy, boy." Hazlett clutched his leash. "We're getting close, fellows, but Speedy's giving us a stress alert. Alexis was scared and injured when they brought her here."

"That's a foregone conclusion," Steve said. "I bet there's a hidden panel ... entrance behind these machines."

Tyrone grinned, tightlipped, at Yeron. "So what's next, Cowboy?"

"I do not see any panels, so I shall move the computers," Yeron said. "Let us hope I find this gate."

He focused on the machine with readouts, the one that agitated Speedy, and tried to move it with his mind. It would not budge. After creating a force field with his gun, he edged the device over the cables and to the side. He then probed the floor but found no panels. The section that caught Speedy's attention housed six machines like the one he moved. He could take hours to push each one sideward the way he did the first, for the Kryszka used levitation-proof equipment. With a deep sigh, he mustered up as much mental power as he could and proceeded to work.

Chapter Twenty-Nine: Botched Escape Attempt

Underground Kryszka Prison, August 30, 7:00 a.m.

Alexis ran through dark tunnels with Shively at her back, lost like Hansel and Gretel. Her hands throbbed. Her right arm clutched her gut. She cupped her mouth with her left hand, trying to quiet her dry heaves. Intense pressure burned through her bladder; she had to urinate.

Blackness settled around her, and the dream replayed itself. The dreams took on a cyclical quality, much like her arthritic flares used to at work. Back then, each four-day stretch began with mild pain. The ache got worse on the second day, and by the fourth, it stung like rusty nails twisting through every joint. The pain receded during her "off" days, and started over during the next work stretch.

Hours later, the veils of blackness parted. Alexis fluttered her eyelids and noticed she was flat out on a metal grid floor in a twelve-meter square room with slate gray walls. She had on her Kryszka tunic, but someone had removed her leg brace and weapon. The overhead light cast a pink glow on her bruised forearms and swollen hands. Awake now, Alexis dry-heaved and gripped her stomach.

"You're awake, Sleeping Beauty."

Alexis whipped her head to the left. Beside her squatted Shively, his blue eyes intent, arms folded across his chest. Shively, Mark's coldblooded killer. Shively, the fighter who led a posse to rescue her mother. Now, they were alone in a foreign laboratory. *Which Shively would surface: the killer or the gentleman?*

Alexis roused herself to a sitting position, but her elbows buckled like rubber. She flopped to the floor. Another try, another. Repeat failure.

"Dammit."

"Easy." Shively dropped onto his knees and looked down at her. "I went through the same shit. Give it some time for the drugs to wear off."

That sounded like the gentleman so far.

"How long have you been awake?"

"About two hours. I'm bigger than you and in better shape, so it wore off pretty quick."

Alexis settled back and looked around. She needed a bathroom. As her vision cleared, she made out control boards laden with flashing lights and readout dials like the kind she'd seen on airplanes. Below the dials and lights she spied a tuba-shaped device.

"Hey, help me up," she said. "I have to piss."

Shively glanced at her, red-faced and bug-eyed. "Are you fucking crazy? This dungeon doesn't have any john."

"That ..." She pointed an unsteady finger toward the tuba device, "...is a Kryszka toilet. It's got a vacuum that sucks your waste. Yeron told me how Kryszka plumbing works." She sighed, watching Shively's set, unyielding jaw. "Never mind. I'll crawl there myself."

She rolled over onto her belly. Her elbows supported her weight, but her legs flopped like cooked spaghetti. She managed, inch by inch, to drag herself to the Kryszka toilet.

"I can't believe this." Shively turned his back toward her and let out a tired moan.

Neither can I. Elbows propped against the rim, Alexis drew herself up to her knees. She gritted her teeth at the pain slicing through her arms. Too bad her levitation wouldn't work. She used her elbows instead and plunked on the seat. The vacuum let loose with a roar.

"Are you done?" Shively asked, burrowing his face in his arms.

"Yes," Alexis said in a tired voice.

"Good." With two strides, Shively was hefting her from the toilet. She pulled up her pants. He eased her to the floor and then sat cross-legged facing her. "What ideas do you have for getting us out of here?"

Alexis took in their surroundings, the flashing dials and readouts, and the paneled walls. "None that involve any mind tricks. If this place is like the one Steve described, guards are outside waiting to shoot us."

"No shit, Sherlock!" Shively's voice reeked with sarcasm. "We can't bust out of here like fools. You know Kryszka, right? Make friends with a guard and lift his radio. Send out an SOS."

"That's assuming I can figure out how to use the radio. By now, Yeron and the others realize we're missing. I'm sure they called the police. You know Steve ..."

"Quit mentioning names, shithead!" Shively shouted. "This place is probably bugged."

Alexis gazed at the ceiling. Solid slate, no sign of cameras. The Kryszka knew how to camouflage surveillance devices.

"If this place is bugged and they understand our language, they overheard your idea about the radio."

Shively heaved a ponderous sigh. "Guess you had a point there."

"Whatever." Alexis shrugged and rubbed her stomach. Already it had thickened, but not enough that people noticed. *It doesn't matter; neither the baby nor I will get out alive.* Renegades aside, she had vomited bright red blood, and lots of it. She had a nasty infection. Her heart burst with a love so intense for Yeron, and at the same time, sorrow. She was going to die without saying goodbye, and she'd be taking his child with her. *Oh, Yeron, I'm so sorry for hurting you this way.* The tears started.

"Cut the waterworks!" Shively yanked her by the shoulder. Ungodly pain speared through Alexis's arms, then she mind-shoved Shively against the slate wall. *Oh shit, I threw him against something that breaks easily!*

"You bitch!" he hollered. "You damn near busted my ribs."

"Let's get one thing straight." Alexis brushed her eyes with the back of a dirt-streaked hand and gave him a scathing glare. "Under normal circumstances, I'd never give those bastards the satisfaction of making me cry. I'm upset because I'm pregnant and sick. I hate dying without telling Yeron goodbye."

"Damn!" Shively shook his head. "Didn't you use any birth control or is that against your religion?"

"What made you so bitter, Shively?"

"I did time in prison after one of my boss Charlie's jobs went bad. It wasn't pretty."

"You want to talk about it?"

"Nope." Shively's eyes hardened, his mouth ungiving. "It's business. Just like the business at the cabin. Right?"

He's talking about Mark. She nodded, wincing. "I'm more awake ... I think. My mind trick is working, so I'm going to stand. I'm not sure how I'll do – whoever brought us here must have taken my brace – but I'll try."

Alexis rolled onto her stomach. Again, she propped herself on her elbows and pushed herself onto her knees. Elbows braced against the wall, she brought her good knee up as if she were genuflecting. *Holding steady.* The left knee came next. She got to her feet, but her legs wobbled and then buckled. Shively caught her before she plopped on her butt. He lowered her to the floor.

"Quit trying before you fucking hurt yourself. What's wrong with you?"

"I threw up a lot of blood and I'm weak." Alexis met his stare with a strange sense of serenity. "Even with the best care, I may die.

The pregnancy will cause complications, too. So do me a favor. If you get a chance, run."

"If you're looking for someone who bails, Mark was the conductor of that train." Shively's deep blue eyes focused on her face.

Thank you for that reminder.

"Kelly's about ready to have the baby if she hasn't done so already. She'll want you by her side," Alexis persisted. "Go home and tell Kelly you love her. Yeron will hate losing me; but if you run, one of us gets out alive."

OMG, Yeron. He must be going through hell. By now, the boys had reported her and Shively missing. She tried assuring herself that anyone who consumed her would get deathly sick from the infection inside her. That idea offered little comfort since that meant her child would die with her. And, she realized, Shively's baby might grow up without a father.

"You think so?" Shively spoke in a measured, patient voice. "Suppose I was the invalid and I told you to run so you could be with Yeron. Would you leave me?"

Alexis shook her head.

"I wouldn't be able to look in the mirror if I did."

"That's my point."

Alexis gazed at Shively with a new respect. A glimpse of his caring side shone through.

"Let's say we escape together. You don't know how to treat whatever's wrong with me. So I'd better say my prayers."

"Why?"

"You and I committed a crime with Mark. Don't give me that look. You pulled the trigger, but I could have stopped you the way I did when you came after me just now. Instead ..."

She gritted her teeth and locked eyes with Shively.

"I held him so you wouldn't miss." *There, I admitted it.* "Then I egged you on. Johnny's death aside, I had my reasons for wanting Mark dead, but I wish you'd used a lethal injection or finished him in the woods."

"I didn't want to risk attention from the walkers, and besides, your loverboy locked up the strong drugs. I wanted to frag Candy Boy, but we didn't bring enough grenades."

"I realize that. Mark was vicious, but not stupid. I think he figured out that you were going to use him for a sacrifice. That's why he tried to run."

"Aw, shit, did Loverboy tell you that?" Shively groaned.

"Yes." One hand went down to her stomach. No movement from the baby. Too early. "We're going to die, so it's not like I'm doing anything with the information."

"Good point. Steve's brother offered himself when they fought Eigil at the old compound. I had orders to dispose of Mark. So I thought I could force him to lure the Kryszka away from us so we could escape." Shively gave a laugh sounding like a death rattle. "Guess the joke's on me."

"The joke's on me, too." Alexis gazed at Shively with admiration. "Your methods may be tough, but you had our backs. I appreciate that. God expected better behavior from me because of my upbringing. I didn't come through and I'm going to die as punishment. I need a few moments to make my peace."

What peace? Can God forgive me, a participant in murder? The battle with the walking dead had been brutal. Johnny bought it; she and Tyrone barely squeaked through. Had Mark succeeded in stealing their weapons, he would have written everyone's death warrant. *Will God factor these circumstances into His equation when passing judgment? I'm not so sure.* According to her aunt, all killers went straight to Hell.

She prayed, commencing with the Act of Contrition, in Kryszka. *Language doesn't matter if prayer comes from the heart. If the Kryszka bugged this room, they'd see that I can speak their language.*

"Oh, my Father ..." She began in Kryszka, then paused. "Father" had to suffice since the Kryszka didn't have a word for God. "I am truly sorry for offending You," she continued. "I hate all my mistakes." No, what she meant was "sins."

"What the fuck are you rambling about now?" Shively gave her a dumb look.

"I'm trying to say the Act of Contrition in Kryszka," Alexis snapped, exasperated. "If the soldiers overhear me speaking their language, this could make things better for us."

"Praying in that gibberish is crazy."

"It doesn't sound like gibberish if you think in triangles. Watch." Bracing with her elbows, Alexis wriggled toward a panel covered with Kryszka symbols. She traced her forefinger over each symbol. "Property of Cybernetic Laboratories. Anyone caught tampering with this instrument shall be subject to discipline up to, and including, termination."

She gave Shively a smile. "Now was that so hard?"

"I still say you're crazy." Shively shook his head, but grinning now. "If you know Kryszka, how about—"

"We find a way out of here?" Alexis shimmied toward another panel, eyes on the symbols. "This one says 'Specimen Chamber.' This might be an exit, you think?"

"Go for it. I'll carry you out of here." Shively stood behind her.

Alexis focused on moving the panel. The panel swung outward, revealing a dimly lit room. Glass cubicles were built into the walls; pink miniature lights above them focused on the infants inside. They heard screeching and hissing. The life forms began to move.

Alexis froze, her heart thudding in her chest. They were not infants after all. The shape of their legs and bodies made them look like people, but they weren't quite human. The rows of needle-sharp teeth, blood-red eyes, and gargoyle faces marked them as a budding race of mutants. The creatures looked angry – angry and eager to kill.

"Jesus, help me!" she cried.

One glass cubicle shattered, and the body hopped out, onto the floor. Another cubicle exploded. Then another. Alexis batted the monsters away with her mind, but then a fourth cubicle broke.

"Get out here and close the damn door!" Shively hollered.

Alexis hovered out of the little room. She shifted her concentration to the panel. It slid shut with agonizing slowness, trapping a mutant's arm.

"Holy shit!" Shively wiped his sweat-drenched face. "That was close."

"Too close." Alexis rubbed her arms. "We'd better stick with praying. Since my prayer didn't translate well, I'll jury-rig one."

"Not again!" Shively sagged against the wall with a groan, covering his ears.

"I'll say one in English, too." She resumed her sitting position again, hands folded. "My dear Father, I am truly sorry for my part in Mark's death. Life is precious but I forgot that for an instant and I cannot fix it. Shively's mate is expecting a child and so am I. I ask You to let me and Shively live. Watch over the people searching for us. I promise, Father, to atone for my part in Mark's death." She then said the traditional prayer in English, concluded both prayers with "Amen," and looked at Shively.

"Feel better now?" he asked, this time without any trace of sarcasm.

Alexis nodded.

"You're all right. So I'll tell you a secret. If we survive and you tell anybody, I'll deny I said it. I'm scared. I keep thinking about Kelly, wondering if our kid will be healthy. I wonder if our kid will grow up in a world continually battling the living dead."

"Shively, I did the best I could. We both did." Alexis laid her hand on Shively's shoulder and rubbed it. "I'm feeling sleepy, so I'm going to lie down for a while."

Chapter Thirty: Interrogation by the Guards

Kryszka Underground Prison, August 30, 9:00 a.m.

In her dream, Alexis wandered through a corridor filled with gray smoke. She couldn't tell if there was a fire because the smoke was so thick. Yeron was calling her, not with his usual self-confidence, but terrified and in pain.

"Yeron! Where are you?"

"I'm here," he replied, his voice growing fainter with each cry.

"Yeron!" Alexis screamed herself out of a fitful sleep. "Yeron, Yeron!"

The images of the smoke faded, replaced by the stark slate walls, blinking control boards, and Shively. Only now, she and Shively had company. At her feet stood two Kryszka men, one tall and lean, the other short by Kryszka standards. Kryszka guards. They pointed plasma guns at her chest. Three others circled Shively.

"Yeron? Teodon?" she pleaded, wondering if these guards had ever met Yeron or Teodon.

She noticed a flash of recognition in the short Kryszka's eyes, and then Tall-and-Lanky shouted something that sounded like gibberish. The last vestiges of sleep kept a stronghold, making their words hard to translate.

"I said, get up!" The sleepiness evaporated. Despite the rough translation, the menace bled through the man's snarling lips and jagged teeth. "We heard you speak our language. Do not make me tell you again."

Arms wrapped around her shoulders, Alexis log-rolled to her side. The dryness in her mouth reminded her of cotton. Blood loss aside, she'd gotten dehydrated. Gathering her strength and her will to survive, she lurched to her feet. The room spun. She tried slow, deep breathing to keep from fainting.

The guards shouted at Shively, too, but he sat cross-legged, mouth gaping, assessing the situation. It took a full moment for Alexis's mind to register that Shively didn't understand one word they said.

"Stand up, Shively!" she said in English, and nudged his shoulder. "They'll kill us right here if we don't obey them."

Shively snapped to his feet.

"This way." Tall-and-Lanky waved his plasma gun toward an open wall panel.

Alexis managed several steps before the nausea assaulted her again. Another step and she pitched toward the tall soldier's back. Shively moved with panther speed and hefted her by the shoulders.

The soldier ahead of her mumbled unintelligible curses and pulled her sideways. "If you do that again, I will fry both of you with my disintegrator."

"I was not trying to harm you." Alexis prayed her watered-down version of Kryszka was understandable. "I am sick and my friend is concerned about me. I am too weak to stand without help because I have a bad infection. If you consume me, you may catch my infection and die."

Whew! That took a lot of work.

"Humans will say anything to save themselves," the sentinel jeered at her. "Walk by yourself or die."

The shorter guard – an olive-complexioned male, Alexis noted with surprise –looked over at her.

"Draekh, the female specimen appears ill," he told the taller soldier. "Allow her friend to help. We need her alive so she can answer our questions."

Questions? What happens if my answers displease them?

"What questions?" The tall, lanky guard gave Mr. Olive Skin an *are-you-crazy* snarl. "Why should I listen to half-breeds like you?"

Half-breed? That explains his coloring.

"Because you have the stupidity of a desert *settva*," the short guard said in a sardonic voice. "Everyone knows it, too."

That sounds like something Johnny might say to Mark. Sobs escaped Alexis's throat. *Oh, Johnny, I hope you're watching over us.*

"Fuck you." The tall guard's lips twisted into a convulsive snarl.

"No, you are fucked if you shoot these prisoners." Alexis lost the translation on the next sentence until he got to "... Quyeba's orders. The female knows our language and will be able to answer our questions."

"Silence, Zoltar!" the tall guard shouted. "Transport her yourself if she needs help."

A breeze surrounded Alexis, and then she was floating, face toward the ceiling, in front of the olive-skinned sentinel. One guard led the way. The other guards moved ahead of them, plasma guns pressed into Shively's back. Shively's face hardened like granite, the way the Kryszka soldiers' did. She tried for a hard stare, but any resolve she mustered dropped off her face when she imagined the medical experiments the soldiers planned for her. Worse, in addition to Yeron, she was leaving her mother without saying goodbye. That part cut to her soul. She rubbed her stomach, longing to hug her child.

They passed through a winding hallway to an auditorium filled with Kryszka men and women, dressed in their regulation blues. The overhead lights cast their glow against the off-white slate walls, bloodstains on most of the soldiers' lips, and names imprinted on each soldier's tunic. White lettering identified the half-breed as "Zoltar" and the yellow gave the tall guard's name as "Draekh." A woman with braids stood head down on a dais facing Alexis. The gemstones sewn into her tunic formed the word "Quyeba." *She must be the leader ... but she looks frightened.*

Two soldiers stationed her and Shively side by side, fastening them to their seats with wire mesh bands. The wires cut into Alexis's wrists, and, despite her best effort at stoicism, hoarse cries escaped her lips. *No one's going to help me because Draekh's taken charge. This is probably just a taste of what's coming. Real torture. The good guys among them probably fear for their own lives.* More tears flooded her eyes.

Zoltar settled to Quyeba's right; the remaining soldiers and Draekh stood to her left, closer to Alexis. Quyeba said something to her entourage and then took her seat, eyes shifting between Alexis and Shively.

Draekh gave Alexis a cold, calculating look.

"We brought you here for questioning. Lie, and you shall die."

"What the fuck did he say to you?" Shively asked under his breath.

"If they catch us lying, they'll kill us," Alexis told him.

"They will, anyway. Tell them I'll answer their questions because I set up the mission."

Alexis grimaced and gagged on the acrid odor permeating the room. She willed herself to ignore the unpleasant sensations and concentrate. The difference between the right and almost-right translation would be a slow, painful death.

"My friend wants to answer your questions because he organized the mission."

"Meaning, he is your leader." Draekh's thin lips curled into a smirk. "He shall answer. You shall translate."

Draekh sat in his chair, eyes focused on Shively, his body arched slightly forward.

"You searched these woods and found our compound." He added something Alexis didn't get.

This is awful, Alexis thought, shivering. *Draekh is such a bastard, he'll probably store anything I don't understand in his internal file to use against us later.*

"How many were with you?" Draekh continued. "Who sent you here?"

Alexis translated the last question, then tilted her head toward Draekh.

"You said something else that I did not understand. What was it?"

"Where did you get your weapons?"

"We purchased the weapons ourselves," Shively said. Alexis translated as best she could, considering that the Kryszka didn't barter, write checks, or use paper currency. They used a microchip that recorded income and expenses. Beyond that, Yeron hadn't explained the Kryszka's monetary system.

"Your troops slaughtered our relatives and friends," Shively went on, "and unleashed an army of zombies on our town. We came here to defend ourselves."

Oh, shit, that's too much.

"Your soldiers attacked *us*," Alexis said, attempting an abridged translation. "They killed our family members. We were defending ourselves."

"It sounds like you left out something," Shively observed.

Alexis shrugged. "I don't know how to say 'zombie' in Kryszka, and besides, they won't believe that."

"Then you'd better figure it out."

Alexis opened her mouth to reply. The wire mesh bands buzzed around her wrists. Sparks shot from the band. Tingling and numbness followed by searing agony flared through her arms and hands. Her muscles spasmed, causing her hands to splay while the cords burned into her skin. Shively jittered in the chair beside her.

"Tell your comrade the private plotting must cease," Draekh warned her. "Next time, you will get a stronger shock. Do you understand?"

"Yes," Alexis managed, tears rolling down her cheeks. "Shively, they don't want us talking amongst ourselves. They think we're plotting against them."

Shively grimaced. "That's bullshit. We're their prisoners, so they'll do what they damn well please."

"Draekh, stop this," Quyeba ordered him. "I will not allow violence or torture of prisoners. A subtle approach will get cooperation, and besides, the woman looks ill. I want her able to answer questions."

"These humans will not understand subtle."

With a snarl, Draekh shifted his attention toward Alexis.

"Your friend appears annoyed. Why?"

"I omitted some information because I do not know the Kryszka words for it."

"Find a way to give me that information. *Now*."

Alexis blinked back tears. No matter how she answered, death was imminent. *Oh, Yeron, I'm so sorry.*

"Someone from your compound kidnapped humans, tortured them, and gave them large amounts of vischlausk. This caused severe um, severe brain damage..."

"We know how vischlausk affects the human brain," Zoltar supplied. "What happened to the humans afterwards?"

"These people became monsters that caught and ... ate other humans. Your soldiers sent these creatures to invade our ..." Alexis hesitated. "...Um, clinic."

Nope. Draekh's angry glare warned that her answer wasn't coming out right.

"They invaded the places where our sick go for help," she shouted, hoping she'd found appropriate words.

She held her breath, waiting for a reply.

Draekh watched their body language but said nothing. In the next instant, he lunged at Shively. Quyeba rushed from her podium and shot Draekh with the blue, sedating ray. Not fast enough. Flames spewed from Draekh's gun, igniting Shively's clothes. His bloodcurdling howls broke the silence. By the time Quyeba's sedating ray took effect on Draekh, yellow sparks engulfed Shively the way the fire from Alexis's gun had fried the walkers. A soldier grabbed a tank—Alexis presumed it was a fire extinguisher—to put out the fire. The air filled with the stench of burning skin and chemical foam.

Alexis sat, lips tremulous, eyes on Draekh, tempted to tackle him with her mind ... and then he pitched to the floor, still conscious. She lowered her eyes toward her gut. She had the baby to consider before making any aggressive moves.

Her eyes turned toward Shively, her breath choking with sobs.

Shively lay slumped in his chair, a limp form, his skin burned charcoal. His dark green overalls were charred. Alexis sat, grimacing at the churning in her gut, her mind trying to grasp the horror of it all.

"Why did you do that?" she asked Draekh, trying for an understandable voice. "I answered your questions."

Draekh moved his hand slightly, as if to reach for his gun, and then smiled. "Because he has good meat," he said in broken English.

The hairs on the back of Alexis's neck stood on end. She opened her mouth to scream, to plead for mercy, but her tightening throat afforded only faint croaks.

"What ... meat?" Quyeba tossed her braids, giving Draekh a censuring glare. "Did you not hear me when I said no violence or torture? We are not barbarians. Your action cost me a valuable informant."

"Beg your pardon, Governor, but I do not listen to any human woman," Draekh told her. "The prisoner lied. No one poisoned by vischlausk has the capability of targeting or infiltrating even primitive security."

"Those creatures had robotic implants," Alexis looked Draekh in the eye. "I was with Shively when your renegade soldiers tried to shoot us."

"Silence!" Draekh shouted. His head swiveled toward the governor. "The prisoners were giving each other signals and plotting in their native language. It is too late to save the man. If he is not dead, he soon will be. Besides, I was getting –"

"Your dinner can wait." Quyeba gave him another scathing look, eyes flashing with anger, then turned toward Alexis. Something flickered in her eyes, but Alexis couldn't tell what. "Tell me your name and how the implants affect the creatures."

Alexis swallowed hard, fighting the urge to upchuck. She retched. When had she last eaten? She couldn't recall.

"My name is Alexis. The implants enabled them to maneuver and shoot. Your soldiers brought these creatures to our cities and ... and ..." She swallowed hard. "...and released them ..."

Another gulp. The stench of cooked flesh was aggravating her nausea. She longed to describe the creatures' sore-crusted skin and foul odor and the grisly way they killed, but she couldn't figure out how to translate these details to Kryszka.

"Who gave you our uniform?" the governor asked in a softer voice. "Did this person provide the weapons, too?"

"Yes." Alexis's voice squeaked. Whatever rumbled in her gut was about to come up any second. "If you are Governor Quyeba, you and this man know each other well. His name is ..."

Yeron, but the bloody vomit jetting from her mouth silenced her. It sheeted down her tunic and splashed on the ground in a crimson rain. Droplets of it blessed Shively and Draekh.

"I am sorry, I must ..." Another fountain of blood-bright puke sprayed from her mouth. *A fountain?* She didn't know she had so much blood to spare. The grayness was closing in; black dots rose before her eyes.

Somewhere through the haze, Quyeba shouted at the halfbreed, "Zoltar, we cannot lose another informant, especially someone who knows our language. Save her."

Sorry, Governor, you don't get a say. Alexis tried to make out the blurry shapes. *Dear God, forgive me for Mark's death. And please look out for Yeron!*

Chapter Thirty-One: Emergency Surgery

Kryszka Colony below Grays Landing, August 30, 11:00 a.m.

Governor Quyeba watched the woman vomit, spraying the other prisoner and Draekh. The grid floor was no longer gray and shiny but crimson with blood from Alexis and her companion. Draekh had gotten out of control. Shooting the humans wasn't in her plan. The prisoners acted fearful, but Quyeba did not detect any hostile signals. Alexis indicated recognition of her name and was answering a question before she lost blood and consciousness.

Zoltar released Alexis's ties. The soldier by Draekh raised his gun at Zoltar. In an instant, Quyeba used her mind to force him to release it, and another split second to shoot the soldier with sedative-laced plasma.

His weapon dropped. The soldier sprawled on the floor next to Draekh. Draekh glared with indignant eyes at Quyeba.

Quyeba met his glare without flinching.

"You had no right."

"Do not give me or my fellow soldiers orders, woman," Draekh shouted. "This prisoner killed our own ... my close friends, so she should die. As for your boy, he ... he humiliated me."

"Maybe because you deserved it." Quyeba stepped around the prisoner, allowing Zoltar room to work, but close enough to inspect the woman's bloated hands. "As a healer, Draekh, you must appreciate the deformities in her hands. She cannot fight."

Draekh worked his lips, forming words, faint but audible to Quyeba's ears.

"Fucking half-breed."

"What did you say?"

Silence. Draekh didn't move; the sedative had immobilized him. She fingered the male prisoner's throat for a pulse. There was none. Her eyes settled on Draekh again.

"I know what you said." Quyeba cast a sideways glance toward Zoltar. Alexis was floating in front of him. He was levitating her toward his operating room. She turned back toward Draekh again. "The woman may be a warrior, but she cannot fight anyone if she is as sick as she appears. Whatever she did, she knows Kryszka well enough to answer our questions. I want her alive and comfortable enough to cooperate. Is that understood?"

Draekh regarded Quyeba with a crooked, malignant grin that reminded her of Eigil.

"When I give orders, I expect obedience." She followed his gaze toward the male. "An android will take the man to the crematorium. I am horrified at your behavior."

Quyeba watched him for an instant. She wanted to execute him, but that would leave her with only two healers. Besides, Draekh might have information about Woehar's secret laboratory and experiments, for they had worked together and taken their meals at the same times. Ever since the cold season, when Quyeba had expelled Woehar, Draekh avoided meetings and gave vague answers to her questions. His behavior had gone too far; but now, her potential informant needed medical attention. Could Zoltar save her? How much care would she need? Quyeba proceeded to the laboratory. In the anteroom, she perched before a window facing the suite where Zoltar worked.

****

In the suite, androids deposited a host of blood samples into high-performance liquid chromatography. Zoltar looked toward the window and spoke into his intercom.

"Our specimen has severe erosion in her abdomen, which caused internal bleeding. I identified a fungus in her blood and a half-breed male fetus. She will continue to bleed unless I repair the perforation."

Quyeba eyeballed the monitors surrounding the woman and suppressed a sigh. Here was her potential source of information, someone cooperative, and the slightest error would send her into oblivion.

"Then do it," she told him. "What about the fungus?"

"I have seen it in the putrescent muscle of dead humans and animals, but not on a live person. I have no antidote for it. Furthermore, she is about to expel the fetus."

"If the fetus can be saved, place it into an incubator. We may need it for a bargaining tool." After another look at the machinery, Quyeba's frown deepened when she saw the squiggly lines on the heart monitor. She knew from her experience as a healer that such erratic heartbeats meant death was imminent. If the woman died, her information would go with her. "She looks fragile, so I suggest you develop an antidote."

"The androids can concoct a formula. I must repair the perforation."

"I do not care how she gets the antidote." Quyeba sighed.

Zoltar made an incision at the base of the abdomen, clamping off the vessels. "This is going to be difficult. Why are we trying so hard to save her?"

Zoltar's question bumped Quyeba back to the day she found the human specimens in Woehar's laboratory. They were dead but somehow not dead. In her mind's eye, she stood before the table inspecting one, grimacing when its hands clamped around her wrists. It took all her concentration to free herself. From what Alexis said, Woehar had found a way to manufacture more of those creatures despite her expulsion from the colony.

Did Woehar infiltrate her compound? Was she implanting microchips to make the dead walk? Who was helping her? She longed to question Draekh or discuss this with Zoltar, but the stranger's arrhythmia warned her that distracting him could prove fatal.

"I do not need to explain myself." She mustered authority to conceal the fear brewing in her stomach. "As I told Draekh, when I give an order you will obey."

"I am not asking you as your assistant. I am asking as your son," Zoltar pleaded. "Has Woehar contacted you, Mother?"

Quyeba lowered her eyes. She could not lie to Zoltar. Despite her gruff voice, the tremor in it betrayed her. She loved him as if he were her biological son.

"No, but I believe Woehar has continued her sordid experiments at another laboratory. I believe our captive is telling the truth."

****

The abdominal repair went without complication. With the help of Zoltar's androids, he aspirated the fetus and placed it into a machine that simulated the environment of a uterus. Later on, Zoltar or his assistant could determine paternity and correct any irregularities in its chromosomes ... or not.

Did the female know about the baby? Did she plan to keep the baby or abort it? Did her plans matter? Of course, Alexis would lie to protect her friends. Quyeba expected it, but persuasion would get the truth. This capture had gone wrong, especially the male's execution. Draekh had a vicious temper. His hostility had worsened after Woehar's expulsion from the compound. Alexis did not fit the profile of a hardened killer.

These notions circled in Quyeba's head the way the soldiers had circled her prone body before they destroyed her beloved mate, Lyrus. Zoltar continued to probe and cut, and call out orders to his androids. The heartbeat remained erratic, and all at once, powerlessness weighed on Quyeba's shoulders. Despite her best technology, it appeared Zoltar would not be able to stabilize the human's heart.

After a while, Zoltar stepped into the anteroom where Quyeba sat.

"I repaired the perforation and salvaged the fetus without complications," he told her. "The androids found an antidote for the fungus, but it is only effective on Kryszka or half-breeds."

Quyeba grimaced.

"Find another," she ordered.

Zoltar bowed his head, his lips quivering.

"I doubt if I can find something soon enough. Someone gave Alexis a chemical that compromised her immune system. Any formula I administer may exacerbate her problems." He paused, regarding Quyeba. "Maybe there is a way."

Quyeba folded her fingers into a steeple position, lips pursed. "Go on."

"Before we left our other compound, Teodon spliced Kryszka and human chromosomes in the human prisoners to cure their diseases. It worked because our cells are immune to most of their bacteria."

"I remember that," Quyeba said through clenched teeth.

"If we splice Kryszka DNA into this human's chromosomes, she will acquire some of our traits and become receptive to my antidote."

"Kryszka chromosomes?" Quyeba stood, her red eyes blazing, nostrils flaring. She was willing to use all the technology at their disposal to treat the infection and make the woman comfortable enough to answer questions. *But fusing genes? That makes me uncomfortable.* Yet the fact remained, the fusion could save her life. Alexis could not provide information if she died. "If I agree, where will you get a blood sample?"

"Woehar would be a good candidate ... if we know where to find her. She was studying human specimens. Or Draekh – it would be a fitting punishment for killing the male human."

"No!" Quyeba shouted. She recalled the deplorable condition in which she found Woehar's prisoners—their purulent gashes and decay wafting from them. "Do me a favor," she continued, her voice softening. "Do not involve Woehar or Draekh."

"I doubt anyone will volunteer a blood sample."

Quyeba imagined Alexis among the other emaciated humans she'd seen in Woehar's laboratory. Or Draekh contaminating the blood sample before Zoltar could use it on Alexis. She longed to explain that death was preferable to such ghastly outcomes. But her eyes caught sight of a black disk on the ceiling, a surveillance device that recorded conversation. Having overheard hushed conversations between Draekh and some of her troops, she suspected that they had sided with Woehar. They might pass along any information that she could use against her and Zoltar.

"No blood samples from Woehar or Draekh are viable," she told him.

"Of course, they are, because they are healthy people. Besides ..." His voice faltered. "Most people trust our soldiers; they will not sympathize with Alexis, let alone donate cells." His face brightened. "Unless, *you* are offering."

Quyeba's eyes widened in dismay at her son's suggestion. As badly as Quyeba wanted her alive, she was not ready to chance a radical procedure. Given Alexis's mental powers, there was no predicting how the fusion might affect her, let alone whether it would invite her cooperation.

"I need to think about this. While I do, find out the paternity and viability of the fetus."

"Consider it done. But Mother ..." Zoltar gave her a somber look. "If you want this woman alive, make your decision quickly. Her condition is critical."

"I am well aware of that."

Zoltar returned to his laboratory and then continued through another exit to the incubation chamber. Three androids hovered around Alexis, watching her vital signs and blood measurements, and adjusting fluids as needed. Quyeba remained in the anteroom, eyes on the heart rhythm monitor. Fast and unsteady with premature ventricular contractions, it whispered a rumor of incipient death. Bending over with her back toward the camera, Quyeba withdrew a portable surveillance device to inspect the compound entrance. Several humans stood talking with a Kryszka male in the outer chamber, but the outlines of his face blurred, making recognition impossible. She pocketed the camera when light footsteps sounded behind her.

It was Zoltar.

"Mother," he said in an excited, yet puzzled voice. "Yeron must be alive; I found residue of his semen in her vagina. So I tested the fetus to determine paternity and he, is in fact the father. That does not make sense. Woehar told us he died in the explosion, but the DNA matches the ones on our records for Yeron."

"That is not possible. Woehar barely escaped with her life."

"I repeated the test twice," Zoltar told her. "I had to because the irregularities in the child's chromosomes would have caused life-threatening birth defects. I corrected most of the chromosomes, enough to avert major complications, but ... Yeron is the father."

"If you are right, this presents further complications." Cold rushed through Quyeba, filling her bones with crushed crystals. Had Woehar lied about Yeron's death? "We must save the child. Who raises it is another matter."

She ran her hands through her hair, losing her bid to maintain a calm demeanor.

"If I donate, how much blood will you need?"

"Three vials."

"I will do it. After Alexis wakes, question her about Yeron and her comrades; ask why she killed our soldiers, and about these creatures with the vischlausk poisoning."

"Mother, she may refuse to answer any questions. After all, she saw one of us shoot her friend."

"There are subtle ways to get someone to talk, son. Use them." She draped her hand across Zoltar's shoulder. "Let us go."

As the panel to the laboratory slid open, Alexis's heart monitor blasted a shrill alarm. The line on it went flat.

Chapter Thirty-Two: Search for Alexis and Shively Continues

Kryszka Underground Laboratory, August 30, 10:00 a.m.

Yeron moved each computer with his mind and prodded around them. He tapped the walls and listened for hollow sounds. Although the Kryszka entrances were not visible, their panels rang hollow, while solid walls gave off dull thumps. Anyone caught knocking on the panels would be recognized as an intruder, but Yeron cared more about finding Alexis and Shively. His rapping knuckles gave off flat thuds. Steve and Tyrone banged the walls with the same results. One more piece of machinery. Yeron moved it aside, this time revealing a small entryway that led into another room. He let out a deep sigh. *Progress at last.*

Hazlett opened his suitcases, pulling out four pressurized suits, with matching helmets, facemasks, and portable tanks. Another suitcase yielded crowbars and other tools. After donning the suits and other gear, the team made its way through the narrow aperture.

Fifteen minutes passed. Speedy circled the area, sniffing the floor, and barked. Still no sign of an entrance.

"Damn!" Tyrone's solemn face glimmered with sweat. "Right now, Speedy's sniffing all over the room. Too bad he can't talk."

"Good point," Steve said. "We'd better stay close together."

Yeron knew Earth animals could sense danger miles away, sometimes even more so than his native people could. Humans, a higher form of animal than dogs, went by gut instinct too; instinct had served Alexis well during battles. Instinct, plus her intellect, had enabled her to survive thus far. To his surprise, she watched him and learned how to retrieve data from secure servers. *I hope her instinct and intellect will be enough to enable her to survive in a Kryszka prison.*

"Yeron, I found something here." Steve slid on his knees.

Yeron tapped the wall in front of Steve and heard an echo. The sound covered an area large enough to accommodate crawling room. It had to be a panel. He concentrated on sliding it sideways, giving way to an opening to a titanium pipe; blackness beyond. These pipes served as ventilation ducts and waterways. He'd once seen a movie about inter- stellar beings running poisonous gases and deadly bacteria through them. *Stop that. This is real life, not one of Alexis's horror films.*

All the same, he tightened his headgear and made sure that his tank was in place. He reached for one of the crowbars. So did Ty- rone and Steve.

"Wait." Yeron held up his hand. "I will go alone. You and Ty- rone have children."

"Yeah ... well, Alexis is pregnant with your child, so you need help." Steve gave him a questioning look. "Besides, Shively and Alexis might need medical care."

"They covered my back more than once," Tyrone told him. "It's my turn to help them."

Hazlett stood by the panel, watching his dog, and frowned.

"Let's not spend hours fighting over who goes. Just make sure your walkie-talkies work so you can contact me."

"Mine works." Steve patted his side. "Alexis might—will need medical attention, so I'm coming with you."

"We may need backup." Tyrone snatched a glance at his radio. "If we run into any trouble, we'll call you, Officer."

"Sounds good," Hazlett said. "If, *when*, you find Alexis and Shively, call me right away."

"We will." Yeron averted his gaze, not caring to remind them that the electrical fields in the compound prohibited calls with Earth devices, including walkie-talkies.

He waited while Steve checked his walkie-talkie. After he fin- ished, he spun around and flashed a grin.

"All set."

"Good." Yeron proceeded to the opening and then turned to- ward Steve and Tyrone. "I shall go in first. Secure your gas masks."

Movie or not, the premise of poison gas was too realistic for his liking. The renegades might have installed a failsafe lock to trap poten- tial intruders, but he was in no mood to dwell on possibilities. His cumbersome suit caused him to waddle. Unlike Kryszka suits, the Earth suits had eleven layers of materials. *But they do protect astro- nauts from the elements of space; surely they could shield me from noxious gases.* With the headgear in place, he could not detect any smells.

"Yeron, you know how your society thinks," Steve said. "Use that to your advantage."

After opening the panel with his mind, Yeron crawled inside. Steve went in behind him and Tyrone was in the rear. When Yeron shut the panel, a reddish haze descended upon them, obscuring their surroundings. Yeron recognized the gas by its color and particulates. This poisonous gas worked like cyanide, preventing the body from utilizing oxygen, and it could kill within minutes. No sign of weakness or breathlessness troubled Yeron, but the sight of this gas kicked his heart into high gear.

"Steve? Tyrone?" He craned his head sideways. "Are you all right?"

"I'm okay." Steve gave him a thumbs-up. "How about you, Tyrone?"

"I'm all right," Tyrone told him. "Whatever you do, don't make any fast moves."

"I'll try not to." Steve smiled.

Further ahead, the passage ceiling raised enough to allow walking room in single file. Yeron increased his helmet light watts, but the red haze blurred most of his view. He tapped the walls on either side, listening for echoes, and toe-tapped the floor for potential landmines. The Kryszka piping system made the human version look like a child's drawing. Installing a hidden landmine was easy. He froze when something clattered behind him.

"Shit," Steve said. "My flashlight came loose."

"Your flashlight won't do you any good," Tyrone said. "Not with all this smoke."

"No kidding," Steve shot a glance over his shoulder. "Yeron, can't you do anything about the haze?"

"I can manipulate doors and invent cures for rare diseases." Yeron sighed. "I have no magic for dissipating poisonous gas."

"So far, the suits are protecting us," Tyrone pointed out.

"They're also adding extra weight. I'm hoping the gas dissipates so I can shed mine," Steve said. "I've got a backpack loaded with IV medications and equipment if ... I mean when we find them."

I know he meant "if." He does not expect to find survivors. Yeron tried to tell himself Alexis was not alone, that Shively knew how to administer first aid. Temperamental as his behavior had been, Shively came through for Alexis when her mother needed rescuing. Since Alexis knew the language, a dignitary might be willing to listen to the truth.

Yes, and as the humans say, tooth fairies exist. Alexis and Shively slaughtered Kryszka soldiers and the Kryszka army protected its own.

They came to a fork. The openings glared through the thinning smoke like the eye pits in a skull. The narrowing passageway forced them to scrunch down again and crawl. Yeron was glad that Hazlett and the dog had remained behind, as these passages would not accommodate his girth or a temperamental animal. The poverty of space underground forced Kryszka to build narrow chambers and pipelines.

Thump, thump, thump. Yeron continued to hit his crowbar against the walls. Sometimes he used levitation, lest a minefield react to hand movement. The muted sounds told him that rocks and dirt surrounded that space in the tunnel. Then, the distant sound of running water, flowing. He did not want to go right, toward the sound, for running water might lead to a reservoir tank, and all the hardware they carried would make swimming impossible.

"I don't like this," Steve said behind him. "Come on, Yeron, talk to me. Which way are we going?"

Yeron's lips set in a grim line. "Let us go through the left fork."

They curved to the left and moved down a straight path. The smoke dissipated, but Yeron dared not remove his mask. He hoped his oxygen would last a long time because most poisonous gases were colorless and odorless. At his former compound, the canisters provided enough liquid oxygen to get workers through an earth-day mission. He would be lucky to realize ten hours on Earth devices.

Moments later, his crowbar elicited an empty sound and his light outlined a plate of stone. Heart thudding, he cracked the entrance. With the men behind him, he crawled through another dark passageway, and then through an opening into a laboratory. Through the dim pinkish lights, he made out glass containers built into the walls. The life forms inside them mewled and howled.

To Yeron, these life forms resembled late-stage fetuses. The shape of their legs and bodies appeared human, but the rows of pointed teeth, yellow eyes, and gargoyle faces were the traits of the *settva*. Someone must have fused the genes of a human with a *settva*. These beings looked ravenous.

"Oh, Lord!" Tyrone hollered.

"Yikes!" Steve cried. "This is worse than Doctor Moreau."

Yes, because these monsters are real and the mad scientist has Alexis. A lead weight of despair settled onto Yeron's shoulders. Part of him hoped he would find Alexis dead for her sake.

"I'm calling Hazlett for reinforcements," Steve said at last.

Your radios will not work down here, Yeron thought sadly, but he remained silent as Steve tried to get Hazlett on his walkie-talkie.

"Can't raise him," Steve said frowning. "We're too far away. We'll lose a lot of time going back for help."

"The hell with it, then," Tyrone said. "Let's keep moving."

Yeron proceeded past the glass cubicles, trying hard not to

look at the creatures in them. His headlight lit up another panel. He reached for his weapon.

Yeron furrowed his brow, concentrating on opening the panel, when the tinkling of glass shards jarred him to attention. He whipped around, as did his teammates. The glass on one of the cubicles splintered. Its inhabitant jumped onto the floor, flopping on its belly, teeth gnashing. Steve fired, and then five more panes shattered. The infant half-breeds hopped on arms and legs toward Yeron and the two humans. Their glittering eyes and gnashing teeth demonstrated intense thirst and hunger.

What they thirsted for did not come in a bottle.

Chapter Thirty-Three: DNA Fusion

A chasm opened before Alexis in the ground, revealing crushed velvet chairs below her and blinking rainbow lights. The colors reminded her of Disney World, right down to the background music, the floral patterns on the walls, and Disney characters carrying glittery balloons.

Tendrils of pink vapor wafted from her under her feet and slid up her legs. The blanket of vapor underneath her was pellucid, enough for her to make out people ... including herself, she noted with surprise, lying on a metal table. Figures in helmets and pressurized suits huddled around her image, obscuring her body, but there was no mistaking her gaunt cheeks and curly hair. They probed her with pointy instruments and tubes. A multicolored waterfall beckoned, drawing her attention away from the table. Sapphires, rubies, and other precious metals dropped into the liquid and became part of the stream.

Pain forgotten, she wanted to run toward the waterfall. *Run?* She couldn't even walk.

"Oh, my God, this is beautiful," she cried with glee. "So beautiful!"

At the waterfall, she collided with Johnny. Alexis recognized the twinkle in his blue eyes. His cuts and gashes were gone.

"Alexis!" Johnny clapped her on the shoulder. "What are you doing here?"

"I missed you." Alexis straightened up and took in the sights. "Things went to hell fast. I got captured by the enemy, got sick, and ... and here I am."

"That sucks," Johnny nodded with commiseration. "Why didn't you stick with Sweetie? He looked out for you."

"I should have." Alexis looked down at her misshapen hands and flexed her fingers. Not a flicker of stinging or throbbing touched her. "Do they have movies and homemade ravioli here?"

"This place has everything," Johnny said. "Even rose gardens."

"*Rose* ... wait!" Alexis's eyes filled with tears. "They won't let me stay. I committed a terrible sin."

"Sin?" Johnny rolled his eyes. "Whatever you've done, it can't be that bad."

"Oh, yes, it was." Alexis lowered her eyes. Johnny was a former coworker and a good friend, someone who deserved the truth. "Meathead bailed and tried to steal our weapons."

Johnny sighed.

"It figures. That guy was a waste of flesh."

Alexis shivered. "Shively was furious ... and so was I. In the heat of the moment, I helped him kill Mark. Is Mark here with you?"

"No, he isn't." Johnny narrowed his eyes. "This is getting deep. Do the police know?"

"Johnny, she can't stay." A male voice of authority rumbled from below her.

"Alexis said she's sorry," Johnny said.

"Alexis has to forgive herself." A tall Kryszka soldier stepped from the shadows. Alexis recognized him from the fight at Trident Mall. He was Teodon, Yeron's dead father.

Teodon stood before Alexis and heaved a deep sigh.

"Yeron warned you not to engage people like Mark. You had to find out the hard way."

"Mark tried to steal our weapons."

"I know. I have watched over you and Yeron since the invasions began."

"Yeron taught me to love life and to fight so I could live. Mark made me so angry; I forgot the sanctity of life. I wish I could undo what happened."

"Done deals cannot be undone." Teodon's voice softened, conceding a reprieve. "You acted out of grief and pain."

"Grief does awful things to people. My mother's going to be heartbroken when she learns of my death."

"She would be ... but it is not your time."

"How can you be so sure? My immune system is shot and no one knows how to fix it. I'm pregnant; and if I die, my baby will go with me."

"That is true, but the healers are trying to save you." Teodon looked down at her. "My son cured the arthritis in your heart. You love him, do you not?"

"I love him." Alexis burst into tears. "My mother must be livid about the baby."

"Your mother may come around. In the meantime, do what you must to survive. You can; you are stronger than you realize, Alexis." Teodon smiled. "Your captors are as frightened as you. That does not make all of them bad."

"Watch out for Crazy Laurel," Johnny told her.

"Tell me about it," Alexis whined.

"Woehar is more dangerous." Teodon rested his hand on Alexis's shoulder, his way of saying goodbye. "That is why you must answer their questions. Make peace with your illness and get on with your life."

"Teodon," Alexis protested, but he faded like a smudge wiped with bleach. So did Johnny. The lights remained ... and then vanished in the smoke.

****

Alexis opened her eyes and found herself restrained. Lights twinkled around her ... no longer the Disney World kind, but like the ones in the room where she had first met the guards. Cables secured her to a table and an IV ... did the Kryszka use IVs? They must, because this one was feeding red liquid into a catheter sutured into her left shoulder. A smaller bag with what looked like saline was piggybacked into the catheter. An IV pump lit up, displaying her vital signs on its front panel, including oxygen saturation at 95 percent. Ninety-five percent? Had Yeron taught her medical terminology in Kryszka? Wires draped across her chest led to a heart monitor. At least it looked like a monitor, but this one gave out electrolyte readings, too.

As she craned her neck to read her electrolytes, sharp jabbing burned through her gut. "Ow!" she cried. "My stomach! That's where the baby—"

Baby. What happened to my baby? Despite the restraints, Alexis managed to raise her head enough to get a gander at her stomach. A sheet covered her body, and underneath, material like a girdle wrapped around her abdomen. Her stomach appeared flat.

A scream lodged in her throat. Her heart raced. *What the hell happened to my baby?*

Another monitor caught her attention. This one measured her urine output, blood cell count, and cranial pressure. Machinery whirred behind her with a slow, steady hum, and ... why would she need a cranial monitor?

The infection, or whatever she came to this prison with, had spread to her brain. The olive-complexioned doctor said she could be useful. *He's plying me with experimental drugs before killing me.* Or maybe ... and this idea had a much more positive spin to it – Yeron had found her and brokered a treatment plan with a doctor.

"Yeron," she croaked. "I'm awake."

Silence, except for the humming of the computers.

"Yeron, where are you?"

An olive-complexioned man emerged through a sliding panel. It was Zoltar, the guard who carried her to the interrogation room. *Maybe he's a doctor, too?* According to Yeron, some Kryszka had double careers.

I should apply for a job here. That will go over well.

You are more valuable to them alive, Teodon said. Alexis sensed that she'd had another out-of-body experience, like the one she'd had when her heart stopped beating during surgery at Jackson Hospital. Zoltar brought her back from the dead, no doubt using the best technology at his disposal.

She tried to sit up until the bubble-type wrap bands chafed her arms.

"Hello." She tried to smile and gave it her best try in Kryszka. "Will you tell Yeron I am awake? Please?"

"Yeron is not here," Zoltar told her.

"Yeron is looking for me," Alexis said. "He told me about you, Zoltar. That is your name, right?"

"Yes, but no one named Yeron lives here," the guard said in a leaden voice. "The microchip worked. You speak Kryszka fluently."

"Thank you ... wait ... what microchip?" The memories came back – Shively's death, the harsh interrogation, and the threats. If Yeron wasn't involved, why was she alive? She longed to ask this stranger, but decided to pretend she knew.

"The one in your brain that will allow you to understand and translate our language. We did this because we need information. Distorting the language will cause inaccuracies in your statements, and you cannot answer at all if you are dead." Zoltar nodded, as if approving the results of his work. "Can you tell me where you are?"

Here we go with the alertness and orientation tests.

"I am in a Kryszka laboratory. Quyeba is your leader. One of your soldiers questioned me and shot my teammate. I vomited blood and lost consciousness and I'm talking now, so I presume you stopped the bleeding."

"Yes, among other measures." The Kryszka doctor paced around her table, eyes on the monitors. As he did so, his left hand rubbed his right, forming a steeple position. "Your heart stopped beating, but I revived you. Your body is septic. Since my medicines are compatible with Kryszka beings, but not humans, I introduced our DNA into your chromosomes."

Chapter Thirty-Four: Alexis Befriends a Guard

He means organ transplant. Despite the stark surroundings and a grim expression on the doctor's angular features, curiosity gnawed at Alexis.

"Which organ?"

"You have a soft tissue infection, the kind found in cadavers, and transplanting an individual organ would not help. So I spliced our DNA into your chromosomes, and I can only do that with white cells." Zoltar added something about blood and chromosomes that Alexis didn't understand, and then continued. "The antidote I had is effective on infected Kryszka, but not humans. My gene fusion was a success. Our medicine is fighting the bacteria that caused your sickness. As time passes, you will acquire some of our traits. Without our chromosomes, the disease would have killed you."

Kryszka chromosomes? My God, he turned me into a ... mutant. Alexis gaped at the monitors and the healer. "Healer" was a Kryszka catchall term for doctors and other medical staff. She told herself she was at the cabin having the granddaddy of nightmares.

The IV drips, machinery, and distaste of fear in her mouth left a bitter dose of reality.

"This cannot be real," she said in a low voice.

"Of course, it is real," Zoltar said without emotion. "DNA splicing between species has been done with success. I did it to save your life."

"But ... but my ..." *religion,* Alexis wanted to say, but Kryszka didn't acknowledge formal religion. Some might believe in spirits or a Higher Power, but the Ten Commandments belonged in a different part of the galaxy. Her voice rose and fell as she plunged ahead. "With plant life, you can splice DNA, but you cannot ... you are not supposed to alter a human being's genetic traits."

Zoltar gave her a puzzled look. "We can with the proper technology. Your eyes are changing. Eye color changes right away. If you do not believe me, here is a mirror." He smiled. "That is right, Alexis. We use basic tools like mirrors."

He retrieved a mirror from his cabinet; an ordinary one with a plastic handle. She looked at her reflection. No changes in skin pigment. Teeth okay, but her eyes looked bloodshot.

"Oh, Jesus!" she cried, and the tears came. Then she remembered that no one here understood English. "What have you done to me? I look like a ... a ..."

"I did the procedure in a controlled environment." Zoltar remained calm. *Just the facts, Ma'am.* "The DNA in our blood and yours is in the white blood cells. I spun a small sample of donor blood at high speed to separate the white cells from the blood fluid. These white cells were what I used for your gene fusion. I did not use contaminated blood. My assistant had corrected any irregularities before we spliced our DNA into you. You will acquire an immunity to bacteria that infects humans. I had no other way to save you. What else could I have done?"

"I do not know." Alexis tried to project a hard stare, but it wasn't happening.

"Why does this upset you? If you loved one of us enough to conceive a child, I assume he must have told you about his background. That would include the technology to do procedures your people consider impossible."

Her child. She'd been afraid to ask.

"He explained some of your technology, but he did not mention DNA fusion." Alexis longed to describe the controversy created when scientists tried to infuse human cells with rabbit sperm, but that didn't explain her feelings. She believed that when scientists tampered with people's genetic traits, they were violating the integrity of humanity. She applauded stem cell research, but that was a long walk from mutating a species. Even if she could translate her thoughts to Kryszka, the healer would shrug and repeat that he had no other options.

"The procedure is not simple," Zoltar conceded. "Quyeba would agree since she donated the blood, but she is attending to other matters now. The choice of donor poses a complication; he or she must be free of infection or other illness, lest they pass it onto you. The chromosomes must not have any defects, and then there is the aftercare. I must watch you for adverse effects and adjust your medicines if necessary. No doubt our DNA will augment your mind-matter interaction, and you will need training on the proper way to use it. Fortunately, most of our machinery and furniture is levitation-proof."

"Is my child ...?" Alexis's voice quivered. She swallowed hard, but her throat burned from the dryness. "Is he, or she ..."

"Your child, a boy, is in an incubator, where he will stay until he is mature enough to survive outside the womb. Under primitive circumstances, he would have died."

"Thank you," Alexis cried with relief. He'd said something about her becoming useful. Might he use her child for leverage? "You took extraordinary measures to save me. Why?"

"I followed Governor Quyeba's orders. When she gives an order, I obey. Besides, I was taught to treat the ill, no matter what they have done."

"Zoltar, I have not done anything—"

"Be silent." Zoltar spoke in a brusque voice, warning that she wasn't off the hook. "You have unique mental powers and you speak our language. Someone taught you how to use our weapons. That much was clear on our cameras; so was the contempt your companion showed for you, and the swelling in your hands. How did they get that way?"

"I have a condition that causes swelling and damage to the joints. It's called rheumatoid arthritis." She enunciated the words in a measured voice. "As for my friend's behavior ... if you had listened to the tone in our voices, you would have realized that he and I made peace. Shively acted out because he was terrified. We both were."

"Fear makes people act like trapped animals." Zoltar spoke with suppressed passion. "I have seen deformities like yours with irregularities in the immune system."

Alexis nodded, resisting the temptation to ask if the fused genes could be a cure.

"You continue to mention Yeron, but someone reported him as dead long ago. Our paternity tests say he is the father of your son. I suspect that a scientist experimented on Yeron before killing him and then impregnated you with his sperm. Why do you call on Yeron like a lover?"

"If I answer, will you shoot me like that soldier did to my friend?"

"As Quyeba said, we are not barbarians." The healer's voice softened. "The one who shot your friend will pay for his stupidity. Quyeba does not donate her genes to people she plans to execute."

You are more valuable to them alive, Teodon's voice echoed in her head. *I should find out what this DNA fusion means.* Alexis dared not ask. Her past experiences working at the hospital had taught her that when patients asked questions about a given procedure, some doctors considered this a prelude to their consent, or at least a willingness to make peace with their condition. Images of the killer mutant infants, no doubt the results of spliced DNA, haunted her thoughts. As far as she was concerned, the road to Hell was paved with spliced DNA.

"I am horrified that humans would send a sickly person to war," Zoltar went on. "But not surprised. Many humans make their underlings work when they are sick. Teodon observed it during his forays above ground."

"Teodon is dead," Alexis told him. "Eigil's soldiers killed him."

"I heard." His voice warmed up to her. "Teodon was my instructor, but he was like a father. He translated things that humans said, and that was how I learned your culture. The unscrupulous humans give their weak underlings duties no one else wants; sometimes dangerous chores. I suspect people made disparaging comments about your deformity."

His words bumped Alexis back to her stay in Jackson Hospital. Before the walkers invaded her floor, the Human Resources Director, Miss Grese, barged into her room and fired her, citing excessive use of sick time. Her absences were due to pain or doctor visits. Miss Grese wouldn't have cared if Alexis died, and Alexis knew this well.

"Some people have," she admitted. "An administrator, ah, *relieved* me of my position because of it."

"You mean terminated," Zoltar corrected her. At her nod, he went on. "If your officers found you and realized how sick you are, they might consider it too much trouble to find a suitable treatment. They might just allow you to die."

"Someone tried ..." Alexis shook her head. Whatever he gave her for pain was loosening her lips, and she didn't like it.

"Someone tried to let you die? I would answer if I were you. Given the severity of your deformity, I doubt your human peers will search for you. They might if they realized the extent of your mental powers because they give you salvage value."

Salvage value? What was that supposed to mean? Her father had used that expression to describe his investments, but she suspected in this alien world "salvage value" had a sinister meaning. *Had Yeron considered this man a friend?*

"Yeron spoke well of you." Alexis shook her head, trying to clear the sleepiness from her eyes. "If he overheard you saying these things to me, he would be furious. He spoke up for me so I would get treatment. I met him on the night one of your soldiers killed my sister."

"He what?" The look on his face said she'd gotten his attention.

"Yeron did not die. He was my healer and we became ... um, mates," Alexis pressed on. "He saw me get sick and begged me to go to a clinic. I refused. We argued about it."

"Argued?" Zoltar smiled; his eyes twinkled. "You mean you disobeyed him?"

"I love Yeron, but he is not my father. Your soldiers did not stop with killing our friends and relatives. They sent out people who smell like they're dead to break into clinics and homes. Shively, our friends, and I decided to find the ones who were making these things because half of our officers were too busy dealing with the casualties and rescuing the wounded. The other half drifted around with their thumbs up their asses." She shook her head again. "You gave me something to make me talk, didn't you?"

At that, Zoltar burst into a soft chuckle. He took one look at the monitors and back at Alexis and broke into loud laughter. Tears streamed down his face. This was not good; well, maybe it was. Alexis lay on the table, eyes flitting between the IV and Zoltar, waiting for the laughter to stop.

"Yes, I have," he said after he composed himself. "It will not harm you. Your last statement makes little sense. Probing the anal orifice is unsanitary."

There you go using slang, a phantom voice chided her. *Nice!*

"What I meant was, instead of trying to solve the problem, they blame other people. Many people do not believe these creatures exist."

"Tell me about these creatures, the walking dead."

"Some of them were live humans with toxic levels of vischlausk. The chemical caused severe brain damage, the kind that destroys your inhibitions. They could walk, breathe, and attack, but not think. Whoever gave them the vischlausk smeared them with secretions from the dead to make them look and smell putrid. In others, someone had implanted microchips that enabled them to lunge and assault. This infection you found ..." She looked Zoltar in the eye, trying to gauge his willingness to suspend disbelief. "It came from those creatures."

Zoltar nodded. "Your infection came from bacteria found in cadavers."

"I fought, destroyed, and examined these creatures. I think their toxins got into a cut I had on my finger."

"You could be right, but I cannot understand why anyone would use vischlausk on humans. The renegade Kryszka kill with disintegrators."

Alexis grimaced. Amidst all this Kryszka technology, not to mention the mixing of genes in her system, she had to get through to this man.

"The renegades consumed humans, too. Whoever examines Shively will find scars on his left arm. They came from a renegade's bite when they first attacked us, and the poison from that bite almost went through his body. Oh! Did you check my back? You'll see scars left by a soldier when she cut me with broken glass."

Zoltar took it all in, eyebrows raised, head tilted. His frown deepened.

"Yeron loved you like a brother," she shouted, exasperated. "Quyeba knew you were part human, but she adopted you. Teodon took both of you under his protection. You must have seen the horrors Eigil was capable of committing. Did you know that Woehar shot her own mother?"

Zoltar's eyes bulged. His mouth gaped like a man who'd sustained a nasty punch in the gut.

"My mother and I left long before the shooting," he said in a low voice. "We're the only ones Teodon told. Quyeba never saw your Kryszka comrade's face on surveillance."

"You might not have recognized him if you did because of his mask. He wears one because we fight with helium. Yeron hates Eigil because he destroyed his entire family. Woehar turned on Eigil and she paid with her life."

"Woehar is not dead," Zoltar said in a leaden voice. "She lived on this compound until my mother exiled her. Where is Yeron now?"

Woehar is more dangerous, Teodon had said in her vision. Alexis's teeth chattered.

"He is somewhere above ground, looking for me."

"Do you have any specimens of these contaminated beings, the ones treated with vischlausk?"

"We did before the house where we stayed caught fire. Yeron and I collected samples and stored them in a fireproof safe. If the slides are still viable, I am sure Yeron will lend them to you."

Zoltar frowned.

"I doubt Yeron will talk to anyone here after what his sister did. She chased him out of their home."

Alexis's jaw dropped. "He said he and his father found his mother's remains."

"I doubt if he remembers what really happened. He may not want to remember." Zoltar backed away, eyes averted. "I should not have told you that."

Cat's out of the bag, Doc. Alexis suppressed a smile.

"I will not tell anyone. Why not go to the burnt-out cabin and grab the safe? The specimens are the last thing on anyone's mind."

"I will send an android to get the safe." He drew in a deep breath. "Tell me everything that happened, starting with your first encounter with my people. Quyeba is interrogating another soldier, but I will record our conversation so she can listen later."

Finally, he was willing to listen. Alexis shuddered at the idea of being part Kryszka. After the infection was gone, she might ask him to undo the fusion. Highly doubtful – *a done deal can't be undone –*

but one never knew with Kryszka technology.

"All right, but I hope you brought your dinner."

"Bringing food into a laboratory breeds bacteria." Zoltar shook his head, frowning again. "Why will I need dinner?"

"My peer worker Laurel is involved, so I will tell you about the day she lost her position. This, my healer, is going to take a while."

Chapter Thirty-Five: The Interrogation Continues

Zoltar's Underground Laboratory, August 30, 8:00 p.m.

Three hours later, Zoltar finished the remains of his supper – cooked steak, she noted with surprise, and bottled water.

Had he acquired the human ability to eat cooked food? I think he has. In any case, he must've gotten hungry enough to put aside his misgivings about bacteria.

"I have more questions," he said. "Have you ever killed for reasons other than self-defense?"

That one got her thinking about Mark. *What possessed me to encourage Shively?* Tyrone was no help either. It was like everyone had chucked their values.

"I helped my friend kill someone once," she admitted at last. "The person was trying to steal weapons we needed to survive. I acted hastily, and I will regret that as long as I live."

"I am not surprised."

"Thank you." Alexis allowed a smile. "May I ask you some questions?"

The doctor shot a glance toward the ceiling, then back at Alexis.

"You may ask, but the surveillance cameras record everything we say. If I feel answering you will risk our safety, I will not do so."

"Fair enough." The words rolled off her tongue as if she'd spoken Kryszka all her life. "Earlier you mentioned placing microchips in my head to help me speak Kryszka better. How do they work? Yeron never taught me medical terms."

"The microchips mirror any past instruction you received from Yeron. They contain directories of words your brain retrieves when you think about them. Sometimes, though, you invent new uses for your words and this might confuse Kryszka."

Welcome to the English language, Doc.

"Our words have figurative meanings. That's why. Do you have any microchips that will allow you to speak English?"

"No, because no one here learned English," Zoltar told her.

"Teodon owned microchips that helped him with several human languages. Governor Quyeba and I never thought we would need them, so we left that technology behind. The microchips were all destroyed when Eigil's compound exploded."

"That is sad, Zoltar." Alexis shook her head. *Like good old Art thinking the street was safe, but gets hit by a car instead.* "I imagine the medical procedures you did will cost a lot. How can I pay you for all of the procedures you have done to keep me alive?"

"Since you have previous scars and trauma residuals, we will not charge you, but you should confirm this with Quyeba."

"Thank you." At least she had tabled the payment issue until she could talk with Quyeba.

"I am concerned that the same renegades who harmed you might go after people here," Zoltar went on. "It would help if you described the humans on your team and gave me their names."

"Those humans are my friends. I do not want them hurt."

"You lost several friends and a sibling trying to handle this yourself," Zoltar pointed out. "If I can profile the victims, it may enable us to track the renegades."

Alexis studied the healer's face, trying to gauge his temperament. Kryszka uniform and gown notwithstanding, he demonstrated a sense of humor and willingness to help. But she couldn't ignore the cameras overhead.

"Since your cameras record everything we say, mentioning names out loud would be unsafe. People who make the dead attack do not forgive *any* mistakes."

"That is true," Zoltar conceded in a sad voice. "My father died because he made a mistake. Can you describe your friends?"

"They wore dark green trousers and shirts when I last saw them. Shively – the man your officer shot – advised us to wear green because it blends with our foliage."

She hesitated, not caring to get into nationality or race; besides, the renegades didn't discriminate when it came to killing.

"One of them is a healer," she said at last. "His skin is light with brown marks on his cheeks. The other, a security officer, is tall and husky with short curly hair and dark brown skin. These men do not understand your language. They began their fight because the renegades harmed or killed their loved ones."

"I can appreciate the strategy. I will discuss this information with Governor Quyeba and see if my android has found any samples."

He stepped away from the bed toward a metal plate on a machine facing her and adjusted its main dial. The soothing humming stopped, and the machine belched out angry whirring sounds. An image flashed across one of the screens above the panel.

"The android found a specimen." Zoltar shook his head, disgusted. "Why would anyone here make those beings? It requires work in unsanitary conditions, something that most Kryszka find distasteful."

"Vischlausk will change your preference, even if you ingest it by accident. Eigil forced a thirst for violence in his followers by giving them vischlausk." Alexis followed this with a hard pause. "Someone tried to poison Yeron with it."

"They did?" Horror crept into his voice. "Not Yeron!"

"I said they tried. It never happened because the assailant did not wear a helium mask. He ran afoul of these ..." *shit, what is the word for balloon?* "... globes filled with helium. I kept a huge collection of them at my bed for protection. His foot caught on their ties and a balloon ... globe broke. He died of asphyxiation."

"Helium globes?" Zoltar arched his brows. His red eyes became holes of terror. "Whatever they are, helium is deadly, even worse than vischlausk. I am surprised Yeron allowed you to keep them."

"The globes frightened him." Alexis giggled in spite of her pain. "His half-sister, Becky, collects them for show and he hates that."

"Becky?" Zoltar's eyebrows lifted and his jaw dropped. "She was the child Teodon had with a human. Is this woman your friend?"

Alexis nodded vigorously.

"We went to school together, and she is the ... ah, mate of one of my human cohorts. She often visited the clinic where I used to work, but she had kept her relationship with Teodon secret from most people."

"Some things are better left unsaid. Eigil's people are cunning. After her expulsion from our colony, Woehar and her team built another compound that adjoins ours. Despite your condition, you found our home and, from the experiences you described, demonstrated excellent marksmanship." His voice tinged with admiration. "Did you engage any Kryszka before the assault on your house?"

"I never met one until the night Robin died, the night of the attacks."

"Has anyone in your family ever contacted our people?"

Alexis tried to imagine her mother and Yeron together. In a wild moment, she might offer him ravioli, despite his intolerance to cooked foods. She imagined her mother placing a platter of steaming hot ravioli before Yeron, hollering *mangia!* At that, she brayed raucous laughter.

Zoltar cocked his head to one side and gave her a bemused look.

"Why are you laughing?"

Indeed. Why am I laughing? What's so funny about killer sepsis, gene splicing, or watching a friend die? She stopped laughing.

"I was trying to imagine my mother and Yeron together. This is hard to describe to someone who has never met my mother. If anyone in my family knew Kryszka, they never told me about it."

"Your Laurel seems bloodthirsty, but Eigil's soldiers would never conduct business with a breed they consider inferior. Yet you believe this happened. Why?"

"I think Laurel may have given Woehar addresses of potential victims, people who cannot fight. That way, Woehar can avoid getting caught. Woehar is not ... *ow!*" Alexis winced. Bright red rockets of pain went off inside her gut. Ditto for the hands. She thought about Laurel and how her mishaps had killed patients. According to Officer Hazlett, she was still missing. The police had found her car and bloody footprints, but no sign of Laurel. She was about to enlighten Zoltar, but the pain took her breath away, making speaking impossible. Zoltar pressed a button near her hand. The cramping slowly passed.

"You required a lot of surgery," Zoltar said, looking down at her. "The next time you hurt, squeeze this button to get more pain medicine."

"Thank you." Alexis let out a deep breath. "Most of the victims were Laurel's enemies. My peers and I reported her actions to our superior. Laurel made serious errors that hastened her patients' deaths." She paused to calm herself, but her voice cracked on each word. "When she was not on duty, she tortured and cannibalized young women in her basement. The night of the first invasion, she disappeared."

"She sounds dangerous." Zoltar gazed at her with sorrow. "I still do not understand how this involves my people. Why do your superiors allow someone like her to treat the sick?"

Because she blackmailed someone, and the bigwigs were too stupid to get around it. Alexis longed to answer, but she wasn't sure if Kryszka ever experienced work politics.

"When I first met Laurel, she performed her work as a decent healer would," she said, hoping for a delicate approach. "She came across as harmless, someone who cared about the sick. Maybe at one time she did, but her work performance deteriorated. So our superior terminated her. Two nights later, your soldiers attacked. The human casualties were people who had, in Laurel's opinion, given her a bad time. Does this clarify things?"

Zoltar shook his head.

"Someone who is mentally unstable will exhibit certain behaviors if you are observant. She may have used extortion to keep her position."

"She blackmailed a superior after she caught him using an illegal drug." Alexis stared at Zoltar. "How did you know?"

"Just a guess. Eigil used extortion to keep his followers. Where is her home?"

"She lives in a city called Philadelphia, a short ride from your old compound."

"A short ride?" Zoltar chuckled. "Our computers rely on coordinates."

"Coordinates?" Alexis echoed. At least she knew the word, but Yeron's explanation of coordinates never made sense. You either went east, west, north, or south, and you turned right or left at a given landmark. An advanced society like the Kryszka would not rely on landmarks. "I am sorry, but I never understood Yeron's explanation about coordinates. It does not matter because Laurel is missing."

"If we searched her home, we might find clues. Can you describe her?"

"If you want to find Laurel, follow your nose. She stinks like a sewer. Unless your renegades gave her a brain transplant, that part has not changed."

"A brain transplant?" A smile crossed Zoltar's lips. *Queeping* issued from the chromatographer, drawing his eyes toward his screens. "My android is testing the specimen it found, so I am watching the screens for results. Continue to talk; I am listening."

Well, Zoltar, she's got six inches and fifty pounds on me. The trouble is, Yeron never got around to explaining measurements in your lingo. "Her hair was dark blonde, but dirty and oily. She stood about half a head taller than me, and she's big. She has tiny lips, skin lighter than mine, but not as pale as Kryszka skin. Her cold blue eyes frighten people when she stares at them, and she says things that do not make sense. She has a nasty look that would make you want your weapon available."

"This Laurel sounds like Eigil."

"Like Eigil, she takes pleasure in torturing innocent people to get human meat. If Eigil were alive, he and Laurel would have made fine mates."

"Eigil would have never mated with a human, even your Laurel. Most Kryszka avoid humans because they consider them inferior. Yet Yeron saw something in you and fell in love. You seem like a caring person, and I am glad that Quyeba's chromosomes saved you. I would think, though, that the microchips should help you with coordinates. You must not have listened at all to his explanation." Zoltar traced his finger across the screens.

Oops. Alexis suppressed a smile.

He shifted to one side giving Alexis a view of the machinery, but the viewscreens were too far away for her to make out any readouts. Instead, she followed the doctor's intent gaze on the numerical values coming through the screen at his eye level. He shook his head, frowning. His body stiffened. His fists clenched and he let out a stream of Kryszka curses.

A perverse urge to tease seized Alexis, tempting her to ask, "Are we having fun yet?" But Zoltar did not look to be in the mood for any jokes.

"Is everything all right?" she asked in a low voice.

Zoltar whirled around and gave her a fearful look. "No, everything is *not* all right."

"Do your reports prove the vischlausk creatures exist?"

Zoltar did not answer. Instead, he took another long look at those messages as if he were staring down a dark cave with a hidden monster, and then he looked back at Alexis.

"Those beings exist, and their tissues carry toxic levels of vischlausk, as you say. That is not all. Because you demonstrated superior mental power, I ran another test before your surgery to see if you were related to anyone living here and I just got the results. Know what I found? You and I are cousins or half-siblings. That explains the similarities in our complexions."

"That is not possible. My mother loved my father and would not mate with another being. I am 100 percent human ... or at least I was before your fusion."

Zoltar did not answer. Instead, he jabbed his fingers against the buttons to Alexis's left. He glanced behind him, cursed to the air, and then jabbed the buttons again.

"Mother, we have a breach in security." Another stream of curses followed. "Fuck it all, I cannot do this. The human and I are related."

Did he say the word "fuck?" He did, by golly! That was the first word I learned in Kryszka. Then there was silence, followed by ...

"How the fuck should I know?"

A panel opened, and without further comment, he tore through the exit. *So much for his mother's interrogation with her soldier.*

What the hell is Zoltar talking about? Dad didn't mention squat about Kryszka contact. Mom would never cheat on him. A strict Catholic, she adhered to the sacredness of marriage. Unless a Kryszka guard had raped her and hypnotized her into forgetting. *There's my aunt, though. She would sleep with strangers to get money for booze. Maybe someone raped her and she drank so she could forget. What about that?* The questions jammed in her mind like shoppers crowding the doors at a Black Friday sale. *Everything's up for doorbuster sales, folks, my sanity, my life, and the world as I knew it.*

The one decent person capable of helping me has gone bonkers. Oh, my God, I'm in so much trouble. This time, despite her best efforts at composure, Alexis burst into tears and cried herself to sleep.

Chapter Thirty-Six: Woehar and Laurel Spy on Alexis

Woehar's Underground Laboratory in Grays Landing, August 30, 4:00 p.m.

Despite Laurel's hope for the contrary, another glance in the mirror showed additional changes to her body. Her head had enlarged, with a bulbous shape. Her sunken blue eyes had faded to yellow. The green coloring of her scales had deepened to the same shade as those on the caged *settva* in Quyeba's compound. Woehar delighted in pointing them out on her viewscreens, saying, "This was where Draekh got your chromosomes."

Chromosomes, my ass. Laurel clenched her talons. *Bitch turned me into a monster.*

She'd gotten too big for the tunics that Woehar had given her. Occasionally, she happened upon a large woman who wore a caftan dress. She wore it after dining on the woman.

Memories of Jackson Hospital haunted her. At one time, she enjoyed health care. Back then, her coworkers acted politely; some engaged her in conversation. Respiratory therapy enabled her to forget the horrible things her mom and dad had done to her. Instead, the headaches came, preceded by Abaddon's orders, and the friendly chatter at work ceased. Like Woehar, several doctors had declared Abaddon a figment of her hallucinations, gifted by a chemical imbalance. When Abaddon appeared, though, his sulfuric smell, pointed teeth, and grating voice seemed plenty real. Now that she had become part *settva*, her Abaddon visions and headaches had stopped. Her incessant hunger and thirst ballooned, and in between feedings, the yearning to treat the sick pleaded to be diminished. *Damn you, Woehar. Why did you make me like this?*

The door panel opened.

"Why are you so glum?" Woehar asked in a clear, cheery voice, as if she'd spoken English for years.

"I'm hungry."

"You have to wait," Woehar said in her happy voice. "Quyeba

has a gift for us."

"Why are you so happy? We lost the connection we had with Mark's microchip. We must have because I've not seen any more recordings involving Alexis and her friends."

"That is right, we did," Woehar said with a dismissive flick of her hand. "Alexis's friends shot him and her lover disposed of the microchip. But we have something much better."

"Such as what? Quyeba hates both of us."

"She is also stupid. Draekh devised a force field that renders this building impervious to intruders and prying cameras, but we can observe the goings-on in Quyeba's compound. Her son is questioning and treating Alexis at a laboratory which adjoins this one by a walkway. When Zoltar finishes repairing the damage Yeron's medicines did, Alexis will be ready for consumption. Her friends are searching for her. They are approaching this compound and they look muscular. You and I shall feast."

Laurel attempted a grin, a lopsided one because of the teeth crowding her mouth. "What treatment is Alexis getting?"

"Something to destroy the infection and undo the damage from Yeron's earlier treatment. Since Alexis speaks our language, Zoltar and Quyeba want her alive and comfortable. Her care distracts them, so I can get into their compound easily and bring her to you."

Standing back, Woehar clicked on a viewscreen. Alexis lay on a cot, hooked up to IVs and other equipment. Her face was scrawny and her arms like matchsticks. She was conversing with a Kryszka male in his native language. Her bloodshot eyes registered fear, but she was directing it at something aside from the Kryszka. The two conversed like friends, occasionally laughing at things the other said. Laurel never understood any of the words because Woehar didn't trust her enough to teach her the Kryszka language.

"What a load of horsefeathers!" Laurel growled. A rasp rose and fell, coming from her nostrils. "How come she can speak Kryszka?"

Woehar shook her head, grinning. "Wrong question. You should ask how soon I can break into Zoltar's laboratory."

Laurel smiled at the prospect of fresh meat.

"Alexis has no meat on her bones, but the people visiting her might." She regarded Woehar fixedly. "Quyeba won't want visitors, but we won't give her a choice."

"Now you are thinking."

Damn straight. Thanks to you, I'm a freak. She longed to shout that out, but it was so obvious. *With any luck, our foray into Zoltar's laboratory will lead to my escape.*

"If Quyeba despises you, so does Zoltar," she said, determined to continue her civil front. "He'll guard Alexis like a prize."

"No, Laurel, their androids will guard her. I know how to de-program an android."

Laurel's gaze shifted to the mirror. She hated what she had become. Why did everyone cater to Alexis's whims, even in this underground hellhole? She swiped at the air with her talons. *Wait until I get you, Alexis. You and Woehar.*

Chapter Thirty-Seven: Deadly Traps Underground

Underground Sewers, Grays Landing, August 30, 2:00 p.m.

The infant creatures slithered across the floor like worms, spiked teeth gnashing, eyes on the intruders. Yeron felt conflicted because he had worked with babies and didn't want to harm them, but these were threatening his life. He doused these creatures with fire. Tyrone and Steve cut to his side, blowing up the ones Yeron missed. Moments later, the charred remains of the infants doused by Yeron lay strewn about the laboratory.

Yeron led his teammates toward the panel ahead, giving the bodies a broad berth. Tyrone murmured something. Yeron whirled toward him, wondering if the creatures had harmed him.

"I'm okay." Tyrone smiled thinly. "I'm asking the Lord for help."

"If your Jesus would listen to someone like me, I should ask, too," Yeron told him.

"Jesus makes time for everyone," Tyrone said, "but you gotta trust."

Yeron was not sure where he stood with Jesus or any other deity, but he never forgot the day his ghost-father had guided him through Alexis's surgery. He had nudged Yeron's hand to the base of Alexis's neck. There, one jagged piece of glass was embedded next to a major artery. With his father's help, Yeron retrieved it, repaired the nick in the vessel wall, and stopped the bleeding. He would give anything for advice from his father now.

Voices jolted Yeron to attention. Two women were speaking in English, but too soft for him to make out the conversation. He crept closer to the entryway, putting his ear against the panel. Clearer now. They were shouting at each other, something about breaking into a laboratory. Both voices sounded familiar somehow.

Steve and Tyrone gave no sign of noticing. No surprise. Shively's team had invented the term "Kryszka ears" to describe Yeron's sensitive hearing.

"Steve, Tyrone. I am going in, so keep your weapons available."

We need more than weapons. We may be stumbling into another deadly trap.

A deadly trap, yes, but the soldiers had brought Alexis and Shively here. Maybe the women he overheard were guarding her. Their conversation continued. Here was his chance to confront the people who might have his Steel Rose.

First, he had to open the panel. He had a plan. He would crack the panel along its inner seams with his mind, tiptoe through the opening, and wait for his partners before closing the panel behind them. He had opened Kryszka panels many times at home with his father. All of the laboratories and clinic rooms including the ones housing Kryszka patients employed paneled doors.

And when he had entered, everyone had greeted him with a smile. Now he was an intruder. To the Kryszka renegades, he sided with the animalistic humans, and their guards would not hesitate to disintegrate him and his comrades. This time, they would shield themselves with helium-proof devices. Yeron knew this as well as he had come to know his love for Alexis.

Do not be ridiculous, his father whispered in his mind. *You are a purebred Kryszka and as good a fighter as they. They might mistake you for an ordinary soldier.*

"Eigil's troops wanted me dead," he whispered.

They still do, his ghost parent said. *Are you going to let that stop you?*

"Yeron, are you all right?" Steve asked in a quiet voice.

Yeron nodded.

"Draw your weapons. I will go in first."

The panel gave way with ease. The pink overhead lights revealed a Kryszka laboratory ahead, a clinic, he noted with surprise, equipped with cubicles, monitors, and trays filled with surgical instruments. A cacophony of wails assaulted his ears from behind the left wall, but no women in sight. He guessed that he was hearing the female voices through a surveillance device built into that wall.

The human occupants lay naked and tied to tables behind each cubicle glass, screaming and writhing. Most of them were missing body parts, mostly fingers and toes. Greenish pus oozed from an elderly man's left eye socket, now empty. Gashes leaking black secretions streaked the prisoners' emaciated bodies. An IV line ran into each victim, young and old alike, the same chemical Yeron had found in the syringe back at Jackson Hospital. Vischlausk.

No sign of Alexis. *Bad omen.*

"What the hell is this shit?" whispered Tyrone behind him.

With a wave of his hand, Yeron motioned him and Steve to the floor. He guided them behind the computers, away from the revealing lights, while darting glances over his shoulder for any sign of movement. That was when something jabbed his shoulder.

He jumped. Steve was squeezing next to him.

"Look over there." Steve pointed.

They crawled behind the machinery. Yeron made out other smaller cubicles filled with human body parts. Behind each glass, disconnected hands and feet flapped about on the metal surfaces. Yeron grimaced. *The madman who made these monsters was cloning body parts or manufacturing mechanical parts to make the monsters more thorough at killing.*

Whoever owned this laboratory had brought Eigil's cruelty to a more depraved level. Yeron feared this person would show soon, and he did not want to be around when that happened. Steve drew his gun, as did Yeron and Tyrone.

"What is this place?" Steve mouthed at him.

"A laboratory for those vischlausk creatures," Yeron told them. "Let us find Alexis."

"I wish we could call Hazlett for backup," Tyrone said.

"Well, we can't." Steve's chest swelled with a sigh. "Let's blow them up with helium. It won't hurt Alexis."

"But it would hurt the prisoners plenty," Tyrone pointed out. "Those people tied down, without body parts and tortured, would be blown up."

Yeron touched his mask, ensuring that it would protect him from the noxious gas. Of course, the renegade Kryszka had devised similar protection from the dreaded helium, but he did not care to point this out to the others.

"Okay, Cowboy, where do we go now?" asked Tyrone.

"We confront the people who own this compound," Yeron told him. "Civilians who live here may not know about this laboratory. I hope I find someone friendly."

"We'd better consult the Wishful Thinking Department." Tyrone sighed.

"I hope it is more than wishful thinking," Yeron said, looking at Tyrone. "The monsters who made these creatures will not allow Alexis to live."

"If Alexis died, she did so from the loss of blood," Steve told him. "Before the monsters got to her. Something tells me she hasn't used all nine of her lives. I hope I'm right, and not only for your sake or Matilda's. Where do we go from here?"

"Straight ahead." Yeron sighted another panel. "Stay behind

me."

At least finding an exit would be easier. The panels further inside the compound were a lighter texture than the surrounding wall, unlike the ones in the chambers closer to ground level. It was not noticeable to the untrained eye, but Yeron recognized the difference, even from several meters away. Where would this new doorway lead? On titanium-stiff legs, he forced one foot before the other, waving the two humans behind him. Before he got within three meters, the door opened.

Kryszka troops marched through the opening, brandishing their plasma guns. Yeron and his teammates retreated a meter, dropping behind a machine, and fired back at the soldiers. The humans' bullets flew and plasma rays flared back and forth without inflicting any damage on the metal. Yeron's human friends made great warriors, but the Kryszka soldiers moved fast. Yeron squeezed off his helium tank, and his shots found purchase. The soldiers kept coming. They did not stumble or show any ill effects from the helium.

Of course, they wore protection. Six of them were moving in on Yeron and his companions. Yeron thought about Alexis again and remembered his mental maneuver, where he devised a force field to repel the soldiers. His father had taught him the procedure, but Yeron had perfected the technique.

With the soldiers closing in, Yeron furrowed his brows and concentrated. No results. The soldiers kept coming and shooting.

Booming voices raised Alexis to consciousness. One sounded like Yeron and the other belonged to a woman. When the cobwebs fell away, Alexis realized the speakers were Zoltar and Quyeba.

Zoltar swept into the laboratory with Quyeba at his heels, screaming at him. She was the governor. Her sequined clothes made her look like a public dignitary, but Alexis found nothing dignified about her outburst.

"Cursing at anyone through a hologram is inappropriate," she scolded him. "Especially around a detainee."

Detainee? Is that an upgrade from "prisoner?" Alexis lifted her brows, but remained silent.

"Mother, Alexis is my ..."

"I am Governor Quyeba when I conduct official business, not your mother."

"Governor, Alexis told us the truth about those creatures," Zoltar shouted. "My android brought tissue samples of the remains from above ground. They harbor the same bacteria that infected her. She was trying to—"

"Zoltar, lower your voice." Panic crept in with the governor's anger. "I saw the vischlausk beings. Woehar said she was making them to intimidate intruders. I ordered her to stop. She did not, and I suspect she sent them to assault Alexis's people. Alexis knows the details, and that is why I need her alive and under detainment." She drew in a deep breath. "Be that as it may, your behavior may have attracted attention through the surveillance, by renegades masquerading as my soldiers. You may have jeopardized my safety, yours, and that of our compound."

"Governor, Alexis and I are related," Zoltar overrode his mother, not caring about security. "What are we? Cousins? Siblings? I have a right to know who my human relatives are."

"Zoltar!" Governor Quyeba glared at him. "I ordered you to

treat and question our detainee. Nothing more. I can only imagine how Alexis feels listening to your declaration."

"My feelings are moot." Alexis's voice came out tinny and distant when at last she spoke. "Zoltar and I are not related. His equipment needs recalibration."

"My equipment does *not* need recalibrating." Zoltar's upper lip jutted out in a pout. "How are we related, Governor?"

"I do not know." Quyeba covered her eyes. "If Lyrus were alive, he could tell you."

"Who is Lyrus?" Alexis raised her voice, but it was like talking through a pane of glass.

"My father," Zoltar replied.

"Your father? He was the one Eigil shot," Alexis said. "I know what happened ... just did not know your father's name. Zoltar ... Governor, I am sorry for your loss."

"Zoltar, what is wrong with you?" the governor shouted. "You should not discuss family matters with strangers. Pull yourself together. Now!"

"Zoltar did not tell me anything about Lyrus," Alexis said. "I found out from ..."

"Quit lying to me!" Zoltar shouted at his mother before Alexis got in another word. The governor said something that Alexis didn't understand. During the shouting, her thoughts turned to Mark and the way he used to belittle the others on their missions. She could have sunk through the floor. She imagined that Zoltar experienced the same feelings, though his mother's quivering lips and darting eyes betrayed fright. Alexis recognized that look, having seen it on her own mother's face the night of the renegades' first attack when the paramedics rolled her, badly hurt, into Jackson Hospital.

Her stomach and wrists burned, reminding her of a time when Mark had hit her with his baseball bat. Images assaulted her mind; she relived a time when he had forced himself on her despite her pleas to stop. She shivered and shrunk into herself, but bad as the past was, she couldn't ignore the future, including possible repercussions resulting from the surveillance camera.

"Governor and Zoltar," she said in a thin voice. "Both of you, please! Time out!"

"Time ... what? What is that supposed to mean?" The governor glared at her.

"Stop quarreling, or at least do your arguing away from the viewscreens." Alexis gritted her teeth. She never thought that Kryszka officials would air their soiled laundry in front of her. Yeron might expect her to remain silent, but the fear in the governor's face hinted of unspoken danger. That, and Alexis couldn't stop thinking about the humiliation she'd endured from Mark. "The situation above ground is uglier than you realize. Yelling will not resolve it."

The governor appeared to consider this.

"No, it will not," she relented after a pause. "Zoltar, I will discuss Alexis's test results with you later. In the future, I will thank you not to curse around me, my assistants, or anyone else." She turned on her heel, gown swishing as she walked to the door.

As she watched the governor's retreating figure, Alexis thought about her psychiatrist, Stan. He had coached her how to use the technique of *listening* as a way to improve her interaction with the hospital staff. Stan's methods had led to her romance with Yeron. Improvising on his lesson might make life easier for her now.

"Zoltar, I know how you can avoid upsetting your mother."

Zoltar looked up at her. He hesitated, as if his curiosity had engendered a willingness to listen.

"How can I keep my mother calm?"

"Curse in a human language. She cannot get angry if she does not understand you. Humans speak many languages, and my parents spoke one called Italian." She regarded Zoltar's bewildered expression and then repeated the word. "Italian."

"Italian."

"If you feel the need to curse, try '*Bah fungule*.'"

Zoltar repeated it several times until he got it right and then regarded Alexis with a grin. "I will increase your pain medicine. My mother and I want you comfortable."

"Would you please untie my hands?"

Zoltar surveyed her intravenous lines and monitors with wary eyes. The smile faded.

"If you try to escape, you will not get far. Your treatment has only begun, and you will die without finishing the protocol. If renegades catch you ..."

"I am not going anywhere," Alexis said, exasperated. "I will never understand your splicing procedure, but I know you did it to save me. I appreciate that. On another matter, I hate to impose, but I was hoping you or your mother would tell someone above ground that I am alive."

"You should discuss that with her." With that, Zoltar tweaked several dials. The bands on her wrists and legs opened, which lessened the burning.

Alexis opened and closed her fists, hoping to ease the stiffness. "Thank you."

"Try to rest. I will work on a counteragent to destroy these beings."

"The plasma gun disintegrated them nicely," Alexis pointed out.

"That may be, but you ruined a lot of vegetation and those beings still killed people you love."

"All right, I will be quiet so you can concentrate."

Alexis watched him tread toward a plate laden with readouts and other buttons. The machines purred with a low-pitched hum that her sensitized ears could now detect. The sound lulled her into sleep, until his shouting woke her.

As the moments ticked by, Zoltar's *bah fungule* index rose. His research, or whatever he was working on, must not have been going well.

At least he's making me feel comfortable. All I need is a platter of ravioli, Yeron, and Mom beside me. Zoltar could arrange a visit if he believed it was safe. By the way, when can I see my baby, even if he's only an embryo? And what's this about Zoltar being a cousin? Alexis had a lot of questions, but Zoltar was too absorbed to answer them. While he cursed, she settled back, pain ebbing, and drifted back into a fitful sleep.

****

Unseen hands lifted Alexis. She lingered in a twilight haze; her limbs dangled like cement blocks. After lying there for at least a half hour, she forced her eyes open and gazed at Governor Quyeba and Zoltar. Someone had strapped her to a chair, wrists dangling over the armrests. The weakness invading her body caused her to sag against the cushions. She looked at the leads taped to her chest and the intravenous lines. Not too different from what Jackson Hospital used, just a little fancier.

"You are awake," the governor said, smiling. "This is good. Zoltar informed me the gene splicing and antidote are working well together."

"They are?" Alexis gazed at her two keepers. "If the medicine is working, why do I feel so awful? I would love to lead you above ground and take you to Yeron. Right now, though, what I want to do is sleep."

"If I let you sleep on that 'bed' too much, you will contract pneumonia," Zoltar told her. "Sitting up is better and you shall begin therapeutic exercises tomorrow. Governor Quyeba has questions about our recording."

"I have a question, too, Quyeba. Excuse me, Governor ..."

"Quyeba." The governor smiled. "Always Quyeba, Alexis. When someone gives me orders in my laboratory, I insist they call me by my given name."

Is this Kryszka humor? If so, I can live with it.

"I never give orders," she said, manufacturing a smile. "The timeout was a *request*."

"Details, details." Quyeba grinned. "What did you want to know?"

"I do not have any means to pay for treatment. How should we address that?"

"It is clear from your wounds and last night's questioning that you were the victim. Zoltar has never worked with a psychokinetic human, and you presented him with a learning opportunity. When you are stronger, I will need you to teach me English. So I shall consider your medication and care as a barter agreement."

"Thank you." Alexis breathed a sigh of relief.

"You sound stronger." Quyeba smiled.

Alexis drew in a sharp breath.

"Then why do I feel so rotten?"

"Your infection is severe and healing will be slow," Zoltar told her.

Alexis wagged her head, trembling. Her smile faded, replaced by tears in her eyes. "I lost three good friends and a sibling because of the renegades," she said more to herself than to her keepers. "This infection happened, I suspect, because of the renegades' vischlausk-poisoned walkers. If my mother realized how sick I am, she would be terrified."

"Of course, she would be. I understand because I am a mother, too." Quyeba tilted her head to one side, voice sad. "The man who disintegrated your fellow soldier tried to harm Zoltar. He has gone missing and could be anywhere."

Alexis tried to recall the events in the interrogation room before she had lost consciousness. She pictured the flames licking at Shively, the stink of his cooking flesh, the terror in his screams. His death had happened before she vomited blood, and then, somewhere through the haze of dizziness, a soldier raised his sidearm, not toward her, but toward …

"Quyeba!" she cried. "I am so sorry."

"Sorrow will not guarantee Zoltar's safety," Quyeba replied with a dreadful sort of patience. "Discretion will. I met these creatures you describe. Humans do not have the technology to conjure such monstrosities, but Woehar and Draekh do, especially if they worked under Eigil. They resent Zoltar because he is half-human. That is why he must refrain from teasing people, outbursts, and cursing. Unfortunately, my son does not listen well."

"I do." Zoltar chuckled. "Most of the time."

Alexis gave Zoltar a smile, then turned her head to face Quyeba.

"Then you realize why I want my mother to know I am alive. Since the complexity of my treatment prohibits my leaving your compound, I hope you or Zoltar can contact Yeron. Yeron can bring my mother here."

Quyeba raised her right hand to indicate her understanding.

"Visiting would not be wise. Most humans fear people like us. Even you, despite your apparent ease with our culture, find our chromosome fusion overwhelming. How will your mother react to your bodily changes?"

"I will tell her my eye color was a side effect of your medicine."

"She will not believe you," Quyeba intoned. "Most mothers, regardless of species, figure out the truth."

"She will be so glad her daughter is alive, she will not care," Zoltar said. "Alexis, what did your mother say about the baby?"

"I did not have a chance to tell her," Alexis replied in a small voice. "She just started to accept my being with Yeron."

The somber nod from Quyeba told Alexis that this didn't surprise her. She leaned against the wall, her eyes regarding Alexis.

"As you pointed out, your mother will be terrified when she finds out. She may need time to accept what happened. I will do what I can to make this easier for you."

Alexis breathed a sigh of relief. At least they no longer regarded her as the enemy.

"However," Quyeba continued, a troubled look crossing her face, "you omitted a lot of details when you described the attacks. Did any of your assailants speak English?"

"I did not notice. I was too busy fighting for my life."

"They must have, because I overheard conversations in your language from our laboratories. That is why I must learn English." Quyeba continued to watch the viewscreens, her eyes moving back and forth. "When did the first invasion by the renegades happen?"

"Before their attack on Jackson Hospital, they invaded a town during our cold season."

"When? What day?" Impatience edged into Quyeba's voice. "You left out the dates and times during the recording."

Shit! I wish I'd learned the Kryszka calendar. Alexis lowered her eyes.

"I am sorry. Yeron never taught me how to keep time in your world."

"I wish he had." Quyeba rubbed the back of her neck. "The microchip will help you remember acquired knowledge, but cannot retrieve what you never learned. I should be glad you had taken the time to study Kryszka before you came here. You shall teach me your language and your calendar."

"It takes ... hundreds of days to become fluent in any language."

"People like me can learn basic elements quickly."

"Yesterday, I think, you told Zoltar I was 'under detainment.' Where I come from, people are detained if the government believes they are a danger to others. Do you think I could harm anyone in my present condition?"

"I sympathize with your plight." Quyeba lowered her eyes; her voice was soft. "Someone here is after you, though, and innocents may die in the crossfire. So ... temporarily you are under detainment. What else can I do, Alexis?"

"I do not know." Alexis's voice came out a plaintive bleat. "Am I allowed visitors?"

"Not until I can guarantee their safety and ours." Quyeba shifted her gaze toward the viewscreens and grew pensive, as if realizing that the monster-concocting scientists made safety a mere fantasy. "First, Zoltar and I shall attempt to repair the breach in security."

"Mother, Yeron or one of their fellow warriors can visit," Zoltar offered, smiling. "Her mother, too, if she is trained in weaponry."

"She is," Alexis chimed in.

"Very well, then." A pleasant smile stretched across Zoltar's face. "Besides, she might know my biological mother."

"Zoltar, no," Quyeba said. "Those warriors consider us the enemy."

"That is true ... except for Yeron," Alexis said. "I find it hard to believe that Zoltar and I are related. My mother would be too emotional to keep something like that secret."

"He is related," Quyeba said. "You must notice the similarities in your complexions. Our blood tests do not lie."

"My father never mentioned a half-breed child," Alexis said.

"How would your father be involved?" questioned Quyeba. "I told you Lyrus is the birth parent. His biological mother was human."

"All right, I am curious," Alexis admitted with a sigh. "Have you met this woman?"

"Yes," Quyeba admitted. "Her hands were deformed like yours, but her skin was light. She had ingested a mind-altering substance."

"Oh, no! Oh, *no!*" Alexis cupped her hand to her mouth. Then noting the puzzled stares of her keepers, she continued. "You are describing my aunt Susan. She could not possibly be the one. Frankly, Zoltar, you are too kind to be related to that woman."

"The tests say I am related to you," Zoltar said. "I would like to meet your aunt."

"It would be a mistake. She mistreated my sister, lied, and stole from my mother so she could buy her mind-altering substances. Besides, the point is moot – my aunt is dead."

Her scrutiny settled on Zoltar.

"Please do not be angry with Quyeba for not telling you. You did not miss anything."

"She is right," Quyeba told him. "Lyrus was an assistant when Teodon tried to crossbreed humans and Kryszka. When the healthy infants – what few there were –matured enough to live outside the incubator, he and Teodon placed them with human families. Lyrus did not want to send you to that woman because of her addiction. As it was, most half-breeds fared poorly in human environments. Lyrus and I were charmed by you and we decided to raise you."

"I appreciate that!" Zoltar smiled, and shifted his gaze between Alexis and Quyeba. "However, I prefer to make my own judgment, not have someone make it for me."

"She is dead, Zoltar," Alexis repeated. "You could meet my mother, who would be your aunt – if Quyeba allows it."

"I will," Quyeba said, "after I establish that the inner and outer perimeter of this building is free of renegades. That will take time because Woehar and Draekh have made a lot of friends among my soldiers. Alexis, I assume you intervened many times for your sister and mother. That I understand; but you surprised me when you spoke for Zoltar. You just met him."

Alexis contemplated telling her captors about life with a disability and a man who raped and ruled with a baseball bat. Under peaceful circumstances, Quyeba might commiserate. She had, in a way, raised a "special-needs" child. She shrugged.

"I considered it the right thing to do."

"People in a frightening environment do not care about propriety," the governor said. "You became distressed when you saw me and Zoltar argue. Most humans in your predicament would not care."

Alexis touched her forehead, fingered an electrode, and then withdrew her hand. How could she discuss Mark with total strangers? *Go ahead, let it rip. Tell her about the days of yore with Markiepoo.*

"I am not like most humans," she said after a pause.

"That much is clear." Quyeba gazed at her like a scientist studying a prized specimen. "Unlike most humans, you speak our language, use our weapons, and move matter with your mind. That does not explain why you would speak up for a stranger."

Alexis shrugged again.

"What can I say?"

"Only you can answer that." Quyeba grimaced like someone

about to undertake a distasteful job. "It would help me guarantee the safety of your friends if you leveled with me."

"I told you everything that happened," Alexis pleaded. She decided against sharing stories about Mark. "Yeron must be worried about me. He is a better historian than I am. If you allow him a visit, he will give you the timelines and dates of the skirmishes, and better details on the renegades and the walkers."

"Mother, let her rest," Zoltar said. "Yeron needs to visit his mate and his child. I will go above ground, find him, and question him."

"No, you will not." Quyeba regarded him with a steady gaze, her jaw set. "Yeron may be glad to see you, but the others will shoot."

"Then allow me to send an android to guide Yeron to our laboratory. He is an experienced warrior and may know more about human armies than Alexis does."

"He does," Alexis jumped in. "He learned about the walkers by invading our army's files."

"Anyone can access your files." Quyeba sniffed. "Your security is simplistic by our standards."

"That is true," Zoltar conceded, "but Alexis needs to be with the man she loves."

Quyeba shot her son a stunned look.

"We have a breach of security – a casualty on the compound, and the risk of exposing innocent people to the renegades. Yet you both are willing to chance all that for love. Do I understand you right?"

"I am not asking for an entire city," Alexis said. "One visitor. A Kryszka. Yeron, a warrior, a kind man. Dates and times matter to you and he can give you those."

The governor shook her head, grimacing as if she'd swallowed a fishbone.

"Yeron is no warrior by our standards. His father sheltered him."

Oh yeah? You haven't seen him in action, my dear governor. Alexis smiled. "You would be surprised at what Yeron can do. I never imagined myself as a warrior, but I promised my father on his deathbed that I would protect my mother and my sister, Robin. When that Kryszka soldier came after Robin and me, I forgot about my health problems and fought. Yeron must be really anxious about me now; he already lost his parents and a sister. No, wait. His sister is alive, but he believes she is dead. So did I."

"Woehar faked her death," Zoltar spoke up. "That does not surprise ..."

"Zoltar," the governor cut in. "Be silent."

Zoltar snapped his mouth shut.

"Your arguments about Yeron have merit, Alexis, but you need to understand our situation. Hear me out, and if you still want Yeron to visit, I will attempt contact."

Is that a concession she's offering? By golly, it is. Quyeba is an okay person.

Alexis gazed at her mangled hands, wondering if Quyeba's chromosomes would reverse the arthritis. It was unnatural, cross-breeding Kryszka cells with human ones, but Quyeba might have given her a hammer with which to fix her medical problems.

"Listening," she said, eyes on Quyeba.

"Yeron's sister—Woehar—told me that Yeron died. She made creatures like yours for an experiment, as I explained. I evicted her, but I continue to overhear dialogue in the human language from a nearby room. Someone might scream, but when I investigate, I cannot find anything suspicious."

Alexis let out a whistle.

"She is smart."

"So are we, so let us think this through. Woehar shot her mother and lied to me about Yeron. If I had known, I would have never allowed her to stay here in the beginning."

"Yeron said she regretted her actions." Alexis leaned back and looked at Quyeba.

"She helped her father escape the renegades, but she let Yeron think she was dead. She might harm him if given the opportunity."

"I warned you about her," Zoltar said to his mother.

"She was Teodon's daughter. I had to let her stay." Quyeba raised her hands and let them drop. "I was wrong. So, Alexis, think carefully about your request for Yeron's company. Woehar may be working with Eigil's soldiers, including the one who shot your friend. I cannot find out who is working with her without a translation of those dialogues. Yeron and your friends and mother may run into Woehar or her soldiers. Do you want them to attempt to visit?"

Alexis rubbed the palm of her hand against her nose. It never crossed her mind that Yeron and her friends could die trying to visit, even with Quyeba's help. The renegades had destroyed three people she loved. Aside from Yeron, her mother and the boys were all she had left. How could she be so selfish not to think of their safety?

"*Bah fungule,*" she said.

Quyeba frowned.

"I detest foul language. Quit using it."

Zoltar snorted a giggle.

"What makes you think I used foul words?" Alexis asked shyly. "You said you do not know the human languages."

More giggling, and then Zoltar burst into rough laughter.

"Humans at Teodon's laboratory said those words, the ones you taught Zoltar. It means the same thing in all languages." She darted her son a black glance. "I do not find this amusing."

The laughter stopped. Zoltar regarded his mother with somber eyes.

"No visitors. At least for now." Alexis considered her keepers, their sad eyes. She tried telling herself that Yeron and the others would be furious about her body changes, but that thought didn't fly. They would be so thrilled she was alive they wouldn't care.

"Can your android locate Yeron and let him know I am alive and getting treatment?"

"He could." Quyeba nodded. "Yeron could give my android times and dates. But we need to warn Yeron that visiting is too dangerous."

"Understood."

"All right. It would help if I knew English so I could translate the dialogues I overhear. Are you ready to begin teaching now?"

"Ready." Alexis scrutinized the computers, wondering what implements she had at her disposal.

The governor turned toward the portal. She took three steps, and the portal slid open. A soldier rushed into the laboratory.

"Governor! We have a security breach. A Kryszka and two humans came in through the lower entrance."

Oh my God! I hope Yeron is one of them. Alexis's heart leaped.

"I will address this emergency right away." Governor Quyeba looked over at Zoltar. "Come along with me. Bring a helium mask for yourself and one for me."

Zoltar looked at Alexis and hesitated. He hated leaving her alone, but he had to obey orders. Quyeba would not jeopardize her entire crew for just one person. He mumbled something about his android while tucking his plasma guns inside his tunic, and reached for the masks.

"Zoltar," Alexis called after him. "Be careful."

You can't be careful around mad scientists like Woehar. "Careful" belonged in another universe. Think about the well of shit where Aunt SusieQ landed. Maybe she went stumbling cockeyed drunk through an alley, and Lyrus picked her up for the egg harvest. More likely, Eigil earmarked her for a good meal and stowed her away with his other prisoners until Lyrus, for unknown reasons, came to her rescue.

"*Bah fungule.*" Alexis shifted in her chair, grateful for the free play with her hands and arms. She thought about her baby, wondering how it was developing inside an incubator. *What color eyes does he have? What color hair?* Zoltar had mentioned some deformities. She prayed her child wouldn't have any mental challenges.

As the moments ticked by, Alexis watched the flashing lights. The feminine looking android, dressed in a navy tunic and trousers, busied herself adjusting IVs, monitoring Alexis's lab values and vitals, but not conversing. The pain was gone. No burning from the IV like at Jackson Hospital. Moments later, she drifted to sleep.

The whisper of sliding panels nudged her awake. A woman in navy emerged through the opening. The set of her chin and tint of her hair reminded her of Yeron. She smiled, but her eyes held a horrid red stare. The irises spun like pinwheels. Behind her, the android lay in a melted heap on the floor. Alexis shivered at the alarms going off in her head.

"Alexis, we finally meet," the visitor said in perfect English.

"Woehar ... that is your name, isn't it?" At the woman's nod, Alexis continued. "What happened to the android?"

"She is not your concern." Woehar gave a forbidding frown, as if daring Alexis to contradict her. "A friend of yours is expecting you."

"What friend?" Alexis asked, tired of volunteering information.

"Do not be coy with me." The woman parted her lips, showing bloodstained, sharp teeth. The glare of the overhead lights turned her face into a ghastly map of clotted blood and gristle. "I met her after she had an unfortunate accident. She told me about you and your backbiting friends."

What accident? Never mind, she's crazy. "You should leave before Governor Quyeba catches you." Alexis's skin prickled with goose bumps, but she forced calmness in her voice. "The governor does not want any visitors here without her consent."

"Quyeba knows about me," Woehar said, leaning close.

Alexis looked at the buds of blood and spittle dripping from her lips. The saliva dropped on Alexis's tunic, dotting it red. She bit back a scream and forced her gaze up toward Woehar's wild eyes.

"Why did you let Yeron think you were dead?"

"Because he is dead ... to me ... for mating with you, an ordinary animal. But I did not come here to chat. You and I shall go for a ride." Woehar unhooked Alexis's IV lines and the leads to the monitors. She stepped behind Alexis and nudged her chair out of its stand.

"Yeron told me about you." Alexis raised her voice and it *was* stronger. She hoped it would dwarf the liquid fear coursing through her veins. "I have a dangerous infection. It will kill anyone who tries to consume me. It says so on the screens."

Woehar stopped in mid-step and turned toward Alexis. Her

lips pulled back in a sneer.

"I do not intend to consume you. What Laurel does is her business."

"My God!" Alexis gasped. Her limbs rashed out in goose bumps. "What's Laurel doing here?"

"She came here to punish her backbiting friends," Woehar replied, heading for the portal. "Especially you. You will meet her shortly, but she has changed. You will not recognize her."

Chapter Thirty-Nine: Shooting from the Renegades

Kryszka Underground Compound, August 31, 1:00 a.m.

The plasma rays blazed back and forth; Yeron deflected them while Steve and Tyrone huddled behind a computer and resorted to their helium. Though one shot of helium could kill the Kryszka, they didn't die. *They must have devised helium-proof masks, too.* Steve and Tyrone had gone through most of their other ammunition. Yeron's firearm had run out of plasma, too. His gun was firing rays without noxious lasers or fire.

The renegades could kill him before he even got a chance to search for Alexis. *By now, her spirit had gone to Heaven, where Kryszka do not go.* He was not sure about the baby. *Jesus, if You exist, save Alexis and our child. Please!*

Yeron fired another shot. Empty.

The tall soldier came forward, his face covered, waving his gun.

"Come out and prepare to die," he ordered.

Yeron, Steve, and Tyrone dropped their weapons. Yeron stared at the soldier with fiery eyes filled with hatred. He and his two companions faced six guards. Attempting to run would guarantee death. Yeron could deflect a shot from two or three soldiers using his psychokinetic powers, but not six. Besides, the renegades could neutralize his power with a combined effort.

Behind him, Tyrone nudged Steve's shoulder.

"We'd better man up and show ourselves," he said.

Yeron was not sure what "man up" meant, but Steve scrambled to his feet, Tyrone beside him. The three stepped out from behind the machinery. Despite the visor covering the speaker's face, Yeron thought that he sounded familiar.

"We did not come here to fight." Yeron tried hard to muster civility into his voice. "We are looking for someone."

"Humans and enemy Kryszka have no business around our compound."

"Oh, yes, I do," Yeron said. "I am Teodon's son and I am looking for Alexis and Shively."

"Teodon's son is dead," the bold soldier barked. "Do not besmirch his memory."

Steve and Tyrone huddled together, their eyes fearful and yet defiant.

"Give me a blood test. It will prove that I am he." Yeron gestured toward the shattered cubicles. "Your barbarism here will set off another war and the officers above will destroy your compound."

The soldier laughed. His eyes telegraphed bloodlust, and then Yeron recognized him. The soldier was Draekh, Eigil's personal healer. "Our technology can disintegrate the human race if we so choose," Draekh told him.

"Let them be."

"Silence!" Draekh raised his plasma gun, ready to deliver the final shot. Yeron could only hope that Alexis had stumbled upon a kindly guard. It crossed his mind to try to deflect Draekh's shot, but the other soldiers also trained their guns on Yeron and his comrades.

A woman's voice shouted from the hallway. Her voice sounded familiar, but Yeron could not place her name. Clad in a sequined crown and matching tunic, she materialized from the shadows, accompanied by a healer—Zoltar, he noted with astonishment—and an android. Blue rays shot from her gun, circling the three soldiers. In the next instant, they dropped to the floor.

"I will not allow you to harm these people," she told them. "Yeron is Teodon's son." She looked over at Yeron. "That is your name, is it not?"

"Yes," Yeron replied, his head slightly askance, looking puzzled.

"Quyeba," the woman said, smiling. "Governor Quyeba. Have you forgotten me?"

"Your uniform looks different."

"I have aged a few years, too," Quyeba said with a wave of her hand. "When these miscreants wake, they will find themselves in a cage with *settva*. Who are your comrades?"

"Tyrone and Steve." Yeron indicated his respective friends. "We are looking for our comrades."

"Alexis and Shively," Zoltar piped up. "I have ..."

"Be still." Quyeba glared at him, and then turned toward the android. "Lock Draekh and his fellow soldiers in the furthest cell. Make sure the lock is secure. I will decide what to do with them later."

The android glided away, with the three soldiers floating before it. Yeron stood close to Steve and watched, arms wrapped around his shivering body. *Why is Draekh here?*

Quyeba then retrieved a radio-like device from the folds of her tunic, pressed three buttons, and listened. Tyrone and Steve gaped at the android as it sashayed down the hall. Yeron guessed that the technology in the Kryszka colony had overwhelmed them. He knew from experience Quyeba was checking the immediate area for surveillance.

"Yeron." Her voice dropped to a faint whisper. "Alexis is alive, but she has a deadly, potentially fatal infection. We isolated a toxic organism and initiated treatment, but she needed our chromosomes to make her cells receptive to the only antidote we have available. I am the blood donor. With time, she will recover."

"And Shively?"

A long silence followed. "One of my soldiers became aggressive with his interrogation and ..." She gave him a look as if to say, *this was not supposed to happen.* "I am sorry."

Yeron translated the news to his partners but edited the part about the Kryszka DNA. Given the humans' beliefs regarding DNA fusions between species, some matters required discretion.

"Shively ... what? My God!" Steve shouted. "I'm surprised Quyeba was able to help Alexis."

"Yeron, ask her what she wants." Tyrone heaved a sigh. "While you're at it, ask about the walkers."

"The humans are wary," Yeron said. "They want to understand why vischlausk creatures attack their people. Since humans do not know how to manufacture vischlausk, it's clear that a Kryszka here is producing it and introducing into the walkers. We found human hostages ..." He gestured toward the cubicles.

"Hey," Tyrone butted in. "I hope you're asking about the baby monsters."

Yeron translated, describing their skirmish with the grotesque infants.

"This is worse than I expected." Quyeba swept her hand over her forehead. "I know about the vischlausk ... I saw these creatures. Woehar never mentioned infants, though. Did she contact you?"

"No. She died when we escaped the old compound."

"No, she came to me and asked for asylum. I let her stay because Teodon had done so much for Zoltar and me. That was a mistake. Woehar used her laboratory to make the vischlausk creatures. I evicted her, but she set up another laboratory near mine. I never saw the infant monstrosities."

Yeron gasped, trembling. Liquid fear ran through his veins sending chills through his body. *I was so sure my sister was dead. The officers found her soiled uniform.*

Think! Yeron channeled his father's way of reasoning. *Woehar must have faked her death. Remember what she did to Mother? Many humans faked their deaths with success, and Woehar has sophisticated technology at her disposal.* Ice-cold terror ran down Yeron's back. He had considered Woehar's so-called remorse as suspect. *I cannot believe she faked her death. My sister!* As Eigil's ally, she would continue his genocide on humanity. Tyrone was right to be wary. Perhaps Quyeba and Zoltar had gone along with Woehar's plans. Yeron eyed them warily.

Steve nudged him.

"What did she tell you?"

"Woehar is alive and producing vischlausk. She uses it to make the monstrosities that came after us."

Steve gasped, hands covering his mouth. Tyrone stared at Yeron and Quyeba with raised eyebrows. He smacked his hand on his forehead.

Shoulders hunched, Yeron riveted his eyes back to the governor. "She apologized to my father and helped him escape during the explosion at our former compound and then disappeared. We found her torn uniform and presumed her dead."

Quyeba sighed.

"Woehar brought me a recording of that battle. She arrived here wearing clothes that humans wear. Later on, after I gave her a position, she told me she was using humans – people who died of natural causes – to develop androids for weapons. I needed to believe her because I promised Teodon I would look after his family." She hung her head. "I regret the pain that my actions have caused."

Yeron regarded the human prisoners, arms folded tightly against his chest. The chills he felt were coming from the sight of the prisoners, who screamed and writhed against their ties. Neither Quyeba nor Zoltar made any move to help them. The vischlausk had made them dangerous, and neither person knew how to help them.

Quyeba drew a protective arm around her son. Zoltar's head drooped, as if he had been lugging a hundred-pound weight.

"Can we save the prisoners?" Yeron asked, forcing calmness into his voice.

"I doubt it." Quyeba's face did not register emotion. Her eyes flicked toward the paneled exit.

"Quyeba, did anyone tell you how my mother died?" Yeron asked.

"Yes," she said, her tone flat and eyes drooping. "Teodon told me he disowned Woehar after that. Alexis confirmed this, but she told us Woehar was dead. She reported invasions from renegade soldiers and vischlausk-poisoned beings, but did not give me dates or times because she cannot convert Earth's calendar to ours."

"Oh, my God," Tyrone whispered in a dismayed voice when Yeron conveyed this to them.

"Something isn't right." Steve's lips set in a grim line. "Why didn't this governor question Woehar? Her dad wouldn't disown her without a reason, right?"

"Good question," Tyrone said, his voice tense.

"Quyeba, you are an intelligent woman," Yeron ventured. "Most civilians at the old compound avoided Woehar because of her foul moods. Did you sense anything suspicious about her?"

"Yes, I did. Most people here avoided her, too," Quyeba said in a sorrowful voice. "I gave her a chance because I owed Teodon. She became evasive when I asked her about the vischlausk creatures. I assumed the stress of the explosion and loss of her family warped her behavior. She reported you and Teodon dead. When she came here, she was dirty and covered with blood. She brought the recording of that battle, the one in which she tried to save her father. So I ordered Draekh to treat her. What would you have done?"

"I do not know." Yeron rephrased her explanation in English and then asked his companions, "What do you think?"

"Woehar's got to be stopped," Tyrone said softly.

"Our governor may have meant well, but she made a tragic mistake with Woehar." Steve inhaled a sharp breath. "I'm glad she's looking after Alexis, but no one's safe until Woehar's caught."

He forked his fingers through his hair. "Yeron, how about Alexis's mental state?"

Yeron nodded.

"Quyeba, Alexis must be terrified."

"She is, but more than that, she misses you, her family, and her friends."

"Well, I am here now and I can help fill in the dates for you," Yeron hoped to appeal to the sensitivity he recalled about the governor and her son. "Let Alexis go home to her family where she belongs."

"I am her family, too," Zoltar spoke up.

At that, Quyeba grimaced.

"He is related, according to our data," she admitted. "Perhaps through an aunt or uncle."

Yeron frowned, trying hard to imagine Matilda or Susan as someone's mate. It would never have happened.

"Alexis must stay for now," Zoltar told him. "Her treatment prohibits her leaving. Even with our technology, she needs more time to heal, and she knows that. She almost died."

"Steve, she will die without treatment here," Yeron told the others, his lips trembling.

"That doesn't surprise me." Steve mopped his forehead. "We'd never figure out how to treat this bug she's got. Ask him if he knows about her arthritis."

"I understand the condition that caused her deformed joints," Zoltar replied after Yeron posed the question. "Since you were working with primitive equipment, the compounds you introduced into her system caused a breakdown in her immunity. She hemorrhaged from her stomach. It was fortunate I could harvest your child."

"*What*?" Yeron clapped his hand over his lips. "Is Alexis going to be all right? What about our child?"

"Alexis and your child ... a son ... will survive." Zoltar mumbled. "I harvested and implanted your son into an incubator so I could correct the irregularities in his chromosomal structure."

"A son." Yeron smiled and looked proud. He relayed the information to his friends, his lips numb. Months ago, he would have settled for a female to stroll through the park with him. Among humans, unions with otherworldly beings happened in science fiction movies and books. Now, he was going to have a son.

He longed to shout with glee, but the mood in the room was serious and it behooved him to approach Quyeba with dignity.

"Did you tell Alexis?"

Zoltar darted a glance toward the governor, and then back at Yeron and his friends. "I did, Yeron, and she is grateful." A grin surfaced on his lips. "I find her amusing. She invents interesting phrases with our language and teaches me foul human words."

The governor stood, shaking her head, but she smiled, too.

"She scolded me in my laboratory because I was too strict with my son. Why would she do that? She never met Zoltar."

Yeron's jaw dropped, surprised Alexis was so free around these strangers. *Whatever drugs they gave her must have loosened her inhibitions.* He thought about the way she had befriended him when she had been his patient.

"Maybe she saw something in Zoltar worth speaking up for," he replied. "She always looks for the good in people."

"Yeron," Tyrone nudged him. "What's going on?"

"My Steel Rose befriended these two dignitaries. She and I are going to have a healthy son."

"Congratulations ... I think," Steve said. "Are you sure Alexis and the child are going to be all right?"

"Yes, so long as they remain here. You cannot give them the kind of care they need." Yeron shifted his gaze between the Kryszka healers and his human teammates, not daring to mention the gene fusion. As it was, his comrades' willingness to trust was tenuous. The one time he mentioned gene fusion to Steve, his comment was, "Do me a favor, Yeron. Don't mention it to anyone else. They'll put you in jail."

"You are hiding something from your friends," Zoltar observed. "Why?"

"I am omitting information they would not understand. It would not be wise to tell my friends that Alexis has become, as humans say, part Kryszka."

"Interesting," Quyeba said. "Alexis does not want her mother to know, either. You should tell your friends about Zoltar and Alexis. Zoltar wants to meet his human relatives."

Yeron regarded the suffering prisoners and wondered if his Steel Rose knew about them. He suspected not. "Why ... how?"

"My father conceived a child with a female prisoner," Zoltar said.

There has been a mistake. Yeron stared at Zoltar, his eyes widening. *Matilda would never mate with a Kryszka male. Never in a million years.*

"The mother can only be one of two women I know," he said at last.

"When I described the female to Alexis, she said it was her Aunt Susan," Quyeba said, and Yeron translated.

Steve whistled. "That explains it. In her drug-induced rages, her aunt mentioned Kryszka scientists. We decided it was the liquor talking."

Tyrone nodded. "I gotta wonder how come Alexis hasn't lost it."
Because this particular rose is made of steel. Yeron smiled.

"How is her emotional state?"

"She grieves for her deceased friends and sister," Zoltar told him. "She and I get along well, but she finds it hard to believe I am a relative, I think, because I am different from her aunt."

"She may be in what humans call 'denial,'" Yeron said. "Their refusal to accept painful realities is a common defense mechanism against emotional hurt. I find it hard to believe this, too. Her mother tolerates me because she respects Alexis's wishes. I cannot imagine her or Susan mating with anyone like us."

"Susan did not mate with anyone," Quyeba told him. "Lyrus harvested her eggs and his sperm. After employing in vitro fertilization, he incubated the embryo. Zoltar was the result."

Yeron swallowed hard. This latest revelation would be harder on his companions than the report on the chromosome fusion.

"Susan has enjoyed excessive liquor for some time. I am sure this affected her judgment," he told his teammates. "Whatever the reason, it happened. What matters now is that Alexis is safe and our son is going to be all right. Much as I worry about Alexis, I am concerned about these hostages, so I will ask about them."

"Good idea," replied Steve. "These folks look like they're hurting badly. Ask them why aren't they trying to make them comfortable?"

"It is impossible to make someone with vischlausk poisoning comfortable," Yeron said after asking and getting the answer to his question. He mentally confirmed this as he looked at the hostages. "Quyeba has found herself, as you say, in deep trouble."

"You've got that right." Tyrone swiped his beefy hand over his forehead. "I can't wait to hear Alexis's take on these folks."

"She is grateful because these people saved her life and that of our child," Yeron told him. "But sad because she misses us."

"I can believe it." Steve nodded in agreement.

"It sounds like she fell down a well of shit and came up with diamonds," Tyrone conceded. "Can these people cure her arthritis?"

"Can you treat her deformed hands?" Yeron asked Zoltar.

"I need to clean her system of the infection before I do any other procedure or treatment," Zoltar said. "I dare not introduce another foreign compound until I repair her immune system. That could take a long time. Her heart stopped beating while I repaired the perforation in her stomach. Her body cannot take more stress at this time."

Tell me something I do not know.

"When may we visit?" Zoltar gave the governor a questioning look. "These people mean no harm. Let me bring them to Alexis after they have gone through the quarantine procedure."

"No." The governor grimaced. "The breach in security is worse than I anticipated."

What breach? What is this woman doing with Alexis? So far, she has saved Alexis's life and garnered her trust. He scanned the governor's face, trying to gauge her emotions. Her eyes held a wavering glance of fright mixed with anger.

"Look at this mess," Zoltar pointed toward the cubicles. He stared at Yeron and his cohorts. "Friendly visitors might motivate Alexis to fight her infection and recover. When she does, Mother, she may thank you by helping you contain this breach."

"Alexis has been cooperative," Quyeba allowed, "but I cannot allow humans in the laboratory yet. Yeron, Zoltar will lead your fellow warriors through Quarantine. I will escort you to Alexis. In the meantime, your assistants may do what they can for these hostages, but do not touch their mouths or release their ties. Vischlausk poisoning has made them dangerous and hungry."

"Understood." Yeron expelled his breath in a whoosh, knowing now that fear motivated her reluctance to help the prisoners.

"When may I see my son?"

"That depends on how your visit with Alexis goes." Quyeba turned toward the hall, lips set in a grim line. In her face, Yeron saw the terrified young girl who had come to his father for help. She moved toward the open panel.

"She will allow me to visit Alexis, but she wants you under quarantine first. A guard will take you to the showers," Yeron told his companions. "Afterwards, you may examine the hostages but do not touch their mouths or ties. They are dangerous."

"Okay," Steve said. "Let us know about Alexis as soon as you can."

"Ask your friend if she has more ammo," Tyrone piped up. "In case those soldiers make another visit."

"My friends and I need plasma," Yeron told Quyeba. "For their security."

"Under the circumstances ..." Quyeba withdrew three guns from her belt and handed them to Yeron and the others. "I am sealing this laboratory with a force field. If anything happens to you or your friends, there will be dire consequences."

Yeron passed the guns to Steve and Tyrone, with her reassurance.

"It sounds like she's sincere about helping us." Tyrone smiled, taking the proffered gun.

"It sure does." Steve clapped Tyrone on the back. "Roll up your sleeves, my friend. We start with cleaning the wounds."

"Huh?" Tyrone's eyes skated toward the prisoners. "I haven't treated any wounds since I was in the Army."

"It's like riding a bicycle. You never forget." Steve grinned. "Especially after you've had your first cup of coffee."

****

"I never expected such cruelty from a child of Teodon," Quyeba said to Yeron as they proceeded down the hall. "I knew Woehar was lying, but I wanted her close so I could watch her. Despite my observation, she has managed to corrupt my soldiers with vischlausk."

"Woehar can be cunning," Yeron admitted. "She inherited that trait from her grandfather, mother's side. He was very cruel toward our mother."

"The vischlausk poison ruined her, too," Zoltar said. "Rest assured that Alexis responded well to the fusion and antidote."

"She must be grief-stricken," Yeron said, "and angry with me because my medicine damaged her immune system."

"She's not angry with you." Quyeba looked at Yeron with saddened eyes. "She misses you, Yeron. Whenever she harkens to Zoltar's voice, she thinks it is you."

"She must miss her mother and other friends, too," Yeron said.

"I will allow other visitors," Quyeba said, "if your visit brings no surprises. The danger is severe enough for me to abrogate the policy about humans and firearms."

"I can appreciate that. As it is, most of us are ill-equipped to handle her treatment. Does Alexis understand that?"

"She understands ... too much," Zoltar said. "She can interpret her laboratory values from my monitors. I had to position her bed away from the viewscreens." Yeron smiled at that, and then stopped walking.

"How can she interpret her laboratory values? I never taught her medical terminology."

Zoltar looked at the governor, but did not answer. Quyeba looked at Yeron, but remained silent.

"You used a language implant," Yeron said in a low voice. "Does she know that?"

"She knows," Zoltar replied, "Worry about you, her friends, and her mother occupies her mind."

"Of course, it would." Yeron clinched his jaw in anticipation. "When she recovers, Alexis will ask a lot of questions. Someone better answer."

"She knows her mind," Quyeba smiled. "She reminds me of myself when I was younger."

Further down a tiled hall, Quyeba stopped before a windowed panel.

"This is where we are keeping Alexis. I should warn you, Zoltar has her attached to many monitors. She is still gaunt and pale. She will not look healthy."

Yeron stepped closer to the door, expecting the familiar hum of the monitors, especially the ones registering vital signs, and the whirr of IV pumps. Instead, silence. The deathly silence left a sick feeling in his stomach.

"I believe she will recover," Zoltar assured him. "She will have to be careful the rest of her life, but my mother's chromosomes will boost her immunity. She may realize heightened senses and other abilities characteristic of our people. Unfortunately, humans consider splicing among species taboo, so she does not want her mother to know." Yeron nodded with the usual stoicism of his people.

"She may look delicate as a flower, but she is made of steel. She will handle this in her way, and if she lets me, I will provide for her and our child."

The panel opened, giving them a look into the laboratory.

Quyeba let out a low gasp. No Alexis. Medical equipment, including IVs, was there, as he and his cohorts had expected, but no readouts. No readouts on the viewscreens. Quyeba and Zoltar scuttled ahead of him, eyes on the monitors. Quyeba hurried to the bed.

"Where is Alexis?" she asked Zoltar, alarmed.

"She was sitting up right here." Then he hurried over to the bed, followed by Yeron.

IV bags leaked yellow fluid onto the table and grid floor. Tentacles of wires dangled over the side of Alexis's pillow. Feeding solution dripped from its IV machine and landed on the floor in huge oatmeal-colored drops. Blood and feeding solution streaked the sheet.

The chair was gone.

Chapter Forty: Failed Attempt at Rescue

"Change ... how? Woehar, take me back to the laboratory," Alexis pleaded, hoping to appeal to whatever sense Woehar possessed. "Governor Quyeba knows about your vischlausk experiments. If anything happens to me, she will come after you."

Grated laughter echoed behind Alexis.

"I have no intention of harming you. As for Laurel's plans, that is not my concern."

Alexis whipped her head around toward Woehar, shocked. Woehar had replied in perfect English. She longed to unleash her mind power, crumpling Woehar's face. Quyeba's DNA had given her mind control more wallop. There was no telling how the infection would impair her ability, though, or how many guards were watching from their hiding places, waiting to pounce.

The incision in her gut burned like a fiery arrow. It was four inches long, and deep. Zoltar must have cut through nerve tissue to repair the perforation. Arthritis raged through her wrists, hands, and arms. *Oh, how everything hurts!* She knew that without the continued treatment, her infection would spread.

Alexis inventoried the white tiles glimmering from the ceiling, the glazed lime wall tiles, and the olive green grid squares on the floor. A lemony scent permeated the room. *I guess the Kryszka use a powerful disinfectant to remove the body fluids.*

"What is Laurel doing here?" she asked.

"You will find out in due time." Woehar's voice reeked with cheer. "According to Laurel, you did terrible things. Aside from causing trouble for your peers, you stood by and let someone die, Mark Adams. You bullied him into fighting your war, so I gave him an implant that tracked your activities. He attempted to steal the weapons, and then you and Shively killed him."

Mark again. It always came down to Mark. Alexis's breath came out in pants, her teeth clenched.

"I never wanted Mark on our team, but Shively was using him as a lure. You are angry because Mark's death ruined your plans."

Woehar snickered. "No one ruins my plans. Besides, I fed, so I am content. Laurel's appetite is bigger than mine, and she would love to have you for dinner."

Cold, definitely cold. The double meaning of that comment wasn't lost on Alexis. Another glance at Woehar. A sea of fiery red surrounded her birdshot pupils. The chilliness radiated in all directions, the way Laurel's did after she screwed with a patient. But Laurel was stupid; Woehar's intellect made her dangerous.

Why didn't I go to the hospital when Yeron asked me? Not that it mattered since the infection would have killed her, leaving her mother devastated. That prospect zinged an arrow through her heart. She gulped twice to fight off tears.

At the end of the hall, two steel gray panels opened into a room lined with metal tables. An acrid stench steamed from the blood filling the grid squares on the floor and the gristle coating the tables. The putrid smell was worst near the opposite wall where a partially eaten body lay. Its bones had been picked clean, except the face and left arm. It still had blond hair with one wisp sticking out, bulging blue eyes, and a mouth shaped into a vast circle of terror. Closer up, she saw a tattoo of a snake on the arm. Alexis recognized the tattoo and blond hair. She was looking at what remained of her former commander and friend, Shively. A cry built up in her throat.

"What ... what ... I thought ..."

Her voice cut off as Woehar mind-hefted her and dumped her on a table. Razor blades of agony sliced through her gut and arms when she slammed onto the metal. Steel bands snapped around her, cutting into her wrists, neck, and ankles. No air cushions here. Her breath came out in short gasps. Clicking followed. Woehar moved her table toward the one belonging to her deceased friend.

"I know. You thought Quyeba's android had taken him to the crematorium, but one of my fellow soldiers intercepted the transport. You would be surprised at how many friends I have in Quyeba's compound." Another sardonic grin. "I thought you might miss your old companion, so you shall spend some time with him."

"The bands," Alexis whispered. "They're cutting into my skin."

"Are they now?" Woehar's voice oozed good cheer again. Someone listening in on the conversation might mistake that voice for intent to help. Alexis, having received a thorough history from Yeron and Quyeba, understood a different truth. She shivered at the terror coursing through her veins.

"When I return, I shall bring Laurel with me, but you will not recognize her." Woehar's lips curled into a skeletal grin. "If you move, the bands will slice a major blood vessel. This will give you a swift death. I suspect, though, you want to give your friends time to look for you. In that case, your death will be slow and excruciating, but you will be dead by the time your friends find you."

On that note, Woehar turned on her booted heels and marched out of the room, into the hall. Black dots rose before Alexis's eyes. The odor was nauseating. She bit her tongue to keep from fainting; the sensation passed. She concentrated on moving the table; she noticed that some of the tables were on wheels. Hers didn't budge. Then she remembered that Zoltar had told her most of the equipment and furniture was levitation-proof.

Alexis heard footsteps in the hall. Woehar was back. It was best that she struggle, cut an artery, and die quickly, but images of her son in the incubator haunted her. If she died and Yeron got killed in the crossfire, he'd grow up an orphan.

"Alexis?" It sounded like Yeron.

Wishful thinking, Dearie. If Yeron were going to find you, he would have done so already.

"Alexis?" Louder now, more urgent.

"Yeron?" she called out in a shaky voice.

The figure emerged from the doorway and it *was* Yeron, his angular features visible without his mask. His moist, wiry hair dangled like coils behind his ears.

"What did they do to you?" His eyes settled on Shively's body. "What happened here?"

"Yeron, watch out for Woehar." Every word dragged; her strength flagged. "She's alive. Draekh killed Shively and ... and ... how did you find me?"

"Zoltar, Quyeba, and I split up to search for you. I was fortunate." Yeron moved like a cat, pressing something at the head of her table. The bands fell free. "My Steel Rose, I heard that Woehar is still alive. Come. Let us get out of here."

Alexis struggled to sit, wincing with each movement. Tears rolled down her face.

"I can't," she wept. "Everything hurts. Woehar stopped my medicine."

"Ignore the pain." Yeron propped her legs over the side. "It is the only way. I will carry you to the laboratory."

"In a minute." She gasped, trying to catch her breath. She bit back a scream as Yeron scooped her into his arms. "Quyeba gave me a—"

"I know," Yeron whispered. "Do not say anything more here."

Voices echoed from the corridor. They belonged to Woehar and someone who sounded familiar. Yeron backed away from the table and rushed to the door.

"Yeron, watch out!" Alexis bit back another cry, as the sensation of rusty nails twisted through her joints.

The panel slid open, revealing Woehar alongside a grotesque being with scraggly light brown hair, and yellow eyes. Its lips drooled brownish red saliva. The gargoyle-like creases on its face reminded Alexis of the movie *Species*, where the hybrid human-aliens took on grotesque shapes. Its covering of greenish plates was reminiscent of the Kryszka reptiles Yeron had described. Rancid odors of dried blood and shit baked off of its tainted clothing, a tent dress that was once blue. It let loose a coughing growl.

Dear God! She looks like a dinosaur ... all those scales and teeth! That can't be Laurel. Of course, it is; Woehar said I wouldn't recognize her. Someone must have fused her chromosomes with a settva. This is worse than the zombies. Any second, she'll tear into me.

The Laurel-thing sidled up behind Woehar, towering over her, claws reaching. Her nails were caked with what looked like uncooked meat. Flecks of meat peppered her scales in the front. The sharpness in her talons ... Alexis knew what damage those claws could do, having received a lesson on *settvas* from Yeron.

Woehar brandished her plasma gun.

"Put the animal down or I shoot."

Yeron eased Alexis to her knees and faced Woehar with steely eyes.

"Before you shoot who? Me? Alexis? From where I stand, you are the real animal. Look at this." He indicated Shively's body. "You left a similar mess when you destroyed our mother. Someone should put *you* out of your misery."

"What misery? I faked my death and fooled Quyeba into believing you were dead." Woehar's grin broadened. "As humans say, you and the governor fell asleep at the helm."

Alexis watched Yeron for signs of confusion. She was surprised that Woehar was fluent in English, especially idioms. She looked at the Laurel-thing, who was grinning and winking at Woehar. Saliva ran down her chin in stringy strands.

"Quyeba knows about you and Draekh," Yeron said, seeming to ignore her observation. "At one time, you cared about me. If you still do, let me bring Alexis to the laboratory. She needs medical attention."

"We shall see how much attention she will need after Laurel is through with her. You will not stop me because you would not choose an animal over me."

Wanna bet? Alexis longed to challenge her. The trouble was, Yeron faced two monsters.

"You think so?" Yeron angled his gun at Woehar the way he had against the walkers.

Another growl came from Laurel, sending frissons of terror through Alexis. Laurel had cracked when she was human, and her chromosome fusion would only make her worse.

Alexis braced one elbow against the table and tried standing. Her legs wobbled and the slightest movement sent kilowatts of pain through the incision. She sank to the floor on her butt and the pain eased to a dull throb.

"Yeron, find Quyeba," she begged him. "She wants me alive and will gladly help you." *I want you to stay alive, dammit. Where are Quyeba and Zoltar? Where are Steve and Tyrone?*

Yeron remained steady, his eyes and gun trained on Woehar. Woehar aimed her weapon at his chest.

"This is so sweet," she crooned. "Listen to your pet, little boy. Eigil taught me the right way to use guns."

Laurel squatted on the floor, emitting soft growls. Alexis had gotten used to Laurel's craziness, but the cold gleam in her yellow eyes, the *hunger* on her face, was awful.

"Yeron, run!" Alexis shouted.

He didn't budge.

"I used to care about you before you made your home with these humans," Woehar told Yeron. "You are no longer my brother."

She cocked her weapon. Yeron squeezed off a blast of fire that engulfed Woehar's body. She let out bloodcurdling screams, then slumped to the floor, burned the color of charcoal. But Yeron hadn't moved fast enough. Her laser caught him near his right shoulder. With a soft groan, he fell to the floor and blood oozed from behind his back.

"Yeron!" In spite of her throbbing pain, Alexis crawled on her hands and knees to her lover. She forgot about Woehar and Laurel. She forgot about her pain. She forgot about everything except Yeron, the man who'd taught her that love didn't hurt. "Yeron!"

A low deep groan escaped his lips.

He was fading. Alexis checked his wrists for a pulse. Nothing. Then she remembered the Kryszka pulse point was under the rib cage. Doctor Hoffman had once told her that heartbeat and blood pressures for Kryszka ran about the same as they did for humans. Sixty was a nice number for a Kryszka pulse. Yeron's ran over a hundred, and thready at that. His skin was clammy and moist.

"Zoltar!" she shouted, praying that Yeron had brought backup. "Quyeba?"

No answer, except Laurel's snarl, sounding like rattling bones.

The hell with it. I'm levitating him to the laboratory myself. Alexis mustered her concentration, and Yeron rose off the ground. A gasp escaped his lips. He was badly hurt, and moving him by mind or brawn aggravated his injury. The issue became moot when Laurel squatted in front of the exit, malignant grin tucked into place.

Alexis lowered Yeron to the floor.

"Laurel, move! Yeron isn't part of this."

Laurel broke into rough laughter.

"You expect me to let you go? That's rich." Her voice was hoarse, sounding like a longtime pack-a-day smoker.

Alexis gasped, surprised that Laurel could talk.

"Yeron never bothered you." The tears were coming again and she was unable to stop them. "I've got to help him. He'll bleed to death without treatment."

Laurel gave her a black look with her brass-yellow eyes. The irises in them spun like pinwheels. Something inside Alexis froze at the sight of them. Laurel replied with two words, but the hate in her voice knifed through Alexis's heart.

"I know."

"What about Woehar?" Alexis's voice came out a dusty croak. "She needs a doctor, too."

"Yes. Both of them need help, the poor things," Laurel replied in her same cold voice, frostier than a Canadian winter. "I'll get it after I've had my supper. I've got three courses. Who will be first?"

Her eyes settled on Alexis. The malice in them dissipated and a cold, hungry look took its place.

"Woehar has taught me interesting things," she said, smiling. "The greatest thrill I've had here was tearing into live flesh and watching the blood gush."

"Laurel, don't touch me!" Alexis recoiled, backpedaling. "I've got an infection fatal to Kryszka. It will kill you if you eat me."

"Ah, but I'm different now. Your flimsy germs can't harm a *settva*." She rolled her tongue across her lips, raising a curtain, revealing her pointed incisors.

The fusion! Alexis had forgotten that she'd come to this fight with a mutation of her own. The noises had gotten louder – the humming of the machines, padding of Laurel's clawed feet – as if the sounds took place in her middle ear. Whispering as Yeron shifted. Faint but audible. Something else was happening. A force swept through her, the kind that could move cars. Didn't Laurel notice any of this?

Of course not, because she's Shit Drawers, according to Johnny. She's crazy.

At that thought, giggles tore from Alexis's throat.

"You've picked the wrong person. I'm not human anymore, either."

"Oh, yeah?" Laurel grinned as she came at Alexis, like a snake advancing on a mouse.

"Look at my eyes!" Alexis shouted, glad she'd found her voice. "Woehar fused your genes with another being, right? Someone did that to me, too."

Laurel froze in mid-step, eyes bulging, and then grimaced.

"You smell like shit."

"I probably do." Alexis revved up her psychokinesis to use on Laurel, when Yeron let out another groan. She turned and studied his shoulder, trying to figure out the source of the bleeding. Capital mistake. A huge silver flare of agony shot through her ass, high up near the small of her back. Alexis went flying ahead a meter and landed on her right side, next to Yeron. She groped for Yeron's gun.

More laughter erupted from Laurel.

"That was for getting me fired. You've got a lot wrong with you. Boy, I intend on making the most of it before I eat you."

Ignore the pain and fight! That's what Yeron would have told her. Alexis focused on Laurel, and the images of Laurel Past came to mind: Laurel who caused a patient to asphyxiate; Laurel who butchered young women in her home. The force that had been brewing earlier ripped through her. Alexis hurled it in Laurel's direction.

An eerie snapping noise followed. Laurel howled with fury and clutched her chest, right side. She staggered backwards, slid on the bloodstained floor, and landed on her butt.

"Ahhhhh!" She howled. "You broke my ribs."

The exertion left Alexis spent and she flopped on her side. Her arm draped over cold metal, and there it was, Yeron's gun. Breath hitching with each movement, she grabbed the gun and propped herself on her elbow.

Laurel's face twisted into the shape of a gargoyle. Her growl crescendoed and sent shivers through Alexis. Her eyes glazed. She shifted her face toward Woehar and spat.

"You bitch!" Laurel hollered at Woehar. "You knew she was part alien, didn't you?"

No answer. Woehar was silent, maybe dead. Alexis didn't give a damn.

"I think she knew," Alexis said, mustering coldness in her voice. "If I were so delectable, she would've had me for dinner long ago."

Laurel nodded. Arm splinting her chest, she waddled toward Woehar and sniffed. A dog-eared smile curled on her puffy face. She squatted before Woehar's prone form and lowered her head. Her lips drew back, exposing her pointed incisors.

"Damn, I'm hungry," she said, ripping open Woehar's tunic.

This looks too easy. Alexis stared at the door. *As soon as I move, Laurel will be on me like a tiger. More likely, she'll go after Yeron.*

Instead, Laurel knelt by Woehar's side, giggling.

"Kryszka meat," she said in a low voice. Alexis shuddered. With her newly sensitized ears, every word came through clear as glass. "Smells good. I'll take my meat, cooked or raw. You'll do as an appetizer."

Head bent, she ripped a chunk of flesh from Woehar's burnt breast.

Alexis felt a hand settle on her shoulder. She gasped.

"Forget Laurel," the familiar voice told her. "Levitate Yeron out of here while you can."

Alexis looked up at the speaker, Yeron's late father.

"I can't—"

Teodon pointed toward Laurel and held a finger to his lip.

"Do not speak out loud. I will understand the answers you think."

Okay, Yeron's badly hurt and so am I. I can't move him without making his injuries worse.

"All right, then I will levitate him. I know how and I will not see him die. Go ahead of us and lead me to Quyeba's laboratory. You must forget your injuries and pain. It may seem impossible, but Yeron needs your help. I cannot carry two injured people safely, and if you stay, Laurel will come after you again."

I understand. Alexis struggled onto her hands and knees.

Harsh chewing and slurping sounds issued from Laurel. Despite the pain wracking her body, Alexis crawled toward the door.

She had to find her way back to the lab. Yeron was moaning, and his cries were growing weaker. Teodon lifted him. He depended on her to lead the way. Any second, Laurel would tire of Woehar and come after her.

Never mind the pain. Find help.

Gritting her teeth, Alexis began her Bataan Death Crawl. Her incisions telegraphed bolts of stabbing pain with each movement. *It doesn't matter; Yeron's life is on the line.* She mind-opened the panel and led Yeron and Teodon through the exit.

Once in the hallway, Teodon hesitated.

"Left or right?"

Woehar had made a sharp right to enter the killing field, Alexis remembered. *Left.*

She edged along the long stretch of hall. The throbbing from her incision and back brought to mind the pain she'd felt from the rheumatoid arthritis during her job as a respiratory therapist. Her chest tightened at the prospect of navigating that long corridor the way it used to when she faced a heavy shift. No painkillers were forthcoming. She kept going.

It was simple. Woehar had guided right from the laboratory, and then a long stretch of hallway, past two sets of doors, before making her right into the death camp. So Alexis retraced Woehar's steps and looked for steel doors on her left leading to the lab. Adrenaline would carry her. She'd once read a tale about a mother whose adrenaline rush allowed her to lift a car off her child's injured body.

Agony bled into her incision with every shift of her knees. The pain was worse in her lower back, where Laurel had kicked her. Sweat rolled down her forehead, dripping on the grid floor. She was leaving bloody handprints and a ribbon of blood. None of that mattered. She strained her ears, listening for familiar voices.

Seconds later, she *did* hear Quyeba and Zoltar. A few paces further, ungodly spasms tore through her back. The black dots returned. She called for help. She last saw Teodon kneel over Yeron, placing something on his wounded shoulder. Behind them, Laurel emerged from the corridor, growling, her mouth opened wide. The dots swelled and the screams died in Alexis's throat as the darkness took her.

Chapter Forty-One: Yeron and Alexis Badly Injured

Underground Passageway to Zoltar's Laboratory, August 31, 6:00 a.m.

The cries assaulted Quyeba's ears as she, Zoltar, their assistant healer Xian, and two androids sprinted through the hallway. The sight she beheld turned her blood to ice. Alexis lay prone in a puddle of blood. Beside her rested Yeron on his back, his tunic drenched maroon. A soldier –Yeron's dead father, she noted with horror and surprise – knelt beside his left shoulder, applying a dressing. Teodon lifted his gaze and pointed.

Zoltar and the two androids scrambled to Yeron's right side, giving no sign of noticing the soldier.

Quyeba's ears tuned into low pitched growling. Teodon jabbed his finger toward a *settva* at the end of the hall.

"Kill it," he mouthed.

At the sight of the *settva* and the dead man, Quyeba opened her mouth for a shrill scream. She clapped her hand over her lips. *Pull yourself together.* She retrieved her gun. The being looked like a crossbreed between human and *settva*, dark yellow hair and human-like limbs, but greenish plates, yellow eyes, and sharp teeth. Plasma would kill it, but she was working in too small an area and the creature too close to Alexis for Quyeba to use her plasma without harming Alexis, too. Instead, Quyeba shot the monster with the sedative.

"Xian!" she hollered at the assistant. "Command your android to lock the beast in a cell."

While Xian conferred with one of the androids, Quyeba rolled Alexis to her back. Blood poured from her stomach wound.

"I need compresses!" she shouted.

Xian retrieved them from her supply kit and handed them to her. Quyeba pressed them against Alexis's lower abdomen.

"Mother!" Zoltar looked up from Yeron's side. "We must bring him to the laboratory. A laser penetrated his right lung, and he is hemorrhaging from his pleural cavity. Someone will come for Alexis when they can."

"All right." Quyeba nodded, trembling, a horrified look of dismay washing over her features.

Alexis's eyes fluttered open. She whipped her head back and forth. Quyeba pressed the dressing pack as hard as she could. How had Alexis managed to crawl here? She was bleeding somewhere from her back, too. *The blood. All that blood! How can we save her?*

Alexis tried to sit up, but Quyeba's hand held firm.

"Be still. Your incisions opened. I am trying to stop the bleeding. You were fortunate that we heard your cries for help."

"Quyeba, Zoltar ... save Yeron." Alexis's voice sounded rough, like someone with damaged vocal cords. "Woehar shot him. She's dead, thankfully. Laurel turned on her. She started to ... to ..." The sobs came hard and fast. "I'm so scared that Yeron will die."

"Easy, Alexis." Quyeba spoke in what she hoped was a soothing voice. "Zoltar and his assistants are doing everything they can for Yeron. He will send someone for you when he can. I'd levitate you to the operating room myself, but your injuries are serious. It will be difficult to control the bleeding and move you safely at the same time."

"I understand. I did not feel comfortable moving Yeron because of his injuries. Besides, you have androids that could move me."

"One android." She made a number one gesture for emphasis. "Unfortunately, because Draekh is under discipline, Zoltar only has our assistant Xian and at the moment, one android."

"One android?" Alexis's breath came out in pants. "I appreciate you trying to spare my feelings, Good Samaritan. Woehar is dead, but Laurel is not. Someone spliced a *settva's* chromosomes into her. She has yellow eyes ... green scales ... I just heard growling."

"I know, I know." Tension edged into Quyeba's voice. "I sedated the creature. My other android is locking it in a holding cell."

"You should have killed the beast like Teodon told you. You saw him in the hallway; I can tell by the spooked look on your face. Teodon came back to settle unfinished business."

Killing the *settva* was not an option. In the narrowed area, the heat from the laser would have burned Alexis's legs. Any attempt at explaining this would have to include her thoughts on Teodon's return from the dead, a discussion she was not ready to have.

"We can talk about that later."

"There is no later. Laurel will wake soon. I hope your android locks her some place with a deadbolt."

"I do not know what deadbolts are." Quyeba shook her head, puzzled. "Our portals work by mind control. Most humans cannot open them."

"Laurel is part *settva*." Alexis enunciated her words as if she were speaking to a hearing-impaired person. "Her brute strength can tear through anything, and she wants Yeron and me for dinner."

"I am perfectly aware of the *settva's* proclivities." Quyeba tried to muster patience. "Getting upset will not help."

Alexis's shaking persisted and wariness stole into her eyes. Despite Quyeba's attempt to staunch the flow of blood, a trickle escaped, planting sloppy kisses between her thighs.

"Your injuries are severe." Quyeba continued trying to find a gentle way to explain the seriousness of her situation. "But Yeron's got priority because they are much worse."

The shivering stopped. Alexis's breath hitched. "I understand, Good Samaritan. Where I live, we follow a similar protocol. We call it 'triage.'"

"Triage." Quyeba enunciated the word, smiling. "Why do you call me 'Good Samaritan'?"

"Back in my history, the Good Samaritan rescued a wounded stranger who had been beaten by ..." Alexis winced and cried out, her face a rictus of agony, "... by scoundrels. He tried to make the man comfortable, like you are doing for me."

"I find that hard to believe. Like most humans, your Samaritan would never approve of our chromosome fusions."

"Hmmmm." Alexis appeared to consider this. "He might if he had grown up in your compound. The point is, he went out of his way to help an injured stranger the way you are doing with me." She yawned. "May I sleep now?"

"No, you may not. You might not ..."

"Wake up? All right, did any humans accompany Yeron?"

Quyeba nodded.

"One of them may be a healer and qualified to treat me. He can donate blood if necessary. Tell them where they can find supplies and I will translate for you." With that, Alexis closed her eyes.

I must keep her awake. I do not want to lose her. Quyeba gave her shoulder a sharp nudge. "Alexis!"

Alexis's eyes flew open. "What?"

"I do not know where Zoltar stores his equipment," she told Alexis. "Besides, I devised a force field to protect your friends, and cannot deactivate it from where we are."

"*Shit!* Why did my friends need a force field? You can bring them here."

"No, Alexis," Quyeba said through clenched teeth. "Not until I decide what to do with Laurel and Draekh. I have locked Draekh in a secure holding cell, but he has befriended other soldiers who may free him. As you pointed out, Laurel is strong and vicious. Draekh and

Woehar may have created other mutant *settvas*, so I have more questions for Draekh. Besides, your human friends are evaluating Woehar's victims for vischlausk poisoning." Quyeba nodded, responding to Alexis's questioning look. "That is right, Woehar and her renegades kidnapped and poisoned humans, making them into the monsters we saw. She constructed another laboratory to continue her deadly activities."

"Oh, my ..." Alexis gasped. Her eyes became dilated orbs; her breath came out in a harsh whistle. Any instant, Quyeba feared, she would scream. "How could she build a laboratory without you or your assistants finding out?"

"She had Draekh to help her, and I suspect their friends covered for them. Everyone requested Draekh for medical treatment because they had misgivings about Zoltar being part human. The androids can deliver good care, but we need live, cooperative people for decision making. Right now, I only have Xian and Zoltar."

"So Woehar started the war that killed my sister ... and two close friends." Alexis gazed at Quyeba, her eyes brimming with tears. "I may not understand your technology, but I know you are trying to do the right thing. Right choices never come easy when you face a nightmare like this."

"No, they do not," Quyeba nodded in agreement.

"A questionable choice may turn out to be the smartest thing you did. For example, the chromosome fusion. I am glad you did it. It augmented my psychokinesis and enabled me to fight Laurel in her *settva* form. Otherwise, Yeron and I might both be dead." Her breath rasped in and out. "I need a favor, though."

"Of course." Quyeba gentled her voice, hoping to offer encouragement. She was ready to promise Alexis a colony if it would keep her awake.

"Quyeba ..." Alexis blinked her eyes. Sweat dripped down her forehead and chills wracked her shoulders. She was going into shock. "The other day, you asked me how I could speak up for Zoltar. It was easy because I used to live with a man, Mark, who belittled me frequently, even in public. He called me awful names and he – how do you say – forced sex on me against my will. Your chromosomes will not erase that kind of pain."

Quyeba took it in, contemplating her own injuries when Eigil's soldiers assaulted her.

"I do not suppose they would."

"Yeron and the other fighters sheltered me from Mark. We suspected that the renegades had implanted a microchip inside him, one that recorded any and all activity near him. He tried to steal our weapons, and that was when Shively and I, um ..." she lowered her eyes, "… how do you say, eliminated him."

"You had a compelling reason." Quyeba kept her voice gentle. She recognized Alexis's pain, having seen it in her own mirror many times. "Did this man hit you?"

"He did." Alexis's voice was barely audible. "I am sure you and Zoltar noticed a big scar on my leg. I did not get that from your soldiers or the walking dead. Mark did that to me with a wooden club studded with nails."

At that, Quyeba gasped.

"He did that after he … after he …" Alexis's face contorted, and then she burst into tears. She shook her head. "It was *not* my fault."

She gulped. "Anyway, I fought back and left Mark kneeling in his blood. It was a long, long time before I let any man touch me again. Then I met Yeron. Using plasma weapons and speaking Kryszka were not the only things he taught me."

"What else did he teach you?" Quyeba asked, glancing down the hall.

"He taught me that love does not hurt. That was more difficult than teaching me your language. Your technology would not have made it easier."

Quyeba shook her head, stunned.

"I suppose not."

"Right, then. My favor. Will you tell Yeron how much I love him and the baby? Please?"

Quyeba shook her head. "Alexis, I cannot …"

"Of course, you can," Alexis overrode her, her voice stronger. "Yeron spoke highly of you. He will listen to anything you say."

"I am not so sure about that." Quyeba's voice wavered. Any moment, she would burst into a spate of sobbing. *Not good.* As a leader, she must keep calm and find a delicate way to word the news about Yeron. The shell-shocked look on Alexis's face reminded her of a soldier who had gotten shot in the chest.

"Yeron is in no condition right now to listen to what I have to say," she admitted at last.

Alexis shook her head.

"Tell him after he recuperates from his surgery. All right?"

Her eyes searched Quyeba's face, hoping for assurance that Yeron was going to be all right. Quyeba had none. Squeaking noises jarred her attention. Someone was wheeling a table toward them.

"Zoltar sent Xian and another android." Quyeba spoke softly. "I am sorry for allowing Woehar to live here. I never imagined any of Teodon's children would join Eigil."

"Art thought the … oh, how it *hurts* !" Alexis clutched her gut and flank. Despite Quyeba's hold on the compress, she writhed with agony.

Xian and her android were wheeling a table laden with equipment, but Alexis gave no sign of noticing.

"Yeron is lying near death because he tried to save me. That means everything."

Before Quyeba could reply, Xian and the android knelt at Alexis's side. Hands flew over the incision, applying a gel solution. Alexis yawned.

"Governor," Xian said, "now we shall move her to the laboratory."

"Do it fast." Quyeba's voice tightened.

Alexis blinked her eyes. Tears rolled down her face, dripping into the blood.

"Before they move me, just how badly is Yeron hurt?"

Quyeba let loose a long deep sigh. "Woehar's laser penetrated his lung, causing a bleed in his pleural cavity. Zoltar will try to save him, but even with our technology, fifty percent of these casualties die during surgery. Another twenty-five die during the first days after surgery."

Chapter Forty-Two: Quyeba Confides in Alexis

Zoltar's Underground Laboratory, August 31, 8:00 a.m.

Fifty and twenty-five. That much sunk in, but the rest didn't filter through Alexis's cloud of pain. Then more came – something about a laser puncturing his lung, or did she mean burning, and ... oh, God, Quyeba was talking about Yeron's survival chances!

She winced, grimacing when the android slapped a rubber dressing over her gut, and again when Xian injected something into her arms.

"Nooooo!" she screamed. "I want to go to Yeron!" She wriggled and thrashed with her elbows, but Xian and the android held her fast.

"You cannot go anywhere, Earth woman. Your injuries are too severe," Xian told her. "I gave you something to make you sleep."

"I do not want to sleep. I need to go to Yeron!"

But her cries grew fainter and her arms flopped. Darkness fell in fast.

****

Voices invaded her consciousness. Alexis slowly opened her eyes. A dull ache burned in her right flank. Someone had rewrapped thick dressings around her gut. Somewhere through the haze, she heard Quyeba addressing someone on an intercom, using medical terminology she didn't understand.

"Good Samaritan," she called after Quyeba finished speaking, "is Yeron ..."

"Yeron is still in surgery," Quyeba replied. "His vital signs are labile, but you should worry about yourself."

"Why? How much damage did Laurel inflict?"

"Damage?" Uncertainty flickered in Quyeba's eyes.

"My injuries." Alexis's voice grew shrill. "How bad?"

"You sustained nerve damage and bruising in your back. Your incision opened and required more surgery. Your friend – Steve – has your blood type. He and some kind citizens here donated blood for transfusions."

"What citizens?"

"People acquainted with Teodon and his family," Quyeba told her. "The gene fusion we performed earlier made your body receptive to human and Kryszka blood. The damage to your internal organs left scarring. You will never be able to conceive again."

"Are you sure? My Earth healers told me that before, and I conceived anyway."

Quyeba sniffed. "They used primitive equipment."

Yeah, right. Of course, human technology leaves margins for error, unlike the gadgets here, but that doesn't make yours perfect. The hell with it. I can't muster the strength for more children. I'm not even sure if I can handle one. Alexis bit back a scream; her pain had gone raw and primal.

"Why is Yeron's surgery taking so long?" she asked.

"Because Zoltar and Xian are trying to stop his internal bleeding. I am to let him know if your condition changes. You responded well to the medicine and other procedures."

"Thanks to your DNA," Alexis conceded. "Your chromosomes enabled me to use my mind on Laurel, too. Can they reverse the effects of vischlausk?"

"Nothing can undo the damage from vischlausk. If you fuse chromosomes in someone poisoned by vischlausk, you will create a monster. You saw what happened to Laurel. Zoltar performed many tests before he recommended the gene fusion."

"That makes sense. I guess I thought that DNA fusion would reverse the damage done to the vischlausk-poisoned victims." Alexis gasped. "Ow. I wish I could visit my son. And if I am hurt as badly as you say, I want my mother near me."

Quyeba furrowed her brows. "Are you sure you want your mother to visit?"

"Why do you ask?"

"Alexis." Quyeba heaved an exasperated sigh. "Your mother had a difficult time accepting Yeron. That was why you never told her about the pregnancy. Am I right?"

Alexis hesitated, trying for a tactful approach.

"Up until recently, most humans did not acknowledge the existence of extraterrestrial life. My mother has come to accept Yeron only because she realizes how happy he makes me. I had planned to tell her about the baby in my own time, in my way."

"There is no easy way, Alexis," Quyeba said in a pained voice. "Like most humans, your mother considers people like us monsters. At the sight of your bodily changes, she will scream."

Alexis shifted her focus toward the overhead mirror. Ruby

eyes aside, fiery red roots peeped from underneath her chestnut curls. She shrugged.

"I will tell her that my changes came from the medicine. Besides, she has worries other than my hair or eye color."

"Do not count on it." Quyeba spoke with a dreadful sort of patience. She sighed in resignation. "Suppose I allow her to visit. How would I approach your friends? What do I say to them?"

"You say, 'Alexis would like to see her mother.' It is not so hard. You will find out when I teach you the English language."

"Which you will do if we can avoid getting shot." The governor rubbed her neck from behind, then threw her hands up in the air and let them drop. "All right, I will consider your request."

"While you do your considering, may I visit Yeron?"

"Yeron cannot receive visitors."

"Why not?" Alexis looked her in the eye. "You lost your mate without a chance to say goodbye. You understand how painful that is. So please, let ..." Her voice broke.

Quyeba was getting up and heading for the portal. "Wait! Where are you going?"

Quyeba spun around and gave Alexis a sad look.

"I am going to look for isolation gowns. We cannot enter a surgical suite without them."

****

With the help of an android, Quyeba loaded Alexis's IVs and portable monitors onto her table. She then draped a sheet and face shield over Alexis, and put on a gown herself.

"I will wheel you to Yeron now. It will be unpleasant," she warned. "Zoltar will not appreciate our visit. He is territorial about his operating room."

"I appreciate his attempt to heal Yeron." In the surgical suite, Zoltar was sealing a dressing across Yeron's chest. He breathed with the help of a ventilator – Alexis was not surprised. It didn't look like any ventilator she had used at Jackson Hospital. This one had smooth black hoses. Air flowed through them into a crevice above his sternum. His legs, chest, and every other visible body part wore a blanket of spaghetti wires and tubes. Somewhere in the wiring, glassy eyes peeped from a bloated face. Each shift in his numbers brought *beeps* from the monitors. His blood pressure seesawed as time ticked by. The man who had taught her about love and weapons barely existed underneath those tubes.

Xian worked alongside Zoltar while two androids called out Yeron's vital sign values. Alexis opened her mouth to ask if he was going to be all right, but instead she burst into harsh sobs. Quyeba's gloved hand gently rubbed her shoulder.

Zoltar looked up. The thoughtful look faded from his eyes, replaced by shock and fury.

"Mother!" he shouted. "Why did you bring her here? What are *you* doing here?"

"Alexis begged to see Yeron. I brought her here because I never saw Lyrus before he died, and I wanted to spare her that pain. Her request was irregular, but in this case, I made an exception."

Zoltar glared at his mother, his eyes reminding Alexis of a parent scolding an unruly child.

"I do not allow exceptions, especially given Alexis's infection. Do you even care about sterile procedures and the bacteria she harbors? Apparently not." He then settled his gaze on Alexis. "You must know that interfering with sterile procedures may harm Yeron ... and yourself."

"I took precautions," Alexis said between her tears, "and you can see that."

She groped through the folds of her gown until she remembered she no longer had her rosary. She'd lost it during her last skirmish above ground. Would God listen to her prayers if she didn't have her rosary? She wasn't sure. Steve's God spoke of kindness and mercy, but the vengeful God of her childhood meted out punishments for even minor offenses. In either case, she knew no other way. When her father had gone out to his special "jobs," her mother, Robin, and she had said the Rosary together; ditto during her father's fight with cancer. The hollowness inside hurt so much, any second her chest would burst.

Somewhere through tentacles of pain clutching Alexis, a tear dropped on her head. It came from Quyeba who was covering her eyes.

"Alexis, this is awful. I cannot stop thinking about Lyrus. Yeron is alive and we must be strong for him."

Alexis shook her head. "I wish I could be."

"I am referring to the surveillance." Quyeba's voice cracked, bordering on hysteria. "We should not cry around the cameras."

"Why are you worried about the cameras? Where I live, adults cry all the time after torture, near death experiences, and the critical injuries of their mates."

"That is enough!" Zoltar shouted. "Leave now, Mother, and take Alexis with you. Yeron may regain consciousness. He does not need to wake to two hysterical women."

Seconds later, a psychic force nudged Alexis's table. It was pushing her and Quyeba toward the exit.

"Out!" Zoltar shouted as the panel slid shut behind them.

Quyeba turned her eyes toward the empty hall and then back

toward Alexis. Her eyes shone with tears.

"I knew our visit would upset him," she said in a sorrowful voice.

"I realize that. Now." Alexis dabbed her eyes with her gown sleeve. "Why are you so worried about the cameras? Grieving is natural."

"Woehar's renegades will use anything they catch on surveillance against us." Quyeba's voice cracked.

"Then why have cameras?"

"Because I need them to monitor activity and possible breaks into the compound." Quyeba brushed the tears from her eyes. "Seeing Yeron was like reliving Lyrus's shooting. The soldiers did not stop with killing. They forced themselves on me the way Mark did with you, and made Lyrus watch. Then they shot him. Teodon treated me for internal injuries."

Alexis hung her head, her face flushing. "Oh, my. I am so sorry."

"The pain never goes away." Quyeba spoke in a low, intense voice. "Sometimes it speaks so softly I hardly notice it. Other times, like today, it goes through my heart like a poisoned arrow. I recalled what you had said about Mark and that was why I brought you to Yeron. Our technology and lives may differ, but I understand your pain more than I can explain."

"What those soldiers did was not your fault. Mark's behavior was not mine. It took me a long time to accept that." Alexis took in the sadness and nostalgia radiating from Quyeba's eyes. "Does Zoltar know?"

Quyeba shook her head. "No, and I ask that you not tell him. Teodon shielded Zoltar and me from Eigil, but I could not protect Yeron or you from harm. Maybe I can protect Zoltar."

Quyeba has her wishful thinking; I have mine.

"I will not mention it to anyone. Will someone tell us if Yeron's condition changes?"

"Of course, they will. Until then, you will go to your cubicle and rest. Maybe then you can be strong for Yeron. I will send your friends to you. If you can teach me the words I need to say, I will ask if your mother is ready to visit."

Alexis spoke and Quyeba listened on the trip through the corridor. At a room past the laboratories, Quyeba helped her from the table into a bed. She gave Alexis a glass of chalky liquid. A sedative, it tasted like vinegar.

Alexis swallowed the liquid without protest. Exhaustion had set in; even an explosion couldn't keep her awake. The trouble was, every time she closed her eyes, she saw Laurel's gargoyle face. The greenish plates. The stink of blood and gristle baking off Laurel's body. Quyeba understood, but the mutiny among her soldiers left no time for counseling. Alexis lay on her left side, in the only position that did not hurt, and cried herself to sleep.

Chapter Forty-Three: Matilda's Visit

Voices. Two men speaking English. Steve and Tyrone! An android walked them to her bedside.

"Hey!" Tyrone smiled. "Got into trouble again, I see."

"Tyrone!" Alexis cried, relief flooding her body. "Steve! I'd hug you both, but I've got too much hardware."

Tyrone glanced toward the android.

"Is that thing recording our chat?"

Alexis laughed. "It won't do anyone good. No one here knows English. My caregivers use these androids for custodial care. So how did you find me?"

"We found another underground lab closer to the cabin," Tyrone replied. "This time, Yeron found an entrance to the compound. He knows Quyeba – that's her name, right?"

Alexis nodded.

"Quyeba told him they brought you here for treatment and questioned you," Steve supplied. "She escorted us to a room with human prisoners who needed treatment, and took Yeron to her laboratory. Their androids or whatever you call them brought us cooked meat, vegetables, and water. A day later, Quyeba informed us in perfect English that you want to see your mother."

"That's right," Alexis told him. "I coached Quyeba on what to say."

"You were fortunate to have someone like Quyeba," Steve said. "Those soldiers would have shot us if your governor hadn't intervened. Things got ugly fast."

"You must have run into renegades." Alexis noted their solemn nods and continued. "Yeron's hurt – bad enough to need a ventilator. Do you remember Laurel Grant and Woehar?" She paused to observe the *oh-my-God* look on their faces. "Quyeba built a refuge here for the citizens fleeing Eigil's evil. Woehar faked her death and came here to set up a new operation. She brought Laurel with her. She, Laurel, and renegade Kryszka soldiers kidnapped humans off the street—mostly homeless and dope addicts—people they thought no one would miss, and zombified them. While you were fighting these soldiers, Woehar and Laurel worked me over in their torture chamber."

Alexis shuddered at the memory.

"Yeron shot Woehar, but she got him, too. Laurel's changed. She's got claws and teeth, and reptile skin. I think Woehar altered her DNA in a bad way. Laurel came after me, but I used my mind trick to fight her. Then I led – crawled – to the hall with my guts hanging out to find help."

"Holy shit!" Tyrone's eyes bulged. "It's a miracle you're alive."

"Tell me about it." Alexis smiled thinly. *Teodon had a lot to do with it.*

"Talk about miracles." Steve retrieved something shiny from his pocket. "I found your rosary intact and in one piece." He handed it to Alexis.

"Steve!" Alexis held it up to her face, eyes misty, watching the glass beads glitter in the light. "Thank you. This means the world to me." She clutched the rosary beads to her chest.

"Sure." He smiled. "Whoever brought you here took a shine to you."

Alexis reminisced about her chats with Zoltar and smiled.

"I'd say so."

"These people seem caring, but strange." Steve looked at Tyrone and back at Alexis. His voice softened. "What's with your eyes and hair?"

"Side effect from their medicine." *Liar, liar, pants on fire!* "Zoltar's tests confirmed that I caught a deadly infection from the walkers and he concocted a formula to treat it."

Steve nodded, frustration crinkling his eyes. "I heard about the infection. Thank God Zoltar was able to help you."

"You've got that right," Tyrone agreed. "Does this infection pass on to the baby?"

"No, but the medicines caused chromosomal abnormalities in the fetus, so Zoltar harvested the fetus to correct them. The equipment here can support a fetus until it matures enough to survive outside the womb.

"Yeron isn't doing well, though. The laser tore apart his right lung. He looks awful. I love this guy and don't want to lose him."

"If they can save you and your child," Steve said, his voice soft, "they can help Yeron."

"From your mouth to God's ears," Tyrone shifted his eyes toward Alexis. "Did the renegades get Shively?"

Alexis burst into a spate of quaking. "They devoured Shively," she said, her voice wavering. "It was brutal. I saw it."

"Alexis, no!" Steve cried.

"Yes. I didn't watch the soldiers tear into him, but I saw the ghastly results." She shivered. "Shively put on a tough front, but underneath, he was a great guy."

Tyrone nodded. "He thought the world of you, but he hated admitting it. Did Quyeba and your doctor meet Shively?"

"Yeah, just before the soldier fried him. Quyeba was plenty upset. She and Zoltar are trying to make it up to me. Quyeba stopped my bleeding. Zoltar mended the tear in my gut, casualties of Woehar and Laurel's ministrations."

"How did Woehar and Laurel meet?" asked Tyrone.

"Woehar said she met Laurel after her accident," replied Alexis. "Maybe after Laurel totaled her car."

"Why did the governor let Woehar get away with her crimes?" Tyrone continued.

"She didn't. Quyeba evicted Woehar from the main compound, and then Woehar built her own little laboratory. In the lab, Woehar fused DNA from a *settva* – a monster with yellow eyes, green scales, and pointy teeth – into Laurel. Laurel is now a mutant *settva*, with a hunger for human flesh that won't quit. Woehar managed to fool Quyeba into thinking she was a victim because she was Teodon's daughter, and Quyeba owed him a lot of favors. Before her jig was up, Woehar shot Yeron. Now no one knows if he will survive, and I can't raise a child alone."

"You've got a lot of friends at home, and you made some here," Steve assured her. "Quyeba gave us weapons – you don't do that to someone you hate. Now she's willing to let you see your mom."

"That may be, but a visit from Matilda is a bad idea right now," Tyrone told Steve. Some of his horror dissipated, but the worry remained. "She'll go ballistic when she sees how badly Alexis got hurt."

"Hey ... I feel like a piece of shit on a rainy day, but do I look that bad?" Alexis tried to manufacture a smile, but wound up grimacing. Her fingers were as swollen as sausages and pain wracked her body. Her burning, aching body and her concern for Yeron's injuries allowed little room for smiling.

"That's not the point," Tyrone whined. "Matilda whaled on Steve."

"What?" Alexis's eyes widened.

"She smacked him. Besides, we'll never get her down here. Poison gas aside, she's not used to climbing a ladder."

"She can handle it if she wears a pressurized suit like us." Steve grinned, then fixed his gaze on Alexis. "Your mother did lose it with me. The renegades left us nasty surprises, including poisonous gas in the shaft. All that's moot, though, because your governor will make sure the going is safe for future travels. I'm more worried about how Matilda will react when she sees your changes."

Alexis rolled her eyes. "Hopefully, glad to see me. Quyeba warned me that a visit might be stressful for both of us."

"There you go." Tyrone shrugged and looked at Steve. "Matilda can't come here because Alexis can't take the stress now. Hazlett had no business bringing her here at least until Alexis is stronger."

Alexis gasped. "I'm surprised he did that. I thought the officers wanted her to stay at a safe house."

"Some safe house." Steve laughed. "The officers put her in a jail cell."

"What?" Alexis tried to picture her mother in prison orange, eating the cardboard food that the inmates no doubt had to eat. If she weren't so worried about Yeron, she'd find it hilarious. Despite herself, she burst into streams of giggles. "My mom in jail? Are you serious?"

"One hundred percent serious. She's furious, too, so don't make any jokes about it around her. She blames me for this mess because I introduced you to Yeron."

"Oh, Steve, I'm sorry." Another burst of hilarity. "If Hazlett was so worried about her safety, why did he bring her here?"

"She insisted on coming, so tell your android to lead the way. Tyrone, let's man up and get her."

"Shit!" Tyrone glared at Steve.

"It's okay, Tyrone. My mother and I need to talk," Alexis told him. "A lot of secrets came out during my stay. For starters, someone made my aunt part of the Kryszka hybrid experiments, and Zoltar is her biological son. That would make Zoltar Mom's nephew."

"What the ..." Tyrone reeled toward her. "You're kidding."

"I wish I was." Alexis yawned. She badly wanted this nightmare to be over. "You must notice that Zoltar and I look alike."

"We noticed." Steve nodded. "During her deliriums, your Aunt Susan used to ramble about a lost child. I thought she was hallucinating."

"Do us all a favor, Alexis. Go easy on the information." A deep sigh escaped Tyrone. "Tell your android we're ready."

The men fell silent while Alexis delivered instructions to the android. The android proceeded to the portal, followed by Steve.

"Damn, she's a pro." Tyrone shook his head and followed the others.

After her company left, Alexis eased onto her side and closed her eyes, but sleep did not come. The pain was a cascade of stones scraping against every muscle in her limbs. Not the ungodly pain delivered by Laurel, but bad enough to prevent sleep.

Sleep meds; that ought to do it. She pressed the intercom with her mind. No answer. Why would anyone respond to a trivial request for medicine when Yeron's injuries demanded what manpower they had?

"Dammit, Zoltar," she said in her native tongue. "You gave me an IV pump so I could get the pain medicine myself." *What happened to it?*

At that, the portal opened. Quyeba peeked in, the steely look on her face a sharp contrast to the dusky blotches around her eyes. She gave Alexis a stern look.

"Zoltar decreased the pain medicine, hoping to make you alert and aware of your speech. Obviously, it has not. I was listening in for intruders when I overheard you say 'dammit' out loud. I did not understand the rest, but I know human curse words. Watch what you say."

"Because of the camera?" Alexis heaved her shoulders. "Sorry."

"Not only the cameras. Your friends are here with your mother. She appears distraught. I hope I did right, allowing her visit."

Alexis watched while Quyeba signaled in the direction of the portal, and then retreated to the side to allow room for Alexis's visitors – Tyrone, Steve, and a woman. All three wore pressurized suits, helmet cradled in one arm. Her mother looked lost in her suit, about thirty pounds lighter than Alexis recalled, with sagging cheeks and deep bags beneath her watery eyes. Though Steve held her by the arm, she lurched with every step. She'd never worn a pressurized suit and had no idea how to maneuver. *That shit-for-brains Hazlett should have kept her in jail, or whatever passes for a safe house. I'm just as guilty for pestering Quyeba to allow a visit.*

"Mom?" she ventured in a small voice. "What happened to you?"

What a dumbass question. Robin died. The zombies attacked. You took this war on the road. Her house burned down, and then you fell in love with, and got pregnant by, an alien.

"Alexis?" Her mother took three steps closer, then recoiled. "*Dio Mio!* What have those monsters done to you?"

Go ahead, tell her they spliced Kryszka chromosomes into yours. As the saying goes, the truth shall set you free. Alexis turned her scrutiny toward her mother. Something inside her died at the sight of her mother's horrorstricken eyes.

"They did surgery and saved my life," she said in a lame voice.

"You look horrible!" Matilda's cheeks paled. *Any second now, she'll swoon.*

"Easy, Matilda." Steve spoke with the voice of a parent coddling an upset child. "She's had multiple operations and spent the last weeks on a battlefield. No one's at their best under those circumstances."

"Dio Mio, her eyes!" Her mother's shrill cry reeked with the anxiety of a layperson witnessing a cardiac arrest. "They're red."

Tyrone shook his head. "Fuck, I'm not doing this," he said, edging toward the portal. "Steve, you know her better than I; you deal."

Alexis looked back at her mother, sensing her cue to fix this – or not.

"Mom, I contracted a rare infection. The people here concocted a formula to treat it, but it's got side effects. In this case, the changes in my eye and hair pigment."

Oh, how that sounded like certified bullshit. Quyeba eyeballed Alexis from the portal, her head tilted sideways, watching with sad eyes.

"I'm the same me; I applesolutely guarantee it." Alexis thought her childhood phrase would bring cheer, but instead, it elicited a frown from Matilda. "I invented nicknames for the people here – Good Samaritan ..." She pointed toward Quyeba, who smiled.

"Alexis, for God's sake, don't give them nicknames."

"Why not? Quyeba saved my life the way the Good Samaritan rescued the beaten man in the Bible." Alexis's eyes caught on Quyeba, who smiled again and bowed. Alexis smiled back, and then continued. "Zoltar prescribed the drugs. He's doing the best he can. I've said the rosary every day."

At the word "rosary," her mother's head jerked. "Something isn't right. Those people didn't give you conventional medicine."

Alexis shrugged.

"Well, it's not the kind you can get at our pharmacy, but the drug's killing the infection. I'd give anything for healthy hands and a peaceful night at home. That's not happening anytime soon, but I'm grateful to be alive."

"Oh, Alexis!" Tears ran down her mother's face. "I'm grateful, too."

"Matilda, sit." Steve nudged her shoulder and led her to a chair by the bed. She gazed at Alexis with stunned disbelief.

Okay, I'll give it a go. Despite sharp stabbing from her incisions, Alexis sat up and mustered her best smile.

"You haven't been idle. What's this about you slugging a renegade with a frying pan?"

"I used what I had," her mother told her. "Those cast-iron pans make great weapons. Our officers are useless. They put me in a jail cell. They called it 'protective custody' and said no one would find me in jail.

Bah fungule!"

"At least they kept you safe." Alexis scratched her cheek, hiding her smile. "The Kryszka soldiers don't know anything about our prisons."

"It's not funny." Matilda's voice sharpened. "I had to wear the same wrinkled uniforms as the real prisoners and eat the same slop every day."

I'd wear a burlap bag and live on bread and water if it would save Yeron. The laughter died in Alexis's throat.

"What about the house? Will the insurance pay?"

At that, her mother heaved with noiseless sobs. Steve rubbed her shoulders, whispering reassurances. Her mother took a cleansing breath, smacked his hand aside, and looked Alexis in the eye.

"The insurance paid, but it's never going to be the same."

Of course, it isn't. Alexis glanced toward Quyeba, but Quyeba's puzzled stare said, *Leave me out of it. I do not even speak English.*

"I realize Yeron makes you happy," her mother went on, "but a baby ..." Her spate of tears continued. "If he cared, he would've put you in a hospital."

Before Alexis's mind could process an answer, her mother launched another question.

"What's this about an incubator?"

Alexis drew a deep breath. "The doctors harvested the fetus and put him in one of their incubators. Most women here let their babies grow in incubators until they're mature enough to survive the environment."

Her mother sniffed. "When your child matures, you'll still have to feed him and change his diapers," she said. "That's going to be hard, given your health problems. I wish you'd been careful."

"Doctor Hoffman said I'd never get pregnant. I believed him."

"Right." Her mother's voice cracked. Her face shone with tears. "I'm so afraid of losing you."

"I worry about *you*," Alexis told her. "You've had close calls with the walkers and renegades. Yeron tried to make me go to a hospital. I wouldn't. I was lucky to meet up with Zoltar and the Good Samaritan."

Her mother shook her head, her cheeks scarlet.

"Why are they keeping you here?"

Quyeba moved a bit, but remained quiet.

"Enough, Matilda," Steve broke in. "Alexis can't handle the twenty-question routine."

"It's okay." Alexis swallowed hard, fighting a lump in her throat. "Our hospitals don't have the proper equipment to treat my illness."

"After what happened to Robin, I wish you could come home."

"I wish that, too, but the Kryszka have the technology to treat my infection and injuries, and we don't. Quyeba had nothing to do with Robin's death. Laurel Grant, my former coworker, teamed up with Kryszka criminals and killed Robin. I've told you about Laurel and the things she did to her patients, didn't I?"

"Yes, you did—months ago, when you were still working at Jackson," her mother allowed, "but the people here didn't give you medicine as we know it. Your eyes remind me of *The Fly*. Your father took me to see the movie when you were about ten. Seth, the hero, experimented with a transmission pod, and something went wrong – his genes fused with those of a common housefly."

Alexis shrugged. "I don't see any flies, Mom."

"Seth became a mutant because of his gene fusion, *bah fungule!* That's what happened to you. They may have had no other way to save you, but their treatment made you part alien." With that, her mother burst into a high, keening cry.

Shit! How did she figure that out? Alexis fetched another deep sigh.

"I would've died without their intervention."

"You don't know that." Matilda's voice hitched.

"I'm afraid I do." Alexis rubbed her chin. "There's more."

"What?" Her mother gasped, mouth opening and closing. "No, no, no."

Alexis shuddered at her mother's terrified, bulging eyes.

"I'm sorry, none of what I'm saying is coming out right. If Dad were here—"

"Your father has nothing to do with this."

For the moment, Alexis forgot about her pain. Her mind flashed to the dream she had during surgery, the one in which she was talking to Yeron's late father. Steve called her dreams "out-of-body experiences." Whatever they were, Alexis would give anything to have her own father here. All her problems—her illness, failed marriage, and Robin's death—had happened after her father's death. She tried telling herself that all of those events were unrelated. Maybe they were, but she couldn't help an idle thought that his death had opened Hell's Gate and unleashed a court of devils in her life.

"If Dad were here, he'd help me explain my treatment in a way you could accept."

Her mother's frown deepened.

"I didn't sign up for arthritis. I didn't make those walkers attack. I did not cause this infection. I only did one thing wrong ..." *Mark,* she almost said. That had to be it. God was punishing her for what she did to Mark. "... one thing, a terrible sin. I should go to confession, but I'm too sick to go to church. Quyeba doesn't employ clergy."

"I suppose she wouldn't." Matilda lowered her head, her eyes threatening another spate of tears. "What have you done that was so awful?"

"That's enough." Steve's expression reminded her of a custodian facing a messy job. "Get up." He wedged his hands under her mother's armpits. "Tyrone, give me a hand."

"About time you shut down this circus." Tyrone moved fast, and between then, they hauled a weeping Matilda to her feet. "She's upset Alexis enough."

"No, Tyrone, they're both upset," Steve replied in a bleak tone of a beaten man. "Get her out of here. Alexis and I need to talk."

"How about you handle Matilda, and I talk with Alexis?"

"I want to examine Alexis, make sure she's all right," Steve replied in a ponderous voice. "At least as okay as she can be under the circumstances."

"Matilda needs a tranquilizer, so you're not sticking me with this one. Alexis, ask your governor to take us out of here." He then eased Matilda toward the portal.

"In a minute." Steve looked back at Alexis. "Give your mother time. She's gone through hell."

"All right." Alexis shifted her gaze toward the governor. "Quyeba, they are ready."

Quyeba approached her bedside and gazed at the overhead screen.

"Your blood pressure is up. That does not surprise me. I warned you about stress."

"I realize that. My mother figured out the truth." Alexis spoke in Kryszka, glad her visitors wouldn't understand. "I cannot fool her."

"No bond is stronger than that of a mother and child. One day, you will learn that." There was no mistaking the sadness in Quyeba's eyes. "Give her time." She touched Alexis's shoulder. "I will escort your visitors where they need to go. Try to rest."

She led the trio to the door. On the way out, her mother burst into loud, raucous sobs.

"She's becoming one of them, the way Seth turned into a fly."

Someone should have pumped me with sedatives so I would've stayed asleep. Better yet, I should've stayed unconscious.

Alexis's eyes settled on the ceiling, where moving cables supported an overhead screen, and three moving cameras. *Quyeba uses the cameras for surveillance, but how does she get readings from a blank screen? Most likely, she does it by mind control, although each screen comes with plenty of dials.*

"I never wanted anyone to tamper with my genes," she said aloud. "But as Dad used to say, if an airplane fell on our house, he'd search it for treasure."

Did her gene fusion come with any treasure? Indeed, yes. She managed to overpower Laurel because of it. Her eyes settled on the dials; she could tweak them with her mind. After a second thought, she yawned. *Better not. I'll ask Zoltar to show me how later.*

She cradled her rosary beads in her hands and thought about her part in Mark's death. Did her gene fusion exempt her from Confession? She doubted it. Steve's wife was a half-breed and she received the sacraments at her church. Since Quyeba's compound didn't offer any confessionals, she'd improvise with the rosary. She chose the Sorrowful Mysteries because she regretted her part in Mark's death.

Footfalls intruded on her Hail Mary's. It wasn't the squeak of sneakers that Steve, Tyrone, and her mother wore, or the whispering steps of Quyeba and Zoltar. The thudding footsteps belonged to a trooper, she saw as he entered the doorway; a cruel being who walked on his own edge of winter. His eyes glittered with bloodlust. Alexis dared not look at his mouth. He smiled, but not with the friendliness she'd seen with her keepers.

"You fool," he jeered. "You've lost your mind power."

Laurel thought that before I busted her ribs. So who's the fool? All at once, the fear that haunted Alexis faded. Perhaps she was going into denial. Denial led to mistakes and the renegades took advantage of mistakes.

"You know too much," he continued. "Do you expect me to let you live? It is time you learned a lesson."

The soldier advanced closer now, gun aimed, coming within shooting distance.

Chapter Forty-Four: Security Breech

A grim-faced Zoltar stood waiting for Quyeba in the hall.

"Mother, I did my best for Yeron." His lips worked, fighting the tremors in his voice. "I am sorry."

"How bad is he, son?" Quyeba asked.

Lips tightened, Zoltar gestured toward his suite, away from the cameras. Quyeba followed.

The news was dire. Yeron was dying and Zoltar did not want to discuss it around the surveillance monitors. Quyeba understood this as well as she'd known the grief lodged in her heart.

"Let us go to *my* suite." Quyeba led him to her workstation, several doors past the operating suites. She paused before the surveillance monitors for a cursory glance at the halls and other suites.

"He contracted a deadly infection." She looked up at Zoltar's somber eyes. "Was that what happened?"

"No infection, but he may die," he replied in a low voice. "Xian and I encountered one complication after the other in him. We transfused twenty units of blood and plasma. The shock to his system caused fluid overload in his healthy lung. If he does not regain consciousness by the next moon, he will die. My knowledge is inadequate, and that was why I lashed out at you and Alexis."

"Zoltar, do not underestimate your abilities or Yeron's will to live. He may survive this." Oh, how Quyeba longed to believe that. "I certainly hope he does. Alexis's health and the cultural barriers will prohibit her from raising that child alone."

"She has her mother and human friends," Zoltar pointed out.

"Her friends, yes. I am not sure about her mother. During her visit, Alexis's blood pressure went up."

Zoltar tapped his forehead.

"Alexis required multiple transfusions and her pressure has been low. Did something or someone upset her?"

"Someone," Quyeba told him. "Her mother is perceptive, and she saw right away we had done the gene fusion. She became agitated, and her companions escorted her from Alexis's bedside."

Zoltar rotated his camera toward Yeron's suite, hoping to see an improvement in Yeron.

"She should be glad her daughter is alive."

"I am sure she is, but humans do not condone gene fusion. The physiological changes in Alexis terrified her. I did not need to know English to understand this."

"Mother, we must help Alexis. Yeron may die because of choices we made."

"You mean because of choices *I* made," Quyeba said through clenched teeth. "We cannot help Alexis if we are dead. I must increase surveillance for signs of renegade activity."

"All right." Zoltar sighed. "In the meantime, Alexis watched someone shoot the man she loves. You do not understand how she feels."

Quyeba recalled her brutal past. The memories sent a cold trickle of fear down her spine.

"I understand more than you think," she told him. "I still have to increase surveillance. We cannot help Alexis unless we survive."

"That may be," Zoltar said, his jaw tight. "Alexis is a sensitive woman. The fusion will not change that. I should have schooled my temper around her."

Alarms rang out from Yeron's suite. A glance at Zoltar's camera told Quyeba why. Yeron's heartbeat dipped to thirty but then stabilized. The control the medicines had over his heartbeat was tenuous. Zoltar stood by his mother's side, eyes on the screen, frowning.

"Your yelling did not upset her," she said at last. "Her pain runs deeper. Believe me, I know."

"Maybe you do. The question is, does Alexis?"

Shouts blasted from the hallway. The patter of footsteps. Jangling sounds. All red flags indicating a breach in security. Quyeba revolved the cameras toward the hall again, and there they were, three soldiers, rushing her workstation. *These troopers are attempting a takeover.* Already, their shots felled a technician and two androids.

"Renegades!" Quyeba yanked down her face shield – since the first break-in, she had not gone anywhere without her helmet – and grabbed two plasma guns. She longed for sleep – she had not slept since Yeron's shooting, but that no longer mattered. What mattered now was that three soldiers, refugees she had welcomed to her compound, were trying to kill her, kill them all. She had no idea how many others had joined Woehar's team. Woehar must have recruited an army to reinstate Eigil's martial regimen.

Thankfully, Zoltar carried his own plasma weapons. It did not surprise her that Woehar and Draekh had recruited reinforcements. Whatever came next, she would protect Zoltar, even at the expense of her life.

Chapter Forty-Five: Alexis Fights with her Mental Powers

Underground Kryszka Colony, September 1, 10:00 p.m.

Alexis couldn't ignore the gun trained in her direction. Why did Quyeba think she was safe here? Too many people wanted her dead. If Quyeba expected to ensure anyone's safety, she was dreaming. She tried telling herself this was the best time to leave, with her mother above ground. *Trouble is, I can't walk, and if I don't stay here I'll die of my infection. That will leave my son an orphan.*

Worse, the soldier was two doors away from Yeron, Zoltar, and her Good Samaritan. Zoltar and Quyeba had made a home in her heart. *They care about me, too.*

"I should disintegrate you now," the soldier said in a jeering voice. "But I feel like having some fun."

"Fun?" *He wants to eat me.* Alexis looked up at his face. He was not smiling. He was *grinning*. "My flesh would poison you because of the toxins in my system."

"Do you think I am stupid?" he asked in a low voice. "Your mental powers are unreliable because you are ill, so we shall play a game. I will cut you, one body part at a time. Your challenge will be to guess which part I will cut before I raise my knife."

"If I guess the correct part, what is the prize?" Alexis asked sarcastically. She cast a baleful look at the fine stitches in her stomach. Zoltar's handiwork, all in vain.

"Your prize?" The soldier cackled. "I will let you know my plans for the governor and her beloved half-breed."

"You *bastard*," Alexis said under her breath, and all at once, she became aware of all the noise around her – the humming of the computers, the splintering sounds from her viewscreen. Something quivered inside her. Seconds later, it crescendoed into a tidal wave of energy, starting at her toes, working its way up her legs and her back, and up to her face. Her fingers clawed for her rosary. She lifted her gaze to the soldier's eyes, ready to rip his head to pieces.

The force rippling through her body tore her rosary apart. Before she or the soldier could react, the beads shot toward his face, miniature missiles that gouged out his eyes. Grayish tissue oozed through the cuts. The soldier's gun dropped. His mouth opened and closed. He lurched several steps toward Alexis before collapsing on the floor.

Alexis promised herself to collect the beads and place them in a small pouch. She would carry it with her for the rest of her life, as a reminder of how she survived. A merciful God existed, and He was giving her a second chance. She'd capitalize on it by bugging out of there.

Her legs might not work, but she'd manage. She eased herself out of bed and sank to her knees. With one elbow braced against the bedside, she drew up her right knee and tried to stand. The site of her stitches hurt with each intake of breath. Her legs flopped like cooked spaghetti. The IV poles limited how far she could move. A chair faced her bed, a friendly stranger waiting to whisk her to safety. She'd have to crawl to the chair; and crawl she did, giving the glass shards a wide berth, nudging the IVs along with her mind. She knelt before the chair, panting, eyes watering. It seemed so easy. She had to hoist herself to her feet, turn, and sit.

"This isn't working," she said aloud. "Too many stitches. IV needles in both hands. I have to use my mind trick."

Can I do that? According to Yeron, some Kryszka self-propelled with mind power. She managed to gouge the soldier's eyes; why not self-maneuvering?

She concentrated hard, trying to muster another wellspring of energy. This time, nothing.

"Dammit!" she cried.

Screams and laser blasts echoed from the hall.

Chapter Forty-Six: Bloodshed at Zoltar's Clinic

Zoltar's Clinic in the Underground Colony, September 2, 01:00 a.m.

Staying to Zoltar's left, Quyeba blasted both guns full force. Zoltar aside, she had to consider Yeron, Alexis, and their child. They, too, were family, and Kryszka looked after their own.

Her son fired several blasts, but Quyeba mustered her psychokinetic power to squeeze and crush a renegade's ribs. She had discovered this maneuver after breaking into Eigil's files, while he indulged in his bloodfests. Now she was dodging sideways, behind one post and then another, while her son continued firing in front. She rallied another swell of psychic energy, harder now. One soldier dropped, and then another, writhing in pain. Before she went after the third, Zoltar fried him with his disintegrator.

"Nice work, son," she said, after ensuring that the soldiers were dead.

"Glad I killed that last soldier," he said in low voice. "He was getting close to Yeron's cubicle."

"Eigil's evil spreads like bacteria," she said. "The humans are safe – they are with the vischlausk victims and are now protected by the force field. But Alexis..." She glanced at the camera again. Static and wavy lines filled the screen. A soldier must have gotten to Alexis and destroyed the camera in her room.

"Zoltar, cremate these bodies," she ordered. "When you are finished, stop at the laboratory to make sure someone has not gotten to Laurel."

She heard moaning. It was coming from Alexis's cubicle. Quyeba tore off in that direction. A trooper lay on the floor, his head and shoulders poking through the paneled entryway to her cubicle. Blood matted his face, and green beads had wedged in his eye sockets, nose, cheeks, and mouth. Blood and grayish matter oozed from around the beads, and the wounds trailed ribbons of blood down his face. He had no pulse. The stones glittered like crystals. As Quyeba stepped over his body to enter, she spotted the trooper's plasma gun on the floor near Alexis's bed.

The buzzing overhead viewscreen was shattered.

Alexis knelt on the floor between her bed and chair, hugging her knees and shivering. Her overhead monitor had exploded, leaving glass fragments on the floor.

"Alexis! What happened?"

"He was about to cut me." Eyes downcast, Alexis spoke in a quiet voice with the spellbound eyes of someone who had gone into shock. "Then I got angry and a force ran through me…a monstrous surge of psychokinesis … and my beads flew in his eyes."

"Beads?" Quyeba drew a deep breath, regretting her decision to send Zoltar to the crematorium. None of what Alexis said made sense. She was bracing her elbows against the bed and drawing one knee up. "Alexis, what are you doing?"

"I am trying to get to my chair. My psychokinesis worked so well when I defended myself, but I cannot use it levitate myself."

"Given your injuries and medications, your power will fluctuate until your body heals. I will help you back to bed."

Quyeba furrowed her brow and levitated Alexis to her feet. With one arm around Alexis's shoulders, Quyeba guided her back to the bed. Alexis's skin felt cold and damp, her breathing shallow and rapid. Quyeba pulled her radio from her side pocket and dialed up her son's image.

"Zoltar, abort your assignment. Someone got to Alexis."

No hologram or reply, just static. Whoever dismantled the camera had obliterated reception to this room and possibly other areas.

"I don't know your word for beads, but I use them for a ritual at home." Alexis, now propped on one elbow, gave Quyeba a pleading look.

"We cannot stay here," she continued. "This place is overrun with renegade soldiers. If we stay here, we will die."

She has a point, Quyeba thought, *but without treatment …*

"Before anything else, I better make sure that this man is dead," she said aloud.

She inspected the soldier. The beads in his eyes looked like crystals. The camera continued buzzing. Alexis cowered in her bed, teeth chattering.

"Alexis," Quyeba began, then hesitated. The sterile environment that Zoltar had tried so hard to maintain had disappeared. She had expected the chromosomes to gift Alexis with more mind control. How much it had she could not tell, because with most psychokinetic people, the power tended to fluctuate during illness or injury.

"I need to go somewhere safe," Alexis went on. "Where no one can find me, Yeron, or our child."

Quyeba looked toward the door. The body lay where she had found it, a gruesome testament to violence. It belonged in the crematorium, but she dared not leave Alexis alone. Instead, she mind-shoved the body to the hall and sealed the panel.

"I cannot transfer you anywhere until your treatment is finished," she said, eyes on Alexis.

"There must be a way. Healers told me I would never conceive. I did. They also said my arthritis would prohibit my employment. I found a way. As humans say, I used my imagination."

Imagination? Quyeba understood that sometimes, imagination enabled people to create ways to work around their limitations, but true safety required careful forethought and planning as well. She longed to explain this, but saw that Alexis was probably too frightened to listen.

"Where did you get these beads?" she asked instead.

"My mother gave them to me. She never expected me to use them as guided missiles." Her teeth chattered. "The one renegade I killed doesn't make a difference because there are many more."

"It appears so. That was why I did not want you to have visitors." Quyeba draped a warming blanket over Alexis. Alexis nodded her appreciation, but the yearning eyes begged Quyeba to provide a safe place. *I cannot promise anyone safety. I expected the chromosome fusion to augment Alexis's thought control, but not enough to convert crystals into guided missiles. What have we done to her?*

Stop it. That treatment saved Alexis's life.

"Alexis." She tried to muster a gentle voice, the kind she had heard Teodon use on Eigil's prisoners. "The soldier who tried to kill you is dead. He cannot hurt you."

"Good." Alexis eased against the cushions, blanket tucked into place. "He told me about the horrible death he planned for me."

"I know. Three of his assistants attacked Zoltar and me near the laboratory. We eliminated them." She sighed. "I consider Teodon and Yeron my family. Family includes Yeron's mate – you – and his child; besides, Zoltar and you are related. We are not the family you grew up with, but we care about you."

"Thank you, Good Samaritan." A trace of a smile crossed Alexis's lips. "I can suggest a place where I can continue my treatment."

Quyeba cocked her ear toward the door, listening for movement. None.

"I am listening."

"Steve has a lot of authority at his clinic. Given our circumstances, he and the other healers might allow you and Zoltar to set up your own laboratory there. Then you can continue treating me, Yeron, and the vischlausk victims. The government might quarantine the clinic, but ..."

"Alexis." Quyeba met her gaze, her eyes resolute as steel. "I am not allowing anyone to force me out of my home."

"You can say that because you are healthy. Yeron and my unborn child cannot fight for themselves. I survived only because of divine intervention."

Divine intervention? Whose? Quyeba creased her brows.

"Don't look at me like that. Teodon came back in spirit form and helped me bring Yeron down the hall. Can you explain that with your technology?"

Quyeba groaned inwardly. Alexis was not going to let go of her vision of Teodon.

"No, I cannot. Define 'divine intervention.'"

"Where I live, we believe in a spiritual being we call 'God.' We chant to Him when we worship. If we have a problem, we call on God for help. We cannot see Him, but He is there. I believe it was He who sent Teodon to protect me and Yeron."

"Teodon came back because he is a brave man and loves Yeron. Yeron is too sick to be moved. The security here is better than anything above ground. Since I cannot guarantee your safety ..." Quyeba reached into her pocket and handed Alexis a plasma gun. "I gave it a full charge. Every resident here carries a disintegrator."

"Thank you." Alexis exhaled deeply. "And everyone also needs sleep. So to make sure that we all sleep and we keep vigilant ... maybe Yeron, you, and I rotate rooms. One night, I sleep in this room, another night, in a room adjoining the laboratory, and we take turns watching so the others can sleep. What do you think?"

Quyeba frowned. Room rotation would never work on the lower deck. The assault on her life had proved that none of the rooms were safe.

"The upper deck holds plenty of private rooms, but rotating would include moving your IVs and other equipment, which would not easily be concealed from troopers who may or may not be working with Woehar. I will consider this. This soldier apparently knew nothing about your chromosome modification, which gave you an advantage. Had he known, you might not have been so lucky."

Alexis gave her a somber nod.

"I am glad my mother left. If she were here, things would have gotten ugly."

"This invasion has already gotten ugly from the way your room looks." Quyeba indicated the broken shards of glass. "I assume the renegade smashed the camera and then tried to cut you. Was that what happened?"

"No, all the glass in the room shattered when the psychic force went through me. That was when the camera broke."

Quyeba's brows knitted together in a frown as she tried thinking of a kind reassurance; the shocked, frightened expression on Alexis's face stayed her silence. Anything she said might come out wrong.

Quyeba did not think it wise to provoke Alexis in any way until she had learned the extent of her power ... that which was untrained and – so far – underused.

"My mind power got out of control," Alexis went on in a low voice. "It happened once before when I first acquired the power after a treatment Yeron gave me."

Quyeba shivered.

"Zoltar can evaluate and train you," she said in a dry voice. "The stress from your mother's visit may have provoked the surge of your psychokinesis."

"Well, our visit went downhill after she realized I had the chromosome fusion. I did not tell her about Zoltar. I think he expected a friendly meeting. That is not going to happen."

"It does not look that way." Quyeba gazed at the camera, mentally estimating the cost of the repairs required. "I will search for a more secure place for you, but first I will have to go where I can get radio reception. I cannot get it here."

"All right." Alexis's voice tensed. "How far will you go?"

"Just two doors down the hall," Quyeba said in a gentle voice. "I need my radio working so I can locate a better room. I will return as soon as I can."

In the hall, she closed the portal behind her and gazed into the frightened eyes of her son.

"I overheard your conversation," he said in an anxious voice. "We should not leave her alone. I would spend more time with her if Yeron was stable."

"What else can I do? I must find another room for her and get someone to repair her camera."

"Mother, she is terrified." With each jab of his right forefinger into the palm of his opposite hand, he counted off Alexis's mishaps. "We must help her."

Quyeba jerked her chin up.

"How?"

"Where she lives, people do not have any androids." Zoltar leaned against the panel and met his mother's gaze. "Can you imagine her bathing a squirming child with her misshapen hands?"

Images materialized in Quyeba's mind, memories of a time when she had recuperated from painful injuries while an android cared for Zoltar. She remembered the hard work involved in raising a child, something Alexis's injuries could make impossible.

"I understand more than you think," she said. "How come you are here now?"

"Visiting." Zoltar gave her a quizzical look. "I had a little time to spend with Alexis, to at least reassure myself that she is all right."

"This is going to be difficult." Quyeba sighed, and she thought about the humans under treatment. Steve and Tyrone meant well, but the language barrier made communication with them impossible without Alexis's help. Then another idea hit her: using an android would enable Alexis to raise her child, should Yeron not live. *Is making an android that is tailored to Alexis's needs doable?*

"Difficult, but not impossible," she said, smiling. "Go ahead and visit. Alexis will need a custom android. It will require time, so do not say anything to her."

Chapter Forty-Seven: Yeron Lingers near Death

Zoltar's Underground Clinic, September 2, 8:30 a.m.

The portal opened, awakening Alexis. She smiled when she saw the two familiar faces emerging through the opening.

"Steve ... Tyrone," she said. *How do I manage to sleep in this hellhole?* "Who brought you here?"

"Quyeba," Steve said. "She seemed upset. What happened?"

"Mom's visit sent my blood pressure up. Oh, and the visit from the guard." In a halting voice, Alexis described the renegade. "He was going to cut me. Then I used my mind trick in a big way. My rosary beads came apart and flew at his head and into his eyes."

"My God!" Tyrone cried. "Any hope of them releasing you soon?"

"Yes, when I get better," Alexis told him. "Whenever that is. I'll find a job and a way to raise my child."

"Your child? You're talking like Yeron's gone." Tyrone leaned toward the bed. "Jesus worked a miracle through your psychokinesis. He'll work one for Yeron, too."

"I certainly hope so. I can't raise any child alone. I suppose I can feed, bathe, and change diapers by mind control, but I can't do any chore that requires fine motor skills. Governor Quyeba means well, but I don't think she gets that."

"She might understand, but she's got a lot on her mind," Steve told her. "If I inherited the mess she did, I'd have trouble keeping it together."

"Hell." Tyrone chuckled. "I gotta wonder how much these folks know about humans. Down here, they've got androids and mind control, and Quyeba might not realize what we go through to raise kids. Have you told her that?"

"I haven't gone into detail," Alexis admitted.

"Spell things out for her," Steve said. "Have patience with yourself and your governor. She looks as frightened as you do."

Alexis nodded. She hadn't forgotten the spooked look on Quyeba's face or the tears in her eyes the first time they visited Yeron.

"She's worried about Yeron, too."

"I think Yeron will get through this, but if he doesn't, well, he kept you in mind when he made his will." Steve lifted his visor and wiped his forehead. "Jackson Hospital paid him a huge sum to join their team. If anything happens to him, fifty percent of that goes to Becky and our kid, and the rest goes to you. That comes to over three million dollars, less his death costs. That should leave you enough money to hire a nanny to help raise your child."

"I don't want Yeron's money," Alexis cried. "I want Yeron!"

Tyron nodded. "Everyone knows how much you care about him."

"He'll make a great father," Steve added.

"He will," Alexis's voice cracked. "If only he'd wake up so I can talk to him."

Steve sighed.

"Give these doctors, the treatment, and Yeron time. Most people in your situation would have trouble holding it together, but you're doing fine. Tyrone and I are in your corner, and you've got friends here, too. Granted, Quyeba has been reluctant to allow visitors, but she finally made that accommodation. That tells me she cares and she's trying to understand."

"Well ..." Alexis lowered her voice. "I've met a cousin ... and Quyeba recharged my weapon and gave it back to me. I've tried to teach her some English, but haven't gotten far because of the attacks by the renegades."

"I know." Steve bent closer, studied her face, and shot a glance toward Tyrone. "When we brought Matilda above ground, she ranted about a movie called *The Fly*. She swore a lot more was done to you besides giving you medicine, and that's why she went off the rails. What say you, Tye?"

"I agree with her," Tyrone replied. "You're not the same girl we started with – your hair and eyes have changed."

Shit! Alexis sagged against the chair.

"The treatment saved me, guys. Isn't that enough?"

"Not according to your mother." Steve shrugged. "It would help to hear the truth so we can lie to her convincingly."

"It's too late for lies. My mom's way too smart."

"C'mon, cough it up," Tyrone plunged ahead. "Did they experiment on you?"

"I can't answer that. If I do, you'll have to report it to Doctor Hoffman since he was following my case."

"Quyeba saved your neck, didn't she?" Tyrone went on. "She acted concerned when she brought us here, so no one's running to the cops. What's said underground stays underground." He nodded to Steve with a grin. "Right?"

Steve smiled. "The police need never know."

Oh, great! Alexis wrinkled her nose.

"The infection I caught was fatal. Zoltar's antidote worked on Kryszka, but not humans. My condition was worsening and the toxins from the bacteria caused a cardiac arrest."

"Was that why Zoltar did the DNA fusion?" Steve prodded.

"Yes. He fused Quyeba's chromosomes with mine, enabling my body to handle medicine designed for Kryszka natives." Alexis searched her visitors' faces for negative reactions. None. Her friends leaned forward like kids listening to a campfire ghost story. "It was a simple procedure, but now I'm part Kryszka. That's why my hair and eyes have changed."

The men looked at Alexis, and then at each other. *Any second now they will scream and run.*

Instead, Tyrone maintained his steady gaze.

"Obviously, it worked. Here you are, talking to us. Do you know if there will be more changes?"

"No, I don't." Alexis swallowed hard. "The infection's going away. My mental abilities have increased, and on two instances, saved my life. Whatever happens with me, please don't be angry with Quyeba or Zoltar. They did what they needed to do to save my life. Since Quyeba was the chromosome donor, I call her my 'Good Samaritan.'"

"Good Samaritan," Tyrone echoed in a soft voice. "I can respect that."

"So can I." Steve leaned back, covering his eyes with one hand. "We'd better watch what we tell people. Yeron described the gene fusion procedure before. His father spliced Kryszka DNA into five humans afflicted with cancer. It killed the cancer cells, but no one studied the long-term effects because Eigil had the people slaughtered." His voice sounded more urgent now. "I told Yeron that this procedure would never fly, that it violated our code of ethics."

"The native Kryszka don't consider splicing a routine procedure. Zoltar did it as a last resort."

"I understand that," Steve conceded. "Doctor Hoffman wouldn't have had any antidote. He hasn't finished rebuilding his research center."

"I think God allowed it so I can raise my kid. I'd give anything for some semblance of normal living."

"What's 'normal' when you're dealing with people from another world?" Tyrone asked. "I can't tell you how to feel; I'm just glad that you're alive."

"You can't tell anyone else about my little operation. Promise me."

"Your secret will go to the grave with me and Tyrone, but one day you might ..."

Steve stopped at the sound of footsteps in the hallway. Alexis recognized Quyeba's gait.

Quyeba smiled and waved at the two men, then turned to face Alexis.

"I am here to watch while the android changes your dressings and gives you a bath," she said. "Our androids are not equipped to handle renegade soldiers."

Alexis nodded. "Understood. I will chase Steve and Tyrone out of here. Is it all right if they visit with Yeron?"

Quyeba heaved a rueful sigh. "It would not be wise until Zoltar allows Yeron to have visitors, but maybe they can observe him from an anteroom."

Chapter Forty-Eight: Decisions about Laurel's Fate

Quyeba's Underground Laboratory, September 2, 10:30 a.m.

Quyeba and the android bathed Alexis and changed her clothes. That meant replacing the dressings, too. Alexis grimaced as Quyeba pulled off the soiled gauze, but she did not yell.

"Your incision looks clean. There is a bit of drainage, which Zoltar told me to expect." She smiled. "Stay out of trouble."

"I will try." Tears brimmed in Alexis's eyes. "I am sorry about your camera. The surge of telekinesis erupted so fast and I could not control it."

Quyeba drew in a deep breath. "You slaughtered a renegade, which saved lives. None of us knew how the fusion would affect your mental power since you had telekinesis when you were totally a human. You should also expect fluctuations in your power because you are still recuperating. When your injuries heal, Zoltar will test and train your ability."

"I appreciate your understanding." Alexis's eyes opened wide as soup plates. "I never thanked you or Zoltar for saving my life."

Now, it was Quyeba's turn to stare. What explained Alexis's sudden calm? Something her visitors had said?

"Steve thinks that you and Zoltar are as scared as we are of Woehar's renegades, and I tend to agree. You must feel like you stumbled into quicksand. Am I about right?"

Quyeba grimaced. "That is about right."

"Steve suggested that I try to be patient with myself. You need to be patient with yourself, too."

Patience? Is she joking? No, she is not. Whatever Steve said carried strength with Alexis.

"There is too much blood on my hands. If I could transport you and Yeron above ground without danger, I would do so now."

"But you cannot," Alexis said in a tight voice. "At least my mother is safe. She may never come back because my looks frightened her."

"Try some patience with your mother. She may come around."

At least I hope she will. Quyeba had once read that primitive societies practiced "shunning," ostracizing family members who did not conform to the norms of the tribe. *I hope this is not the case with Matilda.*

Alexis sat on her bed, legs dangling, a clean tunic wrapped around her.

"My mother is terrified, but she thinks all Kryszka are bad because one of them killed Robin. She cannot understand Laurel's part in the killings."

Quyeba took a seat by Alexis's bed, listening, grateful for an explanation.

"If you had asked my permission to do the fusion, I would have said no. Splicing chromosomes from other species goes against our religious beliefs." Alexis's softening voice offered a reprieve. "That said, Steve said that a lot of people above ground care about me and would miss me if I died. I am alive, in part because of your gene mixture."

Is that genuine gratitude in her voice? Yes, it is.

"So I am glad you did it. My feelings may not matter anyway, because my skirmish exposed me to bacteria and probably ruined my chances of recovery."

"Kryszka chromosomes are hardier than humans. Our traits are dominant, as you can see with Zoltar." Quyeba allowed a smile. "Besides, unlike your former colleague, soldiers and other personnel here must bathe before they enter a laboratory."

"We had too many interruptions for me to teach you English, but I can give you something you need. I think you need a witness."

"A witness?" *Now, what is she talking about?*

"The polygraphs humans use are not accurate. Our officers rely on the testimony of people who saw the incident. I assume Laurel is locked in your prison. So when I am healthy enough to go above ground, I will tell everyone who asks me that you and Zoltar saved my life and cared for me while I was sick. If you extradite Laurel to our authorities, they will regard it as a peace offering."

You are naïve if you think that. It does not matter whether I save twenty lives or whether I extradite fifty prisoners. Your people will remember the disasters that Eigil and Woehar caused. Quyeba drew in a deep, shuddering breath.

"Your people are not capable of handling the monster that Laurel has become. A meeting with your dignitaries may help."

"I do not have such contacts, but Steve's sister does. Steve and Tyrone want to know you better … after you learn our language. I was wondering if you could have a microchip like mine that would accelerate the learning process."

What did this healer tell her? Whatever he said, Quyeba suspected that he was competent in his chosen calling. No doubt, he and Alexis would make great allies.

"Such microchips do not work on Kryszka because our minds are not as open to suggestion the way humans are. It does not matter; I can learn fast ... if we can go a few days without being shot at or attacked." Quyeba made a wry face.

"No rush; you will need extensive physical therapy and training for your new powers. You will watch your child grow, too. But now your place is with Yeron. Would you like to visit him?"

"Please! If I talk to him, he might wake up. Humans can hear even if they are not conscious, and I suspect Kryszka can, too."

"Sometimes we hear better." Quyeba had to smile. Something about the way Alexis talked made her laugh. "Let us go."

****

In the surgical suite, Yeron lay in his cubicle, breathing on a ventilator, eyes shut. He appeared fast asleep. His erratic heart rate, blood pressure, and electrolyte readings spoke to marginal recovery. Zoltar moved from machine to machine, tracing his fingers along the dials, cutting one medicine and adding another. Crimson shadows had appeared under his eyelids. When had he last slept?

Quyeba had her eyes on Alexis. Alexis's lips opened and closed, but no words came. She was fighting another round of tears. Zoltar stood at her side, one hand on her shoulder.

"I am sorry I was rough on you," he said in a quiet voice. "What matters now is that Yeron gets better."

"Will he?" Alexis asked in a tremulous voice. "My mother cannot handle me or the baby. How will I raise a child alone when I cannot even walk?"

"You will walk because Xian has planned a demanding exercise program to build strength into your limbs. It means hard work, but it can be done. I am doing everything I can to save Yeron."

Zoltar takes after his father, Quyeba thought. *He feels compassion for the sick and expresses it well.* She smiled at him with pride, then turned toward Alexis.

"You managed to slaughter an assassin. I think you can handle a child when the chromosome changes take full effect."

Oh, how tactless that sounded. Quyeba tensed, expecting Alexis to break into another spate of tears. Instead, Alexis gave her a quizzical smile.

"I wondered about that. You provided me a tool with which to work my diseased limbs. People can be cruel. Coworkers who never met me made disparaging comments about my hands."

Understanding dawned. *I should not be surprised to hear*

Alexis's positive thoughts about the fusion. Alexis had seen her share of monsters before she met anyone from the compound, the worst being the disease that riddled her body.

"I hope this fusion does what you expect it to do," she told Alexis.

"I hope so, too." Alexis shifted her scrutiny back and forth between Quyeba and Zoltar.

This time, Quyeba's eyes moistened – and that was bad. *If only the humans had access to better technology and were more accepting.* Instead, they saw monsters everywhere and would not recognize any good among her kind.

"If your condition caused ostracism, I shudder to think of how they treated Yeron."

"Most people shunned Yeron, except his half-sister's relatives, me, and the boys who fought with us. I mean the other fighters ... but I call them the boys."

Boys? If you said that around Eigil, he would fry you with his disintegrator. He had no tolerance for casual talk or humor. Laughter bubbled up into Quyeba's throat, but she fought it back when sadness crossed Alexis's face.

"I wish you and Zoltar would quit yelling at each other so much. Yeron and I argued, too, and now he is lying there, unconscious. He may never get to hear me say 'I love you' to him again. You two are healthy, but people want you dead. Somewhere between all the emergencies, make time for each other."

Quyeba stared at Alexis; her jaw dropped. She looked at her son, expecting him to come up with an intelligent comment that he reserved for his patients. Instead, Zoltar gaped at Alexis in stunned surprise.

"Your mother is lucky to have you for a daughter," Quyeba said, looking at Alexis. "Zoltar is a proficient healer; you may still get your chance with Yeron. Would you like to visit with him alone?" She looked over at Zoltar. "My son and I must talk."

"Yes." With that, Alexis eased back into her chair, and Quyeba wheeled her to Yeron's bedside. Quyeba remained silent a moment, watching Alexis and Yeron, and took her son by his hand. They walked toward the door, stopping just before leaving the room.

"I love you as if you came from my body," she whispered to Zoltar. "This compound – and everything that went with it – I created for you. Otherwise, Eigil would have you killed."

"I understand that, Mother. But I do like hearing you say it." Zoltar lowered his voice. "I love you, too, and I am glad you adopted me."

"We may never know how many renegades are hiding out here. I see Yeron lying unconscious, and I realize that could have been you tonight."

"We will get through this," Zoltar insisted. "Woehar is gone – a victim of her monster. Let the human officials deal with Laurel."

"That is the problem. Most of our residents, let alone humans, cannot handle Laurel as she is now." After scanning the surveillance cameras to assure they were off, she told her son about Laurel's gene fusion. Doubt spread across his olive-complexioned face. "You saw Laurel when we found Alexis and Yeron in the hall, right?"

"No, I did not. I was focused on saving Yeron." His frown deepened. "I did not check on her either because you needed me here."

"Then come with me now. I will show what Laurel has become."

"Yes, I want to meet this human-*settva*." Zoltar headed left and followed his mother down the hall that led to the crematorium and prison. "If you are right, I hope someone kept her well fed."

Quyeba retrieved her portable camera from the pockets of her tunic. The camera in the prison laboratory was out of her range. She could not bring up Laurel on camera until she got closer to the laboratory. When she attempted to focus her camera now, she got a snowy screen with a background of static.

"We are too far out of range. We should see something as we approach the laboratory."

As they came to the area where she last saw Laurel, the familiar vanilla aroma and antiseptic odors faded, replaced by a foul stench. *No surprise there. Laurel stank like a sewer. So did Woehar.*

The prison laboratory in Quyeba's compound loomed ahead. She hoped that by now, a technician or android had removed the bodies of Shively and Woehar. It was highly doubtful, though, considering that the job entailed danger of being attacked by Laurel. According to Alexis, Laurel was angry – angry and eager to devour any living thing. *I have to admire Alexis's gumption. Badly hurt as she was, she managed to crawl through the hall and summon help.* Teodon once described the indomitable spirit of humans, but she had not witnessed it until now.

As soon she opened the paneled door at the end of the hall, a bitter, rancid odor hit her. Woehar's skeletal remains lay in congealed blood on the grid floor. Laurel had picked the bones clean, except for the face. Quyeba's mouth quivered. Fear prickled her scalp.

A deep snort followed. Laurel rested on her stomach, stirring her limbs. She opened one eye. Quyeba shot her, sedating her again.

"Mother!" Zoltar protested, raising his armed hand. "Kill her or I will!"

"Not yet." Quyeba stayed his hand. "We should discuss Laurel with the humans' officials before destroying her. At least confer with Alexis's friends. Otherwise, they might consider Laurel's execution an act of war."

"Very well." Zoltar sighed. "I had better go back and see how Yeron is doing. I shall send an android here for the bodies."

Chapter Forty-Nine: Matilda's Offer

Zoltar's Clinic near Grays Landing, September 2, 04:20 p.m.

Loneliness washed through Alexis's soul, for Yeron did not budge or respond when she held his hand. His ventilator delivered slow and steady breaths.

"Yeron, open your eyes," she pleaded in a broken voice.

No movement.

"Yeron, it's me. Steel Rose. I'm here for you."

Nothing.

Alexis burst into a fresh outbreak of tears, unaware of a hand reaching for her shoulder.

"Dammit, Yeron, why didn't you listen when I told you to run for help? You wouldn't be in this mess."

"He's a man!"

"Mom?" Alexis looked up at the speaker.

Her mother stood facing Alexis with her helmet cradled in one arm, Xian beside her. She was wringing her hands, but her eyes were resolute.

"I said he's a man. Men never listen."

Dammit all, with the new onset of shootings, she's got no business being here. What's she doing with Xian? Did she force Xian to escort her to the bedside?

"Xian," Alexis said after finding her voice, "How did you wind up with my mother?"

"Quyeba ordered me to bring her here. Matilda shouted something at the other humans and mentioned your name." Xian's voice saddened. "Quyeba said it is between you and your mother. We must not interfere."

"I understand." After Xian assumed her post by the door, Alexis turned to her mother. "I'm surprised Quyeba let you come here. We've had several shootings, and more renegades are lying in wait. The doctors did what they needed to do to save me, and now they're trying to help Yeron. If they could speak our language, they'd tell you that."

"Steve Leicht told me all about the shooting." Her mother fetched a heavy sigh. "I wish you'd fallen for a human man who works a 9-to-5 job, comes home every night, and tells you he loves you. Steve … Doctor Leicht told me that Yeron took gunfire that was meant for you. If it weren't for him, you'd be dead. He also reminded me that two people here saved your life."

"That's right. My heart stopped during surgery. Zoltar revived me."

Her mother took in Xian's face and looked at Quyeba and Zoltar, who were reemerging through the door. Her voice quavered, but Alexis saw awe in her eyes.

"Please tell these people I said thank you."

Alexis turned her eyes toward Zoltar. "My mother wants to thank you and Governor Quyeba for saving my life."

Quyeba shrugged. "I am trying to make it right."

Alexis settled her eyes on her mother again. "The governor here is trying to make amends for what the renegade soldiers have done."

"This whole thing is wrong," her mother said. "If my Louis were alive, this wouldn't have happened. Ever since cancer took him, nothing has gone right." And she burst into tears.

"She thinks my father's death caused the tragedies in our family," Alexis said, turning toward the Kryszka.

"She could be right," Quyeba replied in a sad voice.

"Mother … Xian … give them time alone," Zoltar said. "Yeron seems stronger. I can watch him on camera."

With shaky hands, her mother wrapped her fingers around Yeron's left hand.

"God knows this whole thing violates the rules of human nature as I understand them," she said. "But Yeron's an ethical man. I'll give him that." Her mother laid a hand on Alexis's shoulder. "I'm sorry I got so upset before. That red in your eyes spooked me. Those Kryszka injected you with their DNA to make you one of them, and don't give me any bull about drugs and side effects. Doctor Steve Leicht tried that and he couldn't look me in the eye."

Alexis shifted her gaze toward Quyeba and Zoltar, who were lingering by the door. Given their furtive glances and hushed voices, she had to wonder if they were whispering concerns about her and Yeron. She then looked her mother in the eye.

"Okay, Mom, no bull. They fused Quyeba's DNA with mine so that my body would respond to their medicines. They did that to save me and you can take that to any bank."

"I don't know whether to shout with glee or cry," her mother said. "Doctor Leicht said he had no treatment for your infection. This fusion ... can it be undone?"

"I doubt it, but regardless of my hair or eye color, I'm the same person. I want to come home soon so I can eat real food. I want to sleep in my own bed and I want Yeron to get better."

"What about this child you two conceived? I never handled a half-breed, but I can figure it out. I've got a soft heart for children. Louis had the street smarts, though; you got some of that from him."

"You're way smarter than you realize, Mom. I don't know anything about half-breed children either, so we can learn together. I think Steve and Tyrone might help me. Quyeba and Zoltar will, too, when they aren't coping with so many emergencies."

"The people here seem to like you. Louis made friends easily, too. You are your father's daughter." Her face darkened. "But you've got a tender heart and sometimes I worry that you're going to get hurt. You've got so much love to give and you don't realize it."

"Quyeba and Zoltar have tender hearts, too. Quyeba's soft side led her to trust Woehar and believe her story. Yeron lost his father in the war and his sister shot their mother, a woman who couldn't defend herself. Losses like that are difficult."

"How well I know it." Her mother's voice was solemn. "Nostalgia crept in with her voice. "Around 1984 – you were about nine – my sister disappeared for about a month. When she came home, she couldn't remember what happened. At least that's what she told everyone. She'd lost a lot of weight, and that's when the rheumatism began."

"Hm." Alexis leaned toward her mother, head tilted. "That would put Zoltar at age twenty-six."

"Zoltar ... the doctor, right?"

"Yes, the one standing with Quyeba. He's half human. You can tell by his skin color. I think of him and Quyeba as Good Samaritans."

"Alexis!" Her mother's voice became stern. "I warned you not to invent nicknames for these people."

"No one's complained." Alexis darted a glance toward Quyeba and Zoltar and smiled. *Things are going well. Is Mom ready to hear about Zoltar?* "My Kryszka buddies are just as capable of laughter as we are. Like you, Quyeba buried the man she loved and raised a special child alone. Zoltar, a half-breed. She loves him like her own."

Alexis stopped, gauging her mother's reaction. "Mom – Aunt Susan is Zoltar's birth mother."

"Susan? *My sister Susan?*" Her mother's eyes bulged.

"According to Steve, the Kryszka ship landed in 1960. I think they spent the first years building the compound where they first lived. When Eigil assumed power, he kidnapped humans for fodder. Aunt Susan became a hostage until their scientists used her for a hybrid experiment. I think they hypnotized her so she would forget what happened."

"No!" Her mother shook her head. "She would remember if she had a child."

"I don't think she remembered consciously, Mom. The first governor, Eigil, made Hitler seem like Santa Claus. He captured humans and dismembered them. What the scientists did to Aunt Susan was ghastly, but they saved her from becoming dinner for Eigil and his minions." She averted her eyes, not caring to admit that Yeron's father was the one who harvested the eggs. "The scientists harvested and fertilized Aunt Susan's eggs. After fertilization, the embryo was incubated. Aunt Susan didn't carry her child in a typical human pregnancy. Zoltar's got our complexion, though, and he eats cooked food." She drew in a deep breath. "Will you pray for Yeron since he's hurt so badly? Please?"

Her mother rested her palm on Yeron's forehead, and looked at Alexis, tears in her eyes. She then threw her arms around Alexis, managing a gentle hug.

"I'll go one better," she said.

"Come again?" Alexis stared at her at her mother, her mouth an open O of surprise.

"Quyeba's got her hands full. God knows how many terrorists are skulking around this place. I have to wonder how other people who live here and trusted her to lead them feel about this. Getting help to care for you and Yeron might allow time to focus on her other problems."

"Where would she find help?" Alexis shrugged. "None of our hospitals have the equipment to treat me or Yeron. Besides, Quyeba wants me here to teach her English."

"I'm not talking about our hospitals." Her mother shook her head. "I'm a registered nurse. If someone shows me how, I'll change Yeron's dressings and manage his IVs like I do any other patient."

"No, Mom!" Alexis covered her eyes. "You almost died delivering my medicines—"

"Yeron almost died saving you. I'll care for him—that's the least I can do. I'll come here every day so that their robots can do other chores."

Alexis heaved a ponderous sigh.

"Quyeba, my mother wants to visit every day so she can help care for Yeron."

"We cannot allow her to travel, given her age. Transportation is dangerous for the men, too, but at least they have formal training in battle techniques and faster reflexes."

Shaking her head, Quyeba moved back to Yeron's bedside, followed by Zoltar.

Alexis shrugged and threw up her hands.

"She offered. Can you move Yeron to a clinic above ground?"

"No, no, no!" Quyeba cried in a tremulous voice. "Yeron is too sick. Matilda does not speak our language. We cannot transport our medicines and equipment."

"I am sure Steve or Tyrone can act as my mother's personal guard," Alexis offered.

"That may be," Zoltar said. "If Matilda honestly wants to help, I prefer that she live here to care for Yeron. She should learn to use our weapons and wear our clothes to blend in with our environment."

Momsy coming to live down here? Mom packing plasma heat? Mom wearing Kryszka outfits? Better batten down the hatches and tie up your androids. Your world will never be the same again. Alexis grimaced, trying to suppress the laughter in her throat, and proceeded to translate to her mother.

Her mother's face paled, and then she nodded. "I'll do it. This way I can be close to you. I've missed you so much. Someone will have to provide food we can eat."

Alexis swallowed another giggle, coughed, and patted her chest.

"I'm sure Steve or Tyrone will send us meals." She then smiled at Quyeba and Zoltar. "My mother said 'yes.'"

Chapter Fifty: Alexis Realizes a Miracle

Zoltar's Clinic, September 19, 9:00 p.m.

Every three days, Steve or Tyrone commuted from their homes in Bernersville, showing up with bags of sandwiches, platters, soups, and other edibles. Matilda took over Yeron's custodial care and IVs, freeing Quyeba's androids to perform other tasks.

Alexis's fevers and vomiting stopped, but the nerve damage gifted by Laurel sent ungodly shooting pain down her legs with each attempt to bear weight. When she wasn't with Yeron, she spent time with Xian, trying to learn to manage her pain, wearing electrical stimulants to heal the nerves and muscles. Quyeba and Matilda assisted her with bathing.

"Your infection is gone," Zoltar told her a week after Matilda's arrival. Quyeba, who accompanied him, took a seat beside Alexis while he examined Yeron. A frown creased his face.

"What about Yeron?" Alexis glanced toward the rear of the lab, where her mother slept.

Zoltar sighed. "His vital signs are much better, but his mental state does not appear to have improved. The longer he stays in a coma, the less likely it is that he will wake."

"Because?" Alexis shuddered and tentacles of fear crept around her heart.

"Because of the extent of his injuries," Zoltar told her.

"Keep talking to him," Quyeba advised her. "Somewhere in a dark part of his brain, he hears you."

"I will do that." Alexis leaned back and looked at Quyeba. "You gave me good advice about my mother and patience."

Quyeba's lips curved into a smile.

"I am still amazed that she agreed to stay here."

Alexis shrugged.

"I am not. She is truly grateful to Yeron because he risked his life saving me. And she wants to be close to me."

Quyeba appeared to be deep in meditation. "This may give me

a chance to defuse tensions between our species. I need time to contemplate the specifics." She draped a gown over Alexis's tunic and wheeled her to Yeron's bedside. "Keep talking to Yeron."

"Yeron." Alexis rested her hand in his and watched his eyes. "Open your eyes."

No movement.

"Everything is going to be all right. The renegades are gone." Now that was a big fat lie. "I'm getting better. My infection is gone."

Silence. No movement. No acknowledgment of recognition.

What else can I say? How much does he understand? She recited the events of the previous day, describing her exercises, her chats with her mother, Quyeba, and Zoltar. She gave him her prognosis on her injuries, assuring him that while she might limp, she would be able to walk without help. An epistle on Laurel's bodily changes followed, with assurances that neither she nor Woehar could hurt anyone now. Through it all, Yeron remained still.

Fatigue settled over Alexis's shoulders again, and set there, like a mantle over a fireplace. *Didn't Zoltar encourage me to rest? Of course, he had, but I won't leave Yeron.* She tried forcing her eyelids open, to keep the conversation going. The medicines were making her sleepy, along with the injuries from which she was still recovering. Moments later, she fell forward into Yeron's bed, right arm draped over his waist, falling asleep.

Stinging pain in her wrist jarred her awake.

Alexis jerked upright, crying. Her fingers throbbed. *Yeron!* Yeron clutched her hand. His eyes were open. He was trying to get up.

"Yeron, stay still!" With a flick of her mind, she disengaged his fingers. "Mom, wake up! Yeron's trying to get out of bed."

Duh! Mom can't help. Before she could come up with another stupid idea, Zoltar burst in through the door.

"Alexis." Yeron's voice was a croak, but the words came through clear as glass. "You are alive."

"Yes, very much alive, and so are you. Our son is, too. Zoltar harvested him and he's in a Kryszka incubator right now."

"Our son?" Yeron's eyes rolled. "I am sorry I hurt your hand."

"Don't worry about it. Our son is almost eight weeks' gestation. Zoltar worked a lot of miracles with me, our son, and now you."

"Alexis." Zoltar nudged her shoulder. "I must examine him. Step aside."

"I will, but first I must say something to Yeron." Alexis gazed into his eyes. "I love you, Yeron. I have loved you for a long time."

A smile creased Yeron's lips.

"I knew that all along. I love you, too, my Steel Rose."

Alexis got up off of Yeron's bed and wheeled herself to her air mattress. She struggled to her feet and flopped on the bed. The movement cost her nasty stinging around her incisions and lower back, but she smiled the biggest smile she had since the war began. Yeron was going to be all right.

Yeron's and Zoltar's voices drifted her way, both speaking Kryszka.

"Can you tell me where you are?" Zoltar asked Yeron.

"I am at Quyeba's laboratory," Yeron replied. His voice carried weak, but Alexis understood him. "Woehar shot me and everything hurts."

"As well it should," Zoltar said. "I will give you something to help you relax." He turned toward Matilda, still speaking in his native tongue. "Watch him. Keep him calm. Any excitement might cause an arrhythmia."

Alexis snickered into her pillow. *Zoltar, dear, what are you thinking? Momsy doesn't know Kryszka.*

A long silence followed. Alexis opened her mouth to translate, but Yeron did it first, his voice faint.

"Matilda, they are giving me a sedative. They want you to watch me because any excitement might cause an erratic heartbeat."

His mind's sharper than a settva tooth. One hurdle over. But she and Yeron faced months of grueling physical therapy, the challenge of raising a half-breed, and God knows how many renegades and zombies.

Chapter Fifty-One: Yeron's Nightmare

Zoltar's Clinic, September 25, 9:00 p.m.

Yeron went back to sleep, aided by the sedative. He dreamt he saw a younger version of himself exiting the clinic where he and his father worked during their years at Eigil's compound, which they called Little Kryszk. Worried about contamination, he changed his clothes before departing the clinic, leaving his gun there as well, per work policy. He strolled home, hoping to discuss treatments with his parents.

Yeron of Little Kryszk headed to the gate leading to the apartment complex where his family lived. He ran his identification card through a scanning device, and then scurried up the granite sidewalk that led to his door.

Adult Yeron tried to scream at the younger version of himself: *Run, Yeron! Leave while you can.*

Instead, the young man stepped into the apartment and gagged on smoke. Gray wisps curled from the bedrooms. Something had caught on fire.

Yeron – the one sleeping in Quyeba's laboratory – tried to dig out of the dream. He sensed that people he loved were nearby in his real life. Hushed voices whispered around him. He strained toward that loving world that waited outside his nightmarish dream, but the sedative Zoltar had given him was too strong. His eyes were only open in his dream.

Yeron of Little Kryszk hesitated. A thick curtain of smoke blanketed the hallway. He forced one foot before the other, seeing charred walls and broken pieces of tile. He gagged on the frightening stink. It was cooked flesh.

The smoke cleared in front of him, and a figure stood in the hallway. It was his sister.

Woehar wore a pressurized suit, but Yeron could not understand why, since the underground colony provided adequate oxygenation and stable temperatures. The glass helmet revealed her pale face and sardonic grin.

Uh, oh … watch out!

Yeron of Little Kryszk gave no sign of hearing. He did not betray any fear. Despite Eigil's dictatorship, he had felt secure at home, at least before today.

"You are home early," Woehar said in her caustic voice.

"What happened here?" he asked as he gazed toward the bedroom. "Was there a fire?"

"Eigil and I mated. I am going to help him rule our colony," Woehar said, ignoring his question. She spoke with thinly veiled contempt. "Why are you here?"

"I live here." Yeron of Little Kryszk gave a short laugh, trying to pass it off as a joke. But Woehar was not smiling. "I came home early because Mother and I must talk. Father developed a new formula to treat her infection."

Woehar advanced toward him, reaching into her pocket.

"Keep it to yourself. Mother will not need any treatment."

Young Yeron shook at the coldness radiating from his sister.

"Why not? She is in so much pain. Father said he would meet me here. Have you seen him?"

Woehar grinned under her helmet.

"Maybe I have."

She waved her gloved hand. The door to their parents' bedroom opened, revealing the source of the smoke: his mother's body, fried, charcoal black and oozing blood. Her features were barely visible. Only her nametag remained intact.

"Mother!" Yeron rooted through the folds of his tunic, then remembered that he had left his gun at work with his uniform. His father stored plasma guns in the cabinet – right behind Woehar.

Before he could decide what to do next, blue rays circled him.

"No, Woehar!" he shouted. "Stop! Why are you doing this?"

In the next instant, young Yeron dropped to the floor. He expected to lose consciousness. Instead, he lay on his back, eyes on Woehar, but unable to move or speak.

Woehar stood facing him, gun pointed.

"I ask the questions. Not you."

Despite the heated apartment, chills wreaked Yeron's body. *What is she planning next?* He tried using his mind to create a force field around himself. It didn't materialize. His mental powers became useless with the plasma sedative.

"That is right, I sedated you." Woehar's grin revealed a mouthful of pointed teeth. "I paralyzed you for long enough to teach you a lesson. So listen and heed me. Eigil is angry with you and Father for rescuing the humans. He asked me to warn you. This is your warning."

She fired a laser. Yeron clenched his teeth, anticipating ungodly agony. The laser left a hole in his tunic but did not puncture his skin. Another shot. Another hole. She kept going, laughing to herself.

At last, he found his voice.

"All right! If it will make you happy, I will leave. Please let me go."

"Do not come back," she warned him. "This apartment belongs to me and Eigil. Next time Eigil catches you helping humans, he will feed you to the *settva*."

Yeron struggled to his feet. His head spun. He shambled toward the door, desirous to leave before Woehar changed her mind.

At the doorway, Woehar grabbed him by the tunic, using levitation.

"Remember," she warned. "You are next."

Yeron scurried down the sidewalk, hoping to meet up with Father. Perhaps he could live at the clinic like Quyeba did. He intended to forget he ever lived in this apartment. He could do this if he tried hard enough, and he planned to start trying now.

When Yeron reached the front gate, his eyes moved quickly, back and forth, looking for a hiding place. His breath came out in gasping pants. Children were playing in a courtyard next door. He hid behind a pillar so as not to scare them. He did not see Woehar or Eigil, but he sensed they were watching him. *From this day on, I swear I will never go anywhere unarmed.*

Yeron didn't move, his feet like lead, his heart pounding. At last the courtyard was empty. Disheveled, Yeron of Little Kryszk scrambled through the gate. It looked as if rats had gnawed through his navy tunic, leaving bite holes the size of his thumb. His eyes rolled like those of a fear-maddened *settva*. He crept to the street corner, cast one last glance at his parents' home – his beloved childhood home – and broke into a run.

He bolted the four kilometers to the clinic. No matter how fast he ran, tendrils of smoke reached for him, creeping down his chest. He imagined Eigil lurking around a corner where he could not see; he couldn't shake Woehar's whispered earworm: *Eigil and I mated.* Yeron ran, screaming, *please do not hurt me,* and in his mind, a spray of fire followed, along with the answer:

You are next, Yeron. More fire.

You are next ...

In the next instant, he did hear blasting, coming from some place outside his dream, gunfire followed by the crack of escaping flames, the stink of sulfur. The adult Yeron's eyes flew open. He let out a weak moan. Matilda stood, her back to him, Alexis beside her, shooting at renegade soldiers who had broken into the laboratory. The room reeked of sulfur. Flashes of fire stitched back and forth, two of them dangerously close to Matilda, followed by the dull thud of falling soldiers. Matilda and Alexis remained standing.

"Mother!" Yeron hollered. "Alexis!"

Soft arms cradled his shoulders. Matilda's arms, but they reminded him of his mother.

"Easy, Yeron. You're safe," she said in a soft voice.

Yeron blinked his eyes. Two soldiers lay prone on the floor. Woehar and Little Kryszk were gone. He was lying in bed with a tube feeding oxygen into his chest. Alexis staggered toward him, one hand rubbing her back. She sank to her knees.

"No, Mother, we are not," he said, having found his voice. "Woehar wants to kill both of us and Alexis is hurt."

"I'm all right, honey." Alexis lovingly glanced toward Yeron, while withdrawing guns from the soldiers' tunics. "I'm hurting from activity my body's not ready to do yet."

Matilda cast a sidelong glance toward Alexis.

"I'm not so sure about Alexis being okay; she's hurting pretty badly, but Woehar's dead, Yeron. So are the hoodlums who came after us."

"Not quite." With a grimace, Alexis trailed her hands down the soldiers' chests. "This one with the burns is, but the one Mom got is asleep." She blasted his face and neck to make sure he was dead, shambled to her chair and flopped in its cushions.

"Asleep?" The older woman's face reddened several shades, eyes glaring. "*Pezzo di merda!*"

Alexis blushed. "Mom, these guns work. You shot him with the sedative, that's all."

"Sedative, *bah fungule!*"

Clattering footsteps from the hall. The panel opened. Quyeba charged into the room, face scrunched up in anger. Zoltar and two androids edged up behind her, drawing out their weapons. With a vigorous shake of her head, Quyeba gave hushed and hurried instructions to the androids. Yeron watched, spellbound, as the androids levitated the dead soldiers. Backs toward Yeron, the androids left. After a cursory glance around the lab, Zoltar stowed away his gun. He nudged Alexis aside and whispered something that Yeron did not get. Alexis shook her head and limped back to her place at Yeron's bedside.

Yeron gazed at the older woman and Alexis, realizing that they were speaking English. The human female's hair was gray and the voice belonged to Matilda.

"Mother ... I am sorry about Alexis. I tried to keep her safe."

"I know." Her gentle voice soothed him. "She's all right."

"How can you be sure? She can barely walk ..." Yeron squeezed his eyes shut. Colors floated in skull-shaped patterns behind his lids. He opened them again, and Alexis's mother stood facing him, regarding him with concerned eyes. She wore a blue tunic that glittered under the pink lights. "Mother ... Matilda, why are you wearing a tunic?"

"Make it easier – call me 'Mom.' Quyeba thought it safest if I dressed like the residents." Matilda darted a worried glance toward the others.

"Yeron doesn't look so good," Alexis said. "He kept calling for his mother in his sleep. I think he had a nightmare."

Yeron sighed. "This nightmare ... Mom, it happened."

Quyeba gasped. "He remembers."

Alexis looked puzzled, then limped to Yeron's bed, left foot dragging, and slumped into a chair beside her mother. She turned toward Quyeba and Zoltar.

"Remember what?"

"What Woehar did," Zoltar said in a low voice. "It is his story to tell."

With that, Yeron described his life with Woehar. Woehar of the vischlausk. Woehar of the bloodlust. Fleeing his home after finding his mother's burnt remains, with Woehar whispering *you are next* in his dreams. He told it in English, then translated it to Kryszka. Sympathetic nods from Alexis, Matilda, and the others encouraged him to continue.

"Honey, I am so sorry you went through that," Alexis whispered, caressing his cheek.

He shook his head.

"I do not want sorrow. My father taught me to be strong."

"You were strong when Alexis needed you the most." Matilda gave him a genuine smile that lit up her eyes. "Welcome to the family."

Chapter Fifty-Two: Forming Alliances

Zoltar's Clinic, September 26, 10:00 a.m.

Alexis spent the next few days with Xian, attempting to strengthen her muscles and control her augmented power. After much pleading with Quyeba to relax the visitation rules, she chatted with Yeron, her mother, Steve, and Tyrone. She ran Quyeba, Xian, and Zoltar through English 101, amazed by the speed with which they picked up the language. She visited Yeron without wearing a mask or isolation suit. Zoltar had given up yelling at her about sterility after the third time he caught her without protective gear. The platters of food cooked by Steve's wife and Tyrone's church friends were tasty, but in her heart, Alexis longed to stroll above ground. She wanted to smell the flowers and feel the heat of the sun. Her mouth watered when she thought of her mother's homemade ravioli. Yet some part of her welcomed the modern conveniences that the Kryszka city offered, conveniences that were arthritis-friendly.

"You look tired," Yeron told her when they were alone one night. "Get some rest."

Alexis conceded. "I do need some. When you're stronger, we will visit our child together. Right now, he's the size of a strawberry. I can make out the face, and he looks like you."

"We owe Zoltar." Yeron caressed her cheeks. "It was fortunate that his DNA fusion worked so well for you."

Alexis leaned forward and jerked her chin. "Who told you about that?"

"Honey, I can tell by your eye color and the red roots in your hair." He stroked her curls. "Why are you so secretive about it?"

Alexis lowered her eyes. "The Good Samaritan warned me that the renegades might eavesdrop on our conversations."

"Good Sa … you mean Quyeba?" Yeron arched his brows. "Does she mind you calling her that?"

"Not at all. Where you grew up, people couldn't afford humor, but Quyeba knows how to laugh." Alexis smiled wryly.

"You still have not told me everything that happened to you. Why are you using a chair to get around?"

"About three weeks ago, Laurel kicked me and left nerve damage. That injury's going take months to heal." In a halting voice, Alexis described the treatment Zoltar devised for her, and brought him up to speed on the goings-on at the Kryszka compound. She flexed her fingers. No pain. She gazed at her gnarled fingers. The swelling had lessened. "Maybe better than I imagined. My arthritis seems to be in remission."

"The DNA fusion will provide resistance to most human diseases. In time, you might notice changes in your bone structure. I contemplated proposing the DNA fusion to the hospital staff, but according to Steven, it is against ethics."

"Good thing you didn't approach Doctor Hoffman with that idea." Alexis snort-laughed. "That would've gone over like an aerial bomb."

Yeron laughed. "I will give you a dollar if you say that around him."

"I might if I could avoid being attacked." Alexis grimaced. "Last time, Quyeba found me in time. She was a great Samaritan."

"She is an excellent fighter, too," Yeron said. "If Quyeba finds Laurel, she might sedate her and hand her over to the police. I do not know about Woehar."

"Laurel's locked up and Woehar's not going anywhere. She's dead, and –"

The door to the anteroom slid open. Zoltar came in, flanked by Quyeba and Xian, the three whispering in tense voices. Zoltar's eyes flitted toward the doorway, then to his teammates. Xian headed over to the readout screens, her eyes focused, making a show of being occupied while Zoltar continued his conversation with Quyeba in panicked, hushed whispers. He then flicked a glance toward Alexis.

"Where is your isolation gown?" He shot Yeron a helpless look. "My cousin never listens."

Yeron laughed.

"No, she does not .... Why did you say, 'cousin?'"

"Let me explain," Alexis said, and then she described the experiments done on her Aunt Susan. "The egg harvest makes my aunt his natural mother. Someone gave her a memory eradication medication, but I think she might have remembered what happened. We will never know."

"Unfortunately, the nightmare is not over." A grim frown surfaced on Quyeba's face. "Laurel and Draekh are missing."

"What?" Alexis raised her eyebrows, eyes on Quyeba. "I thought your android locked Laurel in that laboratory."

Quyeba lowered her eyes "He did, but Zoltar just checked on both of them. They are gone."

Alexis rolled her eyes. "Someone got to them. Right?"

Quyeba looked at her, shaking her head. She apparently didn't want to discuss the matter around Yeron.

"You can talk in front of me," Yeron said. "What happened?"

Alexis wrinkled her nose. "It is easy to figure out. Some renegade got to Draekh, let him out of his cell, and Draekh got to Laurel. Right?"

"That is about right." Quyeba averted her eyes and touched her face. "Woehar and Draekh built their own laboratory. At one time, two thousand people and eight healers lived in my compound. Now I have 1750 residents and three healers: Zoltar, Draekh, and Xian, along with our androids."

"What?" Alexis gasped. "What happened to the other healers?"

"They died—two by natural causes and the others shot, perhaps by renegades. So we manage with the healers we have and the androids. That does not leave us the resources to investigate the whereabouts of the other residents. I assume they live in Woehar's laboratory. She is gone, but Draekh knows how to run it."

"So Woehar's gone and Draekh is running her laboratory," Alexis said, frowning. "I hurt Laurel pretty badly. If Draekh is a competent healer, he will be able to treat her injuries."

"That is true," Quyeba said.

"No one here is safe," Yeron said.

"Draekh cannot run a latrine," Zoltar said. "He is stupider than a *settva*."

"That he is." Alexis laughed. "Laurel will have him for dinner. Literally."

"He is not so dumb." Quyeba shook her head, frowning. "Worse, the hunger has gone to his head. That makes him dangerous. So I need warriors I can trust. Like you, Alexis."

Since when did I become a warrior?

"I will help you when I am more mobile," Alexis said in a low voice.

"The nerve damage will leave you with a limp, but you will walk and fight," Zoltar assured her. "So will Yeron. Xian will make sure that happens."

Alexis made a face. "Xian's machinery tells her how much force I put into the exercises, and she says I am not trying hard enough."

"Because you do not make enough effort," Xian spoke up from the viewscreens.

"Xian is strict." Quyeba smiled. "Good therapists usually are. Listen to her."

****

"I was afraid to trust our soldiers," Quyeba told her son as they left the room.

"So am I, Mother," he said. "They sided with Draekh and Woehar."

"Teodon once told me that humans possess an indomitable spirit," Quyeba said, gazing through the window at Alexis and Yeron. "Our kind does not die easily and Alexis will have that advantage, too. Can you repair the deformities on her hands?"

Zoltar shook his head.

"At Eigil's compound, Teodon had the technology to improve human deformities. It is possible that the gene fusion may arrest her condition and her deformities might correct themselves. I do not recommend rushing into more surgery now."

"I hope you are right, son." Quyeba sighed. "Despite her health problems, she managed to stand tall. Yeron will fight again, too. He and Alexis make a lovely couple."

Zoltar smiled. "You like Alexis, yes?"

Quyeba nodded. "If Lyrus and I had a daughter, I would want her to be like Alexis. Whether she gets help from an android or not, she will need help raising her child. Her mother will need protection, too. Something hurt her mother long before this war."

"Alexis told me that her mother was mistreated."

"Be that as it may, we have to make choices. Some of us possess a fighter's instinct and some do not. Humans and Kryszka can survive troublemakers like Woehar, if enough are willing to fight. Alexis will have a plasma gun as will Yeron. They are excellent warriors and will be willing to fight."

She patted Zoltar on the shoulder. "Come, let us search for Draekh and Laurel. They could not have gotten far."

Chapter Fifty-Three: Laurel Delivers a Present

Grounds outside Jackson Hospital, September 22, 11:00 p.m.

Sated, Laurel hunkered down behind some machinery in the hospital lab while Quyeba and an olive-complexioned Kryszka male entered.

The young man gave a ponderous sigh.

"Why are we here? I told you that Laurel has escaped."

"She may have left clues."

"How can she evade our surveillance? Draekh or Woehar may have built a secret room to hide her. But where?" The young man skirted the tables, making a serpentine route. "She cannot open paneled doors, can she?"

No, but I've got sharp teeth. The better to eat you with. Laurel sniffed at his sweet aroma. *Better leave with Mommy before I get you.*

"What was that?" Quyeba whirled in Laurel's direction. "It sounded like a *settva.*"

"Or at least part *settva.*" Zoltar drew his gun. "Like Laurel, right?"

"That is correct, and we have seen Laurel in her new form." Quyeba waved her hand to the young man. She pointed toward Woehar's body. Beside it lay several partially eaten others. Flies were crawling over the remains. "We should have cremated Woehar and cleaned this room, maybe even discarded some of this machinery. It is outdated. Draekh was sloppy when he disposed of Shively's body, and we do not have adequate workers or androids to the job. We had better dispose of the bodies before the insects on them spread disease."

"What about Laurel?" Zoltar persisted. "We cannot trust anyone else to find her."

"We can search while we work. Here ..." Searching through the cabinets, Quyeba retrieved two gowns, gloves, and black bags. "Help me put the remains of Woehar, Shively, and the others in these disaster bags. An android can dump the bodies at the crematorium."

The panel opened. Neither Zoltar nor Quyeba gave any indication that they heard. Draekh poked his face through the doorway. With one finger held over his lips, he beckoned to Laurel.

Bingo! While Quyeba and Zoltar donned their protective equipment, Draekh levitated Laurel from behind the machinery. He navigated her around the tables and below them, out of sight. Woehar hadn't gifted her with any special powers, but apparently, she'd found an ally in Draekh, who seemed willing to use his to help. He floated her out of the door and set her on her feet.

In the corridor, Draekh ran his right hand over Laurel's gut and grinned.

"You have eaten well here." He draped a gown over Laurel and tucked a filled test tube in its pocket. "So now you shall deliver a present to the Jackson clinic."

What present?

Laurel looked at him, puzzled, but she wasn't arguing with a chance to go free.

"This," he said, tapping her pocket, "contains a virus, something I harvested from Woehar's specimens. Follow me."

A virus? Laurel quietly followed Draekh down the long corridor toward another laboratory. Yeron lay in bed, with Alexis whispering sweet nothings to him. Matilda was— *why was she here?*

Screw them. Laurel was sated so she kept going, hunched low to keep under the radar sensors. *I'm not doing anything to get attention.*

Past the laboratory, they proceeded down another hall and climbed onto a lift. The lift rose. Higher and higher they ascended, until another metal door opened as they reached the landing.

"I trust you to give this to the right people," Draekh said. "The rest is up to you."

With a swift kick in the butt, he propelled her into an unoccupied room. *Another laboratory, from the looks of the machinery and control boards laden with dials.* No people. On the opposite side, steps opened to the outside and freedom.

Voices. A man and a woman shouting at each other.

Shit! Laurel scrambled behind other machinery in time to avoid discovery by two police officers. One officer busied herself taking pictures. The other put on gloves and carefully placed small objects into a plastic bag.

Laurel's stomach rumbled again.

The officers took their time, chatting about their families and vacation plans. *I can ruin your plans fast.* Laurel smiled, but remained hidden.

The chatter about vacations continued until the male officer said, "I think that should cover it."

The female laughed. "I hope so."

"Be careful driving home."

In the moonlight filtering through the opening above, Laurel pulled the test tube from her pocket and examined it. The sealed vial contained yellow fluid. As her stomach gurgled, she slowly looked up and the officers' bodies drew her attention. *So muscular and well built. Fresh meat.* She let loose a rumbling growl. *Healthy meat.*

It wouldn't do to tackle the officers here. Throwing the test tube at them might cause some excitement. *Nah. I'm saving this for Jackson's sacred seventh floor. I'll get one of those cops alone.*

The officers left by way of an ascending stepladder. Laurel waited until their footsteps and voices had faded before climbing. No doubt, the ladder would creak under her weight, drawing attention she wasn't ready for ... yet.

Moments later, Laurel went up the ladder. Above ground, she made out a waxing moon, a bright sphere against the tar-black sky. A ribcage of trees surrounded her. She couldn't see any houses, but what *is this?* A sweet scent tickled her nostrils. Minutes later, she made out a young man jogging through a field. *Hungry.*

She ran – no, galloped – after the man. Her thick legs enabled her to jump over bushes, low tree branches, and other obstacles in her path. Her talons latched onto the man's armband which held his iPhone. Screaming, the young man recoiled. The band stretched taut and then snapped. The iPhone went flying and he tumbled backward into Laurel's arms. He thrashed and kicked, but Laurel knocked him flat. She went for his throat, cutting his cries short.

Satisfied again, Laurel waddled behind a rose bush in a field and lay down. Moments passed, and her eyes grew heavy. Her next stop was Jackson Hospital, where she'd get the remaining people responsible for her dismissal, and bless them with the contents of Draekh's test tube.

First, she needed a nap. She curled up on the grass behind the bush. Later on, she'd deliver her surprise.

The virus in the vial was deadly. Draekh had intimated that much. Infiltrating the hospital without discovery wouldn't be easy. She might have to wait and that was okay. Revenge tasted best when served cold. Laurel nodded off to sleep with a toothsome grin on her face.

About the Contributors

Barbara Custer:

Barbara lives near Philadelphia, Pennsylvania, where she works full time as a respiratory therapist. When she's not working with her patients, she's enjoying a fright flick or working on horror and science fiction tales. She's published *Night to Dawn* magazine since 2004.

Other books by Barbara include *Twilight Healer, City of Brotherly Death, Infinite Sight,* and *Steel Rose*; also novellas *Close Liaisons* and *Life Raft: Earth*. She enjoys bringing her medical background to the printed page, and then blending it with supernatural horror. She maintains a presence on Facebook, Linkedin, Twitter, and The Writers Coffeehouse forum. Look for the photos with the Mylar balloons, and you'll find her.

To contact her, e-mail her at barbaracuster@hotmail.com.

Visit her at:

www.bloodredshadow.com

www.facebook.com/barbara.custer

www.linkedin.com/pub/barbara-custer/10/aa9/bba

https://twitter.com/NighttoDawn1

Dawné Dominique:

Dawné Dominique is a best-selling, multi-published author and an award winning professional book cover artist. With over sixteen years' experience, she devotes her time between creating cover art for numerous publishers and Indie authors, while trying to write the next paranormal/fantasy bestseller.

Being an author herself, she knows how important cover art is to an author. She has humbly accepted many awards and honorable mentions, but she's quick to attribute her success to the diverse authors she represents. Without them none of those accolades would be possible.

An accomplished oil painter and sketch artist, she has dabbled in all mediums of art.

She loves what she does and every covers is a challenge to ex-emplify an author's deepest desire to see their words depicted into art.

http://www.dusktildawndesigns.com/

Teresa Tunaley:

Originating from the UK but residing in the Canary Islands for the last 10 years, freelance artist Teresa Tunaley devotes time to her love of art and painting. For more than 30 years she has been doo-dling with pencils and dabbling with watercolors. More recently she has been painting traditionally in oil and creating large canvasses full of color and life. Sometimes she uses a more modern technique using software such as Photoshop, Corel Draw and Paint Shop Pro to pro-duce her creations for online publications.

During her art career, she has produced countless illustra-tions, book covers and paintings. Along with published stories and poetry, she can be credited with award winning cover art and illustra-tions for author stories. Her work can be seen online and in print across the UK, US, Canada and Europe.

In May 2011, she opened a new Exhibition in Puerto del San-tiago (Tenerife, Spain) entitled Tutto per la vita (All for the life). She has over 30 works on show and is hoping to be selected to participate in the Capitals annual Art Festival. Should she win, there will be invi-tations to exhibit her work in a whirlwind trip across Spain and Italy.

Touching and spectacular "has been the inauguration; Tutto Per la vita" Some thirty of their works appeared, giving you a journey to Spain, Africa, America, Japan and Thailandia. The work was in-tense with feeling, in full color and textures, where figures, landscapes and moments will leave the visitor with a memory of a magical trip."

Jose Francisco Morales

Comisario de la Exposicion (Tenerife)

http://www.artesigloxxi.org

I like to think that I am very versatile in my choice of subject matter - my new surroundings provide the inspiration for me to paint on a daily basis and the fact that others may enjoy my work gives me the confidence to continue.

Website: www.artstopper.com

www.ingramcontent.com/pod-product-compliance
Lightning Source LLC
Chambersburg PA
CBHW020227260626
47156CB00002B/578